Caucasia

Caucasia

D a n z y   S e n n a

Riverhead Books

a member of

Penguin Putnam Inc.

New York

1998

Riverhead Books
a member of
Penguin Putnam Inc.
200 Madison Avenue
New York, NY 10016

Library of Congress Cataloging-in-Publication Data

Senna, Danzy.
Caucasia / Danzy Senna.
p. cm.
ISBN 1-57322-091-4 (acid-free paper)
I. Title.
PS3569.E618C3 1998
813'.54—dc21   97-28911 CIP

Printed in the United States of America
1 3 5 7 9 10 8 6 4 2

This book is printed on acid-free paper. ∞

BOOK DESIGN BY JUDITH STAGNITTO ABBATE

For F. Q. H.

Caucasia

A long time ago I disappeared. One day I was here, the next I was gone. It happened as quickly as all that. One day I was playing schoolgirl games with my sister and our friends in a Roxbury playground. The next I was a nobody, just a body without a name or a history, sitting beside my mother in the front seat of our car, moving forward on the highway, not stopping. (And when I stopped being nobody, I would become white—white as my skin, hair, bones allowed. My body would fill in the blanks, tell me who I should become, and I would let it speak for me.)

This was back when Boston still came in black and white, yellowing around the edges. You could just make out the beginnings of color: red-eyed teenagers with afros like halos around their faces, whispering something about power and ofay to one another as they shuffled to catch the bus; a man's mocha hand on a woman's pale knee. I disappeared into America, the easiest place to get lost. Dropped off, without a name, without a record. With only the body I traveled in. And a memory of something lost.

This is what I remember.

negritude for beginners

face

Before I ever saw myself, I saw my sister. When I was still too small for mirrors, I saw her as the reflection that proved my own existence. Back then, I was content to see only Cole, three years older than me, and imagine that her face—cinnamon-skinned, curly-haired, serious—was my own. It was her face above me always, waving toys at me, cooing at me, whispering to me, pinching me when she was angry and I was the easiest target. That face was me and I was that face and that was how the story went.

In those days, I rotated around Cole. Everything was her. I obeyed her, performed for her, followed her, studied her the way little sisters do. We were rarely far apart. We even spoke our own langauge. Cole insists that it began before I was born, when I was just a translucent ball in my mother's womb. Cole would lean her high forehead down to the pale balloon of our mother's belly and tell me secrets with her three-year-old gibberish genius, all the while using her finger to trace a kind of invisible hieroglyphics against our mother's swollen flesh. Cole believed I must be lonely in there, frightened of the dark, and that her voice and scribblings would soothe me.

Later we perfected the language in our attic bedroom in the brownstone on Columbus Avenue. Up there, amid the dust and stuffed animals, Cole whispered stories, one-liners, riddles to me to help me fall asleep. It was a complicated language, impossible for outsiders to pick up—no verb tenses, no pronouns, just words floating outside time and space without owner or direction. Attempting to understand our chatter, my mother said, was like trying to eavesdrop on someone sleeptalking, when the words are still untranslated from their dream state—achingly familiar, but just beyond one's grasp.

My father described the language as a "high-speed patois." Cole and I just called it "Elemeno," after our favorite letters in the alphabet.

My grandmother wanted us to see a child psychiatrist. She said it was my mother's fault, for teaching us at home, in isolation, around the dyslexic kids, who were my mother's specialty. My grandmother said we must have spent too much time around those "backwards children" and that was why we spoke in tongues. My father also blamed my mother for raising us in that kind of chaos. He said we were suffering from a "profound indifference" to the world around us. My mother said they both were full of shit, and left Cole and me alone in the little world we had created.

Our world was the attic. Up there, we performed for each other with the costumes that were stuffed in a trunk at the end of the bed. The attic had a crooked and creaking floor, a slanted roof so low that grown-ups had to hunch over when they came up there to visit, and a half-moon window that looked out onto Columbus Avenue. Across the street sat a red brick housing project, and beyond that, we could just glimpse the tip of the Prudential. I had some vague understanding that beyond our window, outside the attic, lay danger—the world, Boston, and all the problems that came with the city. When Cole and I were alone in our attic, speaking Elemeno and making cities out of stuffed animals, it seemed that the outside world was as far away as Timbuktu—some place that could never touch us. We were the inside, the secret and fun and make-believe, and that was where I wanted to stay.

I don't know when, exactly, all that began to change. I guess it happened gradually, the way bad things usually do. The summer before I turned eight, the outside world seemed to bear in on us with a new force. It was 1975, and Boston was a battleground. My mother and her friends spent hours huddled around the kitchen table, talking about the trouble out there. *Forced integration. Roxbury. South Boston. Separate but not quite equal. God made the Irish number one. A fight, a fight, a nigga and a white . . .*

One evening, Cole and I lay side-by-side on our big brass bed after dinner. Our bellies were full, and the swelter of the day still stuck to us. We lay with our heads toward the foot of the bed, our legs in the air, as we rubbed our feet against the cool white surface of the wall, leaving black smears from the dirt on our soles. We could hear our parents fighting through the heating vent. Muted obscenities. *You pompous prick. You fat white mammy.* We were trying to block them out with talk of Elemeno. Cole was explaining to me that it wasn't just a language, but a place and a people as well. I had heard this before, but it never failed to entertain me, her description of the land I hoped to visit some day. We whispered questions and answers to each other like calls to prayer. *shimbala matamba caressi. nicolta fo mo capsala.* The Elemenos, she said, could turn not just from black to white, but from brown to yellow to purple to green, and back again. She said they were a shifting people, constantly changing their form, color, pattern, in a quest for invisibility. According to her, their changing routine was a serious matter—less a game of make-believe than a fight for the survival of their species. The Elemenos could turn deep green in the bushes, beige in the sand, or blank white in the snow, and their power lay precisely in their ability to disappear into any surrounding. As she spoke, a new question—a doubt—flashed through my mind. Something didn't make sense. What was the point of surviving if you had to disappear? I said it aloud—*peta marika vandersa?*— but just then the door to our room flew open.

It was our mother. She wore a flowered muumuu from Zayres and her blond hair piled into a loose bun. Lately she'd been acting funny. She was distracted, spending hours on end in the basement. I didn't really understand what went on down there. It was a grown-up land, where my mother held her hushed Sunday meetings with her friends. They would disappear from noon till just before dinner time, and Cole and I were absolutely forbidden, at all times, to go near them. Cole thought they must be smoking pot. I thought it was where my mother hid our Christmas presents. Whatever the case, the door was locked and there was no way around it.

Our mother stood still for a moment in the doorway, arms folded across her chest. "Kiddos, get up. Change into something a little nicer. Your father wants to take you to your aunt Dot's house."

"What for?" Cole asked, already up and heading toward the closet.

My mother crossed the room. She was a big woman, in both directions, and looked like a giant as she stepped over our toys, hunching low so her head wouldn't hit the ceiling. She stared out the window with a grim expression.

"Dot's going away. Far away. And she wants to say good-bye."

I sat up with a start, feeling a twinge of panic. Dot was my father's younger sister and my favorite grown-up. She was two shades darker than my father, a cool, rich brown verging on black, with no breasts to speak of, long legs, and a gap between her two front teeth. She liked to dress like a boy, in overalls or low-slung blue jeans, and wore her hair in a short, neat natural. Her real name was Dorothy, but her mother had shortened it when Dot was just a girl.

Dot was the only relative we knew on our father's side of the family. The grandmother on that side remained a mystery to me. We always referred to her as Nana, to distinguish her from our white one, who was always Grandma. Nana had died when I was still a baby and Cole was three. Cole claims to remember her. She says Nana taught her, at that young age, to have an appreciation for coffee (she would give it to Cole with a dollop of sweetened condensed milk, so it was like coffee ice cream). I was jealous of those memories. All I had was Dot, and now she was leaving.

"She's going to India," my mother explained, still frowning at the street. "To the mountains, to stay with some religious guru of hers. Probably a bunch of nuts. I doubt it'll last long, but it's not clear. She claims she's gone for good. Anyway, hurry up. Your father's already outside."

I asked my mother why she wasn't coming. She didn't go to many parties anymore. She said she didn't have time for boogying. She had rallies to attend, and dyslexic students to teach, and secret meetings in the basement. But this party seemed different. Important, from the sounds of it. I knew she liked Dot and would want to say good-bye. I stood beside her and followed her gaze to the street, where my father's orange Volvo sat parked. "You should come," I said.

She looked tense and shook her head. "No, baby. I've already said my good-bye to Dotty. Besides, there are gonna be people there I don't want to see. Now hurry the hell up. You're late."

Before we kissed her good-bye, she mumbled: "Tell that bastard to have you home before midnight."

My father wasn't alone. Beside him in the passenger seat was his side-kick, Ronnie Parkman, a strikingly handsome man with high cheekbones and deep-set eyes. We clambered into the back of the car. As we rolled toward Roxbury, my father and Ronnie talked politics in the front. Earth, Wind, and Fire crooned from the radio, and my father tapped his hand to the beat against the steering wheel. *You're a shining star, No matter who you are, shining bright to see, what you can truly be . . .*

My father always spoke differently around Ronnie. He would switch into slang, peppering his sentences with words like "cat" and "man" and "cool." Whenever my mother heard him talking that way, she would laugh and say it was his "jive turkey act." In the past year, he had discovered Black Pride (just a few years later than everyone else), and my mother said he was trying to purge himself of his "honkified past."

As we made our way down Humboldt Avenue, my father glanced over his shoulder, smiling at us. "Birdie, Cole, do your papa a favor," he said. "Yell, 'Ngawa, Ngawa, Black, Black Powah!' at those two cats on the corner." He pointed to two young men who stood in front of a barbershop, and muttered to Ronnie, "Check them out. Nypical tiggers, wasting their lives away."

Ronnie chuckled and repeated my father's phrase. " 'Nypical tiggers.' Deck, man, you're crazy."

Cole and I stuck our heads out the window and mimicked the chant at the corner men, who raised their fists in a half-serious salute. I thought it was fun, my head being hit by the wind of the moving car. "Ngawa, Ngawa, Black, Black Powah!" we yelled again in unison, this time at a neat, churchgoing old lady with salt-and-pepper hair. She stopped in her path and scowled at us as we passed by. My father tried to stifle his laughter and ordered us to sit down.

He explained to his friend, "Dot's flaky. Always has been, always will be. Ever since we were little kids she's had her head in the clouds. This latest silliness doesn't surprise me one damn bit."

Ronnie sighed. "Yeah, Dotty sure knows how to pick them."

My father went on, more insistent than usual. He seemed to be trying to get a reaction out of Ronnie. "She sleeps with these white boys, then acts surprised when they don't take her home for dinner. I told her, these ofays just want their thirty minutes of difference."

I was pretty sure "ofay" meant white, and without really thinking, I piped from the backseat, "Isn't Mum ofay?"

I heard Cole snicker into her hand beside me.

My father threw me a sharp look. "Yeah, but that's different."

"How?"

He sighed, about to launch into a long explanation, when Ronnie began to laugh, low and softly, beside him. "Kids are too smart for their own good. Always gotta watch your back."

My father broke into laughter, too, and forgot to answer my question.

DOT LIVED ON the border of Roxbury and Jamaica Plain in a large communal household that grew all of its own vegetables and marijuana in the backyard and was governed by a Hindu philosophy. Usually, no one was allowed to wear shoes beyond the front door. But tonight must have been extra special, because when Dot opened the door, I saw she wore high white platforms and a tight, bright-yellow minidress. Around her head she had tied an orange-and-purple African cloth that made her look regal. She smelled smoky, foreign already, as she wrapped Cole and me in her arms. She held us away from her then, to examine us.

"If it isn't the terrible twosome. Give your auntie a kiss. Look at you two, so grown. Hot damn, Cole, check you out." She spun Cole around in her hands, then said to my father with a wink, "Watch out there, big daddy. She's gonna be a heartbreaker."

Dot hugged my father and his friend then, and kissed them both on each cheek. She seemed unable to stop smiling, full of possibility, as she led us into the dim crowded house, where people lounged around the main room in a swirl of colors, conversation, and smoke. I heard my father whisper to Ronnie, "Check it out. Welcome to the land of miscegenation."

On the couch, a man with a frizzy brown beard and glasses was giving a back rub to a petite dark-skinned woman, while a Puerto Rican wearing a Red Sox cap backward sat beside them, rolling a joint. A red-haired woman sat cross-legged on the couch, nursing a baby at her bare breast, while an small Indian man sat before her on the floor, waving his arms in excited conversation. My father and Ronnie went into a corner to get beers, then stood perched, watching the crowd with critical stares, whispering to each other from time to time. I stood by the doorjamb watching, transfixed, light-headed from the haze of reefer fumes that sifted toward me.

When I reached beside me for Cole's hand, I felt only air. I was alone.

This was always happening to me, in grocery stores, in movie theaters, in crowds. I would wander off, mesmerized by the sight of some oddity—a burned man's face, a dog with three legs, a Bible-thumping evangelist whom everyone else ignored. My mother said that one of these days she was going to get me a leash. Cole was usually the one to find me, on the verge of tears, having realized the danger of my folly.

Cole and Dot had wandered off somewhere. They probably assumed I was close behind. I went down the long hallway in search of them.

The house once had belonged to a family of Hasidic Jews. They had fled Roxbury when it began to change colors, and the building had sat empty and rotting for years until Dot and her motley crew took it upon themselves to restore it. They had been slowly reconstructing the house through lazy Saturdays of hammering, sanding, and painting. But still it had the feeling of a half-finished funhouse. All the floors tilted at an angle, and someone had painted a mural on the long first floor, a row of blissful Indian faces—the disciples of Ramakrishna—women and men with glazed eyes and knowing smiles. The painting was unfinished, and the last disciple, a young woman, was eyebrowless. The mural always had frightened me a bit, and that night I felt a chill as I traced the shape of Ramakrishna's nose with the tip of my finger before moving on through the house.

There were mysteries to be uncovered behind the closed doors that lined the hall, and I turned my attention to the first door, which was open a crack. Angry voices carried out into the hallway. I peeked in. A couple sat on the bed. The woman, a thin white girl with strawberry-blond hair and freckles, was crying. The man wore his hair in a wide, light-brown afro with a headband splitting it in half. He sat beside the girl and said into the air, "You just don't understand. I was trying to help a sister out."

The girl didn't seem to be listening.

"You fucked her, didn't you?" she hissed. Her makeup was smeared and bright like a clown's, and snot was running down into her lips.

"Julie, don't ask questions if you don't want the answers," he told her, shaking his head and looking at the floor.

"You motherfuckers are all alike! All alike!"

She started putting on her jacket, and her eye caught mine.

I stopped breathing, ready to run. But she just sniffled and began sobbing all over again.

I wondered why she couldn't see me, and felt a thrill of anonymity, invisibility, all of a sudden. I wandered away, wondering what else I might find.

I went on like that for a few more rooms, in one finding nothing but clothes strewn across an unmade bed, in another finding four grown-ups giggling madly as they passed a bong around. I was beginning to get bored and to worry where Cole was, when I reached the door at the end of the hall.

It was sealed tight. I had to push hard to open it, but finally it gave.

The light inside was dim, and the room smelled of sweat and cigarette smoke. Books lined the walls, and a desk sat at the far end. It was a strangely conservative room, which stood out from the ethnic and ragtag decor of the rest of the house. It looked somber, like the library in my grandmother's house. But here, a group of men with their backs to me were bent around the desk in an excited huddle, whispering, and letting out little hoots of laughter. I suspected that it was a private meeting and that I should leave. But I wanted to test whether I was really invisible. It was a feeling that thrilled me even as it scared me. I was curious about what all the men were looking at. I opened the door just a little farther, but it let out a loud creak, and one of the men with his back toward me turned in a violent motion.

I had seen him before, though I couldn't place where. Then I remembered. He had come knocking at our door one night a few weeks before. My father had been spending the night away, at a friend's house in Roxbury, but my mother had been at home. I had found them out on the porch together, smoking and laughing, when I came to ask my mother for ice cream. I remember thinking he looked almost like a white man, barely a trace of black at all, except for his tight reddish-brown curls. He had smiled at me and winked and said to my mother, "That your little girl?"

Now he was kneeling in front of me, staring at me with gray-blue eyes, and I stood still as stone under his gaze.

He smiled, and I saw that his teeth were crooked and crowded so that they folded over one another. He had a reddish fuzz over his lip.

"Hey, girl, whatcha lookin' at?"

I shrugged and moved to turn away. But I felt his hand squeezing into my arm—tight.

A voice behind him said, "Redbone, man, get rid of that little girl."

But the man turned toward them, still clutching my arm, and said, laughing, "Nigga, this ain't no ordinary little girl. This be Sandy Lee's little girl. Ain't that right?"

I frowned at him. His slang was awkward and twisted. It didn't seem to come naturally to him. Even I could see that. It reminded me of an old black-and-white plantation movie my father had forced Cole and me to watch one Sunday afternoon. The slave characters in it had been played by white actors who wore some kind of pancake makeup on their faces. My father had laughed whenever they spoke in their strained dialect. Redbone sounded as if he had graduated from the same school of acting.

I glanced over his head at the group. They were blocking my view to the desk.

He laughed. "Girl, you wanna see what's on the desk?"

I stared at him for a moment. I was aching to see, but hesitated, instead looking at one of the men, a friend of my father's, who smiled softly at me, as if he felt sorry for me.

"Yeah, let me see," I said, knowing I would get in trouble for this one, but too curious to care.

Redbone picked me up in his arms in one swift motion. He smelled like sweat, and there were yellow stains, like piss in snow, creeping out from his underarms.

He hauled me over to the desk.

I looked down to see two large rifles, black and shiny, cradled on top of a couple of pillows. They looked like twin sleeping dogs lying there.

Redbone whispered in my ear, "You know what those be?"

"Guns." I leaned forward in his arms to touch one, but he held me back.

"Naw, you don't want to get too close, baby girl. I'd have to teach you how to use it first."

One of the men said, "Redbone, why you showing her this, man? Isn't this a security risk?"

But Redbone was still staring at me. I was trying to hold my breath, trying not to smell him.

"This little girl ain't no security risk, brotha. We gotta raise our children to know how to fight. There's a war going on. We can't be raisin' no sissies. We got pigs in the White House and pigs patrolling the street. Know what I'm sayin', Birdie Lee?"

I tried to squirm out of his arms. Something about the way he had said my name felt wrong. Too familiar.

The other men looked uncomfortable.

Just then the door swung open, letting in a burst of joyful chatter from the party. We all turned to see who it was.

My father stepped in with Ronnie. They were laughing and carrying beers. He froze when he saw Redbone holding me.

I yelled, "Papa! Over here!" and put out my arms toward him.

But he didn't move. He was staring at Redbone with a thin-lipped smile. Everyone was quiet as he slowly handed Ronnie his beer bottle.

Then his voice came out: "What the fuck do you think you're doing holding my daughter over those guns?"

Redbone laughed again, a strained, unhappy laugh, his voice breaking. But he put me down, and I ran over to my father, turning now to stare back at Redbone with my hands on my hips.

"Deck, man, don't be gettin' like that. She came in here on her own free will, and I just showin' her what we was doin'." He paused, and a queer, rather miserable smile came over his face as he said, "Maybe you need to get your head out of them books and put some action behind them high-falutin' theories of yours."

But my father was leaning over Redbone then, standing so close to him, towering over him, though they were the same height. "Don't tell me 'bout the revolution, you fake-ass half-breed motherfucker."

The other men crowded around, pulling them apart, laughing nervously, saying, "C'mon, y'all, we're brothers, ain't no need to fight."

"This ain't no brother. Where did this fool come from, anyway? Can someone tell me that? He shows up a month ago actin' like he been a revolutionary all his life. But no one knows where you came from, Red, do they?" my father bellowed.

Redbone's voice was different now, nasal. He was no longer speaking in his butchered slang as he said, "Deck, watch your step. Don't get black and proud on me. You're the one with the white daughter."

There was a lot of pushing and yelling. Without thinking I grabbed the leg next to me and said, "Stop it! He's gonna kill Papa!"

But Redbone didn't get very far. The men held them safely apart and talked to them in smooth, calming voices. I realized I was clutching Ronnie's leg. He leaned down to my level and smiled, putting his hand on my head.

"Bird, no one's gonna hurt your papa. I'll make sure of it. Now, why don't you go find your sister and your aunt Dot? I think they're in the kitchen."

I nodded and turned to go. Behind me, my father's voice: "If I ever see you near my wife again, I swear, man, it's all over."

I gave one last glance to my father holding his hands in the air and backing away from Redbone, who was looking over his shoulder at me with a pained grin.

Outside of the room I ran down the hall toward the yellow light of the kitchen. Dot sat at the table, smoking, while Cole sat beside her, chopping greens. A woman with bleach-blond hair, darkening at the roots, stood at the stove, singing in a low, Spanish accent.

Dot said to me, "Where you been, girl?" Then she looked at Cole and said, "This sister of yours is always wandering off. You need to keep a better eye on her." She stroked my hair. "Your father's been lookin' for you. He wants you and Cole to perform some dance he taught you."

Cole piped in, "'Member, Birdie? He wants us to do the Bump for everybody."

Dot's smile faded when she looked into my eyes.

"What is it, Birdie, baby? Did someone bother you out there?"

I hesitated and looked over at Cole, who had stopped chopping and held the knife in midair.

Dot shook me roughly by the shoulders, and my head jiggled loosely like my Sasha doll's. "Why you look so funny, Bird? Did someone bother you?"

I shook my head no. Dot hugged me to her bony body and said, "Hey there, now. I didn't mean to shake you. But you tell me if anyone hurts you. You hear me?"

I started to speak, to tell them what had happened, but the words caught in my throat. It seemed secret, what I had just seen, and so I said only, "All right. Let's go rehearse."

Cole and I did the Bump to "Roller Coaster" before a group of swaying, grinning grown-ups, who stood jingling their glasses and shouting out encouragement to us. My father had taught us how to do the dance one silly afternoon in the fading light of our kitchen, but now he stood in the back of the crowd, barely watching our performance, his head cocked to the right side as if weighed down by too much information.

In the car ride home that night, as Cole dozed with her head against the glass, I watched the streetlights fly by and tried to eavesdrop on my father and Ronnie, but their words were swallowed by the smooth bullshitting baritone of Barry White.

I HAD THOUGHT the incident with Redbone was bad. But the real battle began as soon as we got home. I lay huddled next to Cole, twisting one of her curls around my finger. We both were quiet, frowning at the ceiling, listening intently to our parents' muffled shrieks and curses, which came floating up to us from the kitchen.

"Redbone's full of shit!" I heard my father say, his voice tight and indignant. "I mean, Sandy, you've got to be crazy letting that madman into your little group."

"Fuck off, Deck. All right? 'Cause your ass sure isn't helping out with the cause. I mean, there's a war out there. A fucking war. Not just overseas, but right in your own backyard. Shit, Deck. The FBI is trying to destroy everything we've fought for. And all you can think about are the origins of the word 'Negro.'"

Cole claimed to remember the good times between my parents. But I didn't. Seemed like they were always breaking up to make up. After their big fights, they usually got back together with a little ritual: Al Green, a bottle of red wine, and a carton of Chinese noodles. Sometimes they would read aloud to each other from one of their favorite writers, Camus or Richard Wright. Other times they would just stand in the living room, lights off, swaying to the soul music, kissing, and whispering to each other secrets Cole and I would never know.

Even when they were getting along, their union seemed fragile, on the verge of ending. I never heard them say "I love you" to each other. Instead, they said, "I miss you," when they were lying beside each other in bed, or when they walked hand in hand along the banks of the Charles River. "I miss you," they would say, and overhearing this, I didn't understand how you could miss something that was right beside you. Lately, though, they didn't even talk about missing each other. And their fighting had only intensified. As my mother fell deeper into Boston politics, my father went deeper into his book and his ideas about race. Cole said she bet they were going to get a divorce. She said everybody's parents did at some point.

Sometimes I wondered if it were my fault. I knew their marriage had begun to sour at about the same time as my birth. They couldn't even agree on a name for me, which is how I ended up Birdie. My sister had been born when they still got along. They named her Colette, after the French writer, though everyone shortened it to Cole. But when I was born, my father wanted to call me Patrice, as in Lumumba, the Congolese liberator; my mother wanted to name me Jesse, after her great-grandmother, a white suffragette. Cole just called me Birdie—she had wanted a parakeet for her birthday and instead got me. For a while, I answered to all three names with a schizophrenic zeal. But in the end, even my parents grew tired of the confusion and called me Birdie, though my birth certificate still reads, "Baby Lee," like the gravestone of some stillborn child.

Now their words reached us in starts and stops, parts of the conversation missing, so we had to fill in the blanks ourselves. Earlier, at the party and in the car afterward, I hadn't had a chance to tell Cole what had happened with Redbone. So here, in bed, I whispered to her in Elemeno across the blue darkness of our room. She listened sternly. I told her how I had believed I was invisible until I reached that last room. I told her about Redbone's teeth, how they crossed over one another so it looked like he had double rows. I told her about the guns, and about my father's last words to Redbone: "If I ever see you near my wife again . . ." When I was finished with my story, I felt a little guilty. If I hadn't been snooping, Papa never would have gotten in the fight.

Cole just took my hand and said *jasmu billa woola*. Never spy alone.

Downstairs, their fighting continued. My father was shouting, "I've had enough of your antics. It's got to come to an end. I mean, this is insane, what you're running here. The visitors have got to stop."

It always came back to the visitors. They'd been coming for more than a year now. They stayed in the guest room on the second floor. They were a mysterious lot—a steady stream of strangers, hunched and tired, who showed up on the doorstep of our big crumbling brownstone at odd hours of the night. International exiles and just plain-old Americans. Cole and I didn't really understand why these people needed to stay with us. We knew only what our mother told us. That they were wanted by the pigs, the Feds, the motherfuckers in the big house, and that they had nowhere else to go.

Some stayed just a night, others a few weeks or months, before fleeing into the night to the next hiding spot, leaving behind only their thank-you notes and sometimes a piece of them that they had forgotten: a tube of lipstick, a blond pageboy wig, a dog-eared book with notes scribbled in the margins, a comb with missing teeth, a T-shirt with the faded words "Free Angela" across the front, a tarnished silver bracelet from Ghana. When Cole and I came across these objects—found in the back of a closet or under the cushions of the sofa—we always insisted on keeping them hidden in the trunk at the bottom of our bed, buried beneath a pile of costumes, our only proof that those people had existed.

There was an Iranian poet who got drunk one night at a party my mother gave. Cole and I had fallen asleep on the floor in the television room, and he stumbled over our half-sleeping bodies, thinking we were the rug. A gaunt Irish nationalist who held a fund-raising campaign out of our living room. And the most mysterious of all, an emaciated American girl named Sarah Lou, a vegan who never let us in her room and could make her stomach "talk" on command for Cole's and my entertainment. Sarah Lou vanished one morning after a three-week stay, leaving only a note to my mother on the kitchen table saying, "Thanks for everything. By the way. Your husband's an asshole."

Our last visitor had been a black South African named Lucas. A thin, bespectacled man, Lucas had stayed with us most of the spring. He was quiet, polite, and excessively neat, and dressed awkwardly in too-tight polyester shirts and high-water pants. He had left behind a daughter my age in Cape Town, and maybe because of that he took a special liking to me. He taught me how to suck marrow out of a chicken bone, and brought Cole and me a package of Wrigley's spearmint gum each evening after his day of university research. After dinner, Cole and I would smack the gum loudly before the light of the television, chewing each piece until the flavor was gone.

Lucas had been taken away one night by men in suits who said they were immigration authorities, but who my mother told us were "fascist murderers, monsters." My mother had stood cussing at their car on the front steps to our house, while my father had tried to call friends at *The Boston Globe* to help. But Lucas had gone as quickly as he had come, leaving a room smelling of foreign cigarette smoke, a framed picture of his daughter, and a plastic pink lighter with the word "Pretoria" across it. After he left, I pocketed the lighter, not willing to share it even with Cole. I lit it each night in bed, hypnotized by the blue flame, until eventually the lighter fluid ran out.

Our room had turned a deep, dark blue as the street light sifted through our little window. Their voices still came strong through the heating vent. My father was getting nasty, the way he sometimes did. I heard him laugh and call my mother a "walking, talking marshmallow." I knew my mother was fat. At least that's what everyone said. Her very own mother in Cambridge once called her a "whale of flesh" and found every opportunity to comment on her size. But I had never really seen my mother that way—just as big and solid, with a rope of blond hair swinging between her broad shoulders.

He was on a roll now, in the middle of one of his monologues. He said she was ten years too late to be storing radicals, that she never knew when to stop. Didn't know when to stop eating. Didn't know when to stop drinking. And she damn sure didn't know when to stop this game of cops and robbers. The movement, he bellowed, had shifted gears, and she was still living in another time, another era, not realizing everyone else had moved on to other tactics or had dropped out of dropping out.

My mother replied that intellectuals like him were parlor-pink creeps who never really practiced what they preached. At least, she bellowed at him, she was trying to do something to change the world, not just writing about it.

It was true that my mother had always been the practical one. Driving through Boston was like taking a tour of my mother's accomplishments: a community health clinic she had helped to found; a breakfast program for poor kids; and a mural that spanned a whole block, depicting the brightly colored faces of revolutionaries, with the words of some Puerto Rican poet below. My mother liked to tell Cole and me that politics weren't complicated. They were simple. People, she said, deserved four basic things: food, love, shelter, and a good education. Everything else was extra.

But for my father, politics were more complicated. He was obsessed with theories about race and white hypocrisy, and seemed to see my mother's activism as a distraction. My mother said that my father was paralyzed with "the weight of his intellect." "That's the tragedy of your father," she had told us one night. "He thinks too much to be of much use to anybody."

That night there was the sound of flesh hitting flesh, cries and shrieks and doors slamming. The house seemed to shake with their combined rage at each other. I whispered to Cole: *tempa mi walla stu*. This is their worst ever.

The last thing I heard before falling asleep was glass breaking, something hard and porcelain splitting into a thousand pieces.

A COLD DROP hit my forehead. It was the next morning, and Cole was leaning over me, her hair wet, shiny ringlets, water clinging to the ends. She was serious, upset about something. It was in her eyes. She held my face in her hands, and her curls lightly tickled my cheek. *shugaray musunka dalo*. Papa is leaving. They're splitting up for real this time.

A pale strip of light fell across the wood floor. In the distance, I could hear something sharp and angry—the same sound I had fallen asleep to the night before.

I followed Cole to the half-moon window. Outside, the asphalt already shimmered with the heat.

My mother and father looked small and toylike from our window. I was surprised and relieved to see them both standing. Nobody had died during the night. My mother stood on the steps, hands on hips, watching my father stuff a garbage bag into his rust-colored Volvo. They moved their mouths, but from up so high, I couldn't make out their words.

I was barefoot and wore only my mother's T-shirt, which hung down past my knees.

Cole said, "I'm going down there. I'm going to find out what it's about."

She glanced at me out of the corner of her eye, then sighed. "Yeah, yeah, you can come too. But only if you're quiet. They can't see us watching. If they do, we're not gonna find out anything. We're spies. Got it?"

She wore slippers, her glasses (her eyes were already weak at eleven, making her seem more serious than she actually was), and a blue silk kimono from Chinatown. I put on my Dr. Scholls and grabbed her hand. Their voices grew louder as we descended each flight, until the cool morning air hit our faces.

My father was in the middle of a speech. His wire-rimmed glasses had caught the glare of the sun, and they glimmered, shielding his eyes, making it impossible for us to read his expression. My mother stood facing him on the cracked bottom step. She had her back to us, so I couldn't see her face. She still wore the flowered muumuu. She held something balled in her fist and appeared to be on the verge of throwing it at him.

I listened to my father speak. It was never clear exactly to whom his words were directed. They were difficult words, and they seemed to rise above the person before him, as if aimed toward the sky rather than at anything on earth.

"It's a law of physics," he was saying now. "People can't ever truly get away from where they came from. And you, Ms. Sandra Lodge"—he pronounced her maiden name with a venomous clarity—"need to go back to Cambridge."

Even then I knew that this was a sore spot for my mother. Cambridge was where she had grown up, the daughter of a Harvard professor and a socialite wife, both the decendants of old Boston families. Her father had died before I was born. He was the only one in the whole Lodge clan that she spoke of with any real affection. Her mother still lived in Cambridge in the family house on Fayerweather Street, guarded by weeping willows and an ancient barking bloodhound named Gory. We didn't see much of her, and I knew that whenever we did, my mother grew depressed and angry. My father liked to call my grandmother, jokingly, "the last of a noble line," referring to her heritage, which she never let us forget. But my mother called her "the last, thank God, of an evil line" and drove us there only on special occasions.

My father went on taunting my mother: "You belong in the Square, just where I found you, Sandy, no matter how much you try to fight it. You're a Harvard girl at heart." He paused to light up a cigarette, then continued, changing the tone of his voice slightly: "And I need to go to Roxbury. Find me a strong black woman. A sistah. No more of this crazy white-girl shit."

I saw my mother clench her fist around the object in her hand. She forced a harsh sound in her throat, something like a laugh. "Oh my God. Since when do you talk that way? 'A sistah.' Don't blacken your speech around me. I know where you come from. You can't fool me."

My father ignored her and continued putting his stuff away with a methodical concentration. He had been trying to grow an afro, and it was crooked that morning. He was ordinarily so meticulous in his appearance, and the sleep-molded slant to his hair told me something serious was going on. He had changed since last night and was dressed casually, blue jeans and a faded B.U. T-shirt.

Cole leaned over and said, "You think we should try to go with him?"

I shook my head. "No way. He'll be back. This is just an act."

Really, I wasn't sure he'd be back. But I knew I didn't want to go with him. He was so distracted all the time. I thought my mother was more fun, even if she did act wild on occasion.

She was acting pretty wild now, ranting, pacing up and down the sidewalk with her fist still balled at her side. She was in the middle of her own speech: "Let me tell you something, Mister Esteemed Professor of Bullshit. If you think you know everything, then explain this. How can you talk about Black Power and leave your two daughters with their white mother? Tell me that. If I'm such a 'crazy white girl,' how am I going to raise these two?"

He shrugged. "We've been through this already, Sandy. I'm taking them on weekends. And besides, they're going to the school in Roxbury."

I had heard mention of a school in Roxbury before, but wasn't sure what it was all about. Cole and I had never been to real school. Only my mother's school, in between the dyslexic kids who came to be tutored in the afternoons. My mother said she wanted to keep us safe from the racism and violence of the world. She said she could teach us better at home, and prided herself that Cole and I were well above the reading and math levels for our ages. In the beginning, when my parents still got along, my father had agreed that we should be taught at home. He had even contributed to some of our lesson plans. He liked to joke to his friends that Cole and I were going to be proof that race mixing produced superior minds, the way a mutt is always more intelligent than a purebred dog. (My mother agreed with this theory of his. She said that's why Wasps were such a stupid race; like golden retrievers, she said, Wasps were experiencing the effects of too much inbreeding.)

It was only recently that my father had decided that we should go to a real school—that my mother's lessons weren't adequate. And he had picked this school in Roxbury, where some of his new friends sent their kids. He hadn't even consulted my mother first, had just come home one day and announced that this was where we were going. Now my mother stopped in her tracks and turned to him. "Jesus, you've got nerve. If you think some Black

Power school's gonna make up for your absence, it won't." With that, she threw the object that was in her hand—a sock—and as it sailed through the air, I could see it was mine. A red sock with blue polka dots. It grazed his head, then rolled beneath his car. I thought of running to fetch it, but I knew it was against the rules.

My father stared at the sock for a moment with clear disgust, then clicked shut the trunk to his Volvo before walking around to the front of the car, jingling his keys.

My mother watched him start up the engine, her arms hanging loosely so that she looked bewildered, like a girl. "Come off it, Deck. I mean, I guess the school makes some sense with Cole. But Birdie? Look at her sometime, really look at her. Try to see beyond yourself and your goddamn history books. She looks like a little Sicilian."

Sicilian. I didn't know what it meant. Only that it sounded dirty off my mother's tongue. I could feel Cole beside me, studying me, struggling to see something on my face, something she had never seen before. I stuck my tongue out at her, trying to make her laugh, but she looked sad, worried, and turned back to my father, who was starting up the motor of the old Volvo. Soul music from his car floated in the air around us.

He spoke slowly, softly, to my mother now, so I had to strain to hear him. "I know what my daughter looks like, thank you. Maybe you need to cut this naïve, color-blind posturing. In a country as racist as this, you're either black or you're white. And no daughter of mine is going to pass."

He revved the engine of the car, and before he cruised away he shouted out his window: "You should really take a look at my book again. It explains everything."

He was referring to his last book—Wonders of the Visible World—which was about the fate of black people in an integrated society. He tried to read it aloud to Cole a few times, but she always began to rub her eyes and whine that she wanted to go play. Nothing drove my mother more crazy than when he mentioned the book. During his research for it, he had given Cole and me a sort of racial IQ test using building blocks, questionnaires, and different-colored dolls. I was three at the time, and those dolls were the only part of the test I really remembered. Some of them were black, some of them were white; the rest were soiled and ripped stuffed animals he had found at the Salvation Army. He had us play with them in our bedroom, while he sat nearby, his lanky form squeezed into our child-sized blue plastic chair, watching us intently and scribbling notes on a little pad. He had devoted several pages of the book to the results of that test, referring to Cole as "Subject A" and me as "Subject B." My mother had been infuriated, but Cole and I had thought the tests were fun. We got new toys out of it, as well as his attention, uninterrupted, for hours on end.

He was supposed to be working on a new book. This one also would be about race, he had told us one night over dinner at Friendly's, but it would be bigger, better, more groundbreaking than the first. He had said it would cover not just America, but the whole wide world. Cole and I had asked if we could do more experiments. He had only laughed and said, "Don't worry. You'll be in there."

But he was gone now, his car just a distant speck of rust in the distance.

Cole was squeezing my hand tightly, and I could feel a slight moisture between us, though I couldn't tell whose sweat it was.

My mother stood for a moment, watching his car, and I couldn't see her expression, only that her shoulders were hunched angrily forward. Finally she turned around toward the house and blinked in surprise at the sight of us staring at her from the steps.

Cole was the only one to mourn after my father left. She stood frozen for several minutes, watching the street even after his car was out of sight. After we had gone inside, she cried into her cereal bowl, dripping fat hot tears and heaving in shivers, while my mother swept the floor obsessively and, with her eyes averted, talked in a high, quavering voice about how often we would still see him, how close Roxbury really was. I patted my sister's hand, whispering consolations in Elemeno, wishing all the while that I could muster up some tears too. But I couldn't, for I felt a secret relief at seeing him go, a tinge of hope that he might take their fighting with him.

That night I looked at myself in the steamy bathroom mirror while I brushed my teeth, the white toothpaste foaming onto my hand, making me look like a rabid dog, and I tried to think what Sicilian meant by reading my own face. I glanced at my sister's reflection behind me. She was also brushing her teeth, only neatly. Her hair was curly and mine was straight, and I figured that this fact must have had something to do with the fighting and the way the eyes of strangers flickered surprise, sometimes amusement, sometimes disbelief, when my mother introduced us as sisters.

same
difference

I liked to play a game with myself. I would try to imagine the days before I was born—what my parents were wearing, what the weather was like, what the smells in the air were. Sometimes I saw that first meeting, as if I were there with them, floating over them, waiting with bated breath for them to bring me to life. But most of the time the image disintegrated into the people they had become, no matter how hard I tried to see something different. They didn't have a wedding album. It was as if nobody had cared enough to document the event. My only proof that they had even been married was a snapshot I found stuck inside my father's huge encyclopedia. It marked the page that delineated the three racial phenotypes of the world—Mongoloid, Negroid, and Caucasoid. The page included three drawings, the first of a Chinaman, the second of an African Bushman, and the third of a European explorer, but I was more interested in the wedding photograph.

In it, my parents stand on a lawn behind my mother's family home in Cambridge. My mother looks like a missionary in her flowing Guatemalan skirt and peasant blouse; she wears her hair in twin braids on either side of her face. Her transluscent blue eyes are those of a child on her first day of school—terrified, blinking, expectant. My father looks frightened as well in his stiff collar, the kink of his hair cut close to his scalp. The lawn around them is sprinkled with relatives, smiles so tight it could have been a funeral.

Dot stands in the corner of the photo, wearing a silver lamé minidress, the only one whose smile looks sincere.

That discarded photo was the only proof that there had been a before. My father wasn't a nostalgic man and just shrugged, irritated, when we asked him for stories of how they had come to be together. My mother didn't talk about that time either, except to say that she had been drowning in the cream of Cambridge society and that the day she met my father, she came up for air. But I knew that in order to understand how it all fell apart, I needed to know how it all had come together.

I got my chance a few weeks after my father moved out. My mother had been lonely since that day, and each night, seated cross-legged on the living room floor, she put back Scotch or Irish whiskey. Cole and I tried to keep out of her way, sticking to the attic, where we played our elaborate games of make-believe. But one evening my mother called us down to keep her company. She wasn't drunk yet, but moving toward it, and Aretha Franklin belted out from the stereo. Cole and I were dressed in tattered antique gowns that held the faint smells of old women—talcum and dust and Chanel No. 5. We sat on either side of her on the couch. She said she was going to tell us the story of how she met my father. I've never been sure how much of the story was fact, how much was fiction. But as she spoke, Cole and I listened, quiet as we'd ever been, staring out the darkened window as if the scene she described were a silent movie that played on the glass before us.

IT WAS THE COLDEST day of the year, January 17, 1963, and my mother was lost. She was eighteen, less than a year out of high school, and her future sat before her, blank and bleak as the New England winter. She had been accepted to Brandeis but had turned the school down at the last minute. Even then, she thought of school as a kind of prison. She had never fit into the world of the Buckingham School. There, she had been a hefty and pensive girl in a world of lithe and winsome debutantes, girls who accepted their good fortunes with style and manners. The Cambridge boys were no better and had treated my mother as a joke, the one to tease one another about. "You'll end up with that lard-ass, Sandy Lodge, if you're not careful."

She had never really had a boyfriend in all her years at Buckingham. She didn't count the night that three athletes from the boys' school, Browne and Nichols, had followed her home drunk and held her against a brick wall on Lowell Street while each of them felt underneath her skirt, calling her disgusting and ugly, a sloth, even as their pants bulged with desire. In the daylight those same boys had chosen girls more like my mother's own mother, whose hips stuck out beyond the flatness of her belly, whose body was fragile, hard, androgynous.

So the winter after her high-school graduation, my mother found herself still living at home. Her father was a professor of classics at Harvard, and that night she went to meet him in the Square to discuss her future. She walked with her head tilted to the side, toward the light and confusion of Harvard Square, toward her father, the gentle professor. He had sworn there were plenty of options for her. The Peace Corps. A job in publishing. A research position with a professor friend. Her interests were literature, existentialism, and the Holocaust. She was obsessed by the footage she had seen of the Jews being liberated from Treblinka, and often found herself crying over photographs of the sad-eyed skeletons of the camps.

As she walked, wearing a mannish tweed coat and her horn-rimmed glasses, she carried a book under her arm. Her father had bought it for her. He was always doing that—bringing her gifts after a day of teaching: pistachio nuts; a chocolate malt from Brighams; Tintin comics, which both of them shared a passion for. The night before he had come home with *The Notebooks of Albert Camus*. It was Camus's diary, and she had stayed up all night reading it. As she walked, she pondered a line from the book, under the date November 11, 1942: "Outside of love, woman is boring." She read that line over and over and felt an intense emptiness.

She came to the building where her father taught his evening class on Plato and Aristotle. On the lawn around her stood marble bodies frozen in thought. She sat down to wait in her usual spot, on the bottom steps, where, with mittened hands, she read more of Camus's diary. After a while she looked up to the sound of footsteps on the concrete. Her father was coming toward her through the darkening evening air, wearing his black herringbone jacket, a hat perched over his eyes. He looked old to her all of a sudden, like a ghost, and she rose to meet him. Trailing after him, following him out and into the night, were three students—later she would remember the other two, but at that moment they faded like unnecessary scenery. All she saw was the one who stood out, the brown-skinned boy who wouldn't look her in the eye. Her father introduced this student with some amount of paternal pride—Deck Lee. He added, with a note of apology, that the students needed to discuss their papers for a bit at the café at the corner. She didn't mind, did she? Her future would have to wait.

On the sidewalk outside the café, some street musician sang a Pete Seeger song. Inside, the men talked over cups of steaming coffee about the subject of the class: Plato's cave. Given her youth, my mother was still ignorant on the topic, so she sat in the corner with her hot chocolate and muffin, sifting through the pages of Camus's diary. She said she felt a discontent with these, a force willing her to glance up from time to time at the quiet and elegant black man who watched the others talk with a kind of knowing disdain.

What did my mother know of black people at this time? She read the papers often enough to know that the Negroes down South were mobilizing for their civil rights and that the Kennedy administration was getting nervous. She had asked her father about all of this, and he had told her with a look of grave concern that the Negroes had a right to be angry. Her parents had discussed the issues with their friends, mostly Harvard faculty, some Cambridge eccentrics—actors, writers—thrown into the lot, but all with a kind of distance that struck her as odd.

She looked at the man across the table, who was blowing on the steaming mug in front of him. He was immaculately dressed. She told me she had wondered about this fact: Why were Negroes so neat and tidy compared to white people? She had noticed this more than once. She had no particular interest in Negroes at this time—not in them or their cause. Just a sense that they were a mysterious race, full of secrets that the white world would probably never glimpse. The ones she saw on the streets of Boston seemed so different from the happy, smiling brown faces she saw in the movies, on television—the Bojangleses and Hattie McDowells of the world. Outside of pictures, they seemed closed, tense-faced people, forever in a hurry, forever averting their eyes from her.

This student called Deck was steadily ignoring my mother. She supposed it was because of her hefty frame. But she wasn't bothered. She was glad to have a chance to watch him closely, as close to a Negro man as she had ever come, really. He was not very dark, and his features were not very African—it was only his milk-chocolate skin that gave his race away. His face spoke of something other—his high cheekbones, his large bony nose, his deep-set eyes, and his thin lips against the brown of his skin. It reminded her of the drawings in her high-school history book of half-nude natives at the first Thanksgiving. His hair wasn't so woolly, either. It was more like that of some of the Jews she had seen who had afros—black ringlets pleasantly curling into his scalp. Fingers. His were long, darker around the knuckles. Looking at them, she could tell he was nervous. They drummed against his knee under the table, and she wondered what reason he had to be uncomfortable. She had a sudden urge to reach out and pat his hand—a motherly urge—and say, "It's all right. We're on your side." But she wouldn't and didn't do it. Instead she thumbed through more pages of Camus, and later, when they all stood under a clear, starless sky, she shook each of the young men's hands. My father's, she says now, was a weak handshake, not a good sign, as he pulled his soft dainty hand away from her large gruff one and then stuffed it in his pocket as the professor went on with the other two men about something terribly boring. That was when their eyes caught. At first my father's shot nervously away, then came back, resting on her face with a strangely placid interest.

He said to her in a soft voice, "Do you drink coffee at night?"

My mother blushed, and stammered, "No, never. I mean, not usually. It keeps me up."

My father nodded, somehow amused, and my mother wondered if she had misheard his question. Soon her father was ready to go home, and they waved good-bye to the huddle of boys who stood chattering to one another long after they had turned the corner.

She usually spoke everything to her father, but that night, as they walked, she was speechless. Something had shifted inside of her during that interaction, though nothing had happened. She felt separate from her father in a way she never had before. He was quiet as well, and they went home that way, immersed in their own thoughts. It was only when they were close enough to see the house, with the yellow lit windows, and could hear the sound of opera being played loudly from the phonograph that her father spoke to her.

He said it as if they had been talking all along, were in the middle, in fact, of a conversation: "Sometimes I get the feeling that Deck character despises us—even us liberals. It's just a feeling I get, nothing obvious. I think all Negroes despise us, really."

My mother cried out, "But why?"

Her father turned to her and smiled slightly, sadly, as he said, "Because they know we're cowards."

She felt a cry coming on, and turned her face away from him so he wouldn't see her expression.

That night my mother lay in bed, buried beneath her pink, girlish duvet, and flipped through Camus in a distracted state, only half-digesting the words on the page. But something did jump out at her, on the bottom of page 199—Camus's sketches of dialogue for a novel.

X: "Do you drink coffee at night?"
"In general, never."

COLE AND I waited for their reunion. We waited for Chinese noodles, red wine, and Al Green to appear and make everything better. But the Redbone fight seemed to have been the kicker. It had been three weeks, and my father was still in Roxbury. There were no more shrieks or curses or glasses hitting the walls. At first I was relieved with the peace and quiet. But then, as the weeks went on, the vacuous silence of our house began to keep me awake at night, the way their fighting once had.

The visitors were gone as well. They seemed to have evacuated along with my father. Instead, my mother, Cole, and I were left to fill the corners of the big old dusty house. I missed the visitors. It had always been an adventure, waiting to see who would show up at midnight, a dirty knapsack slung over a shoulder. When I asked my mother why the guests had disappeared, she was vague, puffing on her eternal Marlboro and glancing around her shoulder as she said, "Things are getting crazy out there, Birdalee. We can't fool around anymore." But Cole said that my mother was keeping the house empty to get my father to come home.

My mother did seem to be waiting for something. She would sit on the front stoop till late into the night, smoking, and scanning the street as if waiting for someone to show. She was quiet a lot of the time, cleaning the house with a new vigor and watching the nightly news with a studied rage.

Cole and I busied ourselves those long summer afternoons playing make-believe in our attic. We spoke our language and, no matter how hot it was outside, we traipsed around the house in our most elaborate costumes—feathered plumes, long dresses from the forties, a man's stiff black Stetson, an African mask that my father brought back to us from Kenya. I think now that we must have known our days were numbered and that pretty soon we'd be sent out into the world, so our games held an extra intensity. We didn't have other friends, just each other, and sometimes while we drove around in the back of my mother's Pinto, I would stare at the children outside with a newfound interest, wondering which one of them I would become.

It was in late August when my mother drove Cole and me to City Hall to find out where we would be bused. My mother had decided that the public schools would be best—she didn't want us separated from the people. I think now that she wanted to irritate my father by refusing to send us to the special school in Roxbury. I would never get a chance to experience this thing called Black Power. All I knew of it was that my father agreed with it, my mother and her friends supported it, and it had something to do with the length and consistency of my father's hair.

The leaves, tipped with gold already, made a sizzling sound as they brushed together, and the water on the Charles had turned from its summer silver into a murkier indigo. We arrived at City Hall, and the woman behind the desk took one look at Cole and me and assigned us to different districts. I would be bused to a predominately black school in Dorchester; Cole to South Boston, the Irish section, "in the interest of dahvesetty," the woman explained to us in her thick local accent.

My mother laughed too loudly. She wore a pair of gray sweatpants with baggy, misshapen knees, my father's old crew T-shirt, and her hair in pigtails like an oversized school girl. Even at that age, I could see that she had the power to frighten. Her voice would start quivering at some injustice—an inflated price tag, a parking ticket on the Pinto, a doctor's office bill—and before I knew it, passersby would cluck their teeth at her shrieks, the blasphemy flowing from her lips, and they would look at Cole and me with something that was not quite pity, not quite hatred—as if our presence somehow explained her bad behavior.

Her grip tightened around mine, and I heard her say, "No, I don't think you understand. They're sisters. They stick together. You got a problem with that?"

The woman behind the desk sensed something brewing in my mother's tone. She quickly conceded with a brisk, tense smile. "Okay, ma'am, no big deal. Cool down. We'll bus 'em both to Southie."

We were bused together, but it didn't matter in the end. We never got there.

For the first ten minutes of that bus ride, everything seemed ordinary— the children around us slapped and whispered and shouted to one another, shifting restlessly on the sticky green vinyl. Cole and I sat side by side, speaking in hushed tones. *Wichita OrenthaKublica . . .* She was telling me a story about a great fallen king when I noticed we were slowing down. We stopped at the corner of Franklin Park. The bus driver, a thin Puerto Rican man with earrings and a goatee, leaned closer to the radio, listening to a broadcaster whose words snapped and crackled in fragments toward us at the back of the bus. For those long five minutes we were utterly quiet and orderly. I held Cole's hand and looked out the window. The sky was thick and low, the color of smoke, though no rain broke through. The wall of pudding stone that surrounded Franklin Park seemed to have faces etched in it. In the seat beside us, a tiny boy wore clothes so starched they made him look wooden, like a puppet. He began to cry as his big sister patted his hand and whispered to him in Spanglish.

Finally the bus driver stood and yelled to us, "We can't go on. Those motherfuckers are crazy. No place for children."

No school. It seemed some cause for celebration. I looked around, gleeful. But all the other kids seemed to understand something, and they watched me with somber expressions.

We must have been a pitiful sight when we arrived in Roxbury that same morning, shuttling off the bus in our first-day outfits, all spiffed up with no place to go. Cole and I clutched our recently purchased Sesame Street lunch boxes—hers with Oscar the Grouch, mine with Big Bird. We were dressed immaculately in starched white shirts and plaid skirts, buffed Mary Janes on our feet. A group of grown-ups waited on the steps of the local high school, a huddle of worried brown faces, and my mother a shock of blond in their midst. Once we were with her, she held Cole to her side like a badge of entrance, and I tagged along behind them.

There was a television inside the principal's office, and we all crowded around it to watch the news, the image grainy and crackling on the small screen—one lone black man being pulled from his Volkswagen only to disappear under a cloud of white fists. The parents were silent as they watched, mesmerized by the image. I held my mother's hand and stopped breathing, terrified by what I saw. My mother seemed frozen as well. The newscaster talked excitedly over the live footage, saying something about riots and race wars. At one point the man's face rose from the throng, anguished, terrified, bewildered. I was reminded of Lucas's expression the night he left, the two men holding him roughly as they led him down the steps. He had looked slightly surprised, as if he had expected more from our country, as if he had expected more from our house.

I turned to my mother and buried my head in her jacket.

"Make them stop, Mum. Make them stop hitting him."

She tilted my head back to look at me, and something in her expression—a slight smile, but dead-serious eyes—made me believe her when she said: "That's what I'm trying to do, baby."

I had the vague notion that the problem had something to do with the Irish. I knew the Irish lived in one part of town, that black people lived in another, and that we lived in a part that had once been black and Puerto Rican but was now being, as my father had put it, "overrun by settlers." The Irish lived mostly in Southie, which was entirely different from the South End, our neighborhood. My father had to duck down when we drove through Southie. I didn't know any Irish kids, and it had been about a year since Cole and I had had a run-in with a pack of Irish girls in the underwear department of Decelles in West Roxbury. They wore matching windbreakers and had thin dark hair. I had been seven years old, and Cole had been ten, and the girls had smiled at us as if they knew some secret they wanted to let us in on, as if they wanted to be friends, as if they wanted us to join them in something. I stopped smiling only when they shoved Cole into the rack of bras and one of them stuck some chewed bubble gum in her hair. They hurried off then, laughing, but not so fast that I didn't hear what they said: *Go back to the jungle, darkie. Go wash your ass. Go, you little culahd biscuit.* They left her standing, hidden in the curtains of cloth, her bottom lip quivering but not letting go.

I wondered if those girls were the same ones who wouldn't let us come to school today, the same ones who stood in that crowd on the television set—the ones who hooted delight as a baseball bat fell to a scalp, turning it all soft inside.

As we left the building, I heard shouting. It was a familiar voice. It was Redbone. He was standing at the bottom of the steps, surrounded by a small group of parents. I tugged at Cole's sleeve and whispered, "It's him," but she seemed distant, disturbed still by the man on the TV screen. We followed my mother to the huddle of parents, and I stood at the outskirts, scuffing my shoe, feeling scared all of a sudden. My mother pushed through to the front of the group, pulling Cole behind her. I heard Redbone saying, "We need more drastic action. No more of this pussy-footing around these devils— they've proven to us today that they can't handle the peaceful solution. Ain't we fed up yet with getting the shaft? What's it gonna take before brothers and sisters start doin' it for themselves?"

Most of the parents left, shaking their heads, and I heard mutters.

"He's crazy. Doesn't know what he's calling for."

"Looks like a white boy with clown makeup on, if you ask me."

"I heard he was part of that crazy group."

"Bunch of hoodlums, if you ask me."

But my mother stayed. Later, when the crowd had dispersed, she and Redbone talked together in tones of restrained excitement and outrage, leaning into each other as if they had been friends for years.

I couldn't hear what Redbone said to my mother, but in the car ride home, I piped in from the backseat: "That's the guy from the party. Papa said he's bad. Why were you talking to him, Mum?"

Cole backed me up: "Yeah, Mum. Birdie said he was a real freak."

My mother didn't seem to hear us and only turned up the music on the radio and tapped her hands on the steering wheel as we waited at a traffic light. She kept taking her foot off the brake so that we inched forward slightly, over the crosswalk. She ignored us sometimes, and then just when we thought she hadn't heard us, she'd answer. As we started to move, she said, "Well, girls, your father isn't God Almighty. I do have a life of my own. And besides," she said, scrambling in her purse for a cigarette, "he should be happy. I'm sending you to Nkrumah. The Black Power school."

SCHOOL HAD ALREADY BEEN in session for several weeks before she got around to taking us there. Burnished leaves drifted from the trees, leaving stark frames and a chaos of colors. I sat in the backseat of our battered green Pinto, watching the city fly by. Cole sat beside me, humming to herself, holding my hand loosely in her own. I could see my mother's eyes, darting and blue, reflected in the rearview mirror. I could feel my breathing begin to tighten up in my lungs the way it did sometimes. Outside, a clutter of housing projects where Irish kids in bright winter parkas kicked a ball around the pavement. Farther down the road, tenements, boarded up and covered in Spanish graffiti. As we passed under the Washington Street El, the street darkened like a premature nightfall and a train roared by overhead. I closed my eyes as I leaned my head on Cole's shoulder.

When I opened them, we had arrived. We were in Roxbury, and ahead of us I could see a brick building where a red, gold, and green flag waved over the littered street. The Nkrumah School.

We pulled to a halt at the curb, and the Pinto let out its ceremonial grunts and wheezes. My mother turned to us, but fixed her gaze on me. "Well, here we are."

Next door to the school, on the corner, sat an abandoned Jewish synagogue with weeds growing out of the cracks in the stone. Soda cans and gum wrappers lay scattered on its untended lawn. There were words engraved into the temple's pale granite, words that somehow stuck with me later, when we were on the road and all that was just a memory.

Not by might
Nor by power
But by my Spirit,
Saith the Lord

Inside the Nkrumah School, a woman wearing fuscia lipstick sat at the front desk, typing. A cigarette burned in the ashtray beside her, and at its tip was the bright ghost of her lip print. She looked at my mother over the tops of her cat-eye glasses and said in a cool voice, "Can I help you with something?"

My mother held me to her side while Cole wandered around the front office, examining posters on the wall.

"Yes, I'm here to register my daughters for the school program."

The woman looked at us now. She stared hardest at Cole. At eleven, Cole's tight black ringlets hung around her face in a bob. She had turned honey-colored over the summer, though later, in the winter, when she lost her tan, she would turn closer to my own shade of beige. She had my father's kinky hair and small, round nose. Her eyes, however, were my mother's—the color of sea glass, forever shifting between blue, green, and gray.

"Is this our new student?"

My mother gripped my hand, and I suddenly felt sticky, stifled in the small cluttered office. Something smelled of food, and I glimpsed a foil wrapper with a half-chewed bagel and lox peeking out from under a newspaper.

"Both of them are new students," my mother said with that edge to her voice. "They're sisters."

The woman glanced at me now, a wan smile forming on her lips. After a pause, she pulled out some registration papers, stuck them onto a clipboard, and said with something like exhaustion, "I see."

"Who's that?"

"She a Rican or something?"

"I thought this was supposed to be a black school."

The teacher was late, and I kept my head down, reading the scribblings on the desktop and trying to ignore the whispers of the other kids around me. The classroom was small and run down, with battered boxes of textbooks in the corner, a caged and anemic gerbil that sat stone-still in its treadmill, and a mismatched collection of desks—some terribly small, so that our knees pushed against the tops, others so big we had to sit perched on our knees to see over them.

A boy threw a spitball, which hit me square in the forehead. Laughter sprinkled the room. He hissed, "What you doin' in this school? You white?"

All eyes were on me, and I tried to think of something to say. I felt the familiar tightening in my lungs. The children stared at me, mouths hanging open. A terrifying silence had overtaken the room.

Underneath the desk, I could feel dried lumps of bubble gum, and there was something comforting about those lumps, as if they were the writing on the cave wall from some ancient civilization—proof that others had lived through this moment. I moved my fingertips over the gum slowly, as if I were trying to read Braille.

I was about to say "Sicilian," when Mrs. Potter, the teacher, entered. She was a tall, big-boned, camel-colored woman with gray eyes and a thick braid down her back, and, like my mother, her thighs made a swishing noise when she walked. She glanced at me as she passed my desk. "You must be the new girl. Birdie Lee, right? I just met your sister."

She talked in a circular kind of lecture to us that day about Frederick Douglass, Sojourner Truth, Nat Turner. She seemed to fall into a reverie of sorts, pacing in and out of our rows, rubbing her hands together as if concocting a recipe as she spoke. Her voice was tough, scratchy, and she knew how to tell a story. She made each of her subjects seem like superheroes, and even the baddest-looking of boys rested their heads in their hands and just listened. I forgot about the whispers of the other children. At the end of class, she stopped abruptly as if wakened from a sleepwalk, and turned to us, only now remembering we were there.

"Our tradition," she said, looking directly at me, "is that at the end of each class, everyone stands and says, 'Black is beautiful.' Loud and clear. You gotta be proud of where your people came from. We are the first people, and we will be the last. Understand that, and nobody can touch you. Who wants to start? Cynthia?"

A slender girl with thick glasses stood and said the slogan in a bored voice, scratching white lines like dust tracks onto her thin, dark thigh.

Then each student, one by one, stood up and recited the phrase, some with passion, some mumbling.

When it was my turn, I stood. My fingers clenched the cloth of my skirt, and my voice quavered: "Black is beautiful?" It had come out more like a question.

I heard one boy—the same one who had thrown the spitball at me—say into his cupped hands, "Guess you must be ugly."

Snickers filled the room.

"Damn, he called her shit."

"Ali, you so goofy."

"Ali, I heard your mama—"

Mrs. Potter hit her desk with a ruler, and the class went silent. "That's enough. Birdie, you can sit down."

At five o'clock we all gathered in the gym for a fifteen-minute break. Whistles were blown, balls thrown, and sneakers screeched on the shiny wood floor. I sat in the corner by myself, staring down at my fingers. But I felt a hand on my shoulder, and turned. It was Cole.

"C'mon, Birdie, come play. They know you're my sister." Cole had already made friends with a group of gossipy girls.

I sat on the sidelines, watching them jump rope because I didn't know how and was afraid to be laughed at. Cole, meanwhile, played along, jumping in the middle of the flying ropes, clumsy as she wanted to be.

I OPENED THE DOOR to the second-floor girls' room and saw them gathered there by the window, the midafternoon light turning them all golden for a moment. I had been at the school for only three days, but already I knew enough to hesitate. I wanted to turn around, go to the bathroom on the first floor, but they had spotted me at the door already and I knew it was too late. I put my head down and made my way toward an open stall. I recognized one of the girls as Maria Miller, a pretty girl with thick black hair and smooth brown skin. She was a year older than me, and already wore braces. She stepped close to me when I tried to pass her, so that our bodies brushed together.

Inside the stall I felt too afraid to pee, self-conscious they would hear it hitting the water. Their whispers and laughter were muffled beyond the thin piece of wall, and I closed my eyes, trying an old trick my mother had taught me—imagining running water—to help get my own waters flowing. Nothing came for a few minutes, and beyond the partition there was a heavy silence, an occasional bark of laughter as they seemed to wait with me. Finally a trickle came out.

In order to use the sink, I had to stand right next to Maria, and I recognized her perfume, Jean Naté, the kind Cole wore. They sold it at Woolworth's. She stepped closer behind me and looked over my shoulder at me in the mirror. I felt a droplet of sweat rolling down my back. In the mirror I watched as Maria reached her hand up ever so slowly, in an almost tender motion, and I wasn't sure what she was going to do. Then she yanked my ponytail hard, her large brown eyes flashing mischief. She said, sneering, "Why you so stuck up? You think you're fine?"

I tried to smile as if it were all a joke, even as she pulled my head back toward her.

Cathy Murphy, the drama teacher's daughter, who was tall, yellow, and smelled like pencil shavings, moved close to me and said, "She thinks she's all that just 'cause she got long, stringy hair. I say we give Ms. Thang a makeover. Cherise, go get some scissors from the art room."

Cherise, a short, serious girl, crossed her arms and shook her head. "You all can get the scissors by yourself. I ain't getting into trouble."

Cathy sucked her teeth and said, "You're such a baby," shoving past Cherise as she went out the door.

I just stood there with my head tilted toward Maria's grasp.

Cathy returned shortly, grinning, with some small paper scissors in her hand. They had blue plastic handles. I wondered briefly if they were the same ones I had used to cut my mural pictures in art class earlier that day. Those scissors had been blunt, I remembered, barely getting through the construction paper.

Maria grabbed the scissors from Cathy. "You think Ali's gonna like you when you don't got no hair?"

I didn't know who Ali was, but a vision flashed through my mind—of Maria laughing, her silver train-track teeth catching the light as my ponytail swung dismembered in her hand.

I closed my eyes and heard the cool, swift slice of the scissors. When I opened my eyes, Maria was laughing silently into her hand.

"She thought I really cut it. Damn, she thought I was for real."

Cherise said then, her eyes downcast, "C'mon, Maria, leave her alone. Let's go to class before Mr. Murphy catches us."

They left me standing in front of the cracked bathroom mirror, touching my hair gingerly as if I had just discovered I had any, while the echoing sound of voices and laughter bounced off the hall walls in the distance.

THAT NIGHT I lay under the sheets, listening to the angry swell of South End traffic outside. My sister lay next to me on the old brass bed that had once been our parents'.

I told her in Elemeno what had happened in the girls' room. She was quiet, listening. When I finished my story, I curled up closer to her. "I don't want to go back," I said. "I'm scared. They're gonna kill me." I began to whimper. "Don't you hate it there, Cole? Don't you hate it too?"

She turned to me so we were facing each other in our fetal positions. "No, Birdie. I kind of like it. It's fun. I want to stay." She paused. "Anyway, we can't do home school forever."

She wiped a hair out of my eye. Then she said, "Don't worry, Bird. I'll make sure nobody messes with you."

The next day she dragged me back to the girls' room after gym. Only Maria and Cherise were there. I hung back in the corner by the sink while Cole marched right up to Maria.

"You try and cut her hair?"

Maria had been sitting on the whistling radiator, filing her nails. Now she stood up to face Cole.

"I didn't cut nobody. We was just playing. Just 'cause she's white she thinks she's all that." She chewed her gum loudly and glanced over at me standing in the corner. "Besides," Maria continued, "what you gonna do about it?"

Cole grabbed Maria by her long thick hair. I stood back, terrified for Cole. She was also new in the school. But she whispered to Maria, "Listen, metal mouth, Birdie isn't white. She's black. Just like me. So don't be messing with her again or I'll cut off all your hair for real this time."

Maria pulled out of Cole's grasp and said, "Get your hands out of my hair." Then she shrugged, smoothing down her vest. "So now I know."

Cherise stood up and glanced at her watch. "Come on, y'all. We're gonna be late for third period."

And she was right. Without further words, the four of us turned and went single-file out the swinging door, hurrying to make it to our next class.

WORD SPREAD AROUND the school quickly. Cole was my protector. Nobody messed with me, but they didn't talk to me either. I often found myself alone, chewing on my hair and nails with an insatiable hunger, as if trying to eat myself alive, picking at my scabs with a fervor, as if trying to find another body buried inside. I pondered whether it was better to be harrassed or ignored. My insomnia grew worse. Cole slept soundly beside me, and she looked frozen in the blue light of the room, entirely serene and a little waxy, like a doll of herself. I imagined that I was keeping vigil over her. She had a face that betrayed all of its origins, and she wore the expression of the already beautiful—a sleepy confidence that kept other children at her mercy; a face of those accustomed to being watched, used to the approving smiles of strangers.

But even Cole had trouble to contend with.

One afternoon in gym class, she walked into the crowd wearing her blue shorts. She had white knees, and the other children called her out right then and there. I sat in the back on a bleacher, talking to myself in Elemeno. But I saw it and felt for her while the other kids hooted and hollered.

"Check it out! Check out Cole's knees."

"Ain't she ever heard of lotion?"

"Shit, I could write my name in that ash."

After school that day, she dragged herself to the Pinto, head hung low, nearly in tears, and made our mother drive straight to Woolworth's, where she purchased a family-size container of Jergen's lotion. That night she taught herself and me where the trouble spots were—where to focus when buttering up in the morning. Elbows, knees, calves, but especially the feet, where the dust could leave such a thick layer that you actually turned white and dry and cracked and old-looking. Since that day I too used the lotion, in the mornings in the bathroom beside her, though the dust didn't build up so white on me—just a little bit here and there. The Jergen's lotion made me feel like I was part of some secret club.

Then there was Cole's hair.

One Saturday afternoon a month into our stay at Nkrumah, I came downstairs to find her seated cross-legged between my mother's legs, grunting and wincing as my mother tugged on her hair. My mother was talking to the television set. It was the news. She always spoke back to the news, no matter what they were reporting.

"These motherfuckers," she was saying. "These fucking liars. I mean, spreading these lies about Castro. They should be shot for calling this news."

A copy of *Jet* magazine sat open before them, and a bright-eyed new sitcom star grinned up at us under the words "Cute and Sassy Keisha Taylor Tells Her Beauty Secrets." Cole had been obsessing over the picture for the past few weeks, and now the page fell open naturally to it. Keisha Taylor had tight cornrows with gold beads at the end. Just the way Cole wanted them.

My mother appeared to know what she was doing. Her fingers were quick and nimble as they worked over each section of hair, and she chewed loudly, brassily, on a piece of gum, keeping her eyes on the television set. But it was just an act. I could tell she wasn't getting it right. The braids she had done on Cole's head weren't stuck to her scalp the way they were supposed to be, the way they were on Keisha Taylor. Instead they were thick, uneven ropes that sprung out haphazardly. There was no way that Cole would be able to fit even one gold bead around them.

Cole was about to cry. She whimpered, "It hurts, Mum. You aren't doing it right. You're pulling too hard. How does it look, Birdie?"

Before I could answer, my mother shot me a look of warning and said, "It's not even done yet. Just wait. I'm almost there."

I bit my lip and looked away.

My mother had been trying to do Cole's hair for years now, and it always ended in disaster. When Cole was very little, my mother had simply let her run around with what she called a "dustball" on her head. She had thought the light and curly afro adorable and didn't quite understand the disapproving glances of the black people on the street. At one point, when Cole was three, it had even begun to dreadlock in the back. It had been my father who finally noticed what was going on at Cole's roots and made my mother cut out the tangles, made her start picking out her little afro.

After that, every few months, my mother would sit on a chair, with Cole on the floor between her thighs, her head tilted back, tears streaming from

Cole's eyes as my mother tugged and twisted and braided, only to end up with Cole's hair looking just as messy as it had when my mother had started.

Cole muttered to me now, "Birdie, get me a mirror."

I looked up at my mother, nervously. She was patting down her completed job, with a slightly embarrassed smile. "Now, it'll take a few hours to settle into the look, but really, I mean, I think it looks cute. Cuter, really, than that Keisha Taylor. Don't you think so, Bird?"

I mumbled, "Uh, yeah, I guess, in a way."

Cole was fingering one of the braids suspiciously. "I want a mirror," she repeated.

I tore out of the room and came back with the cracked hand mirror from the bathroom. I held it up in front of Cole, and she wrenched it out of my hands.

She stared at herself for a few minutes. It was hard to read her expression. I was biting my nails and scratching my leg and waiting, while my mother had already begun to put the hair tools back into her bag, humming a little song to herself.

Finally Cole threw down the mirror. It had been cracked already, but with the force of its landing the broken half fell out onto the floor.

"Colette!" my mother shouted. "What the fuck was that for?"

Cole's chin had crumpled up in horror, and her eyes were liquid green. She turned to my mother. "You liar. It doesn't look like Keisha Taylor. You can't do it! You'll never do it right. It looks like a bird's nest, the same way it always does."

She was right. It did look funny. Like big snakes growing out of her head, flopping into her eyes now as she stood up to go.

My mother slapped her thigh and shook her head. "I don't believe it. The nerve of this child. This is what I get. I was trying to make you happy, and yeah, sure, it doesn't look exactly like Keisha What's-Her-Name. But it looks cute. Now, I at least deserve a little credit."

Cole turned to me. My own hair was braided on one side—I had done them myself while watching Cole. I hadn't known how to make them stick to my head like corn-on-the-cob either. I could feel them slipping out already. She stared at me for a moment, then burst into tears before running out of the room.

She spent the rest of the afternoon taking the braids out of her hair, playing the Ohio Players, and doing her homework behind closed doors. My mother cleaned the living room noisily, blasting Bob Dylan over the vacuum cleaner and singing along to him, imitating his drunken slur. I sat out on the stoop, throwing pieces of stale saltines to the pigeons and watching a man piss across the street. After she finished cleaning, my mother took me shopping for groceries. She was quiet and seemed upset about Cole's outburst. As we wandered the grocery store aisles, she stared into the faces of the passing black children and their mothers while I held on to the side of the cart and sucked on a Tootsie Roll. As if in some cruel hoax, it seemed that all the children we passed wore their hair in neat, elaborate hairstyles.

I tried to catch a glimpse of each child's skin, to see if it was ashy. As my mother and I turned the bend toward the produce, one particularly pretty cocoa-colored girl with a head of cornrows tipped with rainbow-colored beads came toward us. She was wearing slacks, but I bet that her skin was glowing with lotion underneath. She was laughing and babbling to her mother about school. I glanced at my mother. She was staring at the girl and the mother, and she looked sad. I grabbed her hand.

"It's okay, Mum. You can do my hair."

She peeled her eyes away from the girl and stroked my hair. She seemed to see something funny on my face, and laughed a little. "I know I can, Bird. I know it."

I had worried that Cole would be angry at me. But when we got home I heard her bellow from our bedroom upstairs, "Birdie! Comeer." I tore up the stairs, two steps at a time. I found her lying on our bed, flipping through a magazine, her head wrapped in a silk scarf from the bottom of our costume trunk. I slumped down beside her. She seemed changed. As if she had made some profound decision in just the few hours we had been gone. She looked older, more determined.

She threw the magazine onto the bed. Her eyes were gray. Like the weather outside. She said, "They all laughed at me last week. Just like the time my knees were ashy. 'Cause of my hair. It looks crazy. They were calling me 'Miz Nappy.' None of the boys will come near me. Mum doesn't know anything about raising a black child. She just doesn't."

I nodded but felt a warm pain growing in my stomach, rising up through my chest.

"We talk like white girls, Birdie." She picked up the magazine she had been reading, and handed it to me. "We don't talk like black people. It says so in this article."

I glanced at the article. The heading read, "Black English: Bad for Our Children?"

The magazine was *Ebony*. I knew Cole must have stolen it from the teachers' lounge because the words "Property of Nkrumah" were stamped on the front cover across Billy Dee Williams's perfect smile.

Cole continued: "They have examples in here. Like, don't say, 'I'm going to the store.' Say, 'I'm goin' to de sto'.' Get it? And don't say, 'Tell the truth.' Instead, say, 'Tell de troof.' Okay?"

I nodded, and whispered to myself, "Tell de troof."

My mother's old friend Jane came over for dinner that night. She and my mother had known each other since childhood, from prep school in Cambridge. She had graying brown hair, Indian jewelry, and a bright-colored smock, and she was involved in Boston politics. My mother said she was a real radical.

Cole was quiet at dinner, only occasionally whispering to me in Elemeno and avoiding my mother's eyes. My mother seemed sad and kept trying to speak to Cole, only to be met by silence.

Jane didn't notice any tension and spoke to my mother now in hushed excitement about something she referred to only in code as "the drop."

"It's happening, Sandy. It's really happening. It's major. The shit is going to go down, and I think you should be a part of it. All you need to do is let them drop it. Here."

My mother was quiet and looked at Cole and me with a funny expression I had rarely seen on her before. She was smiling, but it was more of a grimace.

I finally broke the silence as I turned to Jane.

"Jane, pass de butta, please?"

I heard Cole giggling, but my mother and Jane just gave me blank, distracted stares.

That night Cole and I lay face-to-face, touching each other's hair and speaking in Elemeno.

sambosa malengtha kristo. bella warma.

Cole's hair was soft and crunchy at the same time, and my fingers got caught when I tried to run them through it. Mine was thick, but straight, dark, an Indian girl's head of hair, with a cowlick in the back.

barana sipho mundana.

Cole was telling me she was going to get her hair braided by professionals. "Mum better let me. Ms. Green at school told me where to go. She said she sends her own daughters there."

"Are they gonna make you look like the Pointer Sisters?" I asked.

"Yeah, like that, only better."

I could imagine her that way, and smiled slightly as I pictured her in a gold spandex suit, dancing to "Taste of Honey" while I played backup on the guitar.

She got her way in the end. My father was the one to put up the money for her to go to Danny's His and Hers, a black hair salon on Tremont Street. It cost fifty dollars, and my mother still insisted that she could do it just as well. My father also had refused at first, saying it was ludicrously overpriced. Then Cole told him, "Mum just doesn't know how to handle raising a black child, Papa." He had stared out the window of his Volvo for a few minutes, pondering this fact, then handed her the fifty with a pained sneer.

A week later, she came home with a full head of tiny cornrows with gold beads on the ends. Even my mother had to admire the look. Cole was splendid, ladylike, suddenly in a whole new league.

I grinned and jumped around her while she peered at herself in the mirror.

MY FATHER WOULDN'T come into the house. Ever since he had left us that bright July morning, he acted as if the house were contaminated. Cole and I told him that the visitors had disappeared, but still he refused to enter. Instead, he'd just honk outside and Cole and I would go tearing down the stairs together and out into his car. My mother would watch from the window, a scowl set on her face, and I always felt a little guilty leaving her behind.

He usually came for us on Saturday mornings. Cole called it "Divorced Fathers Day." She said all her friends had them too. He'd take us to the Public Gardens if it was nice out, or to the Museum of Fine Arts if it was raining.

Sometimes, if we begged, he would take us to a movie—any kind, any rating, so we always made him take us to slasher films. Once there, he would wait for us in the lobby, reading a book on some obscure topic, while we shoveled popcorn and Jujyfruits down our throats and stared, glassy-eyed, at the horrors on the screen.

I can't say that I enjoyed these visits with my father. He never had much to say to me. In fact, he never seemed to see me at all. Cole was my father's special one. I understood that even then. She was his prodigy—his young, gifted, and black. At the time, I wasn't sure why it was Cole and not me, but I knew that when they came together, I disappeared. Her existence comforted him. She was the proof that his blackness hadn't been completely blanched. By his four years at Harvard. By my mother's blue-blood family wedding reception in the back of the big rotting house on Fayerweather Street. By so many years of standing stiffly in corners, listening to those sweatered tow-haired preppies talk about the Negro Problem, nursing their vermouth, glancing at him with so much pleased incredulity in their eyes. Those Crimson boys with all their asinine questions, all their congratulatory remarks about how they saw him as different, had made him want to disappear. They saw him and all his seeming repose, his sardonic smile, as evidence that the black race was indeed human. The very fact that they needed evidence made him nauseous. But somehow, somewhere, he accepted the terms of their debate, and he spent years perfecting his irony and stale wit in order to distinguish himself from the poor black blokes scuttling around the outskirts of the city. Perfected it so well that when he finally returned to Wally's one night, a small jazz joint on Tremont Street, he imagined that the cluster of brown and yellow and black faces that dotted the smoky air were laughing at him, mocking his stiff posture and tight smile.

Cole was his proof that he had indeed survived the integrationist shuffle, that he had remained human despite what seemed a conspiracy to turn him into stone. She was his proof of the pudding, his milk-chocolate pudding, the small dusky body, the burst of mischievous curls (nappier than his own), the full pouting lips (fuller than his own). Her existence told him he hadn't wandered quite so far and that his body still held the power to leave its mark.

He usually treated me with a cheerful disinterest—never hostility or ill will, but with a kind of impatient amusement, as if he were perpetually tapping his foot, waiting for me to finish my sentence so he could get back to more important subjects.

And strange as it may sound, I had never really been alone with my father. Not that I could remember, anyway. So when I got the chance that fall morning, I felt I was going on a blind date and went toward it jittery, with a mixture of hope and fear.

It wouldn't have happened at all if Cole hadn't gotten sick. It might have been just another outing, me in the backseat, making cat's cradles with my string; Cole in the front, trying to listen to the radio and my father's lecture all at once. But that morning Cole claimed to have the flu, and it was too late to stop my father. He was already on his way over.

My mother stood up in our room, holding the back of her hand to Cole's forehead.

Cole sniffled and looked at me through red, watery eyes. "You go, Birdie." She was being very melodramatic about it, and my mother was buying it hook, line, and sinker. She had already gone out to buy Cole the latest issue of *Jet* and a box of cherry-flavored Sucrets, which Cole refused to share with me.

My mother nodded. "Yeah, baby. You go alone with your papa and have a good time."

I stared at my feet, then turned to go down to his car.

When I approached him, he looked up from his book quizzically, and then his eyes roamed behind me for Cole, the real reason he was here.

"Cole's not coming. She's sick," I told him. I stood beside his open window, hands shoved in my pockets, waiting to see if he'd call the whole thing off.

He squinted at the house suspiciously. He was always accusing my mother of trying to keep him from us—"us" meaning Cole.

"Sick with what?"

"A cold. Mum says she's got a fever."

"Hmmph."

Then he looked at me and smiled, a little shyly, I thought.

"Well, then it'll just be the two of us, Patrice. Right?" Sometimes, when he was being particularly affectionate, he would call me by my old name. This was a rarity, however. It meant he was making an extra-special effort to connect with me.

He was quiet as he drove us to the Public Gardens. It was a beautiful day outside, one of those late-fall days in New England when the ground is carpeted with colors, the sky a bright blank blue. My father was listening to the radio, the way he always did, head cocked to the side in thought, mouth turned down in concentration. It was the public radio station, and they were talking about the imprisonment of some radicals in California. I listened vaguely and chewed on my hair.

"Bird, you see much of that Redbone character around the house?"

I thought about it. I hadn't seen Redbone. But that didn't mean he hadn't been there. My mother's friends came over some Sundays for meetings in the basement. Usually, my mother would send us up to our room before they went down into the cavernous, mysterious basement.

"Nope. I haven't seen him. He's weird. I don't like him."

We were at a red light now, and my father was looking at me, seeming to ponder my features with a scientific interest. He ruffled my hair. "Well, you tell me if he comes around. I don't think your mother knows what she's gotten herself into. You know what I mean?"

I nodded, not really sure what he meant, but excited that we had an agreement. I would be his spy.

He switched the station then, and we listened to music the rest of the way over, singing along to the Stylistics, our voices rising and falling together, cracking at the high notes.

We wandered around the Public Gardens for a few hours, and though we didn't talk much, I felt closer to my father than I ever had before. We held hands and went on the swan rides together. There was a man selling T-shirts, and my father bought me one that said "Wet Paint" across the front in raised multicolored letters that dribbled down like real paint. He took a picture of me in my new T-shirt, worn over my long-sleeved one so that the long sleeves billowed out like a pirate's.

He bought a newspaper then and lay on the grass while I did cartwheels in circles around him. There were other families and couples scattered around, enjoying the unusually mild temperature and the fallen leaves. I think it was when he gave me a few dollars to buy us hot dogs that I noticed the couple. They were walking a dog—a small gray terrier—and they were older, well-dressed. The woman's hair was silvery blond. Her companion was a small and dour man wearing a trench coat and holding a cane. They

watched me, frowning, as I went up to the hot-dog cart and made my pur-
chase. The man had a fierce scowl, but the woman smiled slightly at me, so I
smiled back. I thought maybe my fly was unzipped, but when I looked down,
all was in place.

They continued to watch me as I brought the hot dog to my father, then
ran back to the cart to get us napkins, which I had forgotten.

My father didn't seem to notice, so I put them out of my mind. After we
finished our hot dogs, I lay with my head on his stomach, so that our bodies
made a T. I read the funnies there, occasionally reading jokes aloud to him,
which he ignored, but which I giggled at anyway.

When I was done with the funnies, I watched the sky—the shapes of animals made out of clouds. And when I tilted my head slightly to the side, I
saw again that strange couple with their gray terrier, pointing at me. I didn't
move, just watched it happen with a lazy interest. They were talking to two
men in uniform, the police on their beat, and then the four of them were
trudging across the grass in our direction.

I didn't move until they were nearly upon us. Then I sat up and nudged
my father, who had begun to doze off.

He opened his eyes just as their shadow fell over him.

He sat up abruptly, and the two of us scrambled to our feet. My father
did what he did when he was nervous: adjusted his glasses and cleared his
throat.

One of the policemen was older, with a beer belly, and creases in his
face that made him look angry, even if he wasn't. The other one was a
younger guy, with dark hair and a mustache. He had laughing eyes but was
trying to look serious.

The couple stood off to the distance slightly, petting their dog and whispering.

"All right, brotherman," the younger one said to my father with a smirk.
"Who's the little girl?"

My father looked down at me and laughed slightly. "She's my daughter.
Is there a problem?" His voice shook as he said it, and I could feel his fear
from where I stood.

The older cop looked at me in my Wet Paint shirt over my long-sleeved
one. I understood what was going on, even if I couldn't have explained it at
the time, and my skin was tingling all over like the prickle of salt water when

you stay in the ocean too long. I stared at the couple and had an urge to go over and kick dirt at them.

The cops didn't believe my father. Not even when he showed them a photograph of me and my sister that he kept in his wallet. Not even when he had shown them his identification card, which read, "Deck Lee, Associate Professor, Anthropology, Boston University." What made it worse was that people around us had begun to notice and had moved closer to see what was happening. They whispered among themselves, eyeing me with concern, and that made me feel ashamed.

I stood beside my father, and the policeman—the younger one with the mustache—leaned down and touched my hair in a way that made me flinch. He smiled, and said, "What's your name, kid?"

"Birdie."

"Birdie? That's a funny name. Now, why don't you tell me your real name?"

"Birdie Lee." I said it louder this time.

"All right, Birdie Lee. How do you know this man?"

He looked at my father, who was standing with the other cop. My father was staring at me with a tense smile.

"He's my father."

The cop laughed a little. Then he touched my shoulder and pulled me away from my father and the other cop, so we were leaning into each other. Secretive. He said in a whisper, "You can tell us, kiddie. He can't hurt you here. You're safe now. Did the man touch you funny?"

I felt sick and a little dizzy. I wanted to spit in the cop's face. But my voice came out quiet, wimpier than I wanted it to. "No, he didn't. He's my father" was all I could manage. I wondered what my sister would do. I figured she wouldn't be in this situation in the first place, and that fact somehow depressed me.

The cop seemed disappointed by my answer and stood up, shrugging with exasperation at his partner.

After grilling my father for a few more minutes, they left us alone. But the old couple didn't leave. They watched us as we gathered up our things, our strewn-about newspapers. As we walked the distance across the grass to our car, I turned to see them still watching us. I raised my middle finger and blew a kiss to the couple on it, the way I had seen the Irish kids do on television. I was about to shout something, too, when my father grabbed my arm roughly, pulling me to his side and quickening his pace. "Cut that shit out" was all he said.

When we were in the car, my father buckled me into my seat belt. From his expression I could see that he didn't feel like talking. He played music on the way back. I knew all the words but decided not to sing along. He seemed deep in thought, and before he let me out in front of the house, he smiled at me, crookedly, sadly. "And they wonder why we want to get out of this place. I mean, shit, it's everywhere I go. Everywhere." He stared at me for a moment, our eyes locked. Then he added, "Study them, Birdie. And take notes. Always take notes."

Usually he kissed me on the top of my head before he said good-bye, but this time he just touched my forehead with the back of his hand, as if he were checking for a fever. His own hand was cold, and he pulled it away quickly, as if the touch had burned him.

the body of luce rivera

I learned the art of changing at Nkrumah, a skill that would later become second nature to me. Maybe I was always good at it. Maybe it was a skill I had inherited from my mother, or my father, or my aunt Dot, or my Nana, the way some people inherit a talent for music or art or mathematics. Even before Nkrumah, Cole and I had gotten a thrill out of changing—spending our days dressed in old costumes, pretending to be queens of our make-believe nation. But only at Nkrumah did it become more than a game. There I learned how to do it for real—how to become someone else, how to erase the person I was before.

Cole had already done it. Changed. It had started with the Jergen's lotion, then with her hair, and before I knew it she was one of the more popular girls at the school. She still carried a book wherever she went, but now she was wearing lipstick, talking about boys as she tried to pull me along behind her. I knew I had to make more of an effort to blend in or I would lose her for good.

I started wearing my hair in a tight braid to mask its texture. I had my ears pierced and convinced my mother to buy me a pair of gold hoops like the other girls at school wore. My father was usually scornful of frivolous spending, but he must have sensed some serious desperation when I pleaded with him to buy me new clothes. On one weekend shopping spree at Tello's, with my sister shouting orders to me, I bought a pair of Sergio Valente jeans, a pink vest, a jean jacket with sparkles on the collar, and spanking-white Nike sneakers.

I stood many nights in front of the bathroom mirror, practicing how to say "nigger" the way the kids in school did it, dropping the "er" so that it became not a slur, but a term of endearment: *nigga*.

It took a while, but sometime late that fall at Nkrumah, my work paid off. A smell of burning wafted in the cool autumn air, and mounds of dead leaves were neatly piled on street corners like enormous fallen birds' nests. I had been sitting on the pavement during recess, tugging at my shoelace, when I felt myself being watched. I looked up to see Maria, the afternoon sunlight hitting her from behind, turning her into a gold-spangled silhouette. Her hair was now in braids, with multicolored ribbons woven throughout, and they fluttered in the breeze. Like most of the kids in the school, she wore all ironed and matching clothes. Today she wore black Jordache jeans and a bright-yellow sweater that brought out her reddish undertones. I had been chewing the ends of my hair, and now it hung damp around my face.

Finally Maria spoke. "So, you black?"

I nodded, slowly, as if unsure of it myself.

She sat down beside me and smiled almost wistfully. "I got a brother just like you. We're Cape Verdean."

I didn't know if that was black or white, or something else altogether.

I also wasn't sure whether she was playing another prank on me, so I decided to stay silent.

She pointed across the playground. "See that boy over there in the red sweater? Ali Parkman. He wants to go with you. At least that's what Cherise says. Anyway, I'm goin' out with his best friend, Ronald, so if you go out with him, you can be in the club."

"What club?"

"The Brown Sugars," she said matter-of-factly. "For girls that already got boyfriends. Cherise is in it. Maleka used to be in it, before Michael started going out with Cathy instead. The twins, Carol and Diana, are in it too."

I stared at the boy—Ali. He was the same one who had thrown a spitball at me my first day of school. *What you doin' in this school? You white?* Those were the words he had spoken. He was skinny and brown-skinned and all I knew of him was that he loved to draw spaceships and that his father was my father's friend Ronnie, the one from Dot's party.

Maria blurted, "So, you want to go with him, or not? I need an answer by this afternoon. Otherwise, he's gonna ask Marcia instead."

"I guess so" was my weak reply.

So it was official. Ali Parkman and I were going steady, "talking," as the kids in the school called it. It didn't mean much—we both were shy around each other. He would smile and wave at me in the hallway and sometimes pull my braid, but that was as close as touching got.

And with my new boyfriend came privileges. Soon Maria, Cherise, Cathy, and I were a clique. A new boyfriend had catapulted me into the world of the freshest girls in the school. Now that I had been knighted black by Maria, and pretty by Ali, the rest of the school saw me in a new light. But I never lost the anxiety, a gnawing in my bowels, a fear that at any moment I would be told it was all a big joke.

Maria and I spent our free time in the girls' room, combing each other's hair, talking about boys we liked and girls we didn't. Cole was glad, I could tell, to see I had some friends besides her. We still spent time together on the weekends. My mother wouldn't let me go out without her, so I would trail along after her to the roller-skating rink, where we would whiz around in circles to disco beats, or hunch over video games at a downtown arcade. In the Brown Sugars clique, we each had nicknames. Maria was "Roxy." Cathy was "Baby Curl." I was "Le Chic."

My mother, who was in a neighborhood women's consciousness-raising group, noticed the changes in Cole and me. She came into our attic after dinner one night and found us smearing our faces with her makeup in front of the big mirror. She rarely wore it anymore, but kept it in the back of a dresser drawer, rotting, some evidence of her old self. Cole had rubbed kohl liner on her eyes so that she looked Asian. I had taken the same pencil to make a beauty mark over my lip. My mother watched us for a moment at the door, her arms crossed and an expression of fierce disgust on her face. She came and stood over us, her looming form casting a gigantic shadow.

"You girls are turning into little tarts before my eyes. This is the end, you realize."

"The end of what, Mum?" I said, putting on some bright magenta lipstick so that it went outside the edges of my lips.

"The end of freedom," she said, grabbing the lipstick out of my hand and putting it in her shirt pocket.

Whenever Jane or Linda came over, she would talk in a loud, disapproving voice about us. "Look at my daughters," she'd tell them, a cigarette dangling from her lips, a beer tucked between her thighs. "All they think about is how they look. It's revolting."

Cole and I ignored her. There was no way I was going back to the never-never land of my old self—scraggly hair, dirty knees, and a tomboy's swaggering gait. But I did feel different—more conscious of my body as a toy, and of the ways I could use it to disappear into the world around me.

One Friday, when the trees were just skeletons and Boston hung frozen in a perpetual gray light, I went to Mattapan to spend the night at Maria's house. We left school together that afternoon, catching the 52 bus at the corner. I felt a thrill of urban adventure as I dropped my change into the slot and followed Maria to the back of the bus. Without my mother's and Cole's eyes on me, I felt that anything could happen. I stared at the faces of the bus riders, all various shades of brown, and tried to mimic their bored, exhausted expressions. Beside me, Maria sang softly to herself, off-key, Roberta Flack's "Feel Like Makin' Love," and I listened, staring out the window as we rolled past Franklin Park.

A girl my age had disappeared there a month earlier—and three weeks later her body had been found violated and dead, crumpled in the shadows of the pudding stone near where she had been lost in the first place, as if in some macabre "return to sender" trick. Her name was Luce Rivera, and her picture had been all over the news that month—a photograph of her smiling in her Catholic-school uniform, looking unsuspecting and utterly pure, the way photographs of the recently murdered often do. It was my mother who first pointed out that she looked a little like me. Then Cole noticed it, then the kids at school, who teased me, saying I was the ghost of Luce Rivera come back to seek revenge. The night they found Luce Rivera's body, my mother came into Cole's and my room in the attic. I was curled over my homework, while Cole lay stretched out on the floor, reading a magazine. My mother wiped her tears and announced to us that the police had recovered "Luce's torn and violated body" and that the search had finally ended. She stood silently by the half-moon window, looking out onto the street for a moment, then turned around rather violently. She came to me and squeezed me to her, so that I couldn't breathe. Then, as quickly as she had grabbed me, she pushed me away, held me at a distance, and stroked the hair out of my face. She hissed, spraying me with spittle, "Don't ever go into Franklin Park alone. You hear me, Bird? You be careful in Roxbury. Don't talk to anyone except your school friends. You understand? There are perverts, crazies, dirty old men, and they want little girls like you."

One of the peculiarities about my mother was that after a passionate diatribe, she could return to normal within seconds, as if nothing had been said or done. As soon as she finished her outburst, she went to our mirror and fussed with our pre-teen beauty products. She picked up Cole's black plastic pick and turned it over thoughtfully in her hands. She ran it through her thin hair, staring at herself in the mirror as she did so, with a sad smile. It struck me as odd that my mother hadn't warned Cole not to go to the park, just me. "There are perverts, crazies, dirty old men, and they want little girls like you."

Girls like you.

When she was gone, Cole looked up from her *Jet* magazine and watched me from behind her braids, which hung like bars across her face, dividing her features into sections.

MARIA AND I arrived in Mattapan. Her house sat on a block of twenty identical tract houses with endlessly shuttered windows and garbage-spackled lawns. There were teenage boys sitting on the stoop of the house next to hers, and they waved to her. She blushed, and yelled, "Hey, Darnell!" Then she whispered in my direction, "He's so cute. He said when I grow up he wants to go out. My brother used to hang with him."

As Maria opened the door to her house, a gust of heated air enveloped us. We stepped inside, and it took me a moment to adjust to the darkness. A piquant smell of sweet-and-sour sauce clung to the air.

Enraged and hysterical voices floated from behind a closed door at the end of the hall. Someone screamed, "You bitch! You'll never steal him from me!"

But as I listened closer, I could hear it was just the television. A soap opera.

Maria turned to me, shy suddenly. "You can just throw your stuff on the floor."

I took a minute to simply soak up the most exquisite home I had ever laid eyes on. The pink-and-purple-flower theme was omnipresent. Faux yucca trees sprung from black vases in the corners, and a fruit bowl with wooden apples and pears sat on the coffee table. The back wall was decorated with a velvet painting of two naked and afroed sillouettes—one curvacious and female, the other muscular and male—intertwined in a lovemaking ritual with a backdrop of a bright magenta-and-pink horizon. I wanted to go and touch the painting, trace the bodies with my finger, but held back. The rest of the room's walls, I could see, were mirrored, and a crystalline chandelier hung over the shimmering mahogany dining room set.

I breathed, "Your house is so beautiful."

Maria scoffed. "You think so? It's all right."

But I could tell she was proud. She went over to the wide-screen television set. "My daddy got this for us last Christmas. It's like a movie screen, almost." She whispered, "He works in a TV warehouse and he took it when no one was looking."

I thought about my mother. She sometimes took things when nobody was looking. She would slip candy and barrettes into her pocket when we went to Kmart. But she had never taken anything this big. "Where's your father?"

"Oh, he lives in New York, but he comes up to see us every year. And that's my brother, James. He's in the Army," she told me, pointing to a picture of a grinning, uniformed boy with hazel eyes and skin the color of my own. "He's much older than me."

"Where's your mother now?"

"She's at work. She's a nurse at the hospital. She gets home real late tonight. Like past midnight."

We spent the afternoon slumped in front of her television set with the stereo booming behind us, the heat and lights on full blast. We gorged ourselves and watched her favorite sitcoms—"Chico and the Man" and "What's Happening"—in a green glowing silence.

By six o'clock we were restless and hungry and wandered into the kitchen. Maria's mother had left spare ribs and potato salad in Tupperware in the refrigerator. Maria threw the ribs in the oven and turned it on high. My mother never cooked red meat. I felt I was being let into a secret world I had been denied for so long, and I tried to hide the giddy feeling bubbling away in my stomach as Maria revealed one small luxury after another.

Maria had more clothes than I could even imagine. She played the clock radio beside her bed and sang along—knowing all of the words—as she tossed clothes on the bed.

"This one—this one looks real cute on you," she said, holding up a purple angora sweater with sparkles in the shape of a unicorn on the front. "And we're gonna have to do something about your hair. Do you want me to trim it and curl it?"

The next thing I knew, I was seated on the squishy toilet cushion and Maria was snipping away at my hair. "Just let me even out these split ends," she had said, but by the time it was over, my hair was a full inch and a half shorter.

She saw the look on my face. "It looks fine! Don't worry. I'm not done. It still needs to be curled."

She heated up the curling iron and sprayed my newly shorn hair with Queen Helene hairspray till it was wet. Each time she put the curling iron to a lock of my hairspray-soaked head, it let out a hiss and steam emerged. But I assumed she knew what she was doing, and stayed quiet.

When she was finished, my straight hair was curly. I stared at myself in the fogged mirror, amid the rows of beauty potions, and breathed in the sweet-and-sour spare-rib air of the apartment. The curls Maria had given me softened out my pointed features. As I admired my new look, I imagined myself to be just a girl who lived and had always lived in this splendid pink-and-purple palace where all the furniture matched, a girl whose mother worked late nights as a nurse and whose big brother was in the Army. I imagined my name was not Birdie or Jesse or even Patrice, but Yolanda, and that Maria was one of my many cousins. I imagined myself Cape Verdean.

Maria's voice broke into my thoughts. "Birdie, how do I look?"

I turned to see her standing in the door of the bathroom. She was transformed as well. She wore her mother's lipstick—Revlon's Toast of New York—and matching eye shadow. She had on skintight Jordache jeans over a burgundy leotard that clung to her body.

She leaned in close to me. I could smell the bubble gum on her breath as she fluffed my hair one more time, with an approving wink at her creation.

We spent the rest of the evening eating—soda, popcorn, hot wings—from Maria's endlessly stocked kitchen, watching TV, and listening to music. We gossiped about the other kids from school, and I felt she was accepting me into that bond of "best friend." Cathy was falling out of her favor, and I knew I needed to act right then if I wanted to replace her. At one point she brought me into her mother's room, which had a water bed, and the two of us lay on the sloshing mattress, looking up at ourselves in the smoked-mirror ceiling, singing along to the radio. The tint of the ceiling mirror darkened me, and with my newfound curls, I found that if I pouted my lips and squinted to blur my vision in just the right way, my face transformed into something resembling Cole's. Maria and I lay there for more than an hour, talking about our mutual love for Diana Ross, how we both hoped to marry Billy Dee Williams, and what we wanted to be when we grew up. She wanted to be an airline stewardess; I wanted to be a veterinarian. I asked her endless questions about her family—what her mother looked like, whom she dated, when her parents broke up, how her parents had met. I savored each detail and made a secret promise to myself that I would live in a house like this when I grew up and be just like Maria's mother, who I imagined looked like Marilyn McCoo. We lost track of time, lying side by side on the water bed, speaking to our mirror images that hovered above us like guardian angels.

Before going to bed, we took a bubble bath together using a concoction made from all of her mother's bath products that lined the edge of the tub. I studied Maria's nude body while we undressed in the reeking, steaming bathroom. She had small perfectly shaped nipples like Hershey's Kisses. I hugged myself and shivered, waiting to step in, as she swished the water with her hand to test the temperature.

We sat together in the tub for a long time, until our fingertips were ridged and prunelike and the water around us had turned lukewarm. It had begun to rain outside, softly, and Maria, on her knees behind me, washed my hair, seemingly fascinated by its limp consistency. I had wanted to leave the curls in, but she promised she'd redo them in the morning. She lathered my scalp, telling me what she would do if she had straight hair. I told her I wanted her hair, which she had carefully covered in a shower cap so as not to get it wet.

She asked me if I liked Ali. I crinkled my nose. "He's nice and all, but he's so young. You know, he's still just a child," I said, repeating something I had heard Cole say once about a boy.

We got out of the bath after it became too cold, and dried ourselves in fluffy pink towels. Maria chattered about Darnell, the older boy next door, and I looked out of the corner of my eye at the soft brown slope of her body. I felt ashamed for looking, and hid my face in the wet tangle of my hair.

I lay awake late into the night, listening to the dramatic beeps and yells on the streets outside, pretending that my mother worked the late shift and my daddy stole TVs.

SINCE THE INCIDENT at the Public Gardens, my father hadn't had much to say to me. He went back to ignoring me the way he always had. He didn't come around often anymore. When he did, he would plague Cole with his theories. Our visits to his house had become like drill camp for Cole, as my father seemed more and more anxious that she understand something before it was too late.

During our visits to his place, I was fairly content to be left in front of a television sitcom or reading a comic book in the guest room, my bare feet moving listlessly along his wall. But often I put down my book or turned off the sound on the television and listened in on them, and his message, spoken to some other body, reached me in this oblique way. Some of his ideas I was familiar with, had heard in school, about the Diaspora and the genocidal tendencies of the white man.

Others were new to me—like his theory about America's "love affair with castrated, blind, and crippled black boys," or his notion of how white people find their power in invisibility, while the rest of us remain bodies for them to study and watch.

"Try pointing out to a white boy that he's white, and he'll wince, because you've looked at him, and they don't like to be looked at," my father told Cole one afternoon.

Sometimes, at the Nkrumah School, I found myself repeating some of my father's ideas in class to an amused and surprised Professor Abdul, who blinked at me and said, "Very astute, Birdie."

Cole was interested in his theories only some of the time. She was beginning to notice boys and often seemed restless while he was talking to her. But my father didn't seem to care that she often looked away with an expression of deep ennui when he spoke. He spoke through her, above her, around her, but still to her, as she continued to be the exclusive object of his lessons, leaving me to absorb his platitudes only through osmosis.

One day she sat beside him in the front seat of his car. She no longer sat with me in the back, or played with Sasha dolls, for that matter. She was getting too old. James Brown pleaded from the radio, *Pleeeeeze,* and I sat on the hump in the middle of the backseat, leaning forward, trying to join their conversation. My father pointed to an interracial couple standing on the corner. The woman was dumpy, heavyset, with stringy brown hair and a baby strapped to her body. The man was lanky and ashy, with an afro at half-mast.

My father laughed a little and said, nudging Cole, gesturing toward the couple: "What's wrong with that picture?"

My sister shrugged, blowing on her nails, which were still wet with polish. She didn't seem to remember the right answer—or perhaps didn't care—but I did and, throwing my hand in the air like Arnold Horshack, piped in from the backseat, "Diluting the race!"

My father snorted in place of a laugh, glancing at me in the rearview mirror as he said under his breath, "I guess you could put it that way."

Another time, when we were spending the night at his place in Roxbury, they watched television together on the couch. I jumped up and down on a mattress in the next room, with the door open so I could see them in the flickering blue light. Cole's head rested against his shoulder as they stared somberly at the sitcom. It was "What's Happening" and Rerun was doing a jig across the diner while Raj, playing the straight man, shook his head and groaned. The invisible audience hooted wildly.

My father watched it as if studying some distasteful foreign culture. Cole imitated his expression, although I knew she laughed along to the show when he wasn't around.

He leaned toward her and said with a tight, sarcastic smirk, "What's wrong with this picture?"

From the bedroom, I yelled out in midair above the mattress, "Jigaboo time!" repeating something Mrs. Potter had muttered once while watching television in the front office.

My father didn't seem to hear me, and I heard Cole say, "White people love to see us making fools of ourselves. It makes them feel safe."

He patted her shoulder.

It wasn't unusual to find them slouched together late into the night, seated in the living room on his pullout couch while he read chapters aloud to her from Harold Cruse's *The Crisis of the Negro Intellectual,* and poor Cole squirmed and rubbed her eyes, whimpering about needing to sleep. Other nights I stumbled out of bed to use the bathroom and found them hunched under the dim greasy light of his kitchen, listening to the BBC international news on his shortwave radio (because American journalism was all propaganda), Cole resting her chin in her hands, staring longingly out into the night while my father shook his head and scribbled notes onto a napkin, thoroughly engrossed in what the clipped British accent was saying.

Cole was slipping out of my reach, slowly, inevitably, like water from cupped hands. Not because of our father's preachings, but more because she found herself in an adolescent torpor with no one, including me, to talk to about it. I think each of us was lonely on those visits. As my father tried to get Cole to learn his language, she chose to stay inside herself, thinking secret, languid thoughts, and I tried to get both of their attention by any means necessary.

Sometimes I repeated things I had heard in school that I thought would impress them.

"Salaam Aleikum," I greeted my father one afternoon as I clambered into his car.

Another time I kissed him good-bye on the cheek, saying, "Stay black, stay strong, brotherman," a line from one of Professor Abdul's poems. My father flashed me a fierce look of bewilderment, then burst into laughter as he ruffled my hair, as if he had just discovered I could talk when he pulled the string on the back of my neck.

Other times I tried to get their attention through more slapstick routines—by doing a chicken dance across the living room floor while they tried to watch the news, or balancing a spoon on the tip of my nose, or eating my cereal on my hands and knees on the floor in the pantry, lapping it up as if I were a dog, or making a hideous face and doing cartwheels at the same time. I still had the power to crack Cole's sullen repose, and she would laugh, happy, I suppose, for my comic relief. But my humor was too slapstick for my father, and he would tell me to stop acting the fool.

My mother called my father's campaign "Papaspeak, the art of bombastic and iconoclastic racial tomfoolery." She placed the blame on his shoulders for her growing distance from Cole, but it seemed to me that Cole was drifting away from my mother for other reasons—reasons to do with her body and the way it was changing, reasons that made her private and scowling and bored by the childish Elemeno games that used to amuse us for hours.

My mother was changing as well, and this scared me most of all. Up until that year, she had always managed her activism, her work with the special-education children, with her mothering—putting us to bed at a reasonable hour; cooking us a dinner of chicken and peas and red potatoes, a breakfast of oatmeal and raisins; carting us off to school bright and early, faces scrubbed down, teeth brushed.

But lately her distraction had reached a new level. Weekends she simply disappeared—across town to Jamaica Plain, where her friend Linda lived, or on Sunday into the basement with the multiracial crew of activists that my father found so distasteful. They all would emerge a few hours later, slapping palms and whispering excitedly among themselves. My mother always seemed a little pale after those meetings and would sit by the window for a while, twisting a blond lock and thinking so hard that we knew not to bother her.

One afternoon I came home from school to find her still in her pajamas, her hair a scraggly mess, squatting behind the couch beside the phone, which was off the hook. She was cutting her toenails with a studied precision, leaving the little half-moon nails on the carpet around her. She didn't look up at me until I said, "Mum?"

She whipped her head up and stared blankly at me for a moment before saying, "Huh? Yeah, Birdie, what is it?"

I asked her why she was sitting there in her pajamas.

She didn't answer my question. Instead she said, "Go look out the window, sweetums. Tell me what you see."

I went to the window. It looked pretty normal outside. There was a tiny kid walking a huge Doberman pinscher on a leash; an old woman shuffling by, stooped over from the weight of her groceries; a couple of teenagers loitering on the steps of the housing projects, smoking, and playing music from a boom box.

I shouted back to her, "I don't see nothing."

"Anything! You don't see anything!" she hissed back from behind the sofa.

"Anything," I mumbled. She didn't like my new way of talking. Sometimes a piece of her that she tried to keep hidden seemed to sneak out—a piece of her that had grown up in a big old Victorian house in Cambridge, had been educated at one of the best prep schools, had spent evenings reading Sartre aloud to her father, the Harvard classics professor, in the den off the living room.

"Well, look again, baby," she barked across the room. "See that van?"

Sure enough, there was an olive-green van parked across the street. I had never seen it before. As far as I could see, there was nobody in the front seat.

"Yeah, I see it. What about it?"

"Come back here!"

I returned to the couch, and she yanked on my arm so that I plopped down next to her. She looked funny, with her hair all wild, the pajamas still on in the middle of the afternoon, and I almost started to giggle.

But the expression on her face told me not to. She said: "Those motherfuckers, they're trying to drive me mad. They're trying to drive us all mad. They're everywhere. They're in the house now, you know. They're listening to us as we speak."

"Who?"

She started to cry then, quietly, into her hands. I put my hand out and touched her shoulder, gingerly.

"You want me to go over to the van and tell them to leave?" I didn't know who was in the van. I had no idea. I imagined a little man living in there, with a little kitchen and a little bed and a little toilet, and a pair of binoculars that would watch us from a hole screwed into the wall. The year before, we had had a visitor named Joel, a bedraggled guy with a sharp, pungent odor who my mother whispered to me had lived in his car for three months. I had been fascinated by the thought and had secretly wished he would take me with him when he left, so I could see what living in a car was like.

She shook her head and peeked out at me. "Don't you dare go near there. You hear me?"

I nodded. "Want me to go get Papa? Maybe he can help."

She shook her head and began to sniffle, wiping her face roughly. "No, baby. Your papa's too busy trying to grow a fucking afro. Nothing can help me now."

Later, when the rain came down like sheets of metal outside our window, she came into our room while Cole and I were busy painting our toenails and listening to the radio. She rifled through our trunk of costumes haphazardly, humming along to the music. Cole and I ignored her for a while, until I turned around to see her watching me with our African mask on. It was the warrior mask from Kenya, and she was wearing a granny nightgown with it, creating a strange contrast.

I nudged Cole, who turned and looked at her as well.

"What the hell are you doing, Mum?" Cole said.

I knew what she was doing. It was a game we had played when we were little, a game I'd almost forgotten. She would put on a mask, any mask, and say, "I'm not your mother," in a scary voice. At first Cole and I would laugh, but eventually my mother always took it just a step too far and we'd start to scream and cry and beg her to come back to us. Only when we were nearly in hysterics would she take the mask off, and we'd shower her in kisses and hugs and all would be well again. It was a strange game to play with children. But we must have liked being scared, because once the mask was off and we had wiped away our tears, we always begged her to put it back on.

I giggled, but there was a strain to my laugh. "Put it back, Mum. You look crazy." I was remembering her squatting behind the sofa with all those half-moon toenails sprinkled around her.

She came toward us quietly, her head tilted inquisitively to the side. When she was upon us, standing over us, she said in a fake witch voice, "I'm not your mother. Where's your real mother?" Then she cackled and twisted her body into a hunchback.

Neither Cole nor I laughed. We didn't cry either. We just watched her from the floor, our feet stuck out before us, cotton balls wedged between our toes the way we had seen it done in a magazine.

Finally she pulled the mask off, and her face underneath was red and a little moist from her own breath. She raked a hand through her hair.

"You two are changing on me. You used to be so much fun. What's happening?"

Cole dropped her head back into a book and curled over it, twisting a braid around her finger.

But I patted my mother's leg. "I'm still fun, Mum."

THAT NEXT DAY, my mother woke Cole and me bright and early and informed us we weren't going to school.

We exchanged looks of initial thrill. Then we saw that my mother was fully dressed. It wasn't a day of hooky. She had something planned.

"Why?" Cole said, sitting up and hugging the duvet around her. She had stolen all the covers, and I shivered in a corner with a tiny ratty blanket wrapped close to my body.

"Because!" my mother exclaimed. "We're going to Concord! Let's do something fun for once. Okay?"

Cole shrugged. "But Mum, I'm supposed to hand in a report to Professor Abdul."

My mother scoffed and waved Cole's worry aside. "Silly child. Don't you know? I'm the parent. I get to call you in sick if I feel like it. It's a cardinal rule. Now, do you want to go have fun, or what?"

Cole and I dressed slowly. We wore our disco finest—skintight jeans with elaborate labels, sparkle shirts, and high-heeled sneakers. I was excited, but I could see that Cole had wanted to go to school. She had stayed up late into the night, obsessing over her project. It had been a report about the black Indians of Rhode Island. She was proud of it.

As the Pinto wound around the long, tree-lined main road, my mother pointed at the houses of note along the way, trying to talk over the music that Cole blasted from the radio. "What a world it must have been. Emerson, Hawthorne, Louisa May Alcott. All in the same vicinity. Oh look, girls. We're coming up to the Minute Man National Park. Would you take a look at the size of those trees? Oh man, here's the Concord River. Daddy used to take me on the canoe here. Isn't it lovely—"

Cole and I just chewed our gum, tapping our feet and mouthing along to Natalie Cole booming "This Will Be" from the radio.

My mother seemed to have been overtaken by a fit of nostalgia. While she had nothing but venom for her mother, her father was, as she put it, "a good, decent man, in the best tradition of America."

My mother drove us to Emerson's house—The Old Manse—where her father had taken her to walk among the flowers called "loose strife" and had given her lessons on those trips about the literary history that had been made in that small town. Now it was winter, and the ground was hard, cracked by the cold, devoid of any blossoms.

Later in the afternoon we bought fresh husks of corn at the side of the road, and the locals stared at my mother, the strangely garbed woman—corpulent, blond, boisterous, wearing a Mexican scarf around her neck and her hair in twin Indian-style braids, shrieking at the size and color of the tomatoes this year—and us, her glowering dark daughters, who must have stunk of the urban fiasco most of them had fled.

On the drive home, my mother's good mood evaporated. She grew pensive, her eyebrows furrowed and her mouth moving in a silent whisper as if she were rehearsing lines for some impending performance. She was worried about something. Cole sat in the front next to her, and I lay stretched out on the backseat, munching on an apple.

I heard Cole say, "Can we go back to school tomorrow?"

My mother reached out and stroked Cole's braids. "Of course you can, sweetie. I just needed to get away. From it all. You can hand in your report tomorrow." She sighed then and stared out at the road. "I just don't know when I'll get a chance to come up here again."

When we got back into Boston, we stopped at Star Market to buy some groceries for dinner. My mother's strange mood escalated again. She zigzagged up and down the aisles, throwing food into the shopping cart haphazardly—food we never ate. She usually had Wasp tastes in food, left over from her childhood, but here she was throwing in macaroni and cheese, Doritos, a mammoth box of Cap'n Crunch, and a gallon of no-name soda pop. I skipped beside her, excited, telling her what else I wanted. This was the food I had craved all my life. Not the peas, red potatoes, white rice, broccoli, creamed chicken, and asparagus we were usually force-fed. Cole didn't join in my festivities, though, and walked behind us at a cautious distance, a dubious frown on her face. She kept looking around her, as if afraid someone would see us together.

"Why are we getting all the good stuff today, Mum?" I finally asked, throwing Wonder Bread into the cart. As soon as I'd said it, I worried she'd realize what she was buying and make me put it back.

But she just shrugged. "Because this is how poor people eat, Birdalee. And we're broke, baby. Seriously broke. It's about time we started to act it."

When we were finished, we had more than twenty items, but my mother went into the express line, where it clearly read "10 Items or Less" in bold red letters. Cole whispered to her, "Mum, you're not allowed—" but my mother cut her off. "Can it, Coley. We'll be here all night if you follow their rules."

We were almost at the register when I noticed my mother slipping two Snickers bars into the pocket of her red duffel jacket. I didn't say anything, but looked at Cole to see if she had noticed. She shook her head and rolled her eyes. When we got to the register, my mother began talking in an excited chatter about Lamaze methods to the pregnant clerk behind the register. When we were safely outside she whooped in the air like a fraternity boy who has just gotten laid, and held out the candy to Cole and me. I grabbed mine and ripped in, but Cole just shook her head with disgust. My mother aped Cole's prissy expression, then said, already ripping apart the foil wrapper, "Fine, then, Ms. Goody Two-Shoes, I'll eat it."

She took an enormous bite of the bar, and as we drove out of the parking lot, she spoke through the goo of chocolate, nuts, and caramel: "Cole, you're really missing out. I seriously doubt Star Market is going to notice these two bars of chocolate. Jesus, you'd think you were part of the Republican party the way you're carrying on. I thought my daughters were wilder than that."

Cole ignored her, staring out the window with a scowl on her face.

My mother winked at me where I sat beside her in the front seat, and said, "Now, Birdie. Birdie's a real radical. She likes her candy hot. Don't you, sweet tush?"

"Yes, I do. Let's get more. Mum, go get us two more!" I bounced on my seat, enjoying the show.

Cole groaned from the backseat, "Birdie, why do you encourage her? She's crazy."

My mother screwed up her features and imitated Cole's voice, making it all British and proper: "'Why do you encourage her? She's craaaazy.' Jesus,

Cole. You've been spending too much time with your father. Get a sense of humor, kiddo. It'll get you through the hard times."

Cole stomped her foot onto the floor of the car and crossed her arms. "God, you're such a freak. Get me out of here!"

I tried to enjoy my chocolate, but my excitement had passed. It was difficult to swallow and stuck at the back of my throat in a solid lump. My mother was slipping. I could see it sometimes in her eyes when we walked down the street—the way she had begun to glance over her shoulder—that she was scared of something huge and pressing and unsuitable for children. And I understood in those flashes, her hand clutched tightly in my own, that she had nobody—not my father nor Cole nor the radicals in the basement, not even her own blue-blood Cambridge clan—to protect her from this unnamed threat. Nobody, that was, but me.

golliwog's revenge

A snow storm swept over Boston. It was the biggest in three years, and it brought a silence to the city—a silence like a body smothered by a pillow, muffled out of its misery but still thrashing below the waist. That week, cars were transformed into igloos; sidewalks into tunnels; and Bostonians into Eskimos, traveling with their heads against the wind, their bodies buried under layers of bulky protection.

The weekend the snow began to fall, Cole was staying at our father's, but I had chosen to stay home, in part to avoid having to beg for their attention, in part because my mother said she got lonely when I left and whispered that we would do fun things if I just stayed home for those few days.

"Let them have some time alone together," my mother had told me, sucking pancake mix off her finger. I had wanted to tell her that they were always alone together, even when I was there.

Cole was supposed to come back to us on Sunday, but the heavy silent flakes began falling on a Friday night and continued falling, so that by Sunday everyone was quarantined—Cole in Roxbury, me in the South End.

My mother woke me that Sunday morning wearing nothing but her muumuu and a bandanna tied like Aunt Jemima's on her head. She blew on my eyelids, then dragged me to the half-moon window and pointed to the street below as if presenting me with a gift. The city was a crystal white slate as far as the eye could see. My mother embraced me, and we watched the flakes drift languidly down before us onto the empty street. Her breath in my ear was already sweet and thick with coffee and cinnamon rolls as she said, her words brimming over with excitement, "We're stuck inside. The city's all shut down, and we're stuck inside. Hooky for a week."

And she was right. It lasted all that week. Cole was stuck at our father's, as the streets were closed off, and I stayed indoors with our mother, unable to connect with the outside world except through the phone.

I called Cole each day, but she seemed to be keeping herself busy in Roxbury. She had Nkrumah friends in the area, so she could trudge to their houses. And, she confided in me on Tuesday, our father had a new girlfriend. She whispered, "Don't tell Mum. Her name's Carmen and she's so beautiful, Bird. Wait till you see her. She did my hair up last night in a French twist and we listened to music and she told me about—s-e-x."

She didn't seem to want to talk to my mother, so I acted as the go-between, shouting out messages between them like a translator of foreign tongues.

At night I was lonely without Cole's body beside me, snoring, stealing all the covers. I listened to the hiss of the radiator and the constant drone of the television set downstairs, where my mother sat over a plate of macaroons and a mug of hot coffee mixed with brandy, shouting weather forecasts to me deep into the night. I tried to imagine my father's new woman. All I knew was that her name was Carmen, she was from New York City, and Cole worshiped her.

Carmen answered the phone one evening when I called, and her voice was like I had imagined it would be, bright and fun and yet somehow mysterious. She said, a smile in her voice, "Hey, girl. You must be the famous Birdie. Your sister tells me all about you. Too bad for all this snow. We'll meet when it melts. Unless you can fly."

And then she laughed softly and handed the phone to Cole, who picked it up, giggling.

"Isn't she awesome?" she said, and I whispered, "Yeah, she sounds great," not wanting my mother, who sang off-key to Joan Baez in the next room, to hear me.

My mother watched the news obsessively that week, seated cross-legged on the couch with a dog-eared book open on her lap, looking over the tops of her reading glasses. She told me that she had discovered during the blizzard how solitary and peaceful her world could be—no dyslexic children streaming through our door with demands to be taught, no activists stamping around our basement, not even the mailman delivering the bills that she dreaded. She had found her island of anonymity, silence, contemplation, a rare moment where she was cut off from both Cambridge and Roxbury and was responsible for only herself and, of course, me. She told me at night, lying stretched out on her side next to me, her cream-colored arms glowing in the dark, that she dreaded the melting of the snow, that day when the world would start up again, beckoning her to its aid.

As far back as I could remember, my mother had thrived in states of emergency. She had always thrilled at the prospect of a good crashing storm, and when it came, she would wake me and Cole up and pull the two of us, groggy and groaning, into the kitchen to watch the flash of light against the windowpane. She once told me that the only thing she had in common with my father was a passion for tempestuous weather. "That's why neither of us could live anywhere but New England. The extremities of the seasons remind us that we're alive."

But I felt strangely panicked by the snow, and especially by Cole's absence. I wanted my mother to travel by foot the distance to Roxbury to fetch her. But neither she nor Cole seemed to want to make the effort, each sleepily accepting the snow-padded rift between them, which had been a long time coming anyway.

A BOMB WENT OFF in Berkeley.

I watched the news report with my mother that Wednesday evening—day five of the blizzard.

I sat in the crook of her arm, lazily listening to the newscaster tell of an organization that had claimed responsibility for the blast, which had killed no one but had blown up an empty police car. The television flashed a wild-looking white man with a black beard being led into a courthouse. He raised his fist at the camera and shouted, "Put the pigs in the pokey and the people . . ." His words were cut off by the newscaster before he could finish.

My mother held me tight and watched it with a gloomy concentration, smoothing down my cowlick while the newscaster explained how many years the man might face in prison.

"So, why'd he do it, Mum?"

She looked down at me, and her eyes were somewhere distant as she said, "We live in disgrace. We slaughter our own and we slaughter people overseas who don't think or look like us. This is a sick, sick country, baby girl. I know. Trust me. And the only way to get people's attention is to do something drastic." She glanced back at the television set, where they showed a bunch of protesters outside of the courthouse with placards and angry, shouting faces.

I ran my finger over the pattern of faint freckles on her hand. "Why is this a sick country?"

She smiled and said, "They didn't teach you that in Nkrumah?"

I shrugged, trying to remember Mrs. Potter's last lesson on the slave trade. School seemed so long ago. I couldn't remember.

My mother looked out into the night and said, "Everybody who can will fuck you over. Never trust power, wherever it comes from. It's always"—her voice had raised a notch—"and I mean always, corrupt. You hear me?"

I nodded.

She kissed my head and said, "That man on television is on the right side of history. It doesn't matter what your color is or what you're born into, you know? It matters who you choose to call your own."

On the television screen, the newscaster was introducing the weatherman, who announced an "ice alert." The drizzle of the afternoon had frozen into a thick layer of ice, and the streets were treacherous.

My mother seemed to snap out of her melancholy daze and said, "I've got a great idea! Get up. Get your coat on."

The two of us bundled up, put on ice skates, and went out into the glowing streets. They had been plowed just that day, but the snow blower had pushed the snow to the gutters, building a fortress more than five feet tall.

She held my hand and pulled me along, hooting laughter as we slipped and stumbled over the sidewalk, her breath like fog before her face. She was enormous and she was moving fast, and I followed, feeling the contagion of her spirit. She slipped at one point and the two of us fell onto the soft pillow of newly fallen snow. After our laughter had subsided, she rolled over so that she was leaning above me. She brushed the hair out of my eyes and said, "This is how it should be all the time. No fucking car-r-r-r-r-s! This is when the capitalist wheel comes screeching to a halt."

On our way back to the house, I was shivering, and she blew hot air onto my fingers, rubbing them between her own, telling me she would make me cocoa and popcorn when we got home. She sang a nonsensical and not-quite-rhyming ditty she had made up:

Birdaloo, Birdalee
So much melancholy
In this planet of deceit
I'm so glad we got to meet
Birdaloo, Birdalee . . .

Later, while she tucked me into bed, she whispered in my ear, the tip of her nose still cold, "Sweetie, if anything happens to me, no matter what they try to tell you, remember that I love you and your sister more than anything in this world, and that I did it for you."

I asked her what she meant, but she just tweaked my nose and then left me to ponder it on my own.

THE RAIN CAME, speeding up the thawing process, turning the fortress of snow into a dingy-gray stream that rushed down the gutter. The streets were slick and black as if buffed by shoe polish overnight. It was a week after the first snowbound day, and my mother and I were beginning to circle each other like caged hyenas. Even she seemed tired of being cooped up inside, and that morning we both waited anxiously for my father to return Cole, now that the streets were clear.

I heard his familiar beeping outside and peeked out the door to see his orange Volvo shining in the winter light. The cars parked around them were emerging from under their casts of snow, and their bodies peeked out like bright hard candies. Cole sat in the backseat, and in the front I could make out a vague feminine figure.

My mother yelled from the kitchen, "Tell Cole to get her booty in here and kiss her mother. It's been a week, for Christ's sake."

Cole didn't appear to be budging, and waved nonchalantly at me from inside the car. My father rolled down his window and said, "C'mon, Bird. We're going to Bob the Chef's for brunch."

Bob the Chef's was a soul food restaurant just down the street that my father liked to frequent. They served my favorite breakfast of grits, eggs, and sausage.

I paused, then shouted back to my mother that we were going to Bob the Chef's and would be home soon, wincing as I heard her slam down a pan. I knew she had been preparing Cole's favorite breakfast: hard-boiled eggs served in the green, chipped, family egg cups; raspberry tea; and English crumpets with expensive marmalade. I didn't wait around to hear what I suspected would be an obscene rant against my father. Instead, I went bounding down the stairs to greet him, wearing my old winter parka and my sister's L.L. Bean boots, a size and a half too large.

As I got closer I could hear Brazilian music sifting out from the steamy vehicle.

The new woman, Carmen, sat daintily beside my father in the front seat, a wet smile turned toward him, her hands folded in her lap. As I climbed into the car, my father introduced us. She glanced back at me, and there was something in her look that made me pause—a sort of surprise and hesitation before she attempted a smile and mumbled a lukewarm "Hi." She had glowing mocha-brown skin, a faint feminine mustache, and a small splotch of a birthmark flowering like a coffee stain on her left cheek. As we drove down the street, she snapped my father's suspenders playfully. Other than the mustache, I thought she looked like a black Barbie come to life. Her nails were painted a rosy pink, and she waved her fingers around like a sorceress when she talked.

Cole looked different, more put together, with light expert makeup, her hair tightly bound in a French braid. She wore a soft fuzzy sweater, two-toned jeans, and gold hoops in her ears. On her feet, she wore moon boots in daunting hot pink.

Bob the Chef's was filled with people standing around like a pack of bears who had simultaneously emerged from hibernation. The air was thick and sizzling with the smell of soul food, and the windows were all greasy, blurring the ugliness of the slushy city outside. My father, tall and thin and stooped over, nodded at some of the regulars, and the obese cook—Tony, not Bob—came waddling over to greet us at the door.

"Well, well, well. If it ain't the professor. Professor Lee. How's it goin', man? Looks like it's back to work."

They laughed and slapped palms, and my father slipped into the slang he used when we were in all-black establishments. He introduced Carmen as his "brown sugar." She blushed as Tony's eyes lit up and he kissed her outstretched hand, taking in her sleek figure with his eyes. "That's a fine sister for you, Lee." Then, winking at Carmen, he said, " I could tell you some stories about this cat. We used to roll together, down in the Orchard Park projects. He was always a little bit of the loner, you know. Preaching to us about how he was gonna make it out. And I guess he did. Hahvahd and all that."

My father was laughing, pleased, I could see, to hear this rendition of himself. Carmen slipped her arm through my father's, and Tony led us to a booth in the back.

Cole and I sat across from them and automatically began our old habit of knocking feet under the table. I had felt incomplete outside of her presence, and now felt safe with her beside me. But Carmen seemed to have grown chillier toward me since we entered the diner. She didn't make eye contact with me through the whole brunch, and spoke only to Cole and my father. When I asked her a question, she gave curt, one-word answers, looking at Cole while she spoke, as if I was my sister's ventriloquist dummy.

At some point Cole began to talk about me to them as if I weren't there. She told them I could dance, stand on my head without a wall to support me, that I had memorized whole episodes of "Good Times." "She got an A-plus on her project on Toussaint L'Overture. Mrs. Potter said it was the best in her class."

It sounded, from the high, strained tone in her voice and the way she squeezed my hand under the table, that she was a used-car salesman trying to convince them to buy.

"Professor Abdul put Birdie's report in the front hall with a mural that Ali Parkman drew to go along with it—"

Carmen looked bored by Cole's stories and kneaded my father's shoulder while Cole talked on. At some point, my father cut in and said, "Why don't you tell Birdie about what we did this week?" And Cole paused in midstory, finally getting the hint, and she turned to me, leaving Carmen and my father to their massage.

Cole spoke to me in Elemeno about how much fun they had had all week together, playing card games and reading out loud to one another about Brazil, where we all were going to visit one of these days.

rula mest fundacolo. midge part ridge yazza.

As she spoke, I saw the new life in my sister's face, as if she had found some reflection of herself in this tall, cool woman. I felt heavy with grief as I played with the greasy food in front of me, cutting it up into tiny pieces, then mashing the eggs, grits, and sausage together into a revolting, inedible stew.

THINGS UNRAVEL. Slowly. Without warning. We all had been going through our separate changes for a while. Moving in different directions. My mother disappearing into the basement. Cole disappearing into her adolescence. Me into my life with the Brown Sugars clique at Nkrumah. My father into his book. But looking back on it, I think Carmen was the icing on the cake, so to speak. Others before had made me see the differences between my sister and myself—the textures of our hair, the tints of our skin, the shapes of our features. But Carmen was the one to make me feel that those things somehow mattered. To make me feel that the differences were deeper than skin.

Cole tried. She went out of her way to make sure I was invited along on her and Carmen's activities—trips to the hair salon; shopping sprees to outlets; visits to Carmen's girlfriends' houses, where they sat around the kitchen vaguely watching soap operas and discussing their men. But even then I sat perched on a stool in the corner, chewing on my hair, feeling the ever-present weight of Carmen's silent irritation. It seemed that around my father she made more of an effort, but when we were alone, I sometimes thought I saw her looking at me with muted disgust.

Cole even donated to me many of the gifts that Carmen had given to her—a Peaches and Herb cassette, a gold ankh necklace from a museum gift shop, a baseball shirt with an iron-on unicorn emblem across the front—and we both understood without saying it that our exchange was secret and that Carmen would not find out that her gifts were being funneled my way.

On Cole's twelfth birthday, Carmen took her to get her hair done. I came along with them, at Cole's insistence and Carmen's annoyance. The salon smelled of a pungent mix of hair chemicals and Chinese food, and a fat woman sat at a manicure table eating egg foo young with chopsticks out of a white carton and watching a soap opera with a cynical smirk.

Carmen, it turned out, was an old friend of the hairdresser's, a man named James who wore a yellow blouse unbuttoned so I could see his smooth chest, and his hair wrapped in an orange silk scarf.

Carmen kissed James on both cheeks, then said, pointing to Cole, "This is the one. Deck's girl. Isn't she just gorgeous? She wants braids. Like all the girls are getting them."

James came toward Cole and fingered her hair, which Carmen had picked out into a soft afro around her face. He clucked his teeth and smiled. "She's got a good thick head of hair. Enough for three heads."

Cole wasn't smiling, though. She was watching Carmen with a quizzical expression, her lips parted and her brow furrowed. She then belted out loudly enough for the whole salon to hear, "And this is my little sister, Birdie." I heard an edge to her voice that was somehow combative, and I worried that I'd ruined her birthday. My mother was at home making a special dinner for her and had asked me to stay home and help her chop and dice. I was wishing I had stayed there.

James spotted me then, standing behind Cole, staring at my shoes, and he broke into a smile. "Hey there, little sister. You want braids too?"

Carmen turned to me and frowned. Then, looking back at the man, she said, "Yeah, that's Cole's little sister, even if she doesn't look like a sister." She giggled at her pun rather unhappily, with an anxious expression, and touched my hair as if to show she was just kidding around. James turned away, seeming embarrassed. Before starting on Cole's hair, he handed me a Tootsie Pop out of the drawer at his side and winked at me, saying, "See how long you can suck it before you have to bite." For the rest of the afternoon, as the light turned from yellow to orange on Tremont Street outside and the traffic grew dense and noisy with the ending day, Carmen sat beside James's workstation smoking and gossiping with him about his latest romantic escapades. I, meanwhile, sat in the waiting area, reading back issues of *Soap Opera Digest* and listening to the sounds of the manicurist's tiny television set.

Later, at dinner, when it was just my mother, Cole, and me, it felt like old times. My mother had made lemon chicken, mashed potatoes, and a fancy salad with walnuts; for dessert, an upside-down cake. It was the first time I had seen my mother and sister get along in a while, so I forgot about Carmen and the hairdresser's and enjoyed myself. We sat together around the messy kitchen, giving Cole her gifts. I gave her a diary—a gold notebook from the Museum of Fine Arts with a profile of Anubis' head on the front. My father had helped me pick it out. My mother gave her a stack of tarot cards and a silver locket that had been her grandmother's. On the front were her grandmother's initials, but on the back she had engraved Cole's initials. She made each of us put a lock of hair into it that evening— my mother's fine gold one, my straight brown one, and Cole's wiry black curl. Cole hugged my mother for a long time, and I felt a little left out. They seemed back to the way they once had been. She told my mother that it was the best gift yet, and I could see how much it meant to my mother. Her eyes were all watery, and she seemed unable to speak as she cleared the dishes.

After dinner, Cole lay beside my mother on the couch while my mother fingered her hair and read to her from a Colette novel. I sat on the floor with my knees pulled into my chest, watching them and pretending to listen to the stories my mother read. It struck me how much they looked alike, sitting side by side, their high foreheads and deep-set green eyes, their hands small and delicate. People generally didn't comment on their resemblance to each other, but if you looked at them in the right light—like just then, the two of them tilting their heads toward the book my mother was holding, eyebrows raised in identical expressions of amusement—it was clear that my sister's face held both my mother's and my father's within it, the raw and the cooked in aesthetic harmony.

THERE IS STILL a lot about that spring that I feel unable—or unwilling—to tell. When you've been let in on a secret, told that your very existence and your mother's freedom and even the negritudinal forces of the universe depend on your keeping that secret, you kind of lose the ability to speak it, even after the secret's reasons are no longer clear.

But it is true that one night I was drifting into sleep when I heard a car door slam down on the street below, then my mother's voice, muffled by the windowpane. I lay beside Cole in bed. It was two o'clock in the morning, and now I was wide awake. An indigo darkness blanketed the room, interrupted by bars of light from the street. I could make out only the shapes in our preteen sanctuary. A stuffed animal that, in the darkness, had acquired the profile of Karl Marx. A poster of an afroed Jackson Five that in the half-light appeared as a cluster of dark, swaying lollipops. A sock-monkey doll with red felt buttocks, which in the darkness created a second smile.

I looked at Cole, whose face was turned upward, mouth slack, and I knew she was really out for the night. A man's laughter floated up to the room. I thought then that it must be my father returning home. I went to the window silently. My father was nowhere in sight, and I saw instead a green van and a group of strange men: black men and one or two white men dressed casually in jackets and blue jeans. Men who seemed nervous, tension holding their faces frozen in masks of ivory and gold and mahogany. They came bearing long duffel bags shaped like bodily limbs—and they came silently, speaking in a kind of sign language under the glow of the street-lamps. My mother stood before them—the lone spot of white womanhood in their midst—wearing blue jeans, a dirty T-shirt, her red bandanna in her hair. She had her hands on her hips, watching the men as they climbed in and out of the van, whispering and gesturing directions to one another. I couldn't make out her expression.

There were two metal doors built into the sidewalk that opened to steps that led down to our basement. Usually those doors were locked with a padlock and a chain, and I liked to imagine that they opened not into our basement but to a ladder that went straight through the earth, eventually to Hell, where flames would tickle your toes as you made your way down. Now I watched from above as the men methodically pulled duffel bags out of the van and carried them into the lighted cavern.

I went back to the bed and shook Cole. After I had woken her from her grumpy blur, I told her that there were men down on the street with our mother.

She threw her hands angrily over her eyes. "Damn, I was asleep," she said, rolling away from me onto her side. "It's probably just Hassan and Charles came over to drink wine."

She sighed deeply and began to fall back to sleep. I shook her harder, and she turned violently toward me and said, "What, Birdie? Shit. I gotta get up in the morning."

I hissed in her ear, "I've never seen them before. And they're driving a van and taking big bags into the house."

Her eyes fluttered open. Her curiosity had been piqued, and she came to the window, dragging her blankets behind her.

The two of us stood at the window now, watching as the men unloaded the rest of the long duffel bags and brought them into the open basement. My mother stood at the van door, looking up and down the street, wringing her hands, biting her nails, talking with her face close to one of the men's. Cole and I were silent, our questions floating unspoken between us. We watched until all of the bags had been brought in and our mother had crouched to bolt-lock the basement door and the men had hugged her, raising their fists at her in a silent salute of comradeship as they piled into the green van again, like circus clowns squeezing into a trick mini. They drove away, leaving her on the sidewalk hugging herself. Neither Cole nor I turned to go back to bed until my mother had made her way up the stairs to the house and we could hear her locking our front door behind her.

"Should we ask her what's going on?" I wondered aloud once we were back under the covers.

Cole shook her head. She looked scared. "No, Birdie. If she hasn't told us now, she ain't gonna tell us. And besides, I don't trust her. She's crazy. Papa said so."

Cole said we should spy instead. "That's the only way we're gonna get to the bottom of this." We made a pact that what we had seen would be our secret.

MY MOTHER SAT at the table in the same uniform she had worn the night before, the red bandanna still in her hair. She looked tired, her skin transluscent and tinged with blue. She was building a house out of cards, and a record played distantly from the living room stereo. It was Al Green singing about wanting old-time love.

My mother didn't seem to notice us, even as we went about getting bowls for cereal and milk and juice.

Finally, digging into my bowl of Cap'n Crunch, I said, "Mum, earth to Mum."

She blinked at me over the house of cards, which was getting big and absorbing all her attention. Then she placed a final card on top, knocked down the house with a flick of a finger, and said, "Forget about school today, girls. We need to go visit your grandmother."

"Oh, no," Cole groaned, slapping her hand to her forehead. I guess she was getting sick of my mother pulling us out. "Mum, you can't keep doing this. Papa's right—"

My mother slammed her fist on the table and belted out, "Papa Shmapa!" She rubbed her temples and closed her eyes as she went on, calmer now: "This is important. I need to see her." She stood up. "I'm going upstairs to change. I didn't sleep a fucking wink last night. Now, I don't want to hear another complaint out of either of you. School will be there tomorrow. Be ready by noon."

After my mother had gone, I whispered to Cole, "Let's go check out the basement." I was still thinking about the previous night's activities and Cole's promise that we would be spies.

But Cole was stirring her cereal around angrily and staring at the table with shining eyes. She shook her head. "No, Birdie. Fuck Mum. And fuck the basement." Then she stood up and left, stomping up the stairs two at a time.

It was odd to me that we were visiting my grandmother. Last time we'd gone, more than a year before, my mother had sworn we'd never go back. It had to do with the Christmas presents my grandmother had brought back from England for us that year—that is, the one she had brought back for Cole. When we'd opened them on Christmas morning, mine was a dreary little book for a child much younger than me about a character named Noddy whose car went "parp, parp" instead of "beep, beep." But Cole's present was a doll. Its body was made of cloth and hung limply, like a long-legged puppet. Its face was a perfect black circle, its hair a crescent of steel wool. Its eyes were huge white plastic circles with tiny black pupils, and its mouth a half-moon strip of red felt that sat in a perpetually mocking smile. There had been a tag hanging from its wrist with the words: "Hello! My name is Golliwog, but you can call me Golli," and there had been a card for

Cole from my grandmother that read, "Your mother played with one just like this as a little girl. Hope you like it! Granny."

Cole and I had loved the doll immediately. He looked nothing like the black dolls my father had given us in the past, the ones who looked just like our white ones except for the fact that they were made of brown plastic and their hair was dark and slightly curled and maybe they had strips of African cloth sewed to the hems of their pinafores. Golliwog was completely different—wild, laughing, cool. He wore little tuxedo pants and a bright-red bow tie that matched his lips in color and cloth. This was before Nkrumah, before we had any idea what was wrong with dolls like Golli.

My mother, however, knew damn well what was wrong with Golli. When she'd told us we couldn't keep him, Cole and I had wailed and screamed and babbled obscenities in Elemeno. My mother had tried to explain to us that Golliwog was "a racist tool, a parody, a white-supremacist depiction of African people," but we would hear none of it.

My father had come home later that day to find Cole asleep with Golliwog clutched in her arms. Instead of getting angry, he had thought it was hysterically funny and referred to the incident as "Golliwog's revenge." Cole continued to sleep with Golliwog every night, even now, keeping him far out of my mother's reach, for fear she might try to hurt him.

As we drove over the bridge that led from Boston to Cambridge, my mother puffed on a Marlboro and shouted to us over her shoulder about what we could and couldn't say in the old woman's presence.

"Don't mention the basement. I mean, not a word. She'll freak out if she thinks I'm up to any funny business."

I thought back to the men going in and out during the night and almost opened my mouth to say something about it. But Cole must have read my mind, because she pinched me hard.

Spring had come as a surprise after the long gray winter, and I watched the white blossoms on the trees, thinking maybe things would look up. We had a field trip planned for the next week at Nkrumah, to the Black History Trail. We'd see the African Meeting House, where Frederick Douglass spoke when he came to Boston from the South.

My mother beeped her horn at a stalled car ahead of us, then wound around it, flashing her middle finger at the driver. She went on: "And don't tell her your father's left for good. She still thinks he's with us. And I don't want to give her any fuel."

I glanced at Cole. She had pulled out an Archie comic and was thumbing through it, ignoring me and my mother.

"Oh yeah," my mother added as we cruised down Brattle Street, getting closer now to the destination, "and if she asks you anything about where you're going to school, just say it's a public school. Don't tell her it's called Nkrumah, and don't tell her it's all black. 'Cause she'll flip."

My grandmother traced her family line back to Cotton Mather, the Puritan prosecutor in the Salem witch trials. But according to my mother, there was more class than money left in her family. "Blue-blood bandits and Mayflower madames" was how she described her ancestors. Whatever the case, our family had inherited only two things from the legacy. One was a print of Cotton Mather wearing bushy white curls and a sneering expression, which hung lopsided in our living room. It had been my father's idea to hang it up. He said, chuckling, that Mather looked like an "octoroon dandy" and liked to show it off to friends. The second was a collection of semi-valuable silverware with the family initials engraved on it. My mother washed the silverware in the dishwasher along with our regular stainless steel knives and forks from Zayres, joking, "At least there's democracy in the dishwasher." She was always threatening to sell it to pay off her bills or buy a new car.

My grandmother owned a valuable first edition of Cotton Mather's how-to-spot-a-witch guide entitled *The Wonders of the Invisible World*, which she kept under glass in the library. My father had used a play on the title for his first book. I wasn't sure how the books were related, but I knew that my grandmother had disapproved of his using it. She thought he was mocking her. She was proud of the Mather link and liked to remind me of my heritage every time I came over. She would pull me close to her and say, "You're from good stock, Birdie. It still means something." I always seemed to get the brunt of her attention, while Cole was virtually ignored. I thought Cole was the lucky one because she was allowed to stay locked in the guest room watching television while I had to sit under the old lady's scrutiny, hands folded on my lap, listening to her tell me stories about how good my blood was.

It was strange. While there seemed to be remnants of my mother's family everywhere—history books, PBS specials, plaques in Harvard Square—my father's family was a mystery. It was as if my father and Dot had arisen out of thin air. I knew this wasn't true, that they had come from somewhere, namely my Nana's slight brown body. And there were other facts I picked up: My father had been born in Louisiana, but Dot had been born later, when they had already moved north, to Boston, to the Orchard Park projects. I knew there was some tension between Dot and my father that went back to way before I was born. But I knew little of their real past, their blood, which lay somewhere in the Louisiana bayou, where Nana was born. There was nothing in writing, nothing in stone.

What I did know was what my father had told me: that Nana had been adopted as an infant by "a bunch of piss-colored Creoles" who hadn't realized how dark she was when they took her in. A few weeks after her birth, when her hair began to kink up and her skin turned a rich nut-brown, they wanted to send her back. But instead they kept her and treated her as a stepchild and sometimes maid. At night, her adoptive mother would put a clothespin on Nana's nose and bleaching cream on her skin, and the poor child couldn't sleep. Her hair was straightened so many times, with such chemical force, that by the time she was twelve, it began to fall out in great chunks. The family embraced Nana only when they noticed she was at the top of her class at a black college in Alabama. She had studied Russian, done her thesis on Tolstoy, and had dreams of going to the Soviet Union. After her graduation, she took off instead for the Northeast, New England, with a diploma in her bag and a fantasy of herself in fur, downing vodka shots in a dank pub with a man named Vladimir.

But she never made it to Moscow, and the Northeast wasn't what she thought it would be. Something happened to her there, something broke her. She liked to say that the Great Migration was the worst mistake black folks ever made. She said they were spiritually freezing in the North and that they should have stayed where they were and built a new history on the land they had been tending so long. My mother said that the first year I was born, when she was so busy with Cole and the dyslexic students, Nana had babysat for me and would rock me for hours by the window in the attic, where she would read Pushkin to me in between Creole lullabies. She died working but poor as a nurse at Brigham and Women's, still living in those Orchard Park projects, with a dog-eared copy of *Anna Karenina* beside her bed.

My white grandmother had met her a few times before Nana died, and liked to talk about how "intelligent, dignified" she was, as if that fact were a surprise, proof of something that needed proving.

THE PINTO BACKFIRED LOUDLY as we pulled into the driveway, and I saw a face come to the window of the glass porch out front. I made out my grandmother's tall stooped form and gray bun. The rosebushes that circled the house were in bloom—red and lavender and white and pink—and Gory, the dog, sat watching us with his eternally depressed expression as we climbed out of the car. The gardener, a small dark man, was crouched on his hands and knees, tending to the flowers, and my mother shouted to him, "Hey there, Joe! How's things?"

He laughed, and waved at my mother. "Just surviving, Sandy." He looked at Cole and me. He always seemed amused by us, ready to burst into giggles at just the sight of us, and now he winked at Cole. "Colette sure is getting big. You got yourself a boyfriend yet?"

Cole smiled and blushed. He handed her a pink rose. I wanted one too, but my mother was pulling me by the hand toward the house.

I could feel she was angry already, preparing herself for some sort of offense to come. Edna came to greet us at the door. She was my grandmother's housecleaner, a Caribbean woman with salt-and-pepper hair. She smelled of lemon and wore chunky white nurse shoes and neatly pressed hair. She made everything sparkle, but a faint smell of must lingered.

"Hi, Sandy, your mother's waiting in the living room. Food's almost ready."

"How's her mood today?" my mother whispered to Edna.

Edna looked around, a weary smile creeping across her features. "Let's put it this way. It's not nearly as good as this weather."

My mother laughed. "Well, let me at her."

Cole and I followed her down the hallway. We passed my grandfather's old study, and I glanced in. It was where my grandmother kept her safe. On one particularly nasty visit, my mother had pointed the safe out to Cole and me and told us that was where my grandmother kept her "loot." She had made us memorize the combination number—it was the birth year of Cotton's father, Increase Mather. Apparently there was quite a lot of money in the safe. My grandmother had kept a stash of extra cash handy ever since the Great Depression. My mother said, winking at us, that it might come in useful some day.

My grandmother sat at the window in her usual armchair with her cat, Delilah, at her feet. She had a crossword puzzle folded on her lap and a tragic expression on her face. Cole whispered something to me in Elemeno, and my grandmother scowled at us. "Please speak proper English in my house, girls. It's all I ask. Sandy, I thought you said they had stopped with that twisted little dialect of theirs."

My mother sighed. "They still speak it sometimes. But don't worry, they know how to speak English, and that's all that should matter."

My grandmother looked my mother up and down.

"Sandy, what is that queer uniform you're wearing? Have you put on more weight?"

My mother touched her collar lightly. She wore overalls and a blue-checkered work shirt. I felt sorry for her.

My mother had always been fat. And my grandmother had always been bone thin, even during her first pregnancy. We had a few old pictures from when my grandmother was pregnant with her first child, Randall, before my mother's existence. She looked like a snake in the process of devouring a rat, the bulge on her belly only making the rest of her figure look sleeker. The one time my grandmother had put on an ounce of weight was when she was pregnant with my mother—and she always reminded my mother of that, as if it had been my mother's fault even then, in utero.

Now my mother just laughed bitterly at my grandmother's latest comment and said, "Listen, I didn't come over here to be insulted."

My grandmother sighed. "I didn't mean it that way, darling. I just wish you'd take better care of yourself. You're really quite pretty." Then she turned to me. "Birdie, Cole, have a seat. Edna's bringing you lemonade."

Cole seemed bored and flipped through a *National Geographic*. She wore her glasses, which meant she didn't want to be disturbed. I sat still beside her, listening to my grandmother rattle off to my mother about some production of *Huckleberry Finn* she had been to recently in Harvard Square. "I wish the girls could have seen it. Splendid production. And the most delightful black man playing Jim. So noble."

My mother was sneering at my grandmother, who just ignored her and beckoned to me, "Come here, Birdie. Let me have a look at you."

I came toward her, tentatively. She smelled strongly of Chanel No. 5, and her eyes looked like two bluish-gray jellyfish floating in her head. She took my hand and pulled me closer.

She smiled, her first real smile since we had entered the room. She reached out and stroked my hair.

"Birdie, dear, you look lovely. I think she looks a bit like Arabella, those old photos of when she was young. Don't you think, Sandy?" Arabella was one of my mother's distant cousins from England, whom I had seen only in photographs. As I recalled, she looked nothing like me.

My mother rolled her eyes. "Arabella was blond and blue-eyed, Mummy. Don't you remember?" She leaned toward Cole to see what she was reading, glad, I think, to have me entertain my grandmother.

"Yes, but something in her face structure," my grandmother replied wistfully.

We ate lunch in the big dining room. Edna had made salmon and asparagus, with only butter and lemon juice for seasoning, the way my grandmother liked it. I ate the asparagus with my fingers, but Cole barely touched hers. She had brought the magazine to the table with her, and read it there. Nobody seemed to care. Not even my grandmother. She was too focused on me to notice.

"What have you been doing with yourself, Birdie? Have you started going to a real school?"

My mother and Cole looked up from their plates and watched me with identical expectant gazes. I could feel the cat moving in and out of my legs underneath the table. I turned back to my grandmother. "Yeah, um, me and Cole, we're going to—public school."

My grandmother raised her eyebrows at my mother. "Well, finally. You couldn't keep them at home forever, after all. I never thought it was a good idea. It was beginning to show. They were completely without manners. You're wonderful with those mongoloids, Sandra, but normal children are simply not your specialty."

My mother dropped her knife loudly. I could see she was about to lose it. My grandmother didn't seem to notice, though, and turned back to me. "Well, I hope it's a good public school. Tell me about it, Birdie."

I turned to my mother. Her rage had passed. She was biting her lip while she waited to see what I would say. Cole looked like she was going to burst out laughing, and put the *National Geographic* up in front of her face so that I stared at the pelicans instead.

"Yeah, it's a good school. Super-good. You have to take a test to get in and everything. It's special, for special kids. The smart kind," I said.

My mother was trying with her eyes to get me to shut up. I had said too much.

My grandmother watched me. "A test? For public school? Where is it?" I paused.

My mother jumped in to my rescue. "It's in Boston. And yes, it's perfectly good."

My grandmother pressed on, seeming to sense that something wasn't right. "Birdie, what's your favorite class?"

I knew, even as I said it, that it was the wrong answer. But I went on, and my lips moved as if detached from my body: "I like Mrs. Potter's black-history class. I did a report on Toussaint L'Ouverture. I also like music. Want to hear a song I learned? *We are children of the sun, Survived the boat and genocide—*"

I stopped. A thick silence had fallen over the table. My grandmother was staring at me, mouth agape.

Cole was giggling into her napkin. She looked up and mouthed across the table at me: *sima welta vicu.* You screwed up.

My grandmother let her fork rest, then said, "Sandy, what kind of place is Birdie going to?" I noticed she hadn't asked about Cole. She didn't care what kind of school Cole was going to.

My mother said it as casually as she could. "It's called the Nkrumah School. It's a school that focuses on Afro-American arts and culture. It's in Roxbury. Okay? There you have it."

Then it began.

My grandmother's words seemed to rise up and fall onto my mother's head in sharp blunt cuts.

"It's crazy, child abuse, to send your child into a neighborhood like that. She could be robbed or killed or anything! Jesus Christ, Sandy. I told you I'd pay for them to go to The Friends. I told you."

Cole and I got up to clear the table, eyes to the floor. I glanced an apology to my mother as we left the room. She appeared smaller than ever, curled over her food like a broken doll.

Cole and I waited with Gory in the living room. I could hear my mother's voice in the next room. It didn't sound like her. She sounded choked up, on the verge of tears, and pleading.

"Why are we here, anyway?" I asked Cole, who was rubbing Gory's forehead and searching for the cartoons in a copy of *The New Yorker*.

She shrugged without looking up. "Mum's asking her for money. She's freaking out about something. Whatever."

Cole didn't seem interested, so I decided to spy on my own. I went to the door and peered around.

My mother was standing over the dining room table, arms crossed, waiting, while my grandmother wrote her out a check. My mother's cheeks were red, and I could see she was ashamed.

My grandmother was shaking her head, saying in a disapproving whisper, "I don't know what you need this for, Sandra Lodge, but I hope you're not up to any funny business. I mean, you didn't have to take all this so far. You took it too far."

We left my grandmother's house early, before dessert. My grandmother walked us to the door and put her hand on my shoulder. She looked down at me with some expression that made me feel small and pitiful. I didn't like the feeling, and looked away. She said quietly, "You know, Birdie, you could be Italian. Or even French. Couldn't she, Sandy?"

I expected my mother to bark something back like "Well, she's not, crackerjack. She's black!" But instead she just smiled kind of sadly and said, "Yes, mother, she could be."

It was then that my mother embraced my grandmother. It was a strange and alarming moment, and I saw my grandmother stiffen. They never touched, and my grandmother's hands hung awkwardly by her side as my mother held her for that moment.

Then my mother turned and took my hand, and the two of us made our way across the grass to the car, where Cole sat waiting in the front seat with some Donna Summer hit playing faintly from the radio. Just as we were about to get into the car, I heard my grandmother shout out across the lawn: "Sandy!"

My mother turned. My grandmother looked thin, fragile, standing there on the porch. She shouted to us, "Sandy, you should visit more often." My mother just nodded and lifted her hand in a halting wave.

IN MY MEMORY, this is when things speed up. This is when something starts to dawn on me, begins to clarify, but before I can stop it, it's too late. Like a deer who pauses in the road to watch the oncoming traffic, I froze as well, to watch what was coming at me, what was coming at all of us.

By springtime, I had mastered double-dutch. I jump-roped as if my life depended on it, while the other girls sang around me: "Ice cream soda with cherry on top! . . ." I moved strong and hard, my skirt flapping around my knees. Summertime was just around the bend, and the sky seemed to press down on the world like a bright-blue veil. I squinted across the playground. Ali and a group of boys sat hunched in a circle, getting into trouble. I could see my sister sitting against a wall with a group of the older girls, staring wistfully onto the city streets, leaning secretively into one another while one of them played a love song on her transistor radio. And beyond that I noticed a man at the far corner of the school playground wearing a long sheepskin coat, too warm for this weather, and watching us with a thin smile.

Seeing him there, I stumbled on the rope, nicking my knee against the pavement.

Maria shouted, "Aw, Birdie! You was about to beat your record!" I looked over at her. She was laughing and appeared small and far away. I felt dizzy. I stood up and walked away, saying under my breath, "Someone take over. I gotta go sit down."

I left them there singing and skipping and went to the fence, where I sat down, rubbing my scraped knee with a wet finger. The man at the fence who was watching us all was someone I had met before, and now I looked up to see him moving toward me, still smiling, as if we were old friends.

It was Redbone—same orange-brown kinky hair, same freckled skin, same dirty teeth. It hit me that he looked a bit like our portrait of Cotton Mather, the octoroon dandy. He wore the same slightly sneering expression. He had his hands in his pockets and seemed different somehow. His clothes were more like a businessman's, and his hair was neatly trimmed to his scalp. He stood behind me, on the other side of the fence, gripping the bar. He squatted down so that he was at my level.

"Hey, Ms. Birdie. What you doing sitting by yourself?"

I shrugged. I remembered his fight with my father from way back when. I looked over toward my sister, but she was dancing now before the group of girls, swaying her braids in front of her face.

Redbone said, "How's your mother? I ain't seen her in a while. She chickening out on us?" He paused, looked up at the sky, and closed his eyes as if sunbathing. "You can tell her I said hello."

"Okay. But I gotta go," I told him, pointing across the asphalt at my sister. "My sister's over there." I hoped she would see me pointing.

Redbone squinted at her. "Yeah. I see her. What happened there? You sure you got the same daddy?"

"Yeah, of course we do," I said, trying to sound casual, though I was sweating and feeling my lungs close up. "Well, see you later, now."

He smiled. "Hold up. Not so fast. I was just kidding you. Tell me, how's your daddy doing? I haven't seen him in ages either. He don't got time for the revolution?"

I frowned at him, then said something I remembered my father saying: "No, he's writing a masterpiece. He doesn't have time for you."

His smile disappeared, and he watched me for a moment, fascinated by something on my face. I averted my eyes from his gaze. He said, "You look like a little guinea. Anybody ever tell you that? That's what they used to say to me."

He stuck his hand through the metal bars of the fence and began to play slightly with my hair. The children around me were loud, raucous. I looked over at the red metal door of the school, where Mrs. Potter and Professor Abdul stood talking, holding plastic foam cups. They were deep in discussion and wouldn't hear me if I screamed.

Redbone whispered, "I got a camera. Mind if I take your photo?"

I knew enough to stand up and walk away at that point. I made it a few feet across the playground when I heard him say, "I'm gonna miss you, Birdie Lee."

I wasn't sure I'd heard him right. It was an odd thing to say, and I turned around and looked at him from the safe distance.

"But I'm not going anywhere."

As soon as my words had come out, so had his camera—a small automatic—and he leaned in between the bars, snapping me in two deft flashes of light. I blinked at the flash, trying to dispel the yellow spots that danced before my eyes.

He laughed. "Gotcha."

I turned and ran all the way across the playground to Professor Abdul, falling into his arms. He looked down at me, smiling. "Why are you running so fast, B?"

I was out of breath, and I bent over, my hands on my knees.

I finally managed to say, pointing behind me, still not daring to look, "Redbone."

Professor Abdul looked confused. "Red-who?"

"Redbone," I said again.

Professor Abdul paused, then said, "What did that fool want?"

"He took my picture."

Professor Abdul looked angry then. "You sure you aren't telling stories, Birdie?"

I nodded and only now dared to turn back to where Redbone had been. He was gone from that spot, but in the distance, across the street, I could see a car starting up and, vaguely, behind all that glass, a face, pale and blurred from the distance, staring back.

Professor Abdul said, "Well, next time you see him, you come get me or one of the other teachers. He shouldn't be hanging around here."

On the way home from school later that afternoon, I told my mother and sister what had happened. Cole, seated in the passenger's seat, was sucking on a Blow-Pop. She squealed, "Yuck! Sounds like a pervert," and my mother swerved the car, nearly crashing into an oncoming one in the left lane. She didn't say anything, but I could see that something was building in her clenched jaw as she pulled us into the parking lot of a Roy Rogers on Huntington Avenue.

Cole asked, "We're gonna get dinner here?"

But my mother had no intention of getting out of the car. She turned to me and grabbed my arm painfully, pulling me forward toward her. "Tell me that story again. Slower now."

I told it, my voice trembling as it struck me that I might be in real trouble for talking to this man. My mother had drummed it into our heads time and time again not to talk to strangers. But Redbone, I reasoned to myself, wasn't really a stranger.

When I had finished, she pointed a finger at me and said, "If he ever comes near you again, scream your little head off till someone comes to the rescue. Hear me?"

I nodded.

Her gaze seemed distracted as she searched the parking lot for something. She turned to start up the engine. "Cole, keep an eye on your sister."

She blasted the news while we drove home, and all of us were quiet.

The weekend came with no more mention of the Redbone incident, and I put it out of my mind the best I could. The crocuses were in bloom that Saturday, and my father came by to take Cole and Carmen to a museum. Although he had barely seemed to notice the other times I had stayed home, that day he seemed particularly disturbed that I wasn't coming along with them. Cole and Carmen sat together in the backseat. Cole rested her head against Carmen's shoulder as she described some boy story in great tragic detail. My father pulled me to him at the car door and spoke to me. He wore a coffee-stained T-shirt, his wire-rimmed glasses, and faded jeans with sandals. He stroked my hair back away from my face, staring at me with an unusually attentive expression. Ordinarily, he was distracted when talking to me, but at that moment he was all there.

"Hey, baby, we're going to the Egyptian exhibit at the museum. Your favorite. You can touch Anubis' nose."

I managed a weak smile, taken aback by his affection. "I don't know. I think I'll stay home."

"What, you don't want to be around your papa anymore?"

I glanced quickly at Carmen, trying, without words, to relay why I wasn't coming. Carmen looked up at me from the backseat and said in a bright, false tone, "Hey there, Bernie." She consistently mispronounced my name, no matter how many times my father corrected her. She looked me up and down. I wore jeans and my mother's denim shirt, which fell down midthigh, and I thought I saw a barely perceptible sneer cross her face.

He sensed something and looked disturbed. "Carmen," he called out rather sharply, as if speaking to a small child, "tell Birdie she should come with us. You wanted to take the girls to Filene's tomorrow, right?"

Carmen nodded and looked back at Cole. "Yeah, they have the cutest spring selection, girl. I saw something that would look sharp on you."

My father had finally seemed to notice that Carmen didn't speak to me. I could see it in the way his lips grew thin. He said then, softly, to me, "You're my baby girl. I want to spend time with you, sweets. And I don't know when I'm going to get a chance again soon. We can do something tomorrow, just the two of us, if you want. I'll take you shopping alone. We can go to Copley Square." He looked away, toward the film of pasty clouds that muted the afternoon light. "Things are about to get real tight, baby, and we gotta spend time together now. You know?"

He seemed particularly insistent. I both did and didn't want to be left alone at the house with my mother. There was an aching in my chest that surprised me, and my eyes were watering up against my will.

All morning my mother had been talking to Jane in the bedroom, and their voices had risen and fallen so that I had made out only snippets of their conversation.

"I know they'll trace it to me. I just know it," she had said.

"Don't be so paranoid, Sandy. Jesus. Nobody is going to find out. I mean, how could they?"

"Something just isn't right. I can feel it."

When my mother and Jane came out later, my mother's eyes were swollen. I didn't want to go up there and listen to their whispers. It seemed serious, dark, strange in the house.

I looked back at Carmen. Rifling through her purse for something, she said, "If she wants to stay here with her mother, let her, Deck. But we gotta get going."

My father stared at me for a moment longer. "Well, you want to come, sugar-puff?"

I shook my head no. Cole threw me an apologetic look but didn't ask me to come.

I went up to my room after they drove away, and ran to the window to see the car moving out of sight. I felt a sudden inexplicable panic. I had seen in my father's face a flash of my own, an expression we both wore when we were scared. According to my mother, I had inherited only two things from my father—asthma and eczema, both of which Cole had been spared. Now I felt my breathing shorten, and I felt comforted by that shortness, invisible proof that I was his daughter. I had a brief strange fantasy that he would take me to Egypt that summer to do research, just the two of us, circling pyramids in matching white turbans. He would talk and I would take notes, his little scribe, and at the end of the day we would sit drinking tea and talking over our findings—cross-legged in some tent—while flies buzzed beyond the mesh door.

Just then my mother came bounding into the bedroom, interrupting me from my daze at the window. When I turned, she appeared enormous to me. It struck me that she had been eating lately with a hurricane energy—with even more gusto than usual. She wore a flowered sundress with a thermal underwear top underneath, the fabric stretched tightly across her torso.

She stood over me, hands on her hips, seeming not to notice the wet stain on my cheeks, and said, "Baby Bird, I'm in big fucking trouble. Let's go get a banana split."

As we drove to Friendly's, I kept my feet against the dashboard and fiddled with the radio to find the funk station. In Boston the black-music stations were scarce, and the best, WILD, came on only AM, a fact which "added insult to injury," according to my father. Now it crackled a tinny rendition of Roberta Flack singing "Killing Me Softly." I wondered what my father and Carmen and Cole were doing at that moment. Probably something ordinary and fun, I supposed, like a real family. Meanwhile, my mother was whispering things to herself as she drove, her head at a crooked angle. "Goddamn him. Brazil. What's in Brazil? A book, my ass. Escapist overintellectualized creep."

At Friendly's she wolfed down her banana split, getting chocolate around her mouth and a little dot of whipped cream on the tip of her nose so that she looked clownish, like Golliwog. She didn't say much, except to ask me if I liked my father's new girlfriend.

I confessed to her, stirring my coffee ice cream in its silver bowl, that Carmen adored Cole, hated me, and that I didn't know why.

"She's a bitch," I stated, words I had never said. "I can't stand her."

I expected my mother to look sympathetic, but instead she smiled queerly, as if I had confirmed some theory she had been concocting. She rolled a maraschino cherry between her fingers as she spoke.

"So, Miss Black and Beautiful doesn't think you're good enough, huh? You probably remind her of me, and that's what they're all trying to forget these days, you know—that they ever dabbled in the nitty-gritty land of miscegenation. Well, you can tell her and that righteous brotherman—your father—that it's my white ass that's going to end up in prison!"

She barked these words across at me, and a couple of the roly-poly waitresses halted their gossiping and looked at us, their curiosity piqued. My mother didn't notice them, but she saw the startled expression on my face and whispered across the table, trying to lighten the moment with a playful routine of ours, "Let's split this banana joint, eh, Tanya?"

I was supposed to answer, "Sure thang, Che, baby," but I just shrugged and slipped out of the booth.

In the car ride home she kept her eyes on the rearview mirror, and the car seemed to steam up with the heat of her nervous energy. She lit a cigarette and blew smoke rings into the air in a flamboyant gesture. When we got home there were rings of sweat under the arms of her thermal underwear top.

disintegration
of funk

Aku-Aku is a "tropical Polynesian getaway" just around the corner from Fenway Park. On this particular Tuesday afternoon, the restaurant was empty, shrouded in its perpetually hungover darkness. It was three o'clock, a strange time to be drinking Polynesian cocktails and toasting to our family love, against all odds, through the fire, and all the rest of those clichés. Stranger still that we all were together, my mother and my father speaking to each other in civil, almost affectionate, tones. They had told me it was just a meeting to catch up on old times. But they had pulled us out of school early and they hadn't had a civil conversation in as long as I could remember. Something wasn't right.

A song played overhead that afternoon—a Muzak version of Diana Ross's "Mahogany"—and my father, nursing his Tiki Bowl, with his head cocked to the side as if engaged in a private discussion with himself, laughed when he recognized the bastardized Motown melody, saying, "Damn, I guess nothing's sacred."

He had taken Cole and me to Aku-Aku so many times before, on more banal occasions—birthdays, Easter lunches, or simply his weekly visits. He liked it because it was anonymous and I think also because he enjoyed the racial absurdity of the place, where Chinese men with name tags reading "Charlie" passed as Polynesian and gave out drinks with little brown fat-bellied men and women floating naked in bubbling pink froth. My father had once muttered to us, "These Orientals are making a killing off of the white man's racial fantasy. Niggers need to get in on the action—start opening restaurants with niggerish themes. Bow and scrape, step 'n' fetchit, then laugh all the way to the bank." Then he had chuckled quietly, the way he did when he knew his jokes had gone over our wild-child heads.

Cole and I liked Aku-Aku for different reasons. We thought it glamorous in its over-the-top decor, and we always ordered the pu-pu platter "with a roll of toilet paper on the side," cutting up into hysterics every time, no matter how old the joke got.

But that day I was seeing it all from my mother's eyes, and it spoiled the fun. I could see from her tight expression that some long-suppressed part of her found the place repugnant, classless, hideous. All of a sudden the restaurant's gaudiness was clear to me, the cheapness of the plastic palms and the insidious pink of the vinyl seats. The wall was decorated with a three-dimensional mural lit from behind, depicting island jungle scenes with pretty brown women in grass skirts. The decor, which had once seemed exotic to my child eyes, struck me suddenly as sad and seedy, as did the ferocious warrior masks that once had thrilled me.

It was the first time my mother had come with us, and it was strange having her there, as if we had let her into our hideaway and exposed our little fantasy for what it really was. She sat stiffly in the booth over a tall orange drink called "Doctor Funk of Tahiti" that my father had talked her into ordering. She spoke to my father in whispers, while Cole sat curled over *Jane Eyre* and I kicked my shins, making patterns with spilled salt and pepper on the red linoleum tabletop. My father's and my mother's faces were drawn, heavy, adult.

I nudged Cole and said, "Tell me a story. I'm bored." But really, there were little flutterings in my belly. Cole put down her book and began to speak to me in Elemeno, telling me a story about a girl named Afrodite who would come and take us away to that land called Elemeno, which she said looked like the Lanuki Lounge at the back of the restaurant. I listened to Cole whisper while trying to block out my mother and father's conversation and the sudden melancholy that weighed around our table.

My mother was saying in a loud strangled whisper that seemed to echo throughout the empty restaurant, "It just feels so out of control, like it's taken on a life of its own. Jane seems nearly psychotic these days, and I can't even talk to Linda. I guess I didn't know what I was getting into." She stifled a sob into her Doctor Funk, glanced up at Cole and me, a little wild-eyed, then settled her gaze back on my father. "I mean, couldn't we just leave? All of this. Behind. Right now. Just get in the Pinto and keep driving till we get there. I mean, anywhere. Up to Canada. Just the four of us. Who's to stop us?"

My father forced a weak smile and said, looking down, "Sandy, you know I've got other people to think about now."

My mother rolled her eyes. "Oh, of course. Your little brown sugar, Carmen. How could I forget?"

He barely registered her sarcasm and looked up at the TV screen over the bar, where a baseball game was in progress. "It's more than just her, Sandy. You know that. This country is suicide for a black man. Suicide." He paused. "Besides, Sandy, if you were gonna get involved in something like this, at least have some balls about it. And remember, it was *your* fucking decision. I told you not to mess with those crazy thugs. But now that you have, stop acting like you're still at Buckingham."

My mother leaned forward toward him and said, clenching her drink so that her knuckles turned all white, "And to think, I actually thought you'd approve. I thought I could trust you. But you're just like my mother. In blackface." I thought that would inflame my father, but he only patted her hand awkwardly, looking around the restaurant in some odd display of decorum.

I spilled my virgin piña colada just then, and we all froze, mesmerized as the pale liquid overtook the red tabletop in a slow, gliding motion. None of us moved to wipe it up. Cole saw my chin begin to tremble, and broke the silence. "Don't cry, Bird. You can have some of mine." She thought I was crying over the spilled drink. Later, in the bathroom of the restaurant, Cole stayed in the stall for a long time, not making any noise. I stood in front of the mirror, speaking softly to myself in Elemeno, trying to stay calm. After a while she flushed the toilet and came out of the stall. I asked her what was going on. She avoided my eyes and set to washing her hands with vigor. "Nothing, Birdie. Mum's just freaking out about something, as usual."

When we came outside into the bright light of the afternoon, I was confused, like coming out of a movie into the day and forgetting where and when and who you are. It had seemed that it was the deep of night when we were inside the restaurant, and now the light hurt my eyes.

We drove back to Columbus Avenue in silence, listening to the drone of the sports announcer as he rattled on about the Red Sox's latest losing streak. Cole was quiet, looking out the window. I stared at the take-home menu in my hands. It had a little educational bullet in the corner that read:

Aku-Aku means "Brothers-Brothers" in Polynesian. It means "Guardian Spirit" to the natives of Easter Island in the southeast Pacific, the loneliest inhabited island in the world. On this barren and isolated island, men of mystery built huge stone images—and then disappeared.

It sounded like the land of Elemeno to me. I tried to show it to Cole, whispering to her in our language. *vitiligoo peruschka.*

She glanced over at me, and I saw that she was clenching and unclenching her fist around her little calfskin purse. She stared at my face with an expression I had never seen before. I touched my hair, wondering if there was gum stuck in it. There wasn't. I asked, "What you looking at?"

She shook her head and then turned away, resting her forehead against the car window as she gazed longingly out at the passing street. She wore a purple denim jacket that Carmen had bought her, and new microthin cornrows with gold beads on the tips. She looked older to me all of a sudden, like a very pretty teenager—pulled-together, ironed, and smelling of Jean Naté After Bath Splash. I wondered if she was thinking about a boy she liked, who had given her his gold initial—"A," for Anthony—which hung now from a thin chain around her neck.

When we pulled up to the house, my mother said into her hands, "C'mon, Bird. Your sister's staying with your father tonight."

"She is? But it's a school night."

My mother barked at me, "It doesn't matter. Now come on."

She heaved her body out of the car and stomped up the stairs to the house without looking back. After a moment, I thought I glimpsed her pale form in the window on the second floor. For a minute she remained there, like an apparition, then she disappeared into the shadows.

I guess it struck me then and there that we were parting, and that fact— along with my own foolishness—made me feel thick and clumsy and oddly thirsty as I got out of the car. My father and Cole got out too, but not like they were coming with me inside. They stood side by side, leaning against the car, arms folded across their chests, not speaking.

The weather was confused, both rainy and sunny all at once, a web of drizzle glistening in the light. I followed Cole's gaze down the street to a bunch of girls our age sitting on the stoop, braiding one another's hair. My father pulled me to him suddenly, hugging me so tightly that it hurt, and I was surprised to feel his shirt was wet around his back—from sweat or rain, or maybe both. He told me, still hugging me, his face hidden, that Cole and he were going away on "a little trip."

I pulled away from him, breathing in.

He said, looking over my head, speaking to something behind me: "Boston, America, is a fucking mess and it's only going to get uglier. Real ugly. Black people need to start thinking internationally. We're going to Brazil. Cole and Carmen and me. Just for a while." Then, his eyes flickering down on me, he said, "Take care of your mother. She needs you now."

Cole looked at me, and her eyes appeared like bright shimmering emeralds. She tried to smile, but it turned into a kind of grimace, and all of a sudden I could see that she was scared but trying not to show it. "Tell Mum I love her, okay? Tell her I'll talk to her later?"

They got back into the car then, and my father's face was twisted into some expression I had never seen on a grown man before, like that of a child who has just been abandoned to his first day of school. He turned his face away from me as he cleared his throat and shuffled the newspaper on the seat beside himself before starting up the engine.

It was clear, finally, that they were leaving me—why and for how long were still mysteries then—but I also understood that none of us was going to acknowledge this fact until it was over. Funny, but Cole and I didn't even really say good-bye. She just got in the backseat and waved to me as my father pulled away from the curb, her face—small and doll-like—pressed up against the window. I stood frozen to the spot. Only when they were out of sight, when the Volvo had blended into the other chrome colors in the distance, did the enormity of what had just occurred hit me.

I turned and tore up the steps to the old brownstone, looking for solace, or answers, I suppose, in the arms of my mother. I found her in her bedroom. She was curled fetal on the floor by her bed, and the whole room was suffused in a stench of musk oil. Her dress was twisted around her legs, and she was sobbing dryly, under the golden veil of her own hair. I went toward her, tiptoeing, as if approaching a bear caught in a trap. I thought she was alone, but then I glimpsed a shadow in the corner, and a woman stepped into the light. It was Linda, the Puerto Rican revolutionary. Cole and I had never liked her because she ignored us when she came over, acting as if we were a distraction from something far more important. She held a sponge in her hand and appeared to be cleaning up spilled oil. She held shards of a broken bottle in her hand. She smiled at me brightly, as if everything were fine, and said, "Your mami's a little upset, Birdie. Why don't you go watch television. Eh? 'Sesame Street'?"

My mother peeked at me from under her hair and said quietly, "I must have been a sinner in my former life. I must have done something awful to deserve this."

She slept away the remainder of the afternoon and evening—or at least that's what Linda told me while she pattered around our kitchen barefoot, fixing me a peanut butter sandwich and a glass of milk. Linda spoke to me in a generic high voice, like a woman unused to the company of children. She was an experienced revolutionary who had been organizing marches and writing articles arguing for Puerto Rican independence much of her adult life. I asked her questions: Where were Cole and my father? How long would they be gone in Brazil? Why had everything changed? She didn't answer any of them, but poured me more milk and said, with her eyes on my glass, "Your mother will explain later."

I wondered what I would tell Maria at school the next day.

It was that same night, sometime past midnight, when I lay awake, listening to the sounds of the odd and ordinary. A lost mutt's persistent whimper. Faint and fading music playing from someone's car. A man screaming obscenities at his lover across the street.

A distant phone ringing.

The front door downstairs opening.

At some point my mother's crying entered the symphony of night sounds, and another low voice. I thought I recognized my father, then Cole, and waited—frigid with joy and relief. It all had been a silly gag. A late April Fool's Day prank. I bit my pillow, the sound of my own heart seeming to rock the bed in its intensity.

After a while, someone came into my room. The person pattered lightly across the floor. I could sense it was Cole from her breathing pattern, and felt her standing over me for a few minutes, watching me as I pretended to sleep. Then her hand brushed a hair out of my face, a feathery touch. I opened my eyes slightly and saw her standing there, over me, with her hair tied into a head wrap—it looked African, like Carmen would wear. She was staring at me with a kind of grieving smile, if there is such a thing, and I thought I glimpsed another, larger, figure in the background behind her. She stroked my hair back and said, *palen copio mooliani.* She was tucking something under the covers next to me then, and out of the corner of my eye I could see it was Golliwog, still smiling saucily, his teeth and eyes the only things visible in the blank night. She never let me or anyone else touch Golliwog. It was a sign that I should rise, hold on to her tightly, and make her tell me what was going on, but instead I lay, my body tingling slightly but unable to move—that numbness that sometimes came to me upon waking—as if tied to the bed by invisible double binds.

I T W A S S T I L L D A R K, barely five o'clock, when I was wakened again—this time by someone pulling the blankets off me. At first I didn't recognize my mother. She had a gash of red lipstick across her mouth, and her hair had changed colors overnight. It was now the color of pennies, and she had braided it in twin plaits that stuck stiffly out on either side of her face. There were red streaks on her face, fresh scratches raised just above her skin. As I sat up and scooted backward on the bed, she giggled at the alarmed expression on my face.

"Jeez. It's just me, Bird."

She touched her hair gingerly and said, "It's henna. All natural." She smiled so that only her mouth moved, but her eyes stayed expressionless. Then she said in a deep, almost manly, voice: "Get dressed, Bird. We gotta go." I did what she told me to without questions. As I stumbled about in the half-darkness, throwing random articles of clothing into my duffel bag, she stood at the door with her arms folded, tapping her foot and throwing out orders: "Bring just enough for a few days. We can't carry too much."

"But aren't they—? I thought I heard Cole and Papa—? Where are they?"

She looked away, at the window. Then said, "No, you must have been dreaming. They're gone. Brazil. C'mon, now. We gotta run, baby."

"Where's Linda?"

She shook her head impatiently. She said Linda was gone. That it was just me and her. She paced the room and chattered on while I stuck random objects into my bag. I listened to her whispering to herself. Something about a felony and the fuzz and prison time. "I can't believe I let them talk me into this mess. All I ever wanted was to give food and shelter. Not this shit. Hurry the hell up, Birdie. We've got to get out of here. Now."

I hurried to zip up my bag, taking one last look around my room.

As my mother gripped my arm and pulled me toward the door, my eye glimpsed something in the shadows—a package of some sort, wrapped in the Sunday funnies. I pulled back and asked her what it was.

She looked down and said, "Oh, I almost forgot. Your father brought that by for you. Some things he put together. But open it later, when we're on the road and you have nothing better to do. Now, move it!"

That meant Cole and my father had been in the house that night, and that Cole had actually stood over me in the African head wrap and told me everything was going to be all right. That she had actually left Golliwog. I turned to the bed and sure enough saw his red smile peeking out from under the covers. I pulled out of my mother's grip and ran to fetch him. I put him in the duffel bag with the rest of my belongings.

I shuffled after her down the stairs, noticing along the way the ramshackle appearance of all the rooms—overturned chairs in the kitchen; papers tossed randomly across the floor of the study; and drawers hanging open, clothes spilling out of them like intestines.

The air felt gentle with dew, and the workers of the world weren't even awake. We drove away in the green Pinto with just a few bags and the sleep still stuck to our eyes. Beyond my window, the city appeared colorless and hushed, like footage from a black-and-white silent movie. I was silent, too, as if so many questions had left me mute, and I held the box wrapped in the Sunday funnies close to the flatness of my chest as we made our way to the edges of the city, toward the exit north.

phenotypic peek-a-boos

There was usually some logic to my mother's lunacy. So when she told me she had thought up an "ingenious solution" to our problem of hiding, I had no choice but to believe her.

We sat across from each other at a diner in Maine. I chewed on my French toast while she played listlessly with her own food—a poached egg and toast. Since we had begun running, she had eaten with a restraint that I had never seen her use before. Now it struck me that she was moving like a thin person, with a kind of spiritless grace that resembled her own mother's.

She had been nearly speechless since we'd left Boston, weirdly so, moving us from motel to motel in a mournful hush, seeming for the first time in her life without any desires—for words, food, love, or home. Even our unnamed destination didn't seem to matter then, only that we moved away from the scene of this vague crime of hers. I still didn't know exactly what the dangers were that kept us running, or, most important, why Cole and Papa had gone to Brazil, and when the decision had been made.

The package my father had left me that night of his departure was a shoe box filled with a collection of strange objects. Scrawled in magic marker on the side of the box was the word "Negrobilia." I recognized my father's chicken-scratch handwriting. My mother scoffed when she saw what was inside. He and Cole had clearly thrown the collection together at the last minute. It included a Black Nativity program from the Nkrumah School, a fisted pick (the smell of someone's scalp oil still lingering in between the sharp black teeth), a black Barbie doll head, an informational tourist pamphlet on Brazil, the silver Egyptian necklace inscribed with hieroglyphics that my father had bought me at a museum so many years before, and a James Brown eight-track cassette with a faded sticker in the corner that said "Nubian Notion," the name of the record shop on Washington Street. That, along with Cole's Golliwog, was all that was left of them.

At night in the blankness of the motel rooms—with my mother's body beside me, tranquilized with some sleeping pills she had brought along—our situation hit me the hardest. It was then that I allowed myself to wonder where Cole was at that moment, what sky she slept under, if she too was waking with her face wet and salty, a pain throbbing in the center of her palms, and the feeling that she had been kidnapped. I would wonder deep into the night, until before I knew it, morning was creeping through the motel curtains in stages, revealing the anonymous signs and empty strip of road in the distance. I made up for those lost nights during the day, when I would doze in the car, waking only occasionally to look out on the blurring world with a dull, groggy interest.

I knew only what my mother chose to tell me in those rare breakings of her silence: that the FBI was after us. Each morning we scoured the newspapers, searching for a picture of my mother under the word "WANTED." She seemed miffed that the papers had failed to report on her fugitive status. She believed they were trying to dupe her. "It's bullshit. Cointelpro is clearly in cahoots with the media. I've seen this before." She said the FBI kept secrets from the public, and their war against people like her was one of them.

She said little else in our endless drives in the car, instead busying herself by fiddling with the radio station, zipping back and forth between news commentators. She had answered my questions with only perplexed stares, as if I were speaking in tongues.

So now, in the light of the Maine diner, I was relieved to hear her chattering away to me with her old buoyancy, even if her solution did strike me as odd.

The FBI would be looking for a white woman on the lam with her black child. But the fact that I could pass, she explained, with my straight hair, pale skin, my general phenotypic resemblance to the Caucasoid race, would throw them off our trail. The two bodies that had made her stand out in a crowd—made her more than just another white woman—were gone; now it was just the two of us. My body was the key to our going incognito.

With her new copper hair—she flipped her locks—and me simply relabeled as white, no one would ever suspect the truth. We'd be scot-free, she told me, a couple of new people overnight.

She seemed at that moment like her crooked self, the wild woman we had left back in Boston, the one who stole Snickers bars and played "I'm Not Your Mother" in an African mask. Cole would have left the table right then and there, sucking her teeth and rolling her eyes. *Mum, could you keep it down? I mean, shit, you're embarrassing me.* But I just nodded and took a gulp of my tea.

Her theory made sense. And besides, it seemed like a temporary thing right then, just another one of her games to get us out of a bind.

She continued: "Your name. We've got to think of a new name for you. Any suggestions, Birdaloo?"

But she didn't wait for my answer. Instead she slapped her knee and hooted, "Jesse! That's it! It's a dynamite name. The name of a fierce woman, my great-grandmother, you know, the suffragette. That 'Birdie' business was always too cutesy for my tastes. Jesse has a lot more dignity. And you should be fairly used to answering to it. I mean, I did call you Jesse for a long time. If it hadn't been for that Patrice Lumumba fixation of your father's, you'd have an ordinary name by now."

We spent the rest of breakfast trying to figure out a *nom de guerre* for her. Most of the ones we thought of were indulgent, and even as we said them we knew they wouldn't work. There were a series of "dyke names," as my mother put it—Toni, Bobbi, Pat, Jordy—as well as more predictable revolutionary-on-the-run names—Grushenka (as in Lenin's comrade), Tanya (as in Che's sweetheart), Sojo (as in Ms. Sojourner Truth). There were also the "trailer park names" that she thought fun for their white-trash flavor—Donna, Candy, Flo. But none of them seemed good enough for her to keep.

I was the one to find the name we eventually kept. I found it while my mother went up to pay the bill and left me to scour the newspaper for mentions of her. I saw nothing in the front or metro sections, and flipped to the wedding announcements. It was a face that jumped out at me. She was blond, and looked the way my mother might have looked if she had more control over her appetite, if she had never met my father, if she had stayed in

Cambridge, gone to Radcliffe, married a doctor. The woman was smiling, and hugging her husband in front of some body of water. He was dark, with thick eyebrows and a Roman nose.

Her name was Sheila Dorsett, and she worked as an admissions officer at Wellesley, the women's college.

I showed the article to my mother when she came back from paying the bill, and she read it with a tight, resigned scowl. She flashed me a smile. "Nice work, Sherlock. Just call me Sheila."

We stared at each other across the linoleum for a while, her chewing her toast slowly, me chewing my hair. She looked different already, in those few seconds as Sheila. She looked sensible, the kind of mother I had seen before on television but never known. The kind who lived in the suburbs of Boston and drove their kids to soccer practice and ballet lessons and painted still-life portraits on weekday afternoons. She looked mild.

She pushed her plate away, the food only half-eaten, and said, "Now for the last names. That's a little trickier. We're gonna need to use our imaginations. You know, make up a history for you." She wiped the corners of her mouth with a napkin. "You've got a lot of choices, babe. You can be anything. Puerto Rican, Sicilian, Pakistani, Greek. I mean, anything, really." Then she paused. A slow smile filled her face.

"And, of course, you could always be Jewish. What do you think?"

It was a strange feeling to be such a blank slate. It reminded me of the games Cole and I used to play with that trunk of costumes, but now I wasn't sure I liked the feeling. I shrugged, "I don't know. Italian, maybe? I like spaghetti—"

She cut me off: "Jewish is better, I think."

I sneered. "Does that mean I have to eat gefilte fish?" Whenever we had gone shopping with our mother, Cole and I had always gawked at the jars of gefilte fish in the supermarket. They had looked to us like some kind of scientific brain experiment gone awry.

She ignored my question. And I could see the decision had been made already, in that moment. Those other options—Puerto Rican, Sicilian, Pakistani, Greek—floated away, untapped resources.

As we sat over our plates of cooling breakfast, my mother schooled me on my Jewish self.

She explained that I was the daughter of an esteemed classics professor and so-called genius named David Goldman.

"He's this incredibly brilliant professor of classics. Like my dad was." She paused, stirring her grayish tea and looking out into the equally gray light that quilted the forest outside. "That way, I'll really know what to say when they ask me details about your dad's scholarship. I mean, my father practically raised me on ancient history." She began to rattle on about things I knew nothing about: Sapphic meter, the influence of Plato on Heidegger. I zoned out and tried to imagine this guy who would be my dad. I kept coming up with a lighter-skinned version of my own father, seated in his office beside a mountain of books.

She looked away just then, her expression turning downward to something more melancholy, her eyes turning a murkier shade of blue. She got that look when she was reminded of her own dead father. It seemed she was paying homage to him in the form of this Jewish intellectual.

After a moment of reflection, she was back with a gust of energy, forcing herself to look forward, into the crystal ball of our future. "Okay, picture this," she said. "David was funny as hell with a mop of curly black hair, an afro, the way Jews have sometimes, and he was pretty much an athiest even though he wanted you to know your history, your heritage. For him, Judaism was more like a cultural thing." She leaned across the table and ruffled my hair. "I'll call you my little *meshugga* one. As a term of affection, you know?"

So that morning at the Wellington Diner in Maine, surrounded by the thick smoky scent of pine trees and the broad flesh of country women, I was knighted a half-Jewish girl named Jesse Goldman, with a white mama named Sheila—and the world was our pearl. While my mother read the rest of Sheila's story, I made my way to the ladies' room in the back of the restaurant. I glanced at the men eating their breakfasts at the counter—crew cuts, plaid flannel shirts, red rugged faces, thick fingers—and thought of my father, hunched over his plate at Bob the Chef's, talking over my head about Brazil while he barely touched his grits and bacon.

from caucasia, with love

F or four dusty years we ran between motel and commune.

We ran away from the trouble my mother had left behind on the steps of a Columbus Avenue brownstone. Away from the rubble of revolutionary basements, fisted picks, Nkrumah dreams, and into the underneath—into the world of women without names, without pasts, without documents. Women who didn't exist. Women who had been discarded by the radicals they once loved. And so—bruised, disillusioned, erased from the history books—they found one another.

We ran as if we knew what we were running from, knew what we were running toward. And sometimes it seemed that there was indeed a blueprint—that the zigzag chaos of our route was itself a plan, a ruse to keep them from following our trail. But most of the time our trail of auto exhaust and littered fast-food wrappers seemed completely haphazard. My mother would pull our rumpled, coffee-stained map of the Northeast out of the glove compartment, spread it across a picnic table, and close her eyes as she let her finger glide slowly across the map as if it were our Ouija board.

We stayed longest at a place called Aurora, a woman's commune in upstate New York. And we stayed there so long only because my mother found "Sapphic bliss," as she put it, with an Australian woman named Bernadette who rode a Harley. We were at Aurora for nearly a year, long enough for my mother to break Bernadette's heart. But most places we left after a few months. My mother considered it unsafe to stay anywhere for too long, and so I got used to the constant motion. I remembered those years mostly in fragments, a montage of unconnected images which I would begin to make sense of only later: a drunk Navy kid trying to break into our motel room one night, and my mother scaring him away with a karate kick to his groin; speculums soaking in a sink at Aurora; a huddle of thunder-thighed women sharing a group hug; and always, the blurring world beyond our windshield, glimpsed only in passing.

It was easy to forget that we were, as my mother put it, a part of something bigger. She said there were hundreds, maybe thousands, of others like us, fugitives of noble causes. She also said there was a community of radicals who considered her a heroine and would help her at the drop of a hat. But for safety reasons, she explained, we had to remain isolated from our allies. I can remember only one meeting with members of this network, and it came early on in our flight. A tall white man called Mike met us at a diner one night in Poughkeepsie, where he handed us a thick brown envelope containing materials for our new identities. From then on we had been alone in the wilderness.

There's something unreal about the time we spent on the run. Soft. Unfulfilled. Dreamlike. Something about the unseen, the undocumented, the off-the-record that still feels unmentionable. But I'll mention those years enough to say this: On the road and in the women's commune, the lie of our false identities seemed irrelevant, because there was no world to witness them. The people we encountered seemed—like us—to be in a perpetual state of reinvention. We all were fictive imaginings of our former selves, a fact which somehow neutralized the lies, made it all a game of make-believe. In those years, I felt myself to be incomplete—a gray blur, a body in motion, forever galloping toward completion—half a girl, half-caste, half-mast, and half-baked, not quite ready for consumption. And for me, there was comfort in that state of incompletion, a sense that as long as we kept moving, we could go back to what we had left behind.

At first we lived off the money my grandmother had handed over that strange, tense morning at the house on Fayerweather Street. When that ran out, we lived off a savings bond my mother had cashed in, and the proceeds from the family silverware. My mother had sold the silverware sometime in the weeks before we fled Boston—"a valuable piece of Boston history," the man at the shop had told her, greedily eyeing the well-known initials engraved in the spoon handle—and the money it earned us was enough to last us a few months on the road. When that dwindled, my mother had worked like any other single mother, odd jobs—secretarial, factory—but mostly tutoring "special children"—dyslexic, retarded, or simply bad-natured. The same sort she had tutored in Boston. It didn't matter which town, there always seemed to be a problem child with a desperate mother willing to pay for a miracle worker. And it was true, something about my mother's mixture of roughness and eccentricity seemed to be the perfect combination for these children who had struggled to read or sit still or simply exist. She was kind to them in her own belting way, without ever being squeamish, and her method seemed to work, allowing her to support and feed her own child. She avoided the problem of references by going to meet the mothers directly and, during the interviews, charming the childern into submission. She told them her references had been lost, but by that point they already trusted her. She was white, she was clearly educated, and most important, the children seemed to be tamed by her very presence.

When my mother wasn't busy teaching those disturbed and delayed children, she taught me. Home-schooling was nothing new for me. Nkrumah had been my only year of real school in the outside world. Now I was back at the place where I had started: my mother's strange tutelage. She promised me that when I entered school again, I'd be at least two years ahead of other children. I wasn't certain.

Her lessons hadn't involved textbooks or equations. Instead, they consisted of her line of questioning—barked at me across a kitchen or restaurant table—about the latest books I had read. She was right that I was better read than most kids my age. At her bidding, I had read the Brontës, Charles Dickens's *Hard Times*, Richard Wright's *Black Boy*, the Russians—Chekhov, Tolstoy, and Dostoyevsky. Before bed she would read aloud to me the poems of Emily Dickenson, Langston Hughes, Claude McKay. I did exercises that my mother had taken from the back of *Elements of Style*, and was tested on Fanon's *Black Skin, White Masks*, and Paolo Freire's *Pedagogy of the Oppressed*. My mother swore that I'd be the first child raised and educated free of racism, patriarchy, and capitalism.

She was great when it came to right-brain teaching, but her math lessons were shoddy, and she usually rushed through them. She seemed bored by them and said I needed to know enough only to balance a check-book. She put a bit more energy into science class, but I later learned just how primitive those lessons were. One day, when we passed a can of rotting trash and I asked where maggots came from, she said they were made of garbage and that I was witnessing the origins of life. I believed everything my mother told me, including her pseudoscientific theories on spontaneous generation, which had been disproven more than a century before.

I believed her even when she swore that after four years of silence, my father would return Cole to us, as he had promised he would. She claimed he knew whom to contact when he returned—a friend of the underground who could then track us down. I wasn't allowed to know who this friend was, for my own safety. And, my mother said, we had to stay footloose and fancy free until they returned. The jig wasn't up, the jig wouldn't be up, until we all were back together. When they returned, we could return, she told me. Our bodies would land just at the moment the Brasil Air 747 hit the ground, and only then could our lives go back to normal.

Our names—Jesse and Sheila Goldman—were the only things about us that remained constant. To keep those names was a breach of safety, of course. But my mother said Goldman was the name my father and Cole would know to look for. We had to keep the names for their sakes. But our bodies disguised us. While I grew into a lanky twelve-year-old, my mother shrank. She told me she had lost the weight out of grieving for Cole. And maybe that was true. But sometimes I wondered if it were more intentional than that, just another piece of her disguise, to go along with the auburn hair and horn-rimmed glasses and the new name. Whatever the case, it did the trick. She was unrecognizable.

My mother had never been particularly religious before, but I guess something changed when she became Sheila. She read about all the religions of the world with a vigor that she once had reserved for politics. Her own family had no faith in anything. Wasps were like that, my mother said. But my mother threw herself into religion. She dabbled in all of them: Buddhism, Hinduism, Jewish mysticism, even Islam. She practiced what she liked about them, and discarded what she didn't—which was almost everything. According-ing to her, all religions are fundamentally the same. "Everything that rises must converge, sweetie," she explained. This left her inventing some inde-pendent mantra, which she howled alone in the mornings whether on the front porch at Aurora or in a motel bathroom, seated cross-legged on the floor beside the toilet. Although the actual meanings of the words she uttered were mysteries to me—they sounded like some bastardized Elemeno—I understood they were supposed to reach my sister in Brazil. She told me that she believed in something bigger than herself, but there was some emptiness to those morning howls that made me wonder if she really had any faith at all.

I never joined her, but I practiced my own form of praying. I would sit, fingering the objects in my box of negrobilia, usually humming a little tune (some old, long-gone soul song), while I tried to imagine what Cole was doing at that very moment.

We played up my Jewishness only some of the time; other times we nearly forgot about it. She had bought me a Star of David somewhere along the way, a cheap one from a pawn shop. It hung from a thick gold rope and left a vaguely greenish tint on the skin below my collarbone. Another time she bought me *The Diary of Anne Frank,* a book that had been Cole's favorite once upon a time. Sometimes, when she was feeling particularly paranoid in public places, she would call me her *meshugga nebbish* with exaggerated relish. She enjoyed telling the women at Aurora that I got my dark looks from my Semitic side and that she had been on the verge of converting to Judaism before David died. When we were alone she also liked to remind me that I wasn't really passing because Jews weren't really white, more like an off-white. She said they were the closest I was going to get to black and still stay white. "Tragic history, kinky hair, good politics," she explained. "It's all there."

But mostly my Jewishness was like a performance we put on together for the public. Only in the privacy of our car, on those long drives up and down the eastern seaboard, was I allowed to ask her about our real past. Off limits were questions about the basement, the FBI, anything to do with why we were in this predicament. But the past was okay. So I grilled her about the before, her past, before me, even, looking into it for clues to the present situation.

I was consoled by those stories, by my mother's faith in Cole's return, and by the fleeting nature of our lives, which kept the reality of our situation from ever closing in. And I believed our lives would go on more or less in that darting way until Cole and my father returned to fetch us.

Then one day, four years into our flight, while pulling out of a drugstore parking lot in upstate New York, this Sheila woman, this mother of mine, announced to me that she wanted an end to this purgatory, an end to the squeal of tires on an icy road, an end to ideological phonies. She wanted a home surrounded by good country people; she wanted the salt of the earth in its raw, unadulterated form; and she picked New Hampshire.

the color of underneath

Our van radio picked up only AM, making Patsy Cline sound tinny, washed out, like an echo of music, not quite the real thing. I'd been reminding my mother for more than a month that we needed new wheels, but I figured we were out of money because she'd just run a hand through her hair and say, "We need a lot of things, baby." And then she'd go through the list of all the things we were due for: a job, a house, a Pap smear (for her), new shoes, fresh blue jeans, and new fake IDs. The lamination on her driver's license was peeling at the corners, and it had expired more than a year before. My doctored passport wasn't much better. A pen had leaked in my knapsack, leaving a smudge of blue across my small, anxious face.

Our rule all along had been to switch vehicles every six months, but we'd been driving this one for close to two years. It was a paint-stripped van with a cracked and drafty floor and a vague smell of turpentine wafting up from the corners. It once had been yellow. I could tell because some of the paint was left on the interior, a nice buttery chrome yellow. Now it was no color at all; the color of something stripped clean for the sake of starting over. Some nights the van had served as our home, parked in the darkened lot of a Roy Rogers, our bodies wrapped together in an afghan, limbs twisted around the other's for warmth. On particularly cold mornings the van wouldn't start at all and we just called the space where it had stalled our home, as good as any other.

The town we circled now was to be our latest home. My mother had chosen it a week before, when she had gone on a scouting trip to New Hampshire. She had come back in a state of excitement, saying she had found the perfect place—a town that offered the best of both worlds. It was made up mostly of poor farmers and trailer parks, the world she said she most admired. But it also sat near a university town, the world that could provide her with a job. Academics were a naïve bunch, she maintained, and rarely thought to check her referrals. She could play the part when she needed to, and, these days at least, she looked like an eccentric professor's wife.

Now she pointed to the license plate on the pickup truck in front of us. It read: "LIVE FREE OR DIE."

"That," she told me, "is the official state slogan. Anyway, there's a lot of free spirits living up in these parts." She smiled, and repeated the slogan— "Live Free or Die"—as if savoring the words on her tongue.

I stuck my head out the window. It was summer, and the air here was thick, sweet with the smell of cow manure. I studied the world outside, searching the landmarks for clues to my future. What I saw: a small shack that read "Bing Bros. Guns 'n' Stuff"; an American flag in the center of a town green; a billboard of a shining red apple with a bite taken out of it, advertising fresh produce at some nearby marketplace. It all looked strange to me, like some imitation of life I had witnessed before only in movies— grainy colors, Dolby stereo, flat props to be knocked down after the day's shooting was over. We cruised past a Dairy Queen, where a crowd of listless teens stood in a parking lot, eating Softee cones. They turned to watch our van go by as if they had nothing better to do than wait for strangers. I met eyes with one of them—a thin-lipped, freckle-faced girl with her hand raised over her eyes like a visor. She followed our car with her gaze, sneering in a way that made me blush and turn away, back to the road ahead. The look on her face reflected just how strange I had become. I was twelve, but I dressed like a much younger child, in high-water dungarees and a pair of hot-pink Converse sneakers my mother had stolen off a rack at Mammoth Mart. My T-shirt announced some truckers' convention, and my hair hung unevenly from one of my mother's bungled attempts at hairdressing. I saw myself in that girl's eyes, and I appeared wild and ill-fitting, like a girl raised by wolves.

I looked down at the map that was spread across my lap, tracing the web of thin red and blue veins, in search of Bridgewater Road. My mother had seen the house listed for rent in a local paper the next town over: "Cozy two-bedroom cottage on scenic farmland. Family preferred. References required."

We pulled into a gas station, and she told me, "I've got to call the land-lords, tell them we're on our way." She dug into her pocket, pulled out a couple of crumpled bills, and smoothed them out in her palm. "Want anything to drink?"

"Fanta, please, with a straw. And a beef jerky."

She was out of the van then, and I watched her go inside, roaming the aisles of the little stop-and-go shop; picking out food, drink, and a newspaper for herself. She talked to the boy behind the counter while he rang up her stuff. She was asking him for directions. He was laughing at something she said, trying to flirt with her, while she gesticulated wildly, hamming it up for him. The guy was half her age, a plump baby-faced kid with a baseball cap on to go with his Chevron uniform. When she left through the jingling door, he leaned forward and watched her blue-jeaned butt sashay away. I stuck my tongue out at him, but he couldn't see my face behind the glass reflection. I didn't like it when she flirted with white men. It seemed to be taking our game one step too far, becoming the other woman rather than just playing her.

She was seventy pounds lighter than she had been when we'd left Boston. Back then, white men had never so much as looked at her, except maybe in disgust, the way her own mother did. But now she was the woman her mother always wanted her to be—willowy, fragile, feminine, a shadow of her former self—and I often noticed white men glancing at her butt when we passed them on the street. Which was odd, since she had no butt any-more, just a flat board of a backside and slim boyish hips.

I watched as she went outside to the pay phone. She bent over the receiver, her hair swinging into her eyes so that I couldn't read her expression. I had reminded her that we didn't have references, that they probably wouldn't even bother meeting with us. But she hadn't seemed worried. Now her lips were moving silently to somebody on the other end. She was taking too long. The guy behind the counter was on the phone now, too, watching her through the glass. I felt a familiar lurch in my stomach. I imagined he was calling the Feds. He had seen her face in the post office just yesterday. I could hear him: "Yup. It's her. I'd know her anywhere. Hair's different now, and she's lost all that blubber. Cute little redhead woman with a great ass. But it's her. She's driving a van. Color? Sorta gray or black or something. Like a tin can on wheels. Looks like someone's in the passenger seat, but I can't make out the face. Might be a guy. Yeah, it's a guy . . ." I imagined the conversation and bit my nails, watching the scene play out before me.

The driver's door opened, snapping me out of my thoughts. "Here, catch!" My mother tossed me the Fanta and an apple, not a beef jerky. She peered at herself in the rearview mirror and began fiddling with her hair. She said, holding a bobby pin between her teeth, "Beef jerkys'll kill you. Do you know what they're made of?"

"Yeah, yeah, yeah," I told her, crunching into the apple. "Did you reach the landlord?"

Her hair had been transformed into a loose bun. She looked like a real mother, cool, self-possessed, the kind of mother who would be on a television commercial for Ivory soap. She winked at me. "Sure did, Jess. I think they bought it. I think I got 'em."

LATER, AFTER SHE HAD PRIMPED and changed into appropriate clothes in a McDonald's bathroom, we sat in the van, staring at the house in the distance. It had begun to drizzle on our way over. The defroster was on full-blast, and we were silent, listening to the rhythmic squeak of the windshield wipers. The place did look pretty cozy from the outside, like a gingerbread cottage, promising sweets and familial comfort. It sat at the end of a glimmering field of grass speckled with daffodils. It was two stories high, not really a cottage at all, with dark-brown shingles, white clapboard shutters, a sloping front porch, and an overgrown garden in the front. The yard around it was bare except for a trampoline, which was sagging down in its middle with rainwater, and beyond that, at the edge of the forest of ash trees, a green barn. I wondered whether there were animals inside. The ad hadn't said anything about that. My mother was clenching the steering wheel tightly. She was nervous. I knew she really wanted us to live here, to settle down for a while somewhere. She had said it to me the night before, hugging me in the darkness: "I'm so tired. So damn tired of moving. Please, let this work out. It just has to. Or I don't know if I can go on."

There was a rap on the window, and we both jumped. It was a man, his face grinning, wet, and huge behind the glass. He must have come around from behind. We both just stared at him for a moment, as if we were seeing a ghost, and then my mother hissed, "It's the landlord. Roll down the window, for God's sake."

I did as I was told.

The man said, "I'm Walter. Walter Marsh."

We both stumbled out of the van to meet him. He had bad posture and stood hunched underneath a tattered black umbrella, wearing a trench coat that was too small for his large, gangly form. He looked salty, like the sea, with a big bony nose and two startling-green slits of eyes peering from beneath his tanned, rugged skin. His dirty-blond hair was tousled and streaked with silver, giving his face the touch of the intellectual. He seemed young, despite the gray at his temples. There was something about him that struck me as familiar, and it wasn't until later that I realized he was like my mother's brother, Randall. They shared a certain rumpled charm, a similar destroyed good looks.

I followed him and my mother over the spongy grass, breathing in a faint smell of horses, and listening to her lay it on thick. I hoped she wasn't overdoing it as she said, "We're both stunned by the beauty of the place. I mean, even from the outside I can see it's perfect."

Inside, the place wasn't as homey as it seemed on the outside. The furniture was severe, angled, borrowed. Walter Marsh explained that he had once used the cottage as his study, but now that he had built a study off his bedroom at his home across the forest, the cottage was going to waste.

He pointed to the green barn at the other end of the field and said, "Our horses live in there."

My mother nudged me hard, as if to say, *I told you so, I knew this would be fun,* and winked at me.

After we had finished examining the cottage, we followed him through the woods, where he lived, to "the big house," as he kept referring to it. It was huge, brown, and Victorian, and made ours look shoddy in comparison.

Walter Marsh showed off his latest renovations to my mother while I loitered by the mantelpiece in the living room. There was a clutter of photographs. One of a pretty, vivacious woman who was clearly his wife. Others of a sullen boy with dark hair, in various stages of growth. There were several snapshots of Walter Marsh with a boat. He was a sailor when he wasn't teaching English at the university in the next town over. I looked out to where he stood on the porch, talking to my mother. She was nodding her head, hands on hips, and if I blurred my eyes she could have been somebody who belonged here for real.

We sat with him in the living room, where books held to the walls around us. A familiar smell of must clung to the air. He poured my mother's tea as if he were in the casbah and she were a veiled princess. He hadn't paid much attention to me on the walk over, gabbing instead to my mother about his work at the university.

He looked at me for the first time. "We have a son a little older than you," he said. Then, with a knowing smile at my mother, he added, "He goes to boarding school, though. Exeter. I mean, the schools here are great till the kids reach a certain age. Then the locals start acting like locals, if you know what I mean. Chewing tobacco, loitering. Trailah pahk cultcha," he said, imitating the New Hampshire accent.

My mother had a tense smile on her face, and I could almost hear her thought: *Fuck you, you elitist pig.* But she said only, agreeably, "Oh, of course. Jesse may have to start thinking about boarding school at some point." Sometimes even I couldn't tell whether she was lying. I had a brief surge of excitement imagining myself at boarding school, walking, uniformed, across a green with a huddle of other girls. But then it struck me that we had no money, and even if we had, I wasn't going anywhere far.

Just then a car pulled into the driveway, a silver Saab. A figure stepped out and came running up the steps to the back porch. We could hear the stamping of feet on the wood. It was his wife, Libby. She wore a man's Army-green raincoat and L.L. Bean boots. She was delicate and tan, with a brown ponytail and erect dancer's posture. She laughed as their dog, a golden retriever, danced around her feet, shaking rain from his body. When she had peeled the wetness from herself, she came toward us, smiling approvingly. "You must be Sheila, here to see the little house. I spoke to you this morning on the phone."

They shook hands, and the wife laughed, flashing us big, healthy teeth. "I shouldn't call it 'the little house.' It's really quite spacious. Have you had a look already?"

She settled next to her husband on their bulky red velvet couch, tucking her legs underneath her and grasping his hand in hers.

I was hungry for something unnamable as I watched her lean in toward him and whisper, "Be a dear and pour me a little of that Lapsang Souchong? It smells wonderful."

We sipped the smoky tea from chipped blue cups. They asked my mother inconsequential questions, but I could see it was a way of proving that she spoke their language. They smiled knowingly at her.

What did they see?

A tall, statuesque, blue-blooded woman in her mid-thirties, the delicate etchings of sorrow beginning to creep out from her sapphire eyes. She wore khakis and a white V-neck sweater, her feet in Keds. We had bought the clothes just a few weeks before, in preparation for moments like this. It was paying off. I had never seen my mother so appropriate. Loose strands from her bun brushed against her pale cheek. She shifted next to me and played with the wedding ring on her finger. It was the one my father had given her, Russian-style, three different kinds of gold—white, red, and yellow.

"We've seen the house already," she told Mrs. Marsh. "It's perfect. Just lovely. I was just telling your husband that I want Jesse to get a chance to ride. So it's an ideal situation for us."

A note of desperation had crept into her voice. I looked toward the door, where the dog sat panting, his head cocked to one side. He was staring at me, and I shifted under his dopey gaze, thinking maybe he was on to us.

"Jesse," the wife said, "do you know how to ride horses?"

I glanced at my mother. She was smiling at me through clenched teeth. She hadn't coached me on what to say about this. It was true that I had ridden horses at the stables near Aurora. I had ridden bareback, with Bernadette holding the reins from behind me, while my mother stood on the sidelines in a cowboy hat, waving her arms and shouting excited directions.

I shrugged. "Yeah, I've ridden a little. My dad had a horse once. We called her Bernie and I rode her bareback. Nothing fancy. I nearly got thrown once—"

I caught my mother's eye and cut the story short.

But the wife just smiled and worked on undoing then redoing her pony-tail. "Then I think you'll like it here, Jesse. We've got a couple of mares. Our son, Nicholas, will be back from camp in a few more weeks, and I'll make sure he shows you the ropes." Then back to my mother: "And tell me, Sheila, what brings you to New Hampshire?"

My mother answered their questions like a pro. "I'm a widow—recently. He had an aneurysm. He was young—and I just couldn't bear to stay in the area. We needed a change."

She glanced down and breathed her loss just long enough. Her bony nose, her blue eyes, flickering, nervous—an educated voice. They heard her accent, so like their own, and knew she would do just fine. Never mind that thin, glowering, dark adolescent by her side, they thought. They saw a woman and a child. No man? No problem. They knew she was one of them.

I examined their house while they sorted out the details of the rent and responsibilities. The rugs were tattered Persian artifacts, and dust flaked everything like gold.

My mother's widow act seemed to have done the trick, be-cause the Marshes took pity on her. I think they saw something old-fashioned, almost quaint, about our situation, and took pleasure in the romance of it all. Libby brought us over extra blankets, a potted fern, and dishes that they didn't need, and told my mother where to shop in the nearby towns. Libby spent one wet afternoon introducing me to the horses in the barn. There were three of them. My favorite was a dappled mare whom Libby introduced as Mr. Pleasure, though the horse was clearly female. Libby hadn't explained why, and I hadn't asked. She told me I was free to ride them whenever I pleased, as long as I learned how to saddle them up properly.

The Marshes even helped my mother get a job. Walter came over to tell her about it three weeks into our stay there. A sociologist friend of his at the university was going on sabbatical to write a book and wanted help putting together his notes. My mother would be his research assistant.

"His book's a load of crap," my mother told me after her first day with the sociologist. "He's studying police culture. You know, how there's this brotherhood there, the loyalty they feel toward one another. But the man has no politics. And you can't study police without showing what pigs they are. You just can't. Honestly, now."

She blew smoke from her cigarette toward the ceiling, and I watched it evaporate, float into nothing. "But he's paying me well. Ten bucks an hour to read his chicken-scratch handwriting and put it in a computer. I'll still need to get another job. Walter Marsh said he might know of some tutoring I can do. For special-ed kids. I told him they were my specialty, and he laughed and said there were plenty of slow kids in these parts. God, that man is a snob! But anyway, the point is, he didn't think I'd have any trouble getting work here."

We lay side by side on her bed. There were two bedrooms in the cottage, but I didn't like sleeping alone in this new house. It gave me the creeps. It was all too quiet, removed. Even on the commune there had been the noise to lull me to sleep—raucous women debating politics in the kitchen or just giggling and telling one another stories while they baked the week's bread. Something to assure me that the world wouldn't end when I closed my eyes. Here there was nothing, just an emptiness. The few times I had slept alone here, I had stayed awake till morning, listening to the clock beside the bed tick louder and louder, and playing a game with myself, a game I hadn't played since those first few years on the run. A game where I would try to remember as many details about Nkrumah, the house on Columbus Avenue, my father's Roxbury apartment, Maria's mother's bedroom, as I possibly could. Not the obvious details—the portrait of Cotton Mather, or the mirrored ceiling at Maria's, or even the half-moon window looking out from our attic bedroom—but the small, trivial, utterly forgettable details: the sweet chemical smell of Queen Helene hair grease on Cole's pale scalp; the smudged pencil graffiti on my desk in Mrs. Potter's classroom that read "Tarik Luvs Candice"; the taste of cafeteria chocolate milk gulped from the carton. And Elemeno—the grunts and phrases that were only now beginning to sound like gibberish.

My mother snubbed out her cigarette and rolled over to face me. Her mood had shifted within seconds. Something sad had crossed her mind, and she brushed the hair out of my eyes. She was staring at me intensely, with a kind of anguished hunger. I knew it wasn't me she was seeing. I rolled over so that I had my back to her.

I heard her say behind me: "I used to think that if I could just learn to cornrow, she would stay mine. Remember the way her hair looked that first time she got it done, at Danny's His and Hers, so tight and gold and pretty? She was a gorgeous child, wasn't she?"

I swallowed hard and closed my eyes. There was nothing I could say to make my mother feel better, nobody I could become. I just had to wait for her sadness to pass, till morning, when I would find her transformed, frying an egg at the stove and singing along to some country-western tune on the Realistic. And then we both would try to forget.

MY MOTHER LIKED to call Walter Marsh "the man." She would imitate his aristocratic demeanor, sending me into hysterics. He reminded her too of her long-lost brother, Randall. "They have that same broken preppie look to them—too much privilege leads to bad manners," she told me one afternoon while we sat on the porch of our cottage. I sat on the step in front of her, between her legs, my head hanging forward. She was braiding my hair lazily, a cigarette hanging precariously from her lips. She had pulled the Realistic radio to the window, and it played her old Joan Baez tape. She had an open Rolling Rock beside her; I held a sweating can of Pepsi in my hands.

The air was comfortably cool, and the only noise was the sound of the ash trees brushing against one another. The trampoline at the edge of the field was still filled with water and old leaves, and I stared at the sagging bulge, thinking I should empty it, put it to some use. Sometimes, in moments like this, I thought I could be happy with just my mother. I thought she was the funnest and coolest mother in the whole world.

She was telling me how to spot a real Wasp from a fake one. I could feel her fingers moving on my scalp. I wore cutoff jeans and a T-shirt the women at Aurora had given me on my birthday. It said across the front: "A Woman Needs a Man Like a Fish Needs a Bicycle." I wore a gold-and-green anklet that Bernadette had made for me one afternoon. It was getting dirty, but I didn't want to take it off.

"Now get this straight," my mother was saying now. "I'm talking about liberal Wasps. Not Republican ones. And they might as well be two different races. The liberals have more class than the conservatives, and tend to be more interesting. We never mingled with Republicans growing up." She paused in her braiding to take a drag of her Marlboro. "Your grandmother thought conservatives were vulgar, lacking in modesty. Too blatantly interested in money."

My mother loved making lists. On the road over the years, she had entertained us both with lists about a variety of topics, from the serious to the ludicrous: "How to Spot a Fed"; "Favorite Countries to Visit," in order; "Movie Stars"—men and women—"I Could Fall in Love With"; "Countries to Liberate"; "Great Names for the Children I Never Had."

Here, while the polluted sunset spread orange and gold light over the field before us, between sips of Rolling Rock and drags on her cigarette, my mother laughingly explained to me "How to Spot a Real Wasp." It took one to know one, of course, and my mother grudgingly admitted to being a real Wasp, at least by birth. It wasn't long before I was piping in my own additions to "the list":

A Real Wasp drinks everything out of a gin tumbler, never out of a wineglass.

A Real Wasp speaks with a drunken slur, even when he has had nothing to drink.

A Real Wasp is generally a failure in life, though not always, and is thoroughly self-deprecating. He is comfortable with insults and being the butt of jokes, like someone who has never had to defend his own existence. This accounts for his charm.

A Real Wasp is eccentric, often prematurely white (haired), fascinated by the ironies of history, and often finds salvation in Asian religions late in life.

A Real Wasp doesn't like it when people chew food loudly in his presence.

A Real Wasp doesn't really like food, except eaten standing up in the shadows, hunched over, in guilty little bites.

And finally, in a strange, cruel law of physics, the harder a Real Wasp tries to reject his social caste (e.g., joining a Tibetan monastery, marrying a Jew or a Negro, giving all of his money to the Moonies), the more authentically Waspy he becomes.

She said Walter and his family were Real Wasps. The proof, she said, was the layer of dust covering their house—and the way Walter sucked on a tooth-pick, picked his nose, hacked into his hand, and performed other blatantly rude personal habits in public, oblivious that they might be offensive to the people around him.

We stayed out on the porch till all the light had faded and Mr. Pleasure was just a dark silhouette in the distance. We grew quiet, and I was shivering, hugging myself, though I didn't want to go inside just yet. My mother finally said: "I think I could learn to like it here. I really do. Imagine us here. Living here for real. What do you think, kiddo? Don't you think we should make this our home?"

I was quiet. It was true, there was a certain joy and comfort here. The beauty of the nature around us, and the thrill of sleeping in the same bed each night. Our own place. The first in so long. But I tried to imagine my sister and father here, trying to figure out where they would fit in. Cole would say it was boring, a hick town. My father would say he couldn't live around these rednecks. They wouldn't want him, and he certainly wouldn't want them. I hugged my knees to my chest and rested my chin on them. "You mean, stay here till Cole and Papa come?"

She paused for a moment too long, and I could sense her holding her breath. Then she said, "Yeah, until they come."

In bed beside her that night, I thought about what she had said. Could I learn to live permanently in this place, or anywhere, for that matter? At some point during our wanderings, the gypsy life had grown on me. Staying still for too long felt unnatural. I had begun to savor even that moment upon waking up when I had no idea which city we were in, which day of the week it was, even where we had been just the day before. I felt somehow more lucid in that half-waking state, as if that place of timelessness and placeless-ness and forgetfulness was the only space one could possibly inhabit. I cared in that moment only that my mother was nearby—in the bathroom, bal-anced cross-legged on the floor, doing mantras for her firstborn child's safe return. I wasn't supposed to disturb her during that time before breakfast, so I would curl up in the queen-sized motel bed with the scratchy sterile sheets, a hokey painting of a faraway seascape beckoning to me from the opposite side of the room, and I would whisper to myself in Elemeno, whisper to my sister, finding comfort in these words, this gibberish.

A part of me believed New Hampshire was as temporary as any of those motel rooms. Just another stop along the way. But another part of me yearned, like my mother, to stay still, to land on this broad country earth and make a home, for once.

My mother still had her lapses. Today was one of them. She had remembered what was missing, and there was no cheering her up. I had been trying to ignore her all afternoon, to lose myself in a book smeared with car grease, which I had found in the back of our van. She sat in the kitchen under a haze of gray smoke, trying to scrape the lettering off of the green Rolling Rock bottle with her fingernail, pausing only to rewind the Joan Armatrading tape at her side. She had been sitting like that for hours and had played the same song twenty times now—"Love and Affection"—rewinding without even stopping the tape, so that there was a sick, squealing sound of the song going backward. It was beginning to drive me crazy. I usually liked the song, but after the twentieth time it was too much. Finally I threw down my book on the couch and stomped into the kitchen. It was the expression on my mother's face that made me stop in the doorway. I felt I had caught her in some clandestine act. The fading light outside threw butter-colored bars across the table. Her eyes rose from the bottle and settled on my face, but there was no spark of recognition, no reaction.

"Mum?"

She sighed, and looked back down at the bottle; the painted-on words weren't coming off easily. She took a swig from the bottle. There were four empty ones lined up in front of her.

"What are you doing in here, Mum?"

During our first year on the run, there had been many nights when I would wake to her weeping over my body. It had been more regular then, more constant, this sadness that showed itself to me only in flashes now.

She said to me in a whisper, "I wasn't around for her to get her period. We split up before she could get it. I wasn't there to show her what to do."

I too had wondered this: When had Cole finally gotten her period, and had Carmen been the one to show her what to do? Last time we all had been together, Cole had worried that she hadn't gotten her period yet and all of her friends were getting theirs.

I first got mine when we were living at Aurora. That evening my mother had been out on the fire escape, talking to Bernadette, telling her about her dead Jewish husband while they passed a bong back and forth. I stood in the first-floor bathroom and could hear them talking, their words floating across the night air and into the open window. My mother was telling Bernadette how her husband's death freed her up for such braless jaunts. I stood alone in the group shower, trying to wash the stains out of my underwear while the showerheads around me seemed to stare one another down, ready for a cockfight. I watched as my own dark mess floated into the drain, and thought about Cole, wished she was there so I could tell her, so she could show me what to do. The blood was darker than I had expected, not the cartoonish crimson I had imagined it would be. After my shower, I folded toilet paper into my underpants, dressed, and went outside to break up the herbal rendezvous and tell my mother the news.

My mother was staring at me, the corners of her mouth turned down in anguish. I had to get out of there. The house felt oppressively small all of a sudden.

"I'm going out, Mum. For a ride."

I wasn't sure she'd heard me. She showed no response. I grabbed my denim jacket and left.

Outside, the sky was a wash of powdered pinks and purples, like one of my mother's tie-dyed T-shirts—swirling shades of blue and purple illuminated by the lowering sun. The meadow was turning a sudden simple black. I made my way across the darkness to the barn.

Mr. Pleasure snorted and rustled her tail in greeting. I put my nose to her flat brown one and kissed her long and hard. She smelled of hay and salt, and tried to lick my face as I saddled and bridled her the way Libby had taught me to. I had taken up Libby's offer to use the horses and in the past few weeks had taken Mr. Pleasure for mild walks around the field in front of our house. My mother always watched from the porch, smoking and lazily reading a book. She told me she didn't want me going off the property. I had been thrown once, which had left a big blue lump on my thigh, but I was getting better.

I took Mr. Pleasure out for a canter around the meadow. She whinnied and stomped and galloped around, her breath coming out like white smoke in the darkening air.

I let Mr. Pleasure take me into the forest, let her lead the way, as I sang loudly, way off-key, a Barry White song, trying to imitate his voice, just making up the words I couldn't remember. "Oh, there are some things I can't get used to, no matter how I try, yeah, baby. The more I give, the more you take, and baby, that's no lie . . ."

I hadn't been able to listen to black music for a long time. The music they played at Aurora was mostly folk music, skinny white girls with bad attitudes and bad voices who always sounded to me like they were imitating black women. The only time I got to hear old soul music was when by chance it came on the car radio—and that wasn't too often in the parts we were driving through. The few times it did, my mother would let the tuner linger, and we both would be quiet, not meeting each other's eyes as we listened.

The last time I saw Cole, she had been twelve, the same age I was now. She would be sixteen now. I tried to imagine her in Brazil. Did she have a boyfriend? Did she wear her hair differently? What did Brazilian teenagers dress like, talk like? I had dreamed about Cole just the other night. We were still young in the dream—she was around twelve, I was around eight, and she was pulling me into the ocean with her. I was scared. I kept looking back at the shore, where our parents sat, having a picnic. My mother was still fat, and my father still had an afro, and they were fighting about something. I couldn't hear the words they were saying, just the clipped angry tone of their conversation. They didn't notice us going in. Cole was a better swimmer, and the water looked choppy, violent, and tumultuous. I kept telling Cole I didn't want to go in, but she didn't listen and pulled me along by the hand, laughing. She was wearing an aqua-green bathing suit, and her hair had tightened up into little curls from the moisture. I saw a wave growing in the distance up ahead, so big it created a shadow on the beach. Cole said, "Just ride it, Birdie. Don't fight it." I had woken up before the wave hit us.

Now I was lost. Seriously lost. Mr. Pleasure had turned onto a trail I didn't recognize. An overgrown trail. Branches stung me as they hit me in the face, and I wanted to turn back, but as hard as I pulled at Mr. Pleasure's reigns, she just kept moving. I was breaking my mother's rules. *Stay out of any trivial trouble or accidents that could lead to questions of the wrong sort.* I knew I should have been frightened. But instead I felt strangely exhilarated to be lost in the forest. If I never found my way home, I thought, it wouldn't be my fault.

But then we were coming out of the forest, onto someone's lawn, and there were bright lights from the house before me. It was the Marsh residence, and I was in their backyard, near the big porch that Mr. Marsh had built. Mr. Pleasure had taken the long route, a trail that hadn't been used in a while, but she had known where she was going. Now, as I loosened the reigns, she grazed. There were barbecue supplies cluttering the porch, and from where we stood I could see through the sliding glass door to where the family moved in and out of sight, from living room to kitchen. The screen door was open, and I could hear their voices echoing out into the night.

There was Libby, wearing a long denim skirt and a wool sweater. She had her hair piled up in a French bun and a highball in her hand and was saying, sardonically, in a nasal voice that reminded me of my mother's family, "Christ, Walter, he did not steal our yellow roses. I cut them just this afternoon to bring to Mrs. Stuart for lunch. I think you owe that poor little man an apology."

Walter came into view. He had on reading glasses and was holding a book away from himself and squinting. "Lib, you won't believe what they're saying in here about Jane Austen. That she's gay, for God's sake! It's outrageous."

I edged Mr. Pleasure closer to the porch so I could see clearer. Libby sat cross-legged on a lumpy flowered couch with an oatmeal-colored afghan thrown over her lap. Large paintings hung in muted colors on the walls, and white marble sculptures with sharp edges stood in the corners of the room. These same sculptures, I realized then, stood on the dark lawn around me. Someone was an artist.

Just then their son came in. He was back from camp. He was older than me, a real teenager. He was eating a brownie and looking for something he had lost under the furniture. He kept saying "Shit!" under his breath.

I was just settling back in the saddle to watch the show when their golden retriever, with a big, stupid grin on his face, came bounding around the corner of the house toward me. Mr. Pleasure leapt backward on her hind legs, letting out a wild whinny. I almost fell off but grabbed her gray mane and clung on.

But it was too late—Walter had wandered to the screen door, pulling off his glasses with a perplexed expression on his face. He stood behind it, frowning into the darkness.

I sat very still on Mr. Pleasure, who was pawing the ground now, calming down as the dog wagged his tail and laughed at us.

"Nicky!" Walter called into the air. "Will you check behind the house? I just heard a horse out there and I want to make sure that Sheila character and her queer kid haven't let any of the horses loose."

Nicholas yelled out from some unseen location, "Can't you check? I'm watching the game."

His father looked back into his book and grumbled as he walked to his armchair. "C'mon, Nick, just take a quick look."

I moved Mr. Pleasure to the side of the house now, next to the porch. I kicked her sides hard, pulling the reins to my right, to try to get us back in the woods, but Mr. Pleasure stood stock still, shaking her head with a rattle of metal.

Nicholas, groaning in exasperation, came out into the darkness and onto the porch with big, wooden steps. I peered around the corner. He still had half of the brownie left in his hand. He looked in the opposite direction from me, toward the white sculptures. He whistled, and called, "Here, Pudd'nhead . . . Here, Pudd'nhead!" The dog went up the steps to him, leaping at his feet with his tongue rolled out and dripping.

Nicholas ignored Pudd'nhead and walked in my direction to the side of the house.

I closed my eyes, as if it would make me disappear, and sat holding my breath, waiting to be caught. After a moment, I opened my eyes to see Nicholas staring at me from the porch with surprise and some amusement. He had his mother's dark hair and delicate features.

We stared at each other in silence. Then, slowly, his lips curved into a smile. He yelled out, "Dad, I think it was just Pudd'n getting into some garbage. I'll just take a look."

I heard his mother shriek back, "Well, close the door, Nicholas. There's a wretched draft."

Nicholas gripped Mr. Pleasure by the reins and, without saying a word, led us over into the woods, to the path that I had emerged from.

When we were a safe distance away, he looked up at me. "Well?"

I started to speak. My throat felt parched, and I could feel a hollow thudding in my chest.

"I was just taking a ride, and Mr. Pleasure started off in this direction. I couldn't stop him. I mean her. I guess we got kinda lost——"

Nicholas touched my sneakered foot gently and cut me off, saying in almost a whisper, "Hey, don't worry. No big deal. I know who you are. You're Jesse, right?"

I nodded. My heart was still thudding, and I worried that he could hear it, so I squirmed around on the saddle, hoping the squeaks would drown the sound out.

Nicholas stroked Mr. Pleasure's nose, then glanced back toward the house as he said, "Do you want me to take you back to your place? It's kind of dark out."

I shook my head, blushing, and twisting Mr. Pleasure's mane around my finger so that I cut the blood off. "Nah, you don't have to. I think I can find my way back."

But Nicholas shook his head. "No, you'll get lost. There's a lot of false trails back here. Besides, you shouldn't be out alone in the woods tonight. There's a murderer on the loose. Escaped from the local prison. I won't tell you what he did to little girls, but it wasn't pretty. Didn't you hear about him?"

I watched his face, then said, "Yeah, right. Tell me another one." I tried to sound as tough as my mother, but really I was a little nervous.

He nodded. "It's true. You must not read the papers." Then he smiled mysteriously and said, "Scoot. I'll hop on behind you."

In a flash, he had mounted Mr. Pleasure, who groaned under the weight of our two bodies. Nicholas smelled of chocolate brownie and clove cigarettes. His arms slid around my waist to hold on to Mr. Pleasure's reins. I gripped the horse's mane, and we started at a brisk trot through the woods, back to the small house.

We didn't speak. I watched the patches of star-bright sky through the jungle of trees as we rode, and imagined I was a cowgirl leading my men to safety. I leaned back a little into his chest and made clicking noises to Mr. Pleasure.

When the cottage finally came into view, I felt a well of disappointment rise up in me. I could just imagine my mother going through another six-pack of Rolling Rock on the front porch and singing along with Bob Dylan.

Nicholas rode us into the stable. He slid off the horse, then he held out his arms and helped me down, with his hands around my waist. We stood in front of Mr. Pleasure, looking at each other under the warm light of the barn.

His eyes were a startling indigo blue, striking against his dark olive complexion.

His eyes flowed over my hair, my face, my neck.

"How old are you?" he asked, his voice breaking slightly.

"Fourteen." I was twelve, but had lied automatically, not really sure why.

"That's funny, my parents told me you were going into the eighth grade," he said with a knowing smile.

I shrugged. "I'm retarded and stayed back a grade."

"Somehow I doubt that."

He moved away and unbuckled Mr. Pleasure, then put the saddle and bridle away with quick, knowing expertise. He led Mr. Pleasure into her stall and locked the horse in. With a curious, crooked smile, he turned to look at me.

I stood shivering with my hands in my jeans pockets. I was wearing a T-shirt, and my arms were goose-bumped in the cold.

"Well, you should go inside. It's late. Your mom's probably worried."

"Thanks. I mean, for taking me back and everything." I bit my lip. "Could you do me a favor and not tell anyone that I was back at your house? Please?"

He frowned and walked toward me. His eyes seemed cold all of a sudden, like inkblots. "Why? What were you doing back there, anyway?"

"Nothing. I mean, I just—"

He laughed. "You were spying, weren't you? You're a Peeping Tom."

I looked away, scratching my leg through my jeans. I wondered why he was acting so suspicious of me.

I started to turn away, but he grabbed my arm. "Hey, I'm just teasing you. Don't get all upset. I won't tell anyone."

He was still holding my arm, and I turned to him. I shrugged. "Okay."

He looked me up and down. "Well, I better be getting back. My parents are going to wonder—"

"Yeah, me too. 'Bye, now," I said, hearing my voice crack, like a boy's. I turned to head back to the house. I heard him call out after me, "See you around."

I made my way back to our house reluctantly, dragging my feet, thinking about Nicholas and his family and the murderer in the woods.

Inside, the house was dark. It was later than I thought. I bumped into a chair at the kitchen table, and it made a loud scraping sound. The living room was pitch dark as well, but I could hear music playing. Italian opera. I was making my way over to the tape player to turn it off, when I noticed a figure seated on the couch, and I started.

"Shit, Mum, you scared the hell out of me. What are you doing in the dark?"

"Where in the fuck were you?" was all she said.

My words came out quickly, sounding like lies even though they weren't. "I went out for a ride on Mr. Pleasure, the mare. And I got lost in the woods and ended up behind the Marshes' house. And that kid Nicholas, their son, rode me back home, and he just left. Sorry, Mum. I didn't mean to scare you. It was funny, though. I mean, I almost got thrown off the horse when that damn dog—"

"Spying on the Marshes, huh?" she said, cutting me off. I thought she was just kidding, but then she barked: "Get over here."

I went toward her, tentatively. When I was close enough, she grabbed my arm and pulled me down so I leaned over her.

She said it quietly but clearly, her words floating across the dark air between us like vapor: "Hon, I'm gonna say this once. Don't ever, ever, come home later than you tell me. You hear me? I was scared shitless. I thought I was gonna have to go out looking. I thought they had you. I thought they had found you and were gonna use you as bait." She started to cry, and her grip loosened as she pulled away from me and roughly wiped her face dry. She spoke in a softer tone, sounding broken and exhausted as she said, "Fuck it all. I mean, when are you going to understand that this isn't a game? I learned just a week ago that the Feds got Jane. Found her in Oregon, living on some farm with her lover. She'll probably get a sixteen-year sentence to Marion. They've got her, baby, and they're gonna get us if we aren't more than careful. We gotta watch our asses, not get too close to anybody. You know that. I taught you well. Stay away from those rich fucks across the woods. Hear me? They're just like my own goddamn family—the kind of liberals who would like to see me fry. Remember that."

I just stood there in front of her for a few minutes, my arms hanging loosely by my sides. I felt dirty and guilty.

There was a long pause as she sniffled into her arm. Then she peeked up and said, "She's going to hate me. She's going to think this was all my fault." I knew what, who, she was talking about, but knew better than to say anything.

Finally she said, "Go to bed. Go on."

I left her sitting there, sniffling to herself. Before I went up the stairs, she called after me: "I love you, Baby Bird. Remember that." She sung a line from an old soul song: "You are everything, and everything is you."

I took it as an apology, and shouted back: "I love you too, Mum."

soundtrack
to a pass

It sounded like a child crying or a cat in heat. Unpleasant. Pleading. I covered
my head with a pillow. It was my mother doing her morning mantras out on
the lawn. The sound was grating, unsettling to me. I had heard somewhere
that you pray for only the dead or the doomed. I didn't want to pray for
Cole. I wanted to use more practical methods for tracking her down, like
sending word through the underground to tell her where we were, or simply going to find them ourselves in Brazil. Sometimes when I asked my
mother about trying a new tactic, she would say, "It's not so easy, sweetums. We're still prisoners of those fucking Cointelpro goons. Every move we
make is a risk. We've got to choose the right moment, or we're fucked."
Other times she was more optimistic and would pat my head rather gingerly,
look away, and say, "Don't worry, babe. I've got it under control. It's only a
matter of time."

After the mantras, my mother would do her Tai Chi on the broad field
between the stable and the forest. She usually wore tights with rainbow leg
warmers, a long T-shirt, and her feet bare. Her hair had gotten light around
the roots, and she was due for another henna. From my bed, I often watched
her out the window, her body seeming to be frozen in whatever pose she had
struck. But she only appeared to be still, balanced on one leg with the other
bent in the air, her arms in a delicate karate pose before her. She was actually

involved in a barely perceptible motion, one which I could measure only when I closed my eyes and then opened them a moment later to see she had changed positions.

I should have been asleep during that hour of the morning before dawn. But so often I was awake with the first coming of light, rigid, the tips of my fingers tingling with some vague anticipation, as if waiting for something, someone, during that hour when my mother believed she was alone.

Those days when she worked for the professor, I was left by myself to ride the horses in circles on the lawn, read novels on the front porch, and watch television on the mangled black-and-white TV the Marshes had sold to us for thirty dollars. I missed my mother when she was gone, even for those few hours, and my heart would leap at the sound of our clunker van pulling over gravel.

Sometimes, when the boredom and loneliness got to be too much, I walked the long road into town, where I would wander the aisles of Woolworth's, staring at all the things I couldn't have. The town was run down, depressed, despite the university in the next town over. Most of the shops there looked like they belonged in another era—the candy bars covered in dust, the clothes on the racks dingy and faded. There was one particularly strange shop at the edge of town that never seemed to get any business, Hans's Toy Shop and Doll Hospital. In the front window was a sad little display that included a G.I. Joe doll posed holding his gun pointed at the outside world; a battery-operated monkey with his cymbals poised to crash together; and a huge, black baby doll who wore only diapers and a T-shirt that said "Jackson" across the front.

Some days I went in there because I knew I wouldn't bump into kids my age. The store owner, Hans, an old German man who looked like a gnome with his stark-white beard and small wire-rimmed glasses, let me play with an Etch-A-Sketch that sat beside the cash register. Once, Hans even let me glance in the back room at his prized "doll hospital." A long row of naked dolls, with identical blank expressions, lay side by side on a folding table. All the dolls were deformed in some way: a missing limb, a punched-in face, a chewed-up foot. Beside them on the table was a row of tools. I was at once fascinated and terrified by the sight of the crippled little creatures who waited to go under the knife.

Most days, though, I just wandered the main road, crossing the street whenever I saw other children. There weren't many of them around those summer afternoons. Walter Marsh had told my mother that most of the local kids spent their days at the YMCA camp at the other end of town, or in summer school, trying to pass into the next grade.

I sat at a bench in front of a chili-dog stand one afternoon, munching on a corn dog and reading a book about horses my mother had bought me the day before. A group of girls rode up on brightly colored bicycles. It was sweltering outside, and I wore a pair of cutoff jeans, my hot-pink Converse sneakers, and a thin olive-green T-shirt. It said in bold white letters across my chest, "Join the Army: Travel to distant lands, meet fascinating people, and kill them." Alexis had given the T-shirt to me when we'd left Aurora. Alexis had been the only other kid there. She was the daughter of a battered wife who was hiding out from her ex-husband. Alexis had a fragility to her. My mother said it was a form of posttraumatic stress syndrome. She was forever terrified that her father would show up with a baseball bat to kill her mother. We slept together on a mattress on the floor, and she often woke in the middle of the night, crying, remembering her father's wrath. Alexis and I had become inseparable that year. She had been my last real friend.

I felt a sharp longing for Alexis now as the group of girls walked past me. They all were dressed alike in pastel short-shorts and little half-blouses that showed off their belly buttons. One of them, a blond girl whom I had seen once before, said something to her friends, and they all cackled wildly. I put my book inside my backpack and stood up to leave. I heard one of them say behind me, "What the fuck kinda zoo did she escape from?"

I turned, and they all were looking at me with amused disgust. Another one, who wore a pair of high-heeled sneakers, laughed, and said, "I don't think she speaks English."

I took off running, not caring that I looked crazy, just wanting to get home to the quiet and secrecy of our cottage.

Once I was out of town, I slowed to a walk. I felt stupid for caring about those silly girls. Cole would have stood up and shoved the big blond one. She would have had some witty comeback. "Yeah? Well your mama's so fat . . ." But I had been silent, a coward. Just then I heard a car come up the road behind me. I thought it must be the mean girls from the chili-dog stand, and quickened my pace. But the car didn't pass me. Instead it trailed behind me. I was too scared to turn around and see who it was, so I kept walking, face forward. I imagined it was the Feds. They had finally caught up with me. Then the image distorted into Hans. I wondered if he was a Nazi and had glimpsed the star around my neck. I saw myself on his table of dolls, preparing to go under the knife.

I heard a familiar voice.

"Hey, you. Want a ride?"

I turned to see a silver Saab—the Marshes' car. Nicholas was driving. He looked funny behind the wheel, too young to be driving.

He pulled up to the side of the road, and I walked over to the open window. Inside he was smoking, and blasting some rock song that I didn't recognize.

"You in some kind of a hurry? I saw you running."

I bit my lip, embarrassed, and glanced back down the road toward town. I half-expected to see the gaggle of girls on their bright bikes following me. I imagined them trying to catch me with a butterfly net and return me to the zoo. "Um, I was just exercising. You know."

"Well, are you gonna get in, or are you gonna stand there all day?"

I slid onto the leather seat. Nicholas was wearing cutoffs too, which made me feel less freakish. I sat close to the door, as far from him as possible, and immediately began to twist a lock of hair around my finger.

The music he played sounded like a bunch of trash cans rolling down a hill. But I tapped my fingers on my knee, pretending I liked it and trying to find the beat behind the noise. We were speeding down the winding country road, and I looked up at the trees that curled over us, letting dappled sunlight onto the road. I felt like a teenager and turned my face to the window so Nicholas wouldn't see my smile.

He had to shout over the music: "So, what were you doing in town, Jesse James?"

I giggled at his nickname for me. "I was getting a corn dog. My mom's working today. I was just bored."

He nodded, sucking on the tiny stub of his cigarette, then tossing it out the window. "Yeah, I was fuckin' bored out of my mind, too. I hate this town. It's full of losers." He ran a hand through his dark hair, then glanced at me. He held his eyes on me for a minute, and I felt myself blushing. I couldn't tell what he was thinking. He was smiling mischievously, and his eyes were red and puffy. "You like this town?"

I shrugged. "Nah."

"What was it like where you lived before?"

"Um. You know, upstate New York. Cold. Ugly."

"That's where you went to school?"

I played with the fringe on my jean shorts and tried to think of an answer. I hadn't prepared for his questioning. I was about to describe a public school I had never attended, when I saw, with relief, that we had reached my house.

"So, I'll see you soon, kid," he said, pulling up to the curb, still smiling as if he were holding back a laugh.

I tried to think of something cool to say. I managed only, "Sure. I mean, we should hang out. You know, since we're both bored."

He snickered and sped off. I went inside feeling giddy. I'd really forgotten about the zoo comment at the chili-dog stand. For the rest of the afternoon, I stared in the mirror over my mother's dresser, brushing my hair and practicing different smiles, trying to decide which was the most natural-looking.

On the days my mother had off from work, she never left my side. She told me she needed to prepare me for ordinary school in the fall. She wanted me to start in eighth grade, where I belonged. No child of hers would stay back a grade. This usually involved me reading aloud to her from our novel of the week, borrowed from the university library under her professor's name. While I read to her from Zora Neale Hurston or Simone de Beauvoir or J. D. Salinger, she would lay stretched out before me on the porch, eyes closed, a faint smile on her lips. Afterward, we would drive to the chili-dog stand and discuss what we had learned.

But one day she announced that she wanted me to write a novel, not just read one. She handed me a black-and-white-marbled composition book she had bought me at the five and dime. She said my novel could be about anything I chose, and that if I finished it, I would officially graduate from our seventh-grade class. I was bored and lonely, so I took on her assignment with vigor. I pondered the assignment for a few days and finally decided I wanted to write about a Mexican-American family. I had seen such a family on a news show about alien abductions, and had decided, watching the rowdy, exotic lot, that I wanted to be Mexican. The television family lived in El Paso, Texas, and so that became the name of my novel. "El Paso." It featured a religious, perpetually pregnant mother; a banjo-playing, sombrero-donning papa; and their teenage son, the main character, Richie Rodriguez, who is a bad seed looking for a way out. Throughout the course of the novel, Richie gets in knife fights, beats and impregnates his girlfriend, and fails out of high school. I was in love with Richie and dreamed of him each night, his shining black pompadour hair, his bronze skin, and his leather jacket. I also dreamed about his sexy, abused girlfriend. A few times, alone at the house in the afternoon with only my notebook and the television set, I touched myself while thinking about Richie and his girlfriend intertwined in a lovemaking ritual. I was never a part of these fantasies, and it wasn't clear to me which one of them I was supposed to be identifying with—the burly, macho Richie, who lay on top, or his soft, ultrafeminine girlfriend with the pink lipstick and matching toenails, who lay on the bottom. But I would press the spot between my legs while I thought about them, and feel a pulsing warmth.

It took me a week to write it. When I was finished, my mother read all forty pages of "El Paso" on the porch while I paced around her, wringing my hands. I feared from her pinched expression that she was disappointed. It wasn't about the revolutionary heroine she had imagined. I was afraid she'd keep me back a grade. But when she reached the last page, she put it down beside her and hugged me so tight it hurt. She said "El Paso" was brilliant, absolutely brilliant. Afterward, she took me out for a celebratory graduation dinner at the Hunan Dragon in town.

I felt safe going into town with my mother, even if she did attract hostile stares from strangers. She dressed in long peasant skirts and halter tops with no bra, or tattered overalls and a baseball cap on backward. The men smiled at her as if she were something exotic and amusing. The women sneered, disgusted by the free bounce to her breasts and the sass in her step. But she never seemed to notice. She was in her own world. I wondered if something in her blue-blood upbringing spared her shame, made her feel slightly superior to the people around us. Whatever the case, some of that nonchalance rubbed off on me when I was with her, and I stared boldly into the faces of teenagers, daring them to say something, to test my mother's wrath.

BUT AS TOUGH as my mother was, she was lonely. She had nobody in her life except me and the university professor, whom she hated and referred to as "Morning Mouth" because, she said, his breath smelled of rotten milk. She said she didn't trust the Marshes as far as she could throw them. She even admitted to missing the women of Aurora sometimes. But there was no way we were going back. She had left Aurora on bad terms with them. She had called them crazy dykes and said that my father was right: Women can't organize a movement because deep down, they don't like one another very much. The day we left she had a fight with Zoë, the Israeli who was the founder of the commune. I was never totally clear on what the fight was about. I know it had something to do with my mother referring to feminism as being an excuse for "white, bourgeois bitches to complain about something." As we sped away, my mother had cursed them all under her breath, using every foul word in the English language. But now she missed them. She had taken to drinking at night on the front porch, singing along loudly to some sad melody, while I lay upstairs, hoping her voice wouldn't travel across the woods to the Marshes' house.

On nights when the solitude became too much for her, when my company was not enough, she would drive us to the bar in the center of town. There she would play the only two songs she liked on the jukebox: Stevie Wonder's "Superstition," and Joan Baez's "John Riley."

One Wednesday evening I sat beside my mother at the bar, grimy from horseback riding, wolfing down a cheeseburger and sucking on a coffee milk shake from Dairy Queen. The local farmers were drinking in the back, and the huddle of grisly men kept turning to look at us.

There had been a time when the slightest lingering look from a stranger was enough to send us running. One time, at an Arby's in Syracuse, my mother hadn't even allowed me to finish my roast beef sandwich before she was giving me the sign—a sharp tug to her earlobe—which meant "Get out while you can, but act natural." (A pinch under the table meant "Get out by any means necessary, and don't worry about acting natural.") Then she hadn't acted natural at all but had instead pulled me out of the doors and into the autumn air, whispering, "Don't look now, but that guy in the back, with the newspaper—*The Wall Street Journal*—was a Fed. Just keep walking. Don't look back." I had in fact glanced back, as we peeled away in the lime-green Duster (our getaway car of the moment), long enough to see a bespectacled, wide-jawed man at a window booth watching us with a bemused expression. When we got back to the Howard Johnson's, my mother had paced the room, sweating and cursing, looking out of the closed blinds every now and then, while I stuffed our get-up-and-go life into a duffel bag, trying to beat my own packing record of one minute and twenty seconds.

Here, in this bar at the center of this New Hampshire town, I believed I saw a twinkle—an "I'm gonna get you one of these days" look—in the eyes of one of the thick, brawny men who glanced back at us, whispering and laughing. I believed one of them—all of them—might be Feds, and half-expected my mother to start tugging on her earlobe. But she seemed oblivious to their stares as she played with her cheese fries and gulped down a pint of draft, a white froth forming over her lip.

Just the night before, she had sat on the front porch of our house, smoking and crying until three A.M., while upstairs I lay sideways in my bed, rubbing my feet against the wall and trying to remember my father's living room—the white leather beanbag chair; the glass coffee table with the crack, like lightning, across the middle; the frayed black-and-gold Egypt poster; and beside the television, a pile of books almost as high as me. Downstairs, my mother had wept, talking to herself, words I couldn't quite understand. But here, in the bar, you wouldn't have known it. She was transformed. She wore her hair in twin pigtails, and a long black skirt that made her look like a gypsy as she chattered to me about a book she was reading on the origins of evil.

"There are people in your life who seem good, and people who seem just all right," she told me, twirling a copper strand of hair and chewing thoughtfully on a fry. "But when it comes to a crisis, there are only those who will save you and those who will abandon you."

I thought about Redbone. My mother had informed me one night at a Chinese restaurant in New Haven that it was Redbone who had "sold us down river." She rarely talked about him, but when she did, she called him "that high-yellow Uncle Tom sellout motherfucker"—a phrase she had borrowed from my father. She said he was responsible for our downfall, for the breakup of our family. If I closed my eyes, I could almost smell his breath, the stench that had emanated from his body that night at Dot's when he had carried me to the guns and informed me that the revolution lay inside those long, thin, gleaming objects.

"Think about it this way, baby," my mother continued, becoming more animated with her own ideas. "If the Nazis came to get you, who would sell you out to save their own skin? And who would protect you against all odds? You'd be surprised at who steps forward at moments like that. Who's brave, and who's a sellout. I mean, if the Nazis came to get you, who would you trust?"

"I don't know. I guess you—" I started to say, when the door to the bar opened with a jingle, bringing forth a gust of air and a man wearing a denim jacket, a white beard, and a New York Yankees cap. His age was unclear because of the stark whiteness of his hair against the youthfulness of his features. A couple of the farmers acknowledged him with restrained nods of their heads, which he returned. He glanced at my mother, and his gaze lingered for a minute. He looked surprised and a little amused to see us there, as if we were old friends he had been expecting to meet up with later.

I immediately checked his shoes. My mother told me that you could always tell a Fed from his shoes. He might get the rest of the disguise right, but his shoes would give him away. The clue was usually in the newness—the spanking-white tennis sneaker, or the shiny leather Loafer without any scuffs around the heels.

This man wore clogs, and fairly well-worn ones, from the looks of things. I wondered whether that meant he was safe, or simply good at his job.

My mother had stopped listening to my explanation, and her eyes were suddenly shadowy and secretive as she glanced at the man out of the corner of her eye.

He was also looking at her in a way that made me invisible—erased me from the stool and the bar. I went back to drawing my horses.

AFTER THAT EVENING she and I started going to the bar every Wednesday after I was done riding. The man always came in about twenty minutes after we did, in either cowboy boots or clogs, wearing his slightly belled dungarees, each time daring to look a little longer at my mother. I ignored them, instead watching the callused men who sat hunched over their sweating glasses. I liked to pretend I was one of them—a regular. I would ape their postures, and would nod my head and raise a finger to the beefy bartender, Gus. Most nights Gus humored me in my endeavor, asking if I wanted "the regular" (a Shirley Temple) and if it was to go on my "tab" (my mother). He was an old guy with a bulbous and veiny alcoholic nose and a Boston Celtics baseball cap, and he seemed amused by my presence in this surly male den.

My mother became more and more dolled up for those visits to the bar and even deigned to wear lipstick one particular evening when the sun hung on long over the town, leaving a muted orange light that turned everything into shadows.

That was the night the man approached her. Kenny Rogers was playing on the jukebox. *You gotta know when to hold 'em, know when to fold 'em . . .* I was trying to read, but I could barely concentrate in the dim light of the bar, with the music in my ears . . . *know when to walk away, know when to run . . .* The man came toward us, smiling rather goofily, a beer in one hand and his keys jingling in the other. It struck me that he looked like a thinner version of Kenny Rogers, and I wondered if he had planned his entrance to coincide with the music playing, a soundtrack to his pass.

They spoke softly to each other, like bashful school children. He told her he had been watching her and wanted to know her name.

"I'm Sheila Goldman," she told him. Her cheeks were flushed, and she ran a finger around the rim of her glass. "My daughter Jesse and I just moved here from upstate New York."

She was usually cooler toward strangers, giving them the hint that she wasn't interested in small talk. With strangers, even with Walter and Libby Marsh, she usually cut conversations to a minimum if she could help it. And she had taught me to do the same. *Be a presence that no one quite remembers, the one who blends into the woodwork, so when the Feds come asking questions later on, people will say they only vaguely remember a woman and child. Was the child a boy or a girl? They can't quite remember. Were they tall, fat, thin, blond, red-haired, white, black, poor, rich, serious, or laughing? Did they look anything like the two in this picture? If the neighbors can't recall, you've done your job.*

But that night she let the conversation linger, and I pinched her leg hard under the bar. She ignored my warning, never even wincing or pausing in mid-sentence. She was breaking the rules she herself had drummed into me. She was doing the unthinkable—becoming a presence, making herself memorable, slipping into her boisterous old self, a woman that these small-town folks would surely be able to recall, to identify in a picture. I made a note to scold her when we got home.

She told the man the same lie I was used to hearing her speak for quite some time. But for some reason, at that moment in the bar, the lie sounded different to me, weightier, more like the truth. It was as if the past four years had been only a dress rehearsal in preparation for this opening night.

He told her his name was Jim and that he "fiddled with computers" for a living. He said he lived in a bungalow across the lake. They talked for hours, and it was almost eleven when they exchanged numbers and we all got up to leave. I yawned into my hand and followed them out to the car. There, in the air that had turned cool, they said good-bye, both looking at their feet and interrupting each other in awkward starts and stops. There was something thick in the space between them that even I could feel as I stood watching from the sidelines.

She drove home with the windows down, singing along to a country-western song on the radio. She was blushing, and her lips were moist. She glanced at me. "Don't look so disgusted, Jess. Even mothers need love lives."

She tried to take my hand, but I pulled away.

I told her, looking out at the broad, black, country sky: "Do you really think he's safe? I mean, he's been there every night we're at the bar, Mum. And his name is Jim. You were the one who said they have generic names, the kinds they could think up on the spot. And you heard that: he 'fiddles with computers' for a living." I made a noise in the back of my throat. "I bet he does."

She sighed, and said, "Oh, Jess. I didn't get that vibe from him at all. I mean, he seemed real to me. Just a nice guy. Besides, did you get a look at his clogs? Those weren't Fed shoes. No way, Jose. Trust me on this one."

Staring out into the clear summer darkness, I remembered a night—a night at Aurora, a night with Bernadette, when she had spoken to me as if I were one of the grown-ups. Five women, along with me, had traipsed down to the lake nearby to go swimming, though it was late in the summer and the air had turned crisp and smoky with the coming of autumn. The leaves crackled, and the dry earth crunched beneath our feet. When we got to the lake, my mother and three other women went skinny-dipping, hooting and flipping around in the dark water like pale seals. They looked unreal in the moonlight, shiny and full-bosomed, high on something, though no one had been drinking. I had preferred to stay dry and fully dressed with Bernadette by the side of the water. She smoked a dark, European cigarette and watched the women with a mysterious smile. She spoke, and although I sat nestled beside her bulky warm body, it seemed she was talking more to herself.

"Right now, they think it's as simple as this. They think they've found some kind of utopia here. But just wait. Once they meet a man, all their defenses go to hell. Can't trust them for shit once a man walks in the room. I've seen it before."

Her words had made me uncomfortable, and I wanted to tell her that my mother wasn't like that, wasn't the same as the women she was talking about, but instead I picked at my shoelace and watched the women come toward us up the bank, laughing and shivering together, their lips nearly blue.

So this was what Bernadette had warned me about. Jim was throwing everything off. I said to my mother, hoping to strike a nerve: "I can't believe you would risk it all for a man. Typical."

But it wasn't just that. When I closed my eyes, it was my father, mother, sister, and I that I saw together. No Carmen. And certainly not this shaggy white man in clogs. My mother was supposed to be waiting for my sister, but also for my father, so we could start where we had left off.

She glanced at me, momentarily surprised by Bernadette's words coming out of my mouth. Then she slapped the steering wheel. "Oh, come off it, Jesse. Give me a little more credit than that, please. I have lived a little. I'm not stupid. And don't start quoting Bernadette, 'cause I'm not hearing it. She could criticize me all she wanted, but she acted like a chauvinist pig when it came down to it. I don't even want to hear that kind of crap from your mouth. I'm doing the best I can."

She took a violent drag on her cigarette and held her breath for a long minute before exhaling gray fumes out the open window.

I crossed my arms and stared at the trailer park we were passing. The park was emitting a blue light and a faint electric buzz from the bug-zapper lamps. At one of the trailers, I could see a girl my age sitting on some steps, smoking a cigarette and rubbing her foot in the dirt. In the distance, her cigarette looked like a firefly buzzing before her face. I twisted my head around as we passed her, and realized with a start that it was the girl who had called me a zoo animal just a few weeks back.

My mother turned up the volume on the radio—it was Willie Nelson—and hummed along, off-key and loud enough to halt any further discussion.

Before bed that night, I stared at the bathroom mirror and saw a twelve-year-old girl who might be a boy if it weren't for the scraggly ponytail falling down her back. The dark trace of a mustache over her lip, and eyebrows that met faintly in the middle. There were no curls, no full lips, still no signs of my sister's face in my own. There had been a time when I thought I was just going through a phase. That if I was patient and good enough, I would transform into a black swan. I mouthed the word *shimbala* at myself in the mirror. It was somewhere between a noun and a command in Elemeno, but I couldn't remember what it meant.

OVERALL, JIM'S STORY seemed pretty flimsy to me. He told us he had spent five years, from 1968 to 1973 —during the Vietnam war—living in Jamaica, where he had worked odd jobs, spending most of his time in a pot-inspired daze. He told us he had burned through an inheritance for those years in Jamaica. Now that he was back in America, he explained to us, he had a part-time job programming computers in Boston, where he commuted three days out of the week. In his spare time, he gardened and built furniture.

Not only did it seem absurdly suspicious that he disappeared three days a week to Boston, of all places, and not only was it strange that he seemed to have an endless supply of money from his supposed computer job, but he was vague about what he had been doing in Jamaica. He blamed his bad memory on the pot. Those years, he explained, were a blur for him; it was hard to pin down the specifics, except that he had found something approaching nirvana in the island people he had lived among. He had a few photographs of himself in some tropical setting, his skin a brighter shade of pink, surrounded by poverty shacks and white stretches of sand. But that wasn't enough for me. I had questions. If he had spent those five years in Jamaica, wouldn't he have been draft-dodging? And where were the pictures of the friends he had made, the women he had loved? There seemed to be no people other than himself in the photos. His past was as unclear as our own.

His voice gave me the creeps. He talked in a soft, restrained voice most of the time—so softly you had to lean in slightly to catch every word. He told my mother that he believed in women's lib, and I think he thought his soft-spoken voice made him less threatening, less of what my mother called a "brute." But to me it was just as bad. It forced me to stand closer to him than I really wanted to. And while most of the time he seemed benign, laid back—if not a little goofy—there were moments when I believed I saw the real Jim emerge. Someone stern and red-faced and dictatorial—someone I could imagine wearing mirrored sunglasses and a dark suit—someone I believed was out to get us.

He lived in a little shack filled with Jamaican artifacts and plywood. When he wasn't in Boston, he spent his time shuffling around his house in clogs, playing folk songs on his guitar, gardening out back, and smoking "the almighty ganja." He loved reggae music "more than life itself" and that summer introduced me to the sounds of Peter Tosh, Jimmie Cliff, The Wailers. The house was suffused with a heavy smoke of marijuana. There were green sprinklings, like oregano, around the kitchen table, and strange smoking contraptions set up in the living room. Jim's lips often had little blister marks on them from where the burning spliff had come too close.

"His story's bogus and you know it," I told my mother one afternoon while we stood at the edge of the road just outside the Stop & Shop parking lot, clutching our grocery bags and waiting for Jim to pick us up. He was at the hardware store a few miles down the road. "It's so obvious. I bet he's never even been to Jamaica. It's all an act. The pot. The music. The clogs. I bet he spent those five years killing villagers in Laos. Or no—I bet he never even got his hands dirty. I bet he just gave orders from an office in Washington." I paused and kicked a rock with my sneaker. The sun felt strangely cold on my back, and I shivered. "I mean, don't you think it's a little odd that he disappears to Boston—Boston, of all places—every week? I can't believe you don't see it. I thought you were good at this. I thought you were the expert."

My mother shifted the weight of the bag onto her other hip and stared with a slightly pained smile at the line of pine trees across the wide road. She whispered, though there was no way anyone would hear us, "Oh, come on, Jess. Don't do this. The man has done nothing to deserve your wrath. I understand you're just looking out for me, but Jim is not a Fed. That much I can assure you. They're much easier to spot than that. I've seen them. I know."

"Yeah," I said, scoffing. "Like you did a great job spotting Redbone."

She breathed in quickly and looked at me. "That was different. A lot of us trusted him" was all she said. But I could see I had hurt her. She pursed her lips and blinked her eyes as if holding back tears. I felt a little sorry for her, but also perplexed by her sudden, insurmountable stupidity.

I tried another tactic: "But what about Papa? What's he supposed to do when he gets here and you've got a boyfriend?"

She looked away, a pinched expression making her features pointy, severe, like her own mother's. She glanced at me, her cheeks pinkening slightly as she said, "Babes, your papa left with Carmen. Remember? We were no longer together. That still hasn't changed."

My eyes stung as I looked at the cars swishing by before me. Country cars. Good-old American cars. Brady Bunch cars. Big brown station wagons with fake wood paneling. Suburbans, Buicks, Tonka trucks grown to life size. My father had never had any faith in American cars. He said they were shit. He liked to say that he believed in meritocracy, not mediocrity. The Marshes must have felt the same way. Their old silver Saab had the same feel and smell as his car. It made me want to get inside and close my eyes and just inhale the leather, the dust, the slight gasoline smell leaking from the old European motor.

Watching the cars pass by now, I felt an urge to stick my thumb out and let some stranger take me wherever they were going. A trucker would be the best. We could just keep driving forever. I did put out my thumb then, and stared wistfully into the distance, hoping to annoy my mother. But she just laughed slightly, and I heard tires crunching behind me on the gravel of the roadside. It was Jim's Buick. His silver hair glimmered from behind the windshield. He leaned out the window and said, "Going my way, ladies?" My mother and he grinned at each other.

As I pushed past her to get to the back door, she whispered to me from beneath her smile, in a low, clenched voice: "I got us this far, baby. Now, leave the rest up to me."

ONE DAY, late in July, while my mother and Jim were busy swaddling themselves with coconut-smelling lotion, I meandered along the edge of the town lake, bored by their whispers, to collect rocks. It was late in the day, and Jim and my mother wanted to get in a swim before the mosquitoes got too bad. A gold light coated the surface of the water, and it seemed that the bodies that littered the beach were suffused in a similar yellow gauze. I stopped at some length, plopped down, and began to bury my feet in the sand.

A group of children approached me like a committee. They were the kind of kids that Maria would have called "stanky"—the kind of white people that she claimed had warts on all their fingers, lice in their hair. My mother would have called them "real, honest, working people." They wore an odd assortment of bathing suits, from Goodwill, I supposed, and held hands. Their ages ranged from about four to about eight. None of them was even close to my age.

They watched me packing my feet underneath the sand. Finally, the oldest, a thin blond girl with albino-white skin, said, "You want to play?"

I shrugged. I didn't feel like baby-sitting.

A smaller one piped out, "Want us to bury you?"

I stared at them. They seemed normal enough. And I was lonely. Nicholas hadn't come by to visit me like he said he would. Besides, I was beginning to whisper to myself when nobody was looking. I said, "Sure."

They descended upon the sand with a terrifying enthusiasm. They began to dig a hole next to me, their little fingers working quicker than I had ever seen. Before long, they had created a shallow hole in the sand, as long and as deep as my body.

A stumpy redheaded girl, about six, with a pink birthmark around her eye, said, "Well, aren't you gonna get in?"

I rolled into it, and they began with an equal fervor to fill up the hole on top of me. The sand was cool and heavy. I liked watching my long limbs, my skin, my red Speedo bathing suit that was getting too small for me, disappear under the beige sand. One of them had built a pillow for my head out of the sand, and I rested my head against it, knowing I'd have to wash my hair later to get it all out.

The oldest sat alongside, watching her younger siblings. She seemed bored by their antics, as if she had seen them bury strangers before. She asked me, "Where are you from?"

I glanced back down the beach, where my mother and Jim now splashed in the water together.

"India," I told her without much thought.

The children stopped their shoveling and patting and stared at me.

The oldest girl's eyes widened, and I felt a twinge of excitement as they all waited with rapt attention for more details.

"My Indian parents, they've left me in the care of that couple over there." I nodded my head to Jim and my mother, who were kissing, her legs around his waist as he held her up in the water. I sneered, "They're horrible. They make me scrub the toilet and walk ten miles to school. And he, that guy, he beats me with a switch on the backs of my legs."

The children gasped. "Are you going to run away?"

"Naw, I'll probably just wait till my real parents come get me. There's a war going on, you know. They wanted me out of India until it was safe. We're a pretty important family. I'm a princess. My name's—" I paused, my mind racing for something exotic. "My name's Tanzania." It was a word from the Africa map at the Nkrumah School.

The children had gathered in a circle around my head, the only part of me exposed. They belted out questions, their fascination rising with each of my lies.

Can you do that funny dance where your head moves back and forth from side to side?

Why don't you have a dot on your forehead?

Do you have slaves?

Do you live in a castle?

My words flowed freely, weaving a picture of a pampered princess from Calcutta who threw bread to the beggars and spent afternoons getting pedicures by a coterie of beautiful house girls.

"My favorite slave," I continued, "she wakes me up every morning with a fresh bouquet of roses and a kiss. Then she fans me with palm leaves, and her girls sponge-bathe me in a silver tub filled with tulips . . ."

I went on and on, taken away by my own story. It was a few minutes before I realized, with annoyance, that the children weren't paying attention. They were looking over my head. A shadow had fallen across my line of sun.

Jim appeared from behind me then, arms akimbo, staring down at me with pinched, angry lips. He had gotten too much sun. I could see he'd be in pain later. Tonight his skin was going to be a horrid blazing pink.

"Jesse, what are you telling these children?"

"Nothing," I stammered. I sat up, breaking the blanket of sand on top of me. I scrambled to my feet, wiping my legs. My skin felt like sandpaper. "Let's go."

I turned to the children with a wild smile and said, "'Bye, now. Gotta go. See you around," and began to walk off.

But Jim's hand grabbed my arm and held it tight.

He looked down at me a little sadly, as if to say, "This hurts me as much as it's gonna hurt you, Jesse."

I struggled in vain to pull away. "What? Can we go now? I have to pee. *Bad.*"

"Jess, you know lying's not cool. Now why don't you tell these kids the truth? Go on. Be brave about it and we can stop at Dairy Queen on the way back."

I heard my mother's voice behind him. I hadn't known she was there. "Jim, don't embarrass her. Let's go."

Jim turned to her, incredulous. "Sheila, I don't know what your child-rearing methods are, but allowing her to lie like she does just isn't good for her. You know that."

My mother bit her nails and avoided my eyes.

The children were fascinated by our heated exchange. One of them called out, "Are these the ones? Are these the ones your parents left you with? Want us to get our parents? You can live with us until your real parents get back, Tangaria!"

Jim turned to the kids. "Listen, kids. Her name's not Tangaria, it's Jesse. And we're her parents. She was lying. Now, Jesse, you want to apologize?"

I kicked the sand. The kids were looking at me quizzically, as if they were beginning to lose faith in my story. Jim was blinking at me expectantly, and I got the feeling that he didn't really like me much, that I was getting in the way of something. My mother was staring off, too ashamed, I think, to look at me. Finally, I blurted out to the kids, "I told you they were crazy." Then I ran the length of the beach to the car without stopping.

tintin
in the congo

My father was fading on me. Not the Jewish father. I could see David Goldman clear as day, in a rumpled tweed jacket, a yarmulke bobby-pinned precariously to his loose afro, as he bent over some ancient text. It was my real
father, Deck Lee, whom I was having trouble seeing. First his eyes, then his
nose, then his mouth had faded until all I could see was the back of his head,
his hands drumming on the steering wheel, and his voice, singing along to
something on the eight-track cassette, something falsetto and sentimental
like *the reasons that we're here, the reasons that we let our feelings disappear.* I tried
to see his front side, his face, but he lived only with his back to me while his
words, his music, reached me all the same. I wasn't really sure why it hadn't
happened to me before, this fogging in my memory of him. Maybe the perpetual motion had kept my vision clear. It was as if the blankness of our identities before had left enough room for the old to survive. Now that we had
stopped moving, allowing our new selves to bloom, it seemed the old had to
disintegrate.

I wondered what my father would think of us if he could see us now—
me as a Jewish girl, my mother pantomiming the life of some ordinary white
woman. When we had first chosen Jesse Goldman that day in the Maine
diner, I had thought of it as a kind of game. For those first few months on the
lam I believed my father would see our situation as innocent and practical,

just as my mother liked to see it, as the only way for us to remain free while we waited for him to fetch us. I had even convinced myself that my passing for this white girl, this Jewish girl, this Jesse Goldman, would support my father's research.

I used to fantasize that once I got back to Boston, I would write it up as a report to hand in to the Nkrumah School.

I even thought up a series of potential titles for my report.

"What White People Say When They Think They're Alone"

"Honkified Meanderings: Notes from the Underground"

Or something more casual and funky—"Let Me Tell Ya 'bout Dem White Folks."

I imagined that my report might develop into a pompous Papa-style lecture, the kind I had seen him deliver in university auditoriums. I saw myself presenting it in the Nkrumah School auditorium, complete with a slide show, candid and grainy color photographs of the white folks around me: one of the crew-cut boys loitering in front of Dairy Queen; another of my mother and Jim swaddling each other with sunscreen; a third of those tow-headed girls down the road in their bare feet, short-shorts, and dirty knees. When I was finished gesticulating to the audience of rapt faces before me, I would clear my throat like my father did and step back from the microphone, mumbling, "That's all, folks." The whole school would pause for a moment, then stand at once, applauding wildly, and Professor Abdul would jog onstage to grant me the award for best seventh-grade report. He would shout over the hoots and applause still belting out from the audience: "She's the spy we all love. And she *always* reports back to headquarters. . . ."

Maybe that's how it had been at first. A game. But something was changing here. Something slow and sneaky. At night I stared into my box of negrobilia, fingering the objects—the fisted pick, the Nubian Notion eight-track cassette, the Egyptian necklace, the black Barbie head—and tried to tell myself, "I haven't forgotten." But the objects in the box looked to me just like that—objects. They seemed like remnants from the life of some other girl whom I barely knew anymore, anthropological artifacts of some ancient, extinct people, rather than pieces of my past. And the name Jesse Goldman no longer felt so funny, so thick on my tongue, so make-believe.

Something else changed in New Hampshire, something I never told anyone for fear of being called crazy and sent away, like a girl I had seen on an after-school special. It was simply a sensation I had at times, when I experienced a sense of watching myself from above. It happened only occasionally. I would, quite literally, feel myself rising above a scene, looking down at myself, hearing myself speak. I would gaze down at the thin girl sitting by the fence, the one with her brown hair falling into her eyes, drawing patterns in the dirt, and watch this girl with the detachment of a stranger. And in these moments I would notice things about myself, about my body—the faint dusky mustache that made me look dirty in the wrong light; the bunions on my feet that twisted my toes inward like sad, beaten dogs; the remarkable length of my fingers; the knobby knees; and the flat feet. I saw these things as neither beautiful nor ugly, but simply as facts. I would look at my own body the way that I looked at another's. I would think, "You," not "I," in those moments, and as long as the girl was "you," I didn't feel that I lived those scenes, only that I witnessed them.

SHIATSU CRIMSAY PETULAAA. I whispered the words to Mr. Pleasure. The barn was dank and dark and seemed the safest place to remember, the safest place to practice the language that was becoming harder and harder to speak lately. I had been coming here a lot since Jim had entered the picture. Just to be alone. Just to be away from them. Here I would tell Mr. Pleasure the real story of my father and sister, repeating the same cold facts over and over again as if to convince myself that they had existed. I told Mr. Pleasure about Cole's face and body, her curling hair, ocean-green eyes, and cocoa-colored birth mark. The way her breath felt against my back when I lay beside her. Cole hadn't faded on me. She was still clear as sunlight—her face, her hair, her smell.

I felt someone behind me and turned, startled, out of my trance. It was Nicholas, his hair falling into his eyes. He had strawberry patches on his cheeks like a Rugby player. He wore cutoff Army fatigues, a powder-blue polo, and Top-Siders without socks. It was the first time I'd seen him since our drive home from town that day, though I'd thought of him many times.

"Who are you talking to?" he asked, a laugh spilling from his lips.

I felt my face heat up. "Nothing. I mean, nobody. I was singing a song."

"Strange song," he said, loping up to me.

"Yeah," I said, standing up to his level. I wiped my dirty palms against my Toughskins. "You want to ride Mr. Pleasure?"

"I was thinking about it. But if you were going to——"

Our conversation fuddled on from there, and before I knew it I was being hoisted onto Mr. Pleasure and then Nicholas was behind me, his hands brushing across my sides as we rode out into a glare of green and blue.

He said, his lips brushing my ear, "So, why did you and your mother leave upstate New York?"

"Just 'cuz. My mother didn't like it anymore."

"Is it because of your dad? I heard he died. How'd he die?"

I wanted to get off the horse all of a sudden. I remembered my mother's face as she drilled me one night in a putrid-smelling motel bathroom. *Trust nobody. I mean, nobody. You are no longer Birdie Lee. You are Jesse Goldman, and your father was a professor of classics who died suddenly last year. I'm his widow. He was Jewish, dark, and that's where you get your looks. Repeat after me . . .*

Nicholas's question rung in my ears again.

"Jesse? Earth to Jesse——" He leaned forward and let his chin brush across my shoulder. The horse had stopped now to graze, and Nicholas loosened Mr. Pleasure's reigns. "So, aren't you going to tell me? How'd he die?"

I craned my head to look at him. "He died of a brain aneurysm. He was a genius. He thought too much and it affected his brain." That was a new one. I hoped it wouldn't show that I was bluffing.

"Oh, bummer" was all Nicholas said. I could tell he didn't know what a brain aneurysm was. That was why my mother had chosen that disease. She didn't want me to have to elaborate on anything, and she figured kids wouldn't ask questions if the disease sounded complicated. They wouldn't want to show their ignorance. She was right. Nicholas switched the subject. "You're funny. My dad says he thinks you and your mother are running from something, but he doesn't know what. Is it true? Are you running from something?"

I froze. Then forced a laugh, harsh and throaty, as I said, "No, what do you mean? My mom didn't want to stick around. It was too painful, you know. All those memories of my dad. He was writing a book when he died. He never finished it."

After I had said it, I liked the sound of my story. It sounded dramatic——

tragic. I repeated some lines I had heard in a movie: "He died really suddenly, thank God. You should have seen the funeral. Tons of people came and wept."

Nicholas sounded impressed. "I've never known someone with a dead father. That must be weird."

I picked up Mr. Pleasure's reigns and clicked my tongue. Mr. Pleasure began to walk back toward the barn. "Yeah, it is weird."

Inside the barn, we tied up Mr. Pleasure, and Nicholas ruffled my hair and said, "I think I'll call you Pocahontas."

"Why?" I asked him, unbuckling the thick leather strap of the saddle.

"Because you turn all brown in the sun. Like a little Indian."

He was standing behind me, and stepped closer then, so that I could feel his breath tickling my neck.

My mother disapproved of the time I spent with the Wasps across the forest and said that they were "seductive sons of bitches" and that I should be careful. When we decided to move to New Hampshire, she had envisioned me coming of age with tough farmers' daughters, and it irked her that I had chosen the town's one upper-crust family to make my own. But given her love affair with Jim and my continuing suspicion of him, she couldn't exactly scold me. Instead she teased me about my growing friendship with the Marshes, saying, when we were alone, "It's your blue blood coming back to haunt me. I thought I had washed it all out."

Nicholas was my entrée into the Marsh world. Although he was fifteen, three years older than I was, we both were outsiders in New Hampshire. I was on the verge of joining the exposed world, having been hidden for so long. Likewise, Nicholas was only biding his time in this small town, waiting till the summer ended, before joining his ilk at boarding school. He had been going to private schools and boarding schools all of his life and had no relationship really to the other kids in his town. I became his entertainment until the real show began.

At Nicholas's encouragement, I spent most afternoons just lounging around the Marsh house, pretending it was my own. His parents were fascinated by my mother and me and seemed to like having me around to amuse them with stories. They told me to consider their house my second home, and even gave me permission to enter without knocking.

One time when I had barged in to visit Nicholas, I passed the kitchen and heard my name mentioned. I hid behind the doorjamb, peeking around at them from the darkness.

Walter said, nursing a tumbler of red wine, "Well, she's a saucy kid, eccentric, you know, but awfully well brought up. I mean, I just can't figure them out. The mother hasn't a penny to her name, but you get the feeling she should."

Libby, flushed and bent over a steaming vat of pasta, agreed. "I know what you mean. They're a funny pair, but they both just reek of class." She pulled a strand of linguini from the pot and said, dangling it on a fork, "Taste this and tell me if it's done, sweetums?"

I liked the sound of it—"reeks of class"—and felt a surge of pride. I knew my mother would say they were classist fucks, old-money snobs, but for me it meant that they liked me, that I could keep coming over to be near Nicholas.

Sometimes, when I was with the Marshes, I would secretly imagine I was the daughter they never had. And sometimes I got carried away with my fantasy and would start talking differently, affectedly, trying to imitate Libby's long nasal drawl, and using expressions I had heard Nicholas use, as if they were my own. Fuckwit. Loser. Awesome. Bummer. Neither Nicholas nor his parents seemed to notice, but my mother would, later, when I came home talking that way, and she would sneer and say, "What the hell's got into you?"

IT WAS LATE into the summer. Nights grew darker faster, a prelude to the fall. Libby and Walter sat on their back porch, sipping iced tea and reading, while Nicholas and I brushed Mr. Pleasure on the grass. The air was quiet around us except for a crackling baseball game coming from Walter's transistor radio.

Libby, sprawled out on a deck chair and wearing a broad straw hat, broke the silence. "Jesse's got such classic features. Almost old-fashioned. She looks Italian. Wouldn't you say, Walt?"

Walter, lying stretched out beside his radio with a Boston Red Sox cap balanced over his face, chuckled. "Hmmph. Yes, she does. She reminds me of one of those Byzantine icons, you know, the ones we saw in Venice."

They spoke about me as if I weren't there, as if I were painted on a wall over their head, to be observed and studied, never touched. Nicholas smiled at me from over Mr. Pleasure's back and rolled his eyes.

Every time he looked at me I felt a tingling in the base of my belly and I would catch my breath. I liked to look at him sometimes when he didn't know he was being watched.

Libby sat up and began to brush out her hair, then tied it in a knot so it sat in a messy bun at the nape of her neck. She watched me and Nicholas for a moment with a slight smile. "You kids could be brother and sister. Don't you think they could, Walt? It's uncanny." I grinned back at them, as if I were posing for a camera. She winked at me, then went on, "Oh, by the way, Jess, I saw your mother yesterday, shopping on Green Street with her new friend, that Jim Campbell."

There was a pause, the parents waiting for me to elaborate on my mother's new relationship.

I muttered, "Yeah, they're going out."

Libby smiled. "That's wonderful. I'm glad to see she's not lonely. This can be a lonely town if you don't chew tobacco." She giggled. "Well, tell her we'd love to see more of her. She's very private, isn't she?"

"Oh, yeah, I guess since my dad died she's been that way."

"Of course. It makes perfect sense. Such a tragedy. That must have been so awful for the two of you." She paused, peering at me over the tops of her reading glasses. "Do you look much like your father?"

I glanced up at her. "Oh, kind of, I guess. Except his hair was curlier."

I thought of my father's hair. He had kept his afro short. It wasn't nappy enough to get really big. Cole's hair had been nappier, and she could pick it out into a real afro, the kind that had always eluded my father. My father tried growing it big one year and it looked funny. Someone—I think it was his friend Ronnie—patted it, giggled, and said, "Man, you got a Jewfro!"

"My dad had a Jewfro." I blurted it aloud without really meaning to.

Libby blushed, and said, "Oh, I see. . . ."

I wished I hadn't said it. She was no longer smiling. Walter sat up then and looked at me as well over the tops of his reading glasses.

"Jewfro," Nicholas repeated, clearly liking the sound of it.

Libby said, "So, tell me, Jesse, do you have a lot of family in upstate New York?"

I nodded. "Oh, yeah. I have a grandma. A grandpops. We'll probably go see them at some point. My grandmother makes some killer matzo ball soup. It's delicious."

Libby laughed. "I'm sure it is. What about your mother's parents? Are they still alive?"

I stroked Mr. Pleasure's soft nose. I felt a cool drop of sweat roll down from my underarm. I knew I should change the subject, but couldn't think how. I no longer could remember what my mother and I had agreed on. So I just said, "They're dead. I never met them."

Libby was rifling through the newspapers and seemed distracted as she said, "Oh, yeah? Sorry to hear that. What line of work were they in?"

"Um, my grandfather was a high-school history teacher. And my grandmother was a"—I fumbled—"a beautician."

Libby nodded vaguely. I had lost her attention. She was deep into an article. But Walter was frowning at me, stroking his chin. "Hmm," he said. "That's odd. I thought your mother said her mother was still alive. And I believe she said her father was a businessman. I could have sworn—"

I laughed a loud false laugh. "Oh, yeah, right. He did both. Grandpa ran a business, but he liked to teach too. He was a really talented guy."

Walter and Libby exchanged perplexed looks. I had blown it. My mother was going to kill me, if she didn't go to prison first.

I needed to get out of there, out from under Walter's pale-blue gaze. Nicholas was bent over on the other side of Mr. Pleasure, trying to get a stone out from her hoof, and seemed oblivious to the mounting tension. I said to him, "Nicholas, let's go riding. Anywhere. *Now.*"

WE RODE for more than an hour, until the insides of my thighs were chafed raw. My panic had subsided, and I tried to put the Marshes out of my mind. I'd let my mother use me if she had to. She could say I was still getting over my father's death and had been coping with it by telling lies. She could tell them I was crazy if she needed to.

The sun was setting, suffusing the land in a peach glow, and the heated swelter of the day was turning into something crisper, something fed by shadows. The pain on the insides of my legs had turned numb, but I didn't want to go home just yet, to the kitchen where my mother was seated at the butcher-block table, tutoring a dyslexic boy from another town, and where Jim was building a bookshelf in the living room and sucking on a joint. I wanted to stay here, amid the trails that wound through the forest behind the library.

Nicholas promised me there was an amazing field just beyond the woods. We were mostly quiet for the ride, and I took in the land around me —the patches of moss (a strangely artificial bright green), the tangle of brown limbs and thick brush that surrounded our path and tickled my bare arms, the hum of insects, and the rustling movements of unseen animals. It reminded me of Aurora and brought me back to that place in a flash of memories—the smell of freshly baked bread and soybean stew, the curve of worker women in the garden outside, picking vegetables before dinner, while two female forms—my mother's long golden one and Bernadette's thicker and shorter one—sprawled naked and snoozing on the back porch. Things had been less complicated there. Everyone there had had her own secrets to keep. Secrets were respected.

We were coming to an opening in the cloistered spruce forest, a broad green expanse of land which Nicholas had promised me was his own private spot. There was no one around for miles, but it was a clear day and you could see the town in the distance—the top of the Unitarian church, the billboard of the bitten red apple, the town green with the American flag. From this distance it looked like somewhere I might like to live.

After we had tied the horse to a tree, Nicholas jogged off toward the center of the field and began spinning in circles, his head tilted toward the sky, his arms spread out. I approached him, grinning, my arms crossed over my chest. He was laughing and making himself dizzy, and I just stood with my hand over my mouth, giggling along until he finally fell into the soft earth. He threw an arm over his eyes and lay there, breathing heavily. I sat down next to him and hugged my knees to my chest.

"Hey, Jess?"

"Hmm?"

"Can I ask you a personal question?"

"Uh-huh."

"Have you gotten laid yet?"

"Huh?"

"Are you still a virgin, or what?"

I had done some strange things with Alexis at Aurora. Some nights, on the mattress we shared, I had straddled her in a game we called "honeymoon." She would say, "You be the guy, and I'll be the girl. Pretend you have to hold me down. Pretend you're the boss."

And I would hold her down and rub my body against hers, my face hot and moist in the crook of her neck, while I felt a sharp pleasure that turned to melting between my legs. Afterward I always felt a little bit nauseous and would pretend to be asleep so she wouldn't talk to me. She had wept when my mother and I left Aurora (the only one besides Bernadette who seemed sorry to see us go). She had stood at the edge of the road, watching us as we drove away, and we could see her—a tiny speck of orange hair—for a long time. My mother had glanced at Alexis's diminishing form out of the rearview mirror and said as we sped off, "Jeez, I think that Alexis really fell for you."

"Yeah, I'm a virgin," I said to Nicholas.

"I figured you were," he said. Then blurted out, "I'm not."

I lay down next to him. "I don't believe you." I wondered what girl would sleep with him at an all-boys boarding school. He was only fifteen, after all.

But he insisted, saying, "Well, believe it, Poca. Me and a couple of kids from school went to stay in Amsterdam last Christmas. One of my friends' mothers is this old drunk who lives in this amazing house on the canal there and does a lot of drugs with her German boyfriend. So anyway, hookers are legal there. I mean, you can just buy 'em off a fucking window display. And we went out one night, got totally fucked up on hash, and bought one."

He was quiet.

I was curious. "So, what was it like?"

He said, "Well, kinda weird. She was this fat black chick from Africa or something. They have white girls, too, and some Chinese girls, but they cost more than we had. I heard that black girls were supposed to be good, anyway, so we bought this one. It was all right. We all took turns with her. She just lay there, looking up at us with this blank expression. But if you closed

your eyes you'd kinda forget about it, you could pretend you were somewhere else. She was okay, though. I don't remember her face much."

I turned away from him, onto my side, smelling the damp earth. Something about his story reminded me of Jim, of his talk of Jamaica. Something
about the way Jim talked about his time there always set my teeth on edge.

I ripped up grass in tufts and sprinkled it on the ground before me.
Carmen used to say to my sister that white boys were trouble. She said they
might seem nice at first, but they can never forget your color. It'll come up
sooner or later, and then you'll see that they always saw you as a black
chick—a curiosity, a dabble in difference—nothing more. I thought of Dot
and what my father had said about her, that she liked those ofay boys who just
wanted their thirty minutes of difference.

I felt Nicholas behind me, pulling me over toward him, onto my back,
so that I was looking up at him. I felt dizzy from the glare of the sun behind
him, the loud hum that seemed always to be there, coming from the forest,
like a faint electric buzz, but from some invisible power source. I closed my
eyes, feeling his breath against my face, a pendulum swinging at the base of
my belly, and the prickling sense that something was about to happen.

Then I felt it, wet and grainy against my face, like a dog's kiss, but not a
dog. It was Nicholas's tongue against my cheek, and I opened my eyes to see
him chuckling over me.

"You have a mustache."

"Shut up," I said, rolling over to hide my stinging eyes. I tried to get up,
but he pulled me back down.

He whispered, "I like it. It makes you look dirty, like I could lick you
clean." Then he laughed and rolled away, holding his stomach, while I stood
up and wiped the butt of my jeans.

By the time we got back to his house, it was already five o'clock. No cars
were parked out front. The house stood empty.

"Well, I guess I better get going—" I started to say.

He shook his head and made a face. "Aw, come on, Jess. Why don't you
come up and see my old riding trophies? Remember I was gonna show you
them? I got them out of the attic." He paused, then smiled crookedly. "Don't
worry. I'm not gonna bite."

I nodded, and my own voice surprised me. It sounded quick and unsure.
"Okay. I guess so. I'll come up for a while. That would be cool."

His room smelled sweet and mysterious, and his bedsheets were piled into the shape of a body. I had never been up to his room before. We had kept our relationship confined to the stable or the television room. I sat perched on the edge of his bed, while he threw laundry into a closet hamper. He seemed slightly embarrassed to have me there.

I picked up a comic book beside his bed, *Tintin in the Congo,* and began to flip through it. He sat at his desk across from me, strumming the same notes over and over again on a guitar. The sun was going down outside, and I could faintly hear Pudd'nhead barking in the woods behind the house.

I recognized the tune Nicholas played as a Fleetwood Mac song, something from my mother's music collection. He hummed gently to himself, curled over the instrument so that his hair covered his face. I pretended to read but really watched him.

Finally he looked up at me and asked, "Do your mom and Jim smoke pot?"

"Yeah, of course."

He laughed. "Shit. That's awesome. Your mom's pretty cool. You're lucky. My parents are old fogies. Tight asses. I can't wait to get away from them."

He pulled out a plastic baggie with weed in it and said, "Wanna join me?"

Though my mother and her friends had been smoking pot around me since I was little, I had never gotten high before. My mother wouldn't have let me, and besides, it had always seemed boring—a grown-up game, like drinking—and hadn't interested me. But now, looking at Nicholas's hands, I said sure, as if I had done it before.

Nicholas sat deep in concentration, methodically crumbling the leaves into the paper, then rolling it, licking it.

He lit the joint, taking a long puff. Then he handed it to me, saying in a raspy voice, "Go 'head."

I did, and coughed. He laughed and came to sit beside me on the bed, showing me how to do it better. I felt my head grow lighter after the second puff and wanted more.

When we were done with the joint, Nicholas began to tickle me under my arms and on my stomach, and I shrieked uncontrollably, flailing around wildly on his bed. Before I knew it, he was straddling me, his knees pinning my arms down. I panted beneath him, still giggling from the tickle attack. But he had stopped smiling.

"Jess, how old are you, again?"

"Going on fourteen." As I said it, I reasoned that it wasn't exactly a lie. I was going on fourteen, only next year instead of this one. Besides, we had discussed my age once before, and if he didn't remember, it was his fault.

"That's pretty old," he said, swaying slightly from side to side. He looked dizzy, like he might topple over at any minute. He had smoked most of the joint.

He slid down so that he was lying on top of me. He was heavier than I thought he'd be. He kissed me quickly on the lips, tentatively. "Is this okay?"

I didn't answer. I was thinking about Alexis. Once I had bitten her neck so hard that there was a mark in the morning. When her mother asked her where it came from, she told her I had pinched her during a game of Chinese torture.

Nicholas kissed me again, wetter this time, probing my mouth with his tongue. His mouth tasted of cigarettes. He pulled out my ponytail rather roughly and held a tuft of my hair in his hand. He ground his pelvis into mine and slid a cold hand under my T-shirt. I jumped at his touch on my nipples.

We necked for a while, him rubbing my flat chest and pressing his groin against me, while I played with his hair and kissed him back and tried to feel something. It was difficult. With Alexis I had always been the one on top, the one doing the groping and the grinding, the one doing what Nicholas was doing. I wasn't sure how to act now that I was on the bottom. After a few minutes, he took my hand and gently led it toward his shorts.

"Touch me," he whispered in my ear.

It was warm and hard and soft all at once, and he guided my hand over it. The tip was moist. I felt a slight tingling between my legs, the kind I had felt with Alexis. His breath was coming out quicker, and his hand guided my hand quicker and quicker over his penis. Then he put his hand behind my head and began to push it down, in the direction of his crotch. I heard him whisper, "Suck me, Poca."

I panicked and jerked out of his grip.

He closed his eyes and furrowed his brow, making a pained expression. He said in a tight voice, "You want to stop?"

I liked kissing him. But touching him felt too real, proof that the game had gone too far. It wasn't Birdie, but Jesse, who lay beneath him, who held him in her hand, who made his eyes turn all glassy and his breath come out uneven. I nodded that yes, I wanted to stop. I wondered if he'd think I was a baby, or a crazy dyke, as my mother had put it about the women of Aurora. I wondered if he'd ever kiss me again.

But then he smiled crookedly, back to his old self. He tweaked my nose. "That's cool. Let's just hang out, Poca." He wasn't mad at all, and his features looked pretty. Watching him, I felt a warm flush on the surface of my skin. I wondered if I was in love.

He rolled off of me.

"You kiss pretty good, Jess. Where'd you learn to do that?"

I picked up the *Tintin* comic that had fallen on the floor, and hid my face behind it as I said, "With this friend of mine, Alex. We used to make out all the time."

"Never went all the way, though?"

"Nah. I left town before it went that far." I wondered, as I said it, if it was possible for two girls to go all the way.

He sat up and rubbed his eyes roughly, as if trying to stay awake. "Hey, you want some more weed? My folks aren't back yet."

I felt pretty high already, but said, "Yeah, sure."

We smoked a whole half of another joint, and soon we were laughing over the pictures in *Tintin,* tears streaming down our cheeks. The pictures were horrible, making the Congolese into hideous caricatures, but I laughed anyway at the absurdity of it.

"They've made us look like animals," I said, holding my belly, my vision blurred by the tears of laughter. I cut up again, pressing my wet face into his sheets. They smelled good, and I breathed in.

He giggled into his hand and said, "You said 'us.' You said it made *us* look like animals." The hilarity of my statement sent him into hysterics, and he rolled over, silently quaking beside me. Finally he looked at me sideways through his slittish red eyes. "Shit, maybe you could be colored in the right light. Better stay out of the sun."

I felt a constriction in my chest as he spoke, and turned onto my stomach, hiding my face into his dingy gray pillow. It didn't smell so good all of a sudden.

He lit up again and took a long toke of the joint. He held his breath as he said in a raspy voice, "All right. Get this one. I heard it at school last year. When they're born, what's printed on the inside of every black baby's lip?" He was holding his breath, sucking in deeply to get more out of the hit.

I didn't say anything. I didn't think I could talk.

He let his breath out finally, and I heard him say, " 'Inflate to five thousand.' "

He didn't laugh, just hawked spit loudly and sat up quickly to spit it out the window. "Shit, this stuff leaves a taste in your mouth, huh?"

My breathing was coming out funny, in irregular wheezes, like my father's when he had an asthma attack. He used to make me walk on his back at moments like that, "to push the air out." Cole was too big and too heavy to do it. At the time I was the perfect weight. It must have made a strange picture. My father, all six feet of him, lying flat on his stomach across the linoleum kitchen floor, while I did a kind of cake-walk up and down his spine. I felt useful then, listening to the air come out of his chest, the relief in his voice when he hugged me to him afterward, saying, "You saved my life again, Doctor Birdie." It was a little routine with us. And I would answer, "Anytime, Professor Lee." I felt important, as if only my body could give him air at those moments. I would be too heavy to do it anymore, and I wished I had my own little seven-year-old girl right then to walk up and down my spine and push the air out.

"You all right, Jesse James?" Nicholas said. "Why you breathing so funny?"

I peeked up at him. He smiled slightly, and pushed some hair out of my face. "I was just kidding about you looking colored. I mean, you don't look it at all. You're—" He paused, then turned his face away as he said, "You're pretty. You're gonna look really hot in a few years. I mean it."

His compliment stung, and I didn't say anything, just stared at him blankly. It reminded me of my grandmother, when she would stroke my hair and say what a "lovely child" I was. Even then, her compliments had struck me as sinister, though I hadn't known why at the time. I had known only that Cole was the girl I wanted to look like, Dot was the woman I wanted to look like, and if my grandmother couldn't see their beauty, she must be blind.

I wanted to be outside, near Mr. Pleasure, where I could breathe. Before Nicholas's jokes, I had believed I was falling in love. Now the feeling in my chest—the dropping—had turned to a kind of soreness. He looked stupid all of a sudden, like a golden retriever, his blue eyes vacant and naïve, a boy who had been around the world but at the same time had been nowhere. I felt older than him, though I was only twelve.

Just then I heard a car come rolling over gravel into the driveway.

"Fuck," Nicholas said under his breath.

I wheezed, still feeling high and slightly paranoid from the weed. "I better go. They're gonna find me in here and tell my mom."

He put a finger to my lips and said, "Shhh. Just calm down. Who cares? Your mother won't give a shit. She smokes all the time herself. Just wait here for a little while, until you come down a little. Then I'll walk you home."

We stayed on his bed, beside each other, both of us silent and looking at his ceiling, where there were glow-in-the-dark constellations. In the afternoon light they were just pale-green stickers.

Finally Nicholas's voice cut into my thoughts. "What are you thinking about?"

I snapped out of it. "Nothing. Just wondering where he is."

"Where who is?"

"My father."

He shrugged. "In heaven, I guess. If you believe in heaven."

I laughed. "Yeah, in heaven. I bet it looks like Brazil. Lots of beaches and pretty women in tiny bikinis."

"Huh?" he said, turning toward me.

I turned my face away from him so he couldn't see my expression. "Never mind."

He seemed to accept my answer and threw his arm back over his eyes. I spied on him like that. Only his mouth and the tip of his nose showed from under his arm, flung like a blindfold. His arm was flecked with golden hairs, and his skin had browned from the summer rays, so we were almost the same color. His mother was right. We could have been brother and sister.

After a while it seemed he had fallen asleep. His mouth went slack, and his breathing came louder, more regulated. My own breathing had stabilized, my lungs had opened up, but the room felt small and cramped all the same.

I said softly to the ceiling, "Can I tell you a secret?"

He shifted beside me, making a soft noise in the back of his throat, like a word, but something untranslated from its dream meaning.

I was trembling and I held the Star of David to keep my fingers steady as I said, "I'm not who I say I am. I'm someone else. I mean, I guess what I'm saying is, this isn't really happening to me. The Jewish thing. It's a lie. It's this story we tell to people because if they knew the truth they might figure out who I was, who my mother really was—"

He sighed heavily and turned toward me, throwing his heavy arm across my chest, nuzzling his face close to my neck, so that I could feel his breath against my cheek. It smelled sweet and smoky from the pot.

"Bridge suppa melting for—" he murmured, his eyes still closed.

I said, "Huh?"

"Pumkin cellar—" he said.

Then he was snoring, deeply gone somewhere else, where *Bridge suppa melting for* made sense.

I gently pushed his arm off of me and slid off the bed.

I tiptoed down the stairs. Libby and Walter were out on the back porch. There was a chance I'd be able to slip past them unseen. They both held tumblers of some brown liquor that looked like Scotch. They had their backs to the house. The glass sliding door was open.

When I reached the bottom of the stairs, I heard Libby say, "Why would Sheila need to hide anything from us? I'm sure it's Jesse who's telling the fibs, Walt. Kids do that."

I froze where I stood against the wall. I was still reeling from the joints we had smoked, and the hallway's hardwood floor appeared angled, like a funhouse room.

"Perhaps," Walter replied. "But it did give me the creeps to hear two completely different family histories like that. We never did check references from Sheila. You just took one look at her and said she was our kind of person."

"Oh, Jesus, now you're going to blame me," Libby groaned. "You said the same thing. You said, 'She couldn't be more perfect.' And she is. She pays her rent on time and adds a little color and culture to this hideous little town. And if she has some skeletons in her closet, so be it. I mean, you don't go around announcing that your aunt is a lesbian dog trainer, do you, now?" She paused, and I could hear the ice clinking around in her glass. "Hell, maybe the grandparents are shady, and they're simply embarrassed to tell us the truth. Or maybe Jesse just doesn't know her grandparents. Maybe Sheila was disowned for marrying a Jew."

Walter shook his head. "I don't know, something just doesn't feel right." He took a gulp from his glass. "Did you take the salmon out to thaw?"

"Christ, you've asked me that five times already," Libby hissed. Then the two began to bicker about how they would cook the salmon, in the broiler or on the grill.

I tiptoed to the front door and slipped out, making sure not to slam the screen behind me. Then I took off, racing through the woods as if there were dogs at my heels.

ashes and elbow grease

I avoided the Marshes for several weeks. Instead, I reverted to childish games, lolling around the house, cheating on myself at endless games of solitaire, and watching soap operas with a tub of ice cream on my lap. My mother took notice and seemed concerned that I wasn't friends with Nicholas anymore. I had been putting off telling her about my screwup with the grandparent story. I feared she might do something crazy, like pack us up in the van in the middle of the night and move us to a roadside motel, or find some way to intimidate the Marshes into silence. I also knew it was just a matter of time before I had to tell her.

I finally got up the nerve while I stood on my head on the lawn one afternoon. It was two weeks after the incident. The coast was clear to talk. Jim had taken his Buick into town to get an oil change. He wouldn't be back for at least an hour. My mother had just come home from the professor's office and had stripped out of her denim skirt and clogs and into her Tai Chi uniform. She stood poised a few feet away in a frozen karate chop.

"Mum, just in case somebody asks, what should I tell them about my grandparents?"

She didn't move an inch from her position as she spoke: "I thought we discussed this. Your grandparents on David's side are dead. They kicked the bucket years ago. They were old Zionists. You know, back-to-Israel types, whom David rebelled against by marrying me. And my parents are still alive. My father worked as an executive at a textile company. Grandma was a housewife." She moved slowly, gracefully, into another position. Then added, "Keep it simple."

The upside-down world was making me nauseous, and my head was beginning to get sore, so I let my body fall onto the soft earth.

"Why?" my mother asked then, moving rather abruptly out of her Tai Chi position. She turned to face me. "Did somebody bring it up?"

I stood and looked at my big grubby sneakers. In a guilty mumble, I told her then what had happened at the Marshes'.

When I was finished, I braced myself for her whirlwind response. But she just sighed. "Shit. It's my fault. I should have trained you better. I just knew you were getting too cozy over there."

I looked up at her. She seemed only slightly anxious. Her mouth was fixed into a little point, but basically she was under control. She raked a hand through her hair. "Well, it's not the end of the world. I'll just have to do some damage control."

She bit her nails, and I could see her mind clicking away. After a moment she snapped her fingers. She said that if they asked, she'd simply explain that I liked to fantasize about my Jewish grandparents because they had rejected me while they were alive. "They hadn't wanted David to marry a Gentile, and you spent your childhood cut off from them. Now that they're dead, you've created this fiction. And as for my parents. Hmm. I'll say they did the same thing. They were old anti-Semites who also rejected you, and you built up all these fantasies about them. Got it?"

I nodded, impressed by how quickly she had thought up a ruse. But still it struck me that she didn't seem as worried as I had been. In fact, she seemed fairly jovial about the whole thing. Once upon the time this would have been enough for us to disappear.

She started to go to the house, but stopped and turned toward me. She smiled slightly. "I told you they were out to get me."

I continued to keep my distance from the Marshes until a few days later, when Jim sent me over there to get some lighter fluid. My mother wasn't home to stop me. She was at the professor's office. He was almost finished with his research, and she was working long hours, transcribing taped interviews into a computer in his office. It was the end of August, and I figured

Nicholas was getting ready to go to Exeter. I had hoped to forget him, but when Jim gave me an excuse to go across the woods, I skipped the whole way, slapping the mosquitoes on my arms and legs and trying to suppress a pang of excitement at the thought of seeing him again.

I let myself in the front door. It was cool and dark inside, and there was a faint smell of burning sugar. It was strange to me how their house never seemed to get hot like the rest of the world, even on the most simmering summer days. It always felt damp and cloistered, hidden from even the sun.

I found Libby in the kitchen, reading a cookbook while she pared an apple for baking. The news crackled from the radio on the windowsill. She looked at me over the tops of her glasses.

"Jesse, darling! We haven't seen you in ages."

I stood in the doorway, shy suddenly. "Jim sent me over. Do you have any lighter fluid we can borrow?"

"Sure, sweetie. Let me go get it out in the garage. Nicky's outside. He's got a few friends here from school. He's leaving soon, you know."

I heard faint laughter. It came from the backyard.

Libby said, "Why don't you go say hi? I'll get the lighter fluid for you."

I bit my lip. I didn't want to see him suddenly. I didn't want to meet his friends. Libby frowned, sensing my hesitation, and shoed me out with her arm. "Oh, don't be silly. Go! He'll be thrilled to see you."

Out on the porch, the sunlight sparkled against the light beech wood. There was a bowl of grapes and a couple of open cans of Coke with flies sitting on the rims. Playing cards were sprinkled across the deck from some abandoned game, and Nicholas's stereo played Cat Stevens from his second-story window onto the lawn below. On the grass, Nicholas was playing a lazy game of Frisbee with a boy and a girl I had never seen before. None of them noticed me standing there. Nicholas had his shirt off and a bandanna tied around his head. He had his back to me.

I approached them with my arms crossed, shivering, though it was warm and there wasn't even a breeze. I could see that the other boy had beady eyes and a weak chin and wore a T-shirt that said "Choate" across the front. The girl was pretty, though, in a blond sort of way. She wore a white halter top and cutoff shorts with frayed threads that brushed her thighs. She had small breasts and long, gazelle limbs. As I got nearer I could see that her body was coated in a kind of golden down that glittered under the sun. I wished I had dressed better. I wore dirt-stained dungarees, my old pink Converse high-tops, and a yellow T-shirt with the word "Jujubes" across the front that I'd found in a pile at the Salvation Army a year before.

"Hey, you," I said, and Nicholas whipped around, letting the Frisbee sail past him.

He grinned, and all my anxiety floated away. "Pocahontas! Where've you been?"

He loped toward me. His chest was all burned in splotches from the sun. He was blushing, and smiling a little bashfully, as if he had been caught in some shameful act.

Behind him the girl had begun a series of cartwheels across the lawn, while the other boy had picked up the Frisbee and was throwing it to Pudd'nhead, who chased it with his tongue slapping against the wind.

Nicholas turned to his friends and called out, "Justin, Piper, this is Jesse." Then back to me, he muttered, "They go to my school."

The girl, Piper, sidled up to me, smiling. She said in a scratchy voice, "Oh, you're the little mystery girl Nick told us about. He said your mom's really cool."

I kicked my sneaker into the grass and grunted, "Yeah, I guess." She put her hand on Nicholas's shoulder and rested one leg against the other like a stork. Then whispered to him, eyeing me up and down, "Oh my God. She's so skinny." Then louder to me: "You're so skinny. I hate you!"

Nicholas rolled his eyes at me, but I could see he found her amusing.

She leaned forward then, her hand outstretched toward my neck, and I jerked backward. But she was only trying to touch my Star of David. As she held it, her fingers tickled my skin, and I was afraid she'd see where the star had left a green tinge to my skin. But she didn't seem to notice and wistfully said only, "My best friend, Abbie, is Jewish. I went to her bar mitzvah last year."

I corrected her: "Bat mitzvah."

My mother had explained the difference to me one night while we drove through the darkness. She had said that I would never have a bat mitzvah, since I wasn't a practicing Jew. Just a cultural one.

Piper blushed slightly. "Whatever."

I ignored her and turned to Nicholas. "Well, I was just going to borrow some lighter fluid from your mom."

He frowned and scrutinized my face, then said: "I'll only be around for a couple more days. Come see me before I go, okay?"

I nodded, but I knew I wouldn't. I felt slightly dizzy, a tingling all over the surface of my skin. The girl had moved behind Nicholas now and had slipped her arms around his waist. "Nicky," she whined, "you're such a liar. You said we were gonna get to take the horses on a trail ride. You promised."

He blushed as she slapped her hands in a drumbeat against his flat belly.

I heard Libby shouting to me from the porch, "Jess, doll, I have your lighter fluid."

As I turned and walked away, I heard the girl, Piper, say to Nicholas: "She's adorable. I think she has a crush on you."

THE NIGHT BEFORE SCHOOL was to begin, I lay twisted in the sheets, sweating, trying to control the constriction in my lungs. The clock glowed 2:45 A.M. There were only five hours left before my first day of school, and I wished Nicholas had given me some secret blueprint for surviving this place. I hadn't gone to visit him before he left, but he had come to see me, to say good-bye. He had found me in the barn picking a rock out of Mr. Pleasure's hoof. The rain made a peaceful pattering noise against the barn. I had felt him behind me and turned to see him leaning against the stable door. Beyond him the clouds hovered close to the earth, like a wet blanket, intensifying the sweet, musty horse smell of the stable.

We didn't talk long. Just a few minutes of quiet, shy banter. He had tugged at my braid before he left, and said, "Little Miss Poca. You'll be fine." He had paused before adding, "Just don't get too comfortable." Then he had turned and jogged away with his head bowed down against the rain, until he was swallowed by the moist tangle of ash trees.

It would be my first time in a real school since Nkrumah, and I expected the worst. I knew my reading and writing skills were probably okay, but I had essentially missed four years of math and science. Even at Nkrumah I had been struggling to keep up.

A noise came from the hallway. The door cracked open, and a blade of yellow light cut through the shadows of my room. I sat up, startled, and my mother peeked in, then made her way across the darkness of my room, wearing a thin T-shirt and Jim's boxer shorts.

She sat down on the edge of my bed and held a cool hand against my forehead. She looked pretty in the half-light, and it struck me that the FBI might not even recognize this tall, slender, and elegant woman with the copper hair and the tortoise-shell glasses.

She sighed as she looked down on me, and I could see that one of her moods had crept up on her. It was in her eyes. The flicker of sadness, memory, paranoia, had spread and engulfed her tonight.

"Can't sleep either?"

I shook my head.

"Scoot," she said.

I moved over toward the wall. She slipped under the covers beside me and hugged herself, staring up at the ceiling.

I asked her where Jim was.

"In my bed." She paused, then frowned at me. "I woke up from a nightmare and I didn't remember who he was. I got scared. I mean, for a full minute or so I just couldn't place where I was or who this big white man in my bed was. And when I remembered it didn't matter—because I started thinking all these crazy thoughts about him, you know. Wondering if maybe you were right."

She turned toward me, onto her side, and ran a finger across my eyebrow. She said so quietly that I had to strain to hear: "You've got to be careful at this new school tomorrow. Kids ask a lot of questions, and kids don't keep secrets. I'm happy here, babe. I don't want to have to leave town again. I'm tired. I need a break from all the running. So right now, I want you to promise me to keep it quiet no matter how safe anyone seems. Got it?"

I closed my eyes, feeling the sparks of some new emotion. I dug my fingernails into the sheets and said: "Okay, Mum. I got it. I'm the daughter of a dead Jewish intellectual. My name's Jesse Goldman. I never heard of anyone called Deck or Cole Lee, and we never lived in Boston and you never—"

I felt her hand slap my mouth, clamping it tight. A stinging on my lips. I wondered if there'd be a mark in the morning. I had said the names. She hoisted herself up onto one arm so she was looking down at me, her red hair hanging over us like a theater curtain. I stared up at her, trying to breathe out of my nose.

Her eyes seemed to flow into her face. Tears. Her breath smelled faintly of beer as she hissed into my ear: "Imagine if Cole had come with us. Imagine her in this town. She would have been miserable. That fucks up a kid. Being the only one. A token. I've seen it happen." She had never said this before, had never imagined what it might have been like with Cole with us. Her grip loosened, and I could breathe a little bit through my mouth.

I pulled my face out from under her hand and panted freely, wiping my mouth.

She went on talking in a quick breathless voice, as if she were trying to convince herself and not me: "I think she's happy wherever she is. Your father was a good father, no matter what kind of husband he was. He adored her more than anything. Always did, from the day she was born. And as much as Carmen could be a bitch, she loved Cole too. They're taking good care of her. I just know it—"

"Yeah, right. That's what you've been saying for four years."

She leaned in closer to me. "Listen, don't think a day goes by when I don't agonize about this. About what's happened. But if anyone finds out the truth, you're going to wish you were back here. You're going to wish you were still Jesse Goldman. I'll be sent away—*for life*—and you'll end up in foster care somewhere."

"Yeah? Well maybe that would be better. Maybe I'd get adopted by a normal family and I wouldn't have to pretend anymore."

She shook her head. I had hoped to hurt her, but she only laughed a little and said, "You think anyone's gonna adopt a kid as old as you? And a half-black twelve-year-old, at that? Not on your life, kiddo. You'll be shuttled around for years, until you're old enough to be considered an adult. Then you can come visit me in jail. And by then I'll be a four-hundred-pound dyke with a 'Mommy' tattoo."

She started to giggle, and I joined in, despite my wish to stay angry. I had an image of her in jail, her hair cropped close to her scalp, a whale of flesh in zebra-striped jail costume. It had hit us at the same moment, and our bodies shook silently against each other as tears ran down my cheeks and into my mouth. It struck me that we hadn't laughed this way together since we had arrived in New Hampshire.

I heard the sound of a toilet being flushed. We both caught our breaths.

A moment later, a shadow appeared at the door. A man, his silver hair shimmering. Jim. He pushed open the door to my room.

"What's going on in here?" he whispered. "Having a little middle-of-the-night pow-wow?"

My mother sat up. I heard anxiety in her voice. "Yeah, sweetie. Jess couldn't sleep. First-day-of-school jitters. I was trying to convince her that she'll be fine tomorrow."

Jim smiled at me, squinting into the darkness of my room. "Aw, Jess. I know how you feel. I remember my first day at a new school when I was about your age. It can be hell. Waddaya say I make you some cocoa? Might help you sleep?"

I nodded, unable, really, to speak.

He winked at the two of us. "You two look beautiful in the moonlight. Sheila, baby, want some cocoa too?"

She started to move out of the bed. "Sure, I'll come down and help you in a sec."

He nodded, pausing for a moment. As he turned to go, he looked back over his shoulder at us, and I caught a flash of something on his face: the expression of somebody who has stumbled upon two strangers in the act of something sordid.

When he was out of sight and hearing range, my mother turned to me and said, "Okay, Jess. Remember what I said. At school, when they ask you where you're from——"

I cut her off. "Are you sure about him?" My eyes were on the door.

She paused, and followed my eyes toward the light of the hall. Then she said: "Yeah, I'm pretty sure. I mean, of course I am. Jim's cool."

Then she was up and gone, toward the kitchen, to help him make cocoa.

THEY WORE ALLIGATOR SHIRTS and chinos and Top-Siders without socks. Their hair hung ragged as if chewed around their faces. The students at the school were townies, born and raised, eventually married and mated to one another, in this same small town. My mother said their parents were the "workers of the world." Jim said they were "decent country folk."

But neither Jim nor my mother ever made friends with any of the parents, just looked upon the townspeople from an admiring distance.

My mother and I watched them in silence from our van. Finally my mother said, "You'll be fine. You'll make plenty of friends in no time at all."

The engine was running and the windows were sealed tight, but it was freezing inside nonetheless. The weather had turned a sharp seasonal corner, and I rubbed my hands together, feeling the sting of early morning. The heating system in our van was either broken or had never existed, so my mother carried around a ratty afghan for warmth. I had it on my lap, but it wasn't doing much good.

I glanced at my mother. The look I had seen in her eyes the night before, the fear and panic, had disappeared, and now she dug around in her jeans pocket for lunch money for me and sang under her breath to the music on the radio.

After Jim had fixed us both our cocoa, he and my mother had curled up on the couch together, while I had pattered up to my room to drink mine in bed. Later in the morning, I had woken up with a dry throat, my lips parched and cracked. I had tried to drink what was left in the mug beside my bed, but it was only the muddy dregs of the cocoa from the night before, so sweet and thick and cold that I gagged.

My mother handed me two crumpled bills and some change. She paused, looking at me, then licked her finger and smoothed down my cowlick. "Buck up, Jesse Besse. These kids have nothing on you. You're a *survivor.*"

Then the look came over her face—the look of the before, the forgotten, the better-left-unsaid. "Think about Cole. She would want you to be brave."

Her words about Cole made me shiver, and I said, "You act like she's dead. You talk about her as if she's gone for good."

She started to say something: "Oh, mush . . ." Somewhere along the way she had shortened "meshuggana" to "mush."

I didn't let her finish. I was out the door, stepping down from the van into the moist morning light, and striding toward the school, blending into the stream of bodies that flooded through the heavy red doors.

———

I DIDN'T KNOW HOW completely cut off I'd been until I reentered the world that morning. I wandered through the locker room, staring in a kind of dazed stupor at the townie girls clustered around one another like football players in a huddle, planning their next move. They were the ones I had run into at the chili-dog stand over the summer, the ones who had called me a zoo animal, and watching them, I felt my face burn. I saw in their reflections the girl I failed to be, someone ordinary and alive and public, girls with one face, one name, one life. Wandering through them, I felt a yearning that surprised me. Something I hadn't felt at Aurora. A yearning to belong to something ordinary, the same way I had felt at Nkrumah. I looked at these girls with their clownish makeup, their brassy bubble-gum faces, and felt an urge to be one of them. I saw myself from above that first day, saw with a rush of embarrassment what a strange creature I really was: a pitiful creature called Jesse for lack of a better name; a girl who dressed in oversized tomboy clothes, her hair in twin braids, who tapped her fingers against her lips in a rhythmic pattern, a nervous habit that looked like some religious tick. She looked old-fashioned to me. Like someone who has been kept in a box, missed a century, collected dust.

At Aurora, when I was with Alexis, everything beyond us became the generic outside. And we had become the inside, where I had wanted to be. With her, at Aurora, it had been okay to be nobody, to be nameless, just a blur girl who roamed the hallways of that dank farmhouse playing make-believe, because there everybody had been playing make-believe. Everything had seemed secret and intimate and playful. Here, in this locker room, with the smell of dirty sneakers, the violent clang of metal, the siren bell that rang every hour to announce the next period, and the glare of the fluorescent lights overhead, everything seemed suddenly real to me, utterly public, and I yearned to be a part of it. The visible world.

I WENT INTO the girls' room on my third day of school, only to find the cluster of girls from the summer standing by the open window, blowing smoke rings out into the cold air. They checked me out from head to toe. The blond girl had been the boldest, and I could see from her posture that she was the leader. I ignored them and went to pee. As I sat reading the graffiti on the wall of the bathroom stall, I heard them whispering.

"She's that weird chick from the summer."

"Yeah, the fuckin' freakazoid."

"Where's she from?"

"Fuck if I know. She looks like she's from another planet. Why don't you ask her?"

"I heard she lives with her mom on the Marsh land. Where that cutie Nick Marsh lives. I heard someone saw them hanging out over the summer."

When I came out to wash my hands, they all were staring at me with pinched smiles.

It was the blond leader of the pack who spoke first.

"You know Nick Marsh?"

I turned to them, leaning back against he sink. "Yeah, I live over on his land. Me and Nick are friends," I said. They had big hair and frosted lipstick, and one of them—a pudgy one—held a can of diet cola in her hand, which she kept sipping nervously while she eyed me up and down. I added, using some lingo I had picked up at Aurora, "We smoked together, you know, Maui Wowie."

I turned back to the mirror and saw the girls exchange impressed glances. One of them said, "Nick Marsh is fuckin' hot. Totally." The blond girl came up behind me. She wore her hair in stiff layers, and a baseball shirt with an iron-on unicorn emblem across the front. She inhaled deeply on her cigarette, watching me in the mirror through her smoke, then said, "So, what kinda music do you listen to?"

Besides my mother's folk and country-western, the last group I had really loved on my own was Earth, Wind, and Fire. I was glad I had befriended Nicholas over the summer. I repeated some of the groups he had played for me: "J. Geils Band. Kim Carnes. Hall and Oates. You know. Rock."

The girl smiled and said, "I'm Mona. What's your name?"

I told her I was Jesse. I had said the name so many times before, but this time it felt more significant.

Mona glanced back at the girls. "Jesse's an autumn. Don't you think?"

They nodded vigorously. I didn't know what she was talking about.

"An autumn what?"

"That's your season. It tells you what colors look good on you and what don't. You know. I'm a winter. Dawn's a summer. I'll show you sometime. My mom's got a book at home."

I was surprised at how easily they had let me in, and stumbled after them for the rest of the day in a pleasant state of shock. I kept reminding myself that I was pretending, that they didn't know the real me, that this was all part of the game. But I had forgotten the pleasure of sitting around a cafeteria table with a huddle of gossipy girls, popping french fries in my mouth and gabbing about who was who, what was what. There was something safe about it. It reminded me of being with my sister and Maria and Cherise and Cathy. I welcomed the company, moved with it, forward, down the corridor.

IT WAS LATER that same afternoon that I sat beside Mona on the curb, watching our classmates mill around us. I was waiting for Jim to pick me up. My mother couldn't come. She had to be at the university for the afternoon, helping her sociologist enter data on police bonding. So Jim had said he would pick me up and he seemed excited about it, excited to have a chance to act like father and daughter. There was a school bus in front of us, and I watched the students who were lined up to get on. A redheaded boy kept snapping a girl's bra and then running away before she could see who had done it. A fat boy with a crew cut held a smaller boy in a headlock, while the smaller boy's face turned redder and redder from lack of oxygen.

Mona pointed at them and whispered their faults. "She's a total bitch. A man stealer. And watch out for him. Pervert. He tried to finger fuck me last year."

I watched the kids, their faces settling behind the school-bus window. One face caught my eye, and I breathed in sharply. It was a girl I hadn't seen before today. My books tumbled out of my hand onto the pavement, and I heard Mona say distantly, "What's your problem?" I didn't answer. I was staring too hard at the face behind the window.

The girl was black like me—half, that is. I could spot another one immediately. But her blackness was visible. Deep-set eyes, caramel complexion. She looked tired, with dark bruises of exhaustion around her eyes. Her features were a jumble of tribes and unplanned unions—full lips, a tangle of half-nappy black curls that she wore pulled away from her face with a headband. She was staring rather languidly out the window, at nothing, but she must have felt my gaze on her because she looked down at me, abruptly, meeting my eyes.

She blinked, bored, it seemed, by what she saw on my face, then sighed and put her head in her hand and closed her eyes as if to take a nap.

Mona followed my eyes to the girl's face and said, "Oh, yeah, that's Samantha. She just moved here last year from Maine. She's disgusting. We call her 'Wilona,' you know, like the lady on 'Good Times.' The boys call her 'Brown Cow.' She's got tits already. She's on the baton squad. Fucking bitch. I was supposed to make it."

Jim's car pulled up just then, and I stood abruptly. "I gotta go."

She looked at Jim, who was waving wildly in my direction. "That your dad?"

I shook my head. "Naw, he's just my mom's boyfriend. See ya." Then I was jogging toward his car, trying not to cry, while my book bag banged heavily at my side.

Inside, Jim's car was comfortable, the way American cars are, with big bucket seats and the smell of cigarette smoke embedded into leather. The car didn't really suit Jim. It seemed governmental, sterile except for the red, gold, and green beads he had hung from the rearview mirror.

"Hey there, Jess," he said, starting up the engine. It purred, unlike my father's old clunker, which had spat and sputtered and coughed before going anywhere.

"Looks like you got a new buddy there."

I didn't answer.

As we stopped at the red light beside the school bus, I craned my head up at the windows, where the faces sat in a row like stuffed animals at a shooting gallery. A couple of boys saw me staring at them from the car below, and one of them put his lips against the glass and blew so that his mouth and cheeks opened up with air. He looked like some strange form of fish in a bowl. Some other kids waved and laughed. I ignored them and searched the windows until I saw the girl again. She was looking down at me with an expression I couldn't read.

Our car moved forward, ahead of the bus, and we turned off onto a side street toward home. Jim was humming to the radio. *If you like piña coladas, and getting caught in the rain . . .* He turned to me and ruffled my hair. "Cat got your tongue, kiddo?"

I shook my head. I was trembling and digging my nails, hard, into the sides of my blue jeans. Jim didn't seem to notice and began to sing louder, with real passion, carried away by the song. *If you like making love at midnight, in the dunes of the Cape, then you're the one that I've looked for, so come with me, and we'll escape . . .*

HER NAME WAS Samantha Taper. She was in the eighth grade, too. She had only one friend—a tiny white girl named Nora. Nora was the town genius, a prodigy who had already skipped two grades and was constantly away on math tournaments, leaving Samantha to wander the halls and cafeteria alone. The two of them were inseparable when Nora was around. Visually, they were an odd pair—a tiny eleven-year-old genius with Coke-bottle glasses and a cowlick in the back of her wispy blond hair, and a thirteen-year-old black girl who walked unusually upright because, as I would find out, she had scoliosis and had to wear a back brace.

As I became closer to Mona and her gang over the next few weeks, details about Samantha Taper trickled down to me, and I held on to those facts, turning them over and over again in my mind, as if they would hold clues to my own disappearance. She was adopted. Only three days after her birth, she had been left on the steps of a church with a note stating her name and birthday. She had been adopted by a Quaker couple who had been unable to bear children. Nobody, not even her adoptive parents, knew the truth of Samantha's origins. They could only imagine.

She was smart. Not as smart as Nora, but she had made it into all the advanced classes. Her main forte was baton twirling. She was a master at it and had beaten Mona out of the prized baton-squad spot. She carried her baton—a silver rod decorated with red, white, and blue tape—at her side wherever she went, like a weapon.

I didn't mention Samantha to my mother. I told her about the other kids, about the teachers, about the books I was reading, but I left Samantha out of the equation. I did ask my mother and Jim one night over dinner what scoliosis was. Jim, who loved facts, loved being right, answered excitedly, "It's curvature of the spine. Common among girls your age. Why do you ask?" I told them that a girl in my class had it, and they accepted that answer, which was true.

I didn't talk about Samantha, and I didn't speak to her, either, but I did watch her with a wary fascination, glancing over my shoulder at her in the hallway, never stopping to look too closely, rubbernecking, the way one slows to look back at a freeway accident.

Her hair especially stood out to me.

It tried hard not to be nappy, tried hard to consider itself just a little frizzy, but I saw what was happening in the kitchen of her skull, at the base of her neck—what she tried to hide with scarves and upturned collars. I knew, watching her, that she should have either let it go natural or straightened it, but she did neither. Instead she settled for the in-between, the half-hearted frizzies with the naps in the kitchen.

Her eyes were a color I had never seen on eyes before—a dark charcoal gray, the color of slate, of dirty blackboards. I imagined what a field day Maria could have had with her, a bottle of Queen Helene hair grease, some cocoa butter lotion for her skin, which was now so dry it appeared to be covered in a layer of dust, like the books on the Marshes' shelves. Ash-colored, like the dead. I knew something better lay underneath. A slathering of sweet-smelling lotion would make her brown skin glow, but she seemed oblivious to this simple fact. I once caught her wetting a finger, drawing a wet line in the dust that coated her, drawing what turned out to be an X there on her gray knee, the way you sign your name through the steam in the fog of a car window. And I could see what color then lay underneath. The color of cinnamon.

MONA LIVED IN A TRAILER with her mother, a young, wiry, chain-smoking factory worker with spiky black hair and a foul mouth. She and Mona got along like sisters—sometimes fistfighting on the bed over a pair of earrings or a tube of lipstick, other times laughing and cooking brownies together on a Saturday afternoon. Mona had a half brother named Dennis, who lived across town in a place with two other guys. Her mother had given birth to Dennis when she was only fourteen, and blamed him and his runaway father for destroying her life. She referred to Dennis as "that fool" and liked to slap him on the head when he did something stupid or bad, which was often. She had been slapping Dennis all of his life, Mona told me, and now, at twenty, he was skinny and mean with a chipped front tooth and a tattoo of a demonic leprechaun on his shoulder. He chewed tobacco, his bottom lip packed so tightly it bulged, carrying as his spittoon a Dunkin' Donuts plastic cup filled with the swirling black liquid from his mouth.

Dennis had dropped out of the high school years before, but he continued to hang around in the park across the street from school, selling pot, buying liquor for the underaged, and hitting on jail bait. He made me uncomfortable, the way he always found a way to touch Mona—giving her a wedgie when she walked by, whipping her with a wet towel, snapping her bra, and teasing her for "growing titties."

But Dennis showed up only on rare occasions, and when he wasn't around, I liked nothing better than to escape to Mona's trailer. My mother didn't seem to mind that I would disappear there for whole weekends. She and Jim concluded that they liked Mona. "She's a great little fighter. You can see that she's struggled," my mother said. Jim agreed. "Tough cookie. New Hampshire's in her blood." I didn't know about all that, but I liked watching her mother get ready to go out for pool on Friday nights. She'd put on sparkly blue eye shadow and "vixen red" lipstick, and Mona and I had to help her slide into her skintight jeans while she lay stiff as a board on the trailer bed that she and Mona shared.

I preferred trailer life to the world of my own house, but Mona always wanted to be at my house and thought Jim and my mother were "stoners, really fuckin' cool." We spent a good amount of time fighting over whose house to spend the weekend at.

I was playing catch-up with Mona, learning how to be a girl. There were little things the women at Aurora hadn't taught me—how to apply lipstick properly, how to stick in a tampon, how to stuff your bra with shoulder pads ripped right off a department-store mannequin.

One lazy weekend, when her mother was out shopping, Mona showed me in the privacy of the trailer's tiny bathroom how a real woman got off.

She held up a bath plug. "This," she said, winking, and snapping her Bubble Yum, "feels great against your clit."

I watched with rapt attention as she washed the round, flat, white plastic disk with its finlike handle and then stuck it in her underpants, with the fin sticking up into the lips of her vagina. She walked around before me, saying, "Oooh, feels good. I wear it around just for kicks some days."

I had always been afraid of sticking things inside me—I was still squeamish about using a tampon. Now, with Mona's eyes on me, I stuck the object in and pulled up my panties. She sat on the toilet, watching me, her eyebrows raised. "Well? How's it feel?"

It felt like a bath plug in my underwear, hard and uncomfortable. But I smiled and told her it felt great.

Jɪᴍ ᴡᴀs ʙᴜɪʟᴅɪɴɢ a skylight in the living room. It was something he had seen on the PBS show "This Old House." He said he wanted my mother to be able to see the stars from inside, even in the deep of winter. It wasn't his only renovation on the house. Walter Marsh had given him full permission to improve the place. Lately it seemed like every time I turned around, there was something new and improved—a leaky faucet had been mended, the stairs no longer creaked, the bathroom had been retiled. And the more Jim improved our little cottage, the more he seemed to think it was his own. It had gotten to the point where he slept over almost every night. He even had a toothbrush and razor in the bathroom. Often I fell asleep to the sound of the bed squeaking behind the wall, their breaths coming faster and faster, until I heard Jim's inevitable groan.

I no longer whispered warnings to my mother about Jim. It was clear to me that she wouldn't listen. I knew I had to find some kind of evidence against him if she was to believe me.

So one morning, deep into the fall, I decided to take matters into my own hands. While they were outside doing their Tai Chi on the lawn, I crept into my mother's bedroom. I had no real idea of what I was looking for. Just a vague sense that it was probably hidden in the closet, in Jim's overnight backpack. As I fumbled in there, I imagined what I might find. A notepad with scientific descriptions of my mother's and my every move. An FBI identification card with his real name on it. A Wanted poster with a crude police sketch of my mother's face. A book of interrogation methods. A Vietnamese child's dried ear inside a tin box, a souvenir from his days as a murderer in the war.

But as it turned out, his backpack had nothing of much interest in it. I did find a black diary, but when I flipped through it, I saw that there were only notes on how to renovate the house, and a couple of Bob Marley lyrics, with crude drawings of a sun and palm trees drawn around them. He was better than I thought at his job.

The closet smelled of my mother—a mixture of the jasmine oil she wore on her wrists, plain old soap, and something sharp and mysterious that made it her own. I picked up her shirt and inhaled. As I did so, I noticed a bag underneath. It was the one she didn't let me go through—a silver men's sports duffel that was tearing at the seams. She hadn't let me see what was inside all those four years we'd been on the run together. She said it was filled with "grown-up stuff." I had never tried to look in it before, assuming it was sex devices. Now I picked it up. I wondered if there would be answers in there—answers to the questions I had asked myself so many times: *Where are they? What did you do that was so big, that could make us run so hard and so long, that could make us disappear?*

Inside, it was mostly what I'd expected—a diaphragm, a photo of her and Bernadette nude, *The Joy of Sex,* and *Our Bodies, Our Selves.*

But there was something underneath all of that. A book, at the bottom of the bag, beneath the KY jelly. I pull it it out. It was a first edition of Fanon's *Wretched of the Earth.* I remembered my father giving it to her so many Christmases ago.

I glanced out the window at her and Jim, now riding Mr. Pleasure and the other mare, Sky, side by side, lazily, in circles on the grass. I could hear their voices, muted giggles behind the glass. I pulled the book out and stared at it. My mother had told me she had kept nothing but the clothes on her back when we left Boston. She had told me that holding on to the past would have been a big mistake, a surefire way to get caught. But she had kept this. On the first page was my father's inscription to her. *To my slick, sly, ever-fearless Sandy—for now and forever. Missing you as we speak. Deck.* I stared at the words for a while, then turned the page. An envelope fell out and floated to the floor. I picked it up and opened it.

A photograph of my parents. The old-fashioned kind, sepia-toned, with a scalloped edge. It must have been the year she met him, when he was a graduate student at Harvard and she was reading Camus. In the photo, they are standing on some steps in front of a marble statue. My father wears an old-mannish tweed coat, and stands behind my mother, his arms wrapped around her waist, his head resting on her shoulder. They both are smiling. But their smiles are tight, frozen, fierce, as if they are clenching their teeth, as if they are biting into something soft and slippery, and their eyes—grasping, solemn, despite the smiles—seem to search the invisible photographer, as if looking for solutions in his lens. I felt sad looking at them. It seemed that the threat was already there, pressing in on them from the outside.

The next photograph was of my sister and my mother. It was taken while my mother was pregnant with me, when my sister was only three and wore her hair held in two afro puffs, with a zigzag part down the middle—my mother's sloppy invention. My mother is holding her on her lap, and the two of them are reading a book together—I couldn't read the cover, but could tell it was *Stuart Little,* my sister's favorite all throughout her child-hood, the one she couldn't get enough of. And my mother—so young, still chubby, her hair in pigtails and wearing a psychedelic-print minidress, me still an invisible lump buried in her flesh—is pointing at the page in front of them, while my sister's head lolls against her chest. Cole has her thumb stuck in her mouth, and her eyes are lazily focused on the story before her, and she seems utterly content. Behind them you can just make out the cor-ner of a poster—one that hung on our living room wall, opposite the Cot-ton Mather print—a poster of a black child's afroed silhouette, the words "Not Yet Uhuru" above the face. When I was little, I thought the child looked hungry and imagined that Uhuru must mean "dinnertime" in another language.

Looking at those photographs, I remembered how my parents had never said "I love you" to each other. How they had said only "I miss you." At the time, I hadn't been able to figure out what this meant. But now it seemed clear: this was how they defined their love—by how deeply they missed each other when they were together. They felt the loss before it happened, and their love was defined by that loss. They hungered even as they ate, thirsted even as they drank. My mother once told me to live my life as if I were al-ready dead. "Live each day as if you know it's gonna be gone tomorrow," she had said. That was how my parents loved each other, with a desperate, melancholy love, a fierce nostalgia for the present.

There was something stuck in the middle of the book, like a bookmark, but bigger. I opened to it. A postcard. Of somewhere familiar. The silver slab of the John Hancock building against a bright blue sky. The word "Boston" emblazoned beneath it. Tiny pedestrians in bright coats could be seen milling around at the bottom like M & M's. I turned the card over, expecting to see my father's handwriting, sharp and tiny. Instead, it was big loopy letters, female script, that went across the entire postcard, leaving no room for an address or stamp.

S: I don't know if this will reach you, but I am giving it to someone who swears they can get it to you. I am back in America. So much to tell you. So much has changed. Are you okay? Alive? Is B with you? Boston is deserted, not a family member in sight. Everyone has disappeared, including my brother. Somehow, send word. 46 Montgomery Street. Apt 2. Love and blessings, Dot.

I didn't breathe for the whole time that I looked at the postcard. There was no postmark, so I didn't know where it had come from, when it had come. The fact that she hadn't mentioned it to me made me cold. Suspicious. It reminded me of the day we left Boston, when she had lied to me, telling me that my father and sister had never been there when in fact they had. I stuck the card in my back pocket, placed the photographs carefully back where they had come from, into the duffel bag, and shut the closet door. I could hear the front door opening downstairs, my mother calling out my name. I hastily made my way back to my bedroom and closed and locked the door behind me. I put Dot's card into my box of negrobilia and tucked it into my closet. Afterward, I lay with my face down on the bed, biting into the pillow as hard as I could, till my teeth were sore.

The next morning, when my mother and Jim had gone into town to buy some food for brunch, I sat at the edge of the couch, my hands trembling, as I called Boston information.

"What city?"

Her accent was thickly Boston. Working class. Nasal. I had a brief fear that she had been expecting my call. That she had a picture of me and my mother on the wall beside her, with the word "Wanted" across the top. Maybe the whole city of Boston was out to get us. But I forced myself to speak.

"Boston."

"What name?"

"Dot. Dot Lee."

"Address?"

"Forty-six Montgomery."

Clicking sounds as she entered the information. Then a sigh. "No listing. No such person. Is that all?"

I didn't say anything. Just hung up in her face.

THERE WAS A TIME when I told my mother everything. But the post-card was the end of all that. It seemed there was nothing more to say between us. I began to watch her with a distant suspicion. Jim was no longer the focus of my investigation. My mother was the betrayer, had withheld vital information from me—information that might help us find Cole and my father.

She tried talking to me, but I was sullen, hostile even. She told Jim I was just going through puberty, but I think even she knew it was more than that.

Mona was my way out of the house, out of my mother's world, and I became her shadow over the next few months. Jim liked to say we were connected at the hip. Around school, we were known as the awesome twosome. But it was a strangely cold friendship on my part. There was none of the intimacy that there had been between me and Alexis. Around Mona, I was usually performing, trying to impress her, but never letting her in. From the outside, it must have looked like I was changing into one of those New Hampshire girls. I talked the talk, walked the walk, swayed my hips to the sound of heavy metal, learned to wear blue eyeliner and frosted lipstick and snap my gum. And when I heard those inevitable words come out of Mona's mouth, Mona's mother's mouth, Dennis's mouth—nigga, spic, fuckin' darkie—I only looked away into the distance, my features tensing slightly, sometimes a little laugh escaping. Strange as it may sound, there was a safety in this pantomime. The less I behaved like myself, the more I could believe that this was still a game. That my real self—Birdie Lee—was safely hidden beneath my beige flesh, and that when the right moment came, I would reveal her, preserved, frozen solid in the moment in which I had left her.

JIM FINISHED INSTALLING the skylight sometime in November. My mother wanted to celebrate Jim's work-well-done with a ten-dollar bottle of Cabernet Sauvignon and a spinach and cheese quiche Lorraine—her specialty. She said we would have an indoor picnic underneath the skylight.

Jim came to my room to ask Mona and me to go food shopping with him and my mother. Mona and I were lolling on my floor side by side, lazily flipping through Archie comics and popping huge Bubble Yum bubbles. Mona said she was Betty, the blond, and I was Veronica, the dark-haired rich girl. She thought I was rich because I lived on the Marsh land.

"You gals want to join us?" Jim said, leaning against the doorjamb, a dish towel looped through his belt.

"Nah, we'll just stay here," I told Jim.

He frowned and crossed his arms. "No, young ladies. I don't think you will. We're gonna need help carrying bags. Now move your tushies."

Mona giggled and stood up. She liked hanging out with Jim and my mother, watching them kiss in public. I glared at Jim but followed him downstairs.

As we drove to town, my mother and Jim sat in the front, singing along to a song—*Take this job and shove it, I ain't workin here no more*—while Mona and I lay in the back of the van amid spilled tools. Mona was telling me a story about Dennis, how he had been arrested the week before for drunk driving and how she and her mother had to drive to the police station in the next town over to pick him up. "My mom was ripshit. Ohmigod. You should have seen her."

The grocery store was crowded with Saturday shoppers, and Mona and I walked together, leaning in toward each other conspiratorially. My mother had relented and had finally taken me shopping for new clothes. I wore Nikes, Jordache jeans, and a fluffy pink angora sweater with silver sparkles sewn in. Mona's mother had cut my hair into layers so that it feathered around my face.

The women who milled around us wore housedresses with bright floral prints. I stared hungrily into their shopping carts as they walked past me, stared at the lumps of ground beef and the Kool-Aid and the boxes of powdered mashed potatoes—food my mother never let me eat anymore, food that seemed exotic somehow in its trashiness. Ahead of me, my mother wore a Guatemalan smock and silver cowboy boots, and her copper hair in two braids like an Indian princess. Just the week before she had finally given her hair another henna. I had helped put the green clay on her head. Jim had come over in the middle of our beauty shop, and had been surprised to find that my mother wasn't a real redhead. I was worried, but my mother had simply laughed and said he would have found out one way or another.

The women who passed by my mother whispered to one another, checked her out with clear disdain, and I felt my face burn at her visibility. She held Jim's hand and laughed loudly, girlishly, slapping him on his butt. She was as oblivious as she had ever been to the stares she got. Mona stared up at them dreamily. She thought it was romantic.

I was standing in front of the cereal rack when I heard Mona whisper in my ear, "Uh-oh. It's Wilona. Clear the deck." At the very same moment, I heard the crack of broken glass and a gasp. I looked up. A few feet ahead of us, my mother had dropped a jar of jam, and it lay at her feet, a splatter of purple lumps. She stood still as stone, staring at the vision walking toward her.

Samantha Taper and her mother. My mother had never laid eyes on either of them before this moment. I knew I should have told her about them, but I hadn't.

Samantha's mother was petite and blond, her flaxen hair cut into a blunt bob that swung around a pointy face. She was dressed in a gray tweed coat and a cornflower-blue scarf. She looked like the kind of mother I had fantasized about—a pretty, quiet, TV mom who wouldn't draw the eyes of strangers so readily.

Samantha walked beside her, her hand resting on the cart as if it needed extra guidance, her eyes averted nervously from Mona and me, the way losers learned to do at our school.

It struck me, looking at her now under the bright lights of the supermarket, that she was on the verge of being beautiful, something I had missed before, as she worked so hard to hide it in dark colors, ashy skin, and baby fat. She wore an old ratty down coat with a faux-fur collar, and sneakers on her feet, her hair confused, the way Cole's used to be before she went to the Nkrumah School, before Carmen got her hands on it. But still, the potential for beauty shone through.

My mother stood before them, frozen and pallid, her hands by her sides in a helpless gesture as she watched Samantha and her mother strolling in our direction, lingering over the boxes of cereal. Jim was on his knees, cleaning up the raspberry jelly with a handkerchief, looking up from the mess in bewilderment. "Sheila, Sheila, what is it?"

Other women around us had turned to stare, and I saw on their faces some twisted pleasure. Seeing my mother this way had confirmed something for them. Made them feel safe. Assured them that things were as they appeared.

Mona said, "What's up with your mom? She's freaking."

I wasn't embarrassed. More frightened that she was about to blow our cover. That she was about to make the mistake that would give it all away. I should have warned her about Samantha. Shouldn't have let her find out this way.

My mother glanced around, seeming to have forgotten where she was, what store, town, city, or state she was in. She turned to me and blinked. "Birdie?"

She hadn't used my name in more than two years. In the beginning she used to slip up regularly, but she'd fought hard to learn Jesse and eventually the name Birdie had disappeared.

I felt Jim's and Mona's eyes on us, and I came to her side, saying, "It's me, Mum. Me, Jesse," as I touched her arm gently. My heart was hammering in my chest. Jim stood up beside us. He touched my mother's shoulder. "Who's Birdie? What is it, babe? You okay?"

She was looking at Samantha and her mother, who were nearly beside us, arguing over some potato chips Samantha wanted to get.

"They're no good, Sammy. Put 'em back. I already got some corn chips."

My mother looked away from them, her cheeks pinkening as she seemed to realize that she had been staring. She turned to Jim and gazed at him as if he were a stranger on the street. Then she sauntered down the aisle ahead of us just like nothing had happened.

Jim turned to me. "Any clue, Jess?"

I gnawed at my fingernails. "I don't know. She gets like that sometimes. Must be getting the curse." Then I dashed forward after her, leaving Mona and Jim behind.

My mother didn't speak until we were outside, loading groceries into the back of the van. When she turned to get a bag from me, she looked spooked, pale, and fragile, like one of the dolls at Hans's Toy Shop and Doll Hospital, as she said, "Is that girl in your school?"

I shrugged. "Yeah. She's adopted."

Mona stood beside me, ripping into a chocolate bar. She piped in, "You mean Samantha? She moved here last year. Everybody hates her."

Jim was busily opening a jar of peanuts and digging his hand into it. "Jeez, I'm famished. You know, Sheila, it might be hunger that's got you so dizzy."

My mother ignored him and narrowed her gaze at me. "Why didn't you say hello to her?"

I shrugged again. "Like Mona said, she's a loser. Everybody hates her. Nobody speaks to her except the school genius, Nora, and she's a loser too."

I avoided my mother's glare, looking toward the electric poles and trees in the distance. I could see that her arm was shaking from the weight of the groceries. Jim was smacking away at his peanuts, and Mona was teasing her hair and gazing at her reflection in the van's window.

My mother's voice sounded thick as she said, "A loser? Jesse Goldman, I never thought I'd hear you talk about another human being in such terms. What the fuck have I been trying to teach you all these years? That girl is no different from you. Do you hear me?"

"You mean we're both black?" It had come out before I could stop it.

My mother breathed in sharply, and we stared at each other.

I heard Mona beginning to giggle. She had her hand over her mouth and was trying to stifle her laughter. She said, "Sorry, Mrs. Goldman. It's just what Jesse said. It's kinda funny."

I looked at Jim. He appeared confused and was looking back and forth between my mother and me, wiping the salt and peanut grease from his lips.

My mother put her hand to her temple, as if to stop a migraine. Then she began to giggle as well, loudly, in a way that made even Mona's smile disappear.

sit
and spin

I had dreamed it once before. That I woke to the sound of Stevie Wonder playing faintly from the driveway. When I went to the window, I saw a flash of rust-colored chrome from between the trees. The same color as my father's Volvo. I tore down the steps, nearly knocking Jim down the stairs, and out into the yard. I was still in my pajamas, and it was cold outside, frosty, not yet spring. Icy grass crunched under my bare feet. When I came to the driveway, an orange Volvo was parked behind Jim's Buick, and a girl who looked a little like my sister sat in the passenger seat, wearing sunglasses and an African head wrap. She was nodding her head to the music. The hood to the Volvo was open, and a man stood with his head bent into the engine, fiddling. I called to them—"Yoohoo!"—but they didn't seem to hear me over the music. Finally I barked loudly, "Papa!" The man pulled his head out from under the hood and looked up at me, squinting in the morning light. It was someone else. Someone I knew. But not my father. A red-haired man with skin the color of burnt sienna. He smiled and said, "Hey there, little girl. Bet you thought we weren't coming for you." When I looked back at the passenger seat, the girl I thought was my sister had taken off her sunglasses and was staring at me. She was no one I knew. She was deformed. Her face was swollen and pink, and there was a deep scar running jagged down the middle, making her face look like an overripe fruit that had been split, then stuck roughly back together. I wanted to run away, but couldn't move.

When I woke from the dream, my sheets were soaked and my face was wet. It was still dark. I hugged my knees to my chest and sobbed dryly now. When I had a nightmare, when I was little, my sister would sometimes wake before I did, as if she could hear danger coming from inside my head. She would push me gently, saying, "Birdie, wake up. It's only a dream."

My room looked strange in the darkness—the Bruce Springsteen poster over my desk, the horse calendar by the window, the makeup and perfume and blow-dryer cluttering the top of the dresser—the objects suddenly unfamiliar, like props. I slipped out of bed and fetched the box of negrobilia from the top of my closet. I brought it downstairs to the kitchen and put on a pot of coffee. Jim liked gourmet coffee from Kenya and brought some back each week from Boston. He got it at some café on Newbury Street. My father had preferred Dunkin' Donuts brand and always drove with a cup in one hand, the other hand on the steering wheel. He had mastered this balancing act so that no matter how quickly he stepped on the brakes, the cup of coffee didn't spill. I used to watch him, holding my breath, waiting for the burn that never came.

My mother and Jim wouldn't be up for another few hours. It was summertime, and we slept as late as we pleased. Jim was going to Boston only a few days a week. He said he wanted more time at home. My mother had been getting up early all year, to do her mantras out in the backyard. I'd hear her out there, that strange monotone song, and I'd know what she was praying for, whom she was praying for. But it was four-thirty, too early even for her mantras, the light across the kitchen gray and milky and soft, like a dream.

I fixed myself a cup of coffee—pale and sweet—and sat at the kitchen table. It was rare that I got this much time alone. I opened the shoe box and stuck the black Barbie head on the end of my thumb, like a thimble. The shoe box was getting crowded. I had begun to steal things lately, adding them to the box like offerings to some greedy god. It had started with the postcard from Dot. Then there had been Jim's photograph, the one I found in his cabin one afternoon while he and my mother were out swimming in the lake. I had been snooping through his desk drawer, looking for evidence, and had come across it beneath the papers, stuck to a patch of spilled glue on the bottom of the drawer. I had been careful not to tear it, gently pulling it out from the sticky mess. In the photo, Jim looks younger, with dirty-blond hair, and he has his arm around a lean brown woman in a halter top; the two of them sit under the red greasy light of a tropical bar. It was the only proof that he actually had been to Jamaica, that he actually had known the Jamaican people as well as he claimed.

There were other, smaller things I had stolen and added to the box. Things that didn't make as much sense, but that I had taken anyway, for reasons I couldn't explain. A baseball card of Jim Rice I had found, crushed and soiled, on the floor of our school gym; a red, gold, and green friendship bracelet that Jim had left on the edge of the bathtub to dry one night; a stray piece of Samantha's hair, which I had plucked from her sweater when she sat in front of me one day in social studies. She had felt my hand brush her back and had turned around to see what I wanted. But my hand was underneath the desk by then, her hair between my fingers, and I just raised my eyebrows at her and smiled slightly and said nothing.

My latest addition to the box was a page I had ripped from a library book on Brazil. It described a religion there called Candomblé, something that had started in West Africa a long time ago but which the Afro-Brazilians had made their own. I had spent the better part of a summer afternoon curled up in a green vinyl chair by the library window, hiding from Mona and the rest of the gang, reading about this religion while the world rushed by outside. I became especially interested in one of the gods—Exu-Elegba—who the book said represented potentiality and change. It said that although many people thought Exu was the devil, he was really just a trickster, always shifting his form, always at the crossroads. I had a feeling that Cole would like Exu. The page I ripped out showed an ancient clay sculpture of him. In it he looks a little like a fetus, his eyes tiny and squinting, his face amorphous, unfinished.

I wondered if Cole practiced Candomblé in Brazil. I could see her doing that. She had always loved magic and ceremonies. She liked Ouija boards and tarot cards when we were little, and had ordered Sea Monkeys and love potions from the backs of our comic books, believing that the invisible might exist. I could see her with a shrine to Exu. But not my father. He would have laughed at the believers. He didn't believe in things he couldn't explain with logic.

I looked at the picture of Exu. I didn't know why I had stolen it from the book, or why I kept it here, in this box of negrobilia. My mother said it was okay to steal a book from the library now and then, but not to deface a book. Books were sacred. But I had wanted a piece of Brazil, a piece of Cole and my father as they were now, not just the stale artifacts my father had left me with from that other time. And something about this god's face—this squinting creature entering the world—had made me want to keep it close by my side.

My coffee had turned cold, and I went to put the mug in the sink. Outside, the light had risen and hit the dew on the grass, letting off flecks of color. A few years before, I wouldn't have believed that my mother and I could end up here, in this life. I had been so afraid when we first arrived. Of not fitting in. Of never making any friends. Of failing my classes. But it turned out I had nothing to fear. I had blended in perfectly.

My first school year had come to a close, and most surprising to me, I had done well in my classes. I had struggled at first in science and math but had quickly caught up and made it through without much trouble. In my other classes, though, I was second only to Nora in school performance. My mother was proud of me, and proud of herself, too. She had been my teacher all those years on the run, and clearly she had done something right. "See," she told me when we were alone, "didn't I tell you my curriculum was the best?" The teachers were sometimes surprised at how much I knew. Sometimes I even worried that I had revealed too much of myself to them. Like when I quoted from Fanon, or when I repeated things my mother had said about the stages of revolution, or referred to Simone de Beauvoir in my reports. They wondered. I could see it in their eyes, and Mrs. McGuire, my history teacher, a short unhappy woman with huge goggle glasses, had asked my mother at Parents' Night what kind of schools I had been to before this one: "Seems like they had a very unusual curriculum," she had said suspiciously. But even Mrs. McGuire was impressed. She told my mother and Jim that I was way ahead of my grade, that in high school I could skip ahead to advanced English and history and social studies if I wanted.

I would turn fourteen in September, older than Cole had been the last time we'd seen her. High school was right around the bend. And somewhere closer to the equator, Cole was seventeen, probably on her way to college. Sometimes I stared at the girls around town who were her age, at their bodies, and I couldn't believe that my sister, the long-legged twelve-year-old in the training bra, looked something like that. I wondered if I'd recognize her if I were to meet her on the street. I wondered if she'd recognize me.

A truck rolled by on the road outside of our house, a dairy farmer on his way to work. My mother and Jim would be waking soon. Jim was going to Boston that day. My mother had a student coming at ten o'clock. An autistic kid who she believed was a hidden genius and wanted to cure. I knew I should put the box away. I stared down at Exu-Elegba, the unformed face, the squinting eyes that searched the world for answers, and I whispered under my breath a little prayer that I made up. A prayer in Elemeno. A prayer to Exu, the God of Change, the God of Potential, to bring some kind of change.

NICHOLAS WAS AWAY for the whole summer on an exchange program in Paris. He wouldn't be coming home again until Thanksgiving. Whenever my mother asked Libby Marsh how Nicholas was doing, she looked strained, unhappy, and offered only a slight "Oh, you know. He's at that age." I wasn't quite sure what she meant, but I imagined him with Piper, her long downy limbs wrapped around him, her golden hair in his eyes. I could still hear her voice: "I hate you! You're so skinny." And I remembered his face, how strangely embarrassed he had looked to see me there. I wasn't sure if he had been embarrassed of me or of them. I fantasized about joining him at Exeter, about becoming a girl like Piper, a casual rich girl who played Frisbee and lacrosse and sang along to Cat Stevens.

But I wouldn't fit in there. I was a New Hampshire girl now. I had a gang—Mona and Dawn and Kelly—and we were inseparable, bored together, waiting for high school to begin, for our world to move forward. It was mid-July, and the days seemed longer than ever, lazy and claustrophobic. Most afternoons we went swimming at the YMCA, just after the flock of little camp kids had finished their swimming lessons and the water was warm with their piss. After swimming, we would hang out in front, sometimes eating Softee cones, but most of the time just biting our nails, always waiting for some boy to come along and distract us from ourselves, from one another.

One particularly hot day after swimming, we stood on the gray stone steps in our little girl cluster. We were jittery but trying to keep our cool. A group of high-school boys had pulled their car up to the curb. Mona's half brother, Dennis, was in the passenger seat. The boys were eating cheese fries and sucking on lime rickeys, while heavy metal music blared from their radio. We swayed our hips together, mouthing the words to the song and closing our eyes as if we meant it.

Mona was smoking a cigarette, sucking in deep and making rings, while the rest of us leaned against the wall, watching her. Our hair was wet at the ends from swimming, and our skin smelled faintly of chlorine. We dressed identically: cutoff jean shorts, halter tops that exposed our tan bellies, and jelly shoes on our feet. We had bought the shoes together, each picking a different color. I had been stuck with the clear ones, and they made my feet sweat and stink inside of them.

Mona winked at me and said, "Watch this." With her back to the boys, she proceeded to bend over to buckle and unbuckle her jelly shoe, so that her shorts rode up her thighs even farther. The boys laughed and hooted as she lingered down at her shoe, her butt high in the air for them to view, while the rest of us girls snickered into our hands at her audacity.

She stood up and ceremoniously pulled out the wedgie she had created. She flicked her hair and whispered in my direction, "Were they looking? They want it so bad. Too bad none of them are gonna get it."

We laughed, and our laughter was louder and shriller than normal, canned for the sake of those boys who sat just outside our circle.

Just then something hard hit me on the back of the head.

I let out a loud "Ouch," and when I looked at the ground, I saw a penny, as shiny and copper as my mother's hair. I heard giggling from the car behind me, and a voice, high and nasal: "Want another one?"

Mona rolled her eyes and said: "Don't pay attention to them. Pretend you didn't feel it."

But then another flying penny hit me in the center of my back. It didn't hurt, but my face burned as I heard one of them yell, "Yo, you in the blue!" I was wearing blue, and I turned.

He was in the backseat and wore a baseball hat. When he smiled it was all silver with braces. "You want another? I know you do." He was looking at my chest, not my face, and for a moment I thought he was admiring my breasts.

I looked down as if to check whether they had grown overnight. But they were flat as ever.

I looked up. He was still smiling at me, but his face was half-curled into a sneer. "Fuckin' kike. I'm talkin' to you. Do you want another penny?"

I looked down again, this time noticing my Star of David, thick and gleaming in the sunlight. I only realized then that they were throwing pennies at me because I was Jesse Goldman, daughter of David Goldman. I felt a pang of loyalty toward this imaginary father, and touched the necklace.

The boys' car shone brightly, warbling slightly under the heat. They were grinning at me, waiting to see what I would say. I felt an aching in my fingers, then in my fist, an urge to go to the one who had said it, punch him so hard that his face would stay permanently dented in like a car fender. I could see my mother doing something like that. But not my father. Never my father. He would have turned to me with a tight smile and spoken softly: *They're primitive. Pity them for their lack of sophistication. See how they work, see how they play. Watch them, baby, and learn.* These words came to me like a memory, but I wondered if he had ever really said such a thing.

I turned back to the girls, who were smiling at the ground with dazed expressions, as if they hadn't heard anything.

Mona was the only one to defend me. She turned back to the boys and shouted, "Cut it out, you little pricks! Dennis, I'm gonna tell Ma!" The other boys laughed and began to pull the car away from the curb. But as they drove off, the boy who had thrown the penny at me leaned out the window and gave us the finger as he shouted, "Sit and spin, cunts!"

We turned back to one another, and Mona flicked her hair, unfazed, it seemed, by the encounter. My fingers were shaking slightly as I held the star's weight. Mona looked at it as she took a puff of her cigarette, squinting down at me through the smoke, an imitation of some adult she had known.

"So, are you Jewish, or what? I mean, is that what that necklace is for?"

I let out a rather harsh laugh and looked away.

There had been one other Jewish girl in the school. She had played the clarinet and also wore a Star of David, only hers looked like real quality gold and had a diamond on it. She had gone away for the summer, telling us all at the end of school that she wouldn't be coming back. That she was going to boarding school. I wondered if she'd be at the same school as Nicholas. If they'd be friends. I bet they had plenty of Jewish kids at boarding school. Piper had said that her best friend, Abbie, was Jewish. I bet there was even an exclusively Jewish boarding school. I'd ask my mother if I could go to one when I got home, but I knew she'd say no, that she didn't have any money.

I looked back at the girls. They were waiting for an answer, and it struck me that they had discussed this before, outside of my presence. That something unspoken rested on my answer. I said, "Well, not *really* Jewish. I mean, only my dad was, and he's dead. And to be really a Jew, you have to have a mother who is Jewish. It's like the religious law or something."

Mona looked at the other girls and laughed blandly, bored already by the topic at hand, as she said, "I *told* you guys she wasn't really Jewish."

It was sometime that same week that I took off the Star of David and put it at the bottom of my underwear drawer. My mother didn't notice.

IN AUGUST, I LEARNED that a black boy was coming to the high school. Mona told us one bright afternoon while she painted her toenails on the steps of the trailer. It was a little past noon, and the sun glared over the field. A family was having a barbecue some distance away, and the smell of smoke and cooked flesh wafted over to us.

"He's a football player. The high-school coach drafted him from another town. Heard he's pretty good."

I felt a gnawing in my belly and tried to change the subject. "I hope we don't have to take Freshman gym in the fall. I suck at sports."

But Mona persisted: "His name's Stuart Langley. I've never known any black guys, just Samantha. Wonder if they got big dicks, like everybody says."

They often talked like this around me. My grandmother in Boston used to say that "the Negroes should stop obsessing about race. Then maybe everybody else would." But I was finding that in New Hampshire, the white folks needed no prompting. It came up all the time, like a fixation, and there was nothing I could do to avoid it.

Now I felt myself floating, looking down at us, the three of us, almost identical in our blue jeans, polo shirts, scuffed flats, our feathered hair falling around our faces. I saw myself as I sat there kicking the dirt, trying to disappear under my overgrown bangs.

Dawn pitched in: "Shit. We're gonna look like little niggers if we stay out in the sun any longer. Especially you, Jesse."

Mona looked me up and down, then said with a laugh, "Shit, Jess. You never burn. What's your secret?"

I looked over at the family across the lawn. They were fat, and the adults sat sprawled out in lawn chairs. In front of them, a little boy was tormenting a dog—pulling its tail, dragging it around like that while it yelped and squealed.

I stood up abruptly, and they all looked up at me.

"Where the hell are you going?" Mona asked.

"To take a leak."

In the bathroom, I stood at the sink, splashing cold water on my face. I was breathing in little asthmatic wheezes. I closed my eyes and thought of my father's face and of Cole's hand holding mine on the first day at the school in Roxbury. I thought of her sticking up for me: *She's black. So don't be messing with her.* I thought of a game I had long since forgotten, a game the four of us, still one family unit, used to play. A game we played when we wandered into enemy territory, into Southie, home of the Irish, or the North End, the quaint Italian neighborhood with the cobblestone streets, or when we circled the streets that surrounded the white ghetto in Brookline called Whiskey Point.

My parents called the game "Now You See Him . . ." My father would pull out the raggedy plaid blanket we had in the backseat and hunch down real low in the passenger seat, making a tent out of the cloth. Cole and I thought it funny to see him disappear like that, transformed into a plaid lump hidden under the dashboard, all folded up in a cocoon like a caterpillar. My mother, as she maneuvered the car, leaning forward and squinting at the street signs, would say: "Look, girls. Papa's gone away. Papa's disappeared." And we would squeal with delight, "Papa, Papa, come out and play." And often he was quiet, but sometimes he would play along and speak in an ogre's voice or a wicked witch's voice: "Your papa can't come out. The monster's eaten him all up. Yum, yum." He made chewing and gnashing sounds, and we played along, clutching each other and screaming, "Mum, Mum. Make the monster let Papa go! Make him stop." Sometimes he went on too long—made the sounds of chewing too believable—and we would start to really get scared.

My mother, smiling slightly, would say: "Calm down, girls. Just cool it. Your papa's just playing. Deck, cut it out."

They wouldn't stop the game till we were out of the neighborhood, on safer ground, and then she would say, "Coast's clear, Deck."

"Jesse?"

The trailer around me. Flimsy walls made of fake wood paneling. A strong smell of something pink, something fluffy, something there to cover up the bodily odors. A potpourri in a ceramic elephant on top of the toilet. My face staring at me from the small chintzy mirror.

"What did you do, shit yourself in there?" came Mona's voice from beyond the door. "We're going to get milk shakes without you."

"Hold your horses," I called back. "I'll be right out."

I came outside smiling, composed, and we made our way over the grass together toward the chili-dog stand, flicking our feathered hair in unison, like a strange flock of birds.

AT THE DAIRY QUEEN, we all sat huddled in our favorite booth with our drinks, making a list of boys we liked. Just as we were scratching off a name, the bells on the door jingled and we looked up to see who it was.

Samantha had been away all summer. Someone had mentioned that her family had rented a house on Cape Cod and that she wouldn't be back until high school began. Now, in the neon lights of the Dairy Queen, I saw that she was back with a vengeance, a new person, as she came striding through the door with her head in the air.

She looked like an "After" picture from a magazine makeover. She must have discovered lotion over the summer because her skin glowed, cinnamon brown, no longer ashy gray. Her hair was still a little confused, half-nappy and pulled into a high ponytail, but it didn't matter. We all were speechless for a moment as she made her way to the counter and asked for a strawberry milk shake. Nora tagged along behind Samantha like a mad scientist with her creation. She was still bespectacled and skinny, but she now wore her hair in a feathered bob, and also a halter top just like Samantha's.

In the past, Samantha had tried to camouflage her skin in dark colors. Now she stood before us in a hot-pink miniskirt and a light-blue halter top. Her body, we all could see, was at least as developed as Mona's—she had pert, small, but undeniable breasts. We had never really seen her in this light

before. She had always worn layers to cover up the back brace for her scoliosis. Now the brace was gone, and she stood revealed, no longer embarrassed by the flesh she had discovered.

She wore too much makeup. So did the rest of us, but the heavy makeup
was more visible on Samantha because it didn't match her skin color. Didn't
match mine either, but my mother wouldn't let me go overboard—she had
told me I looked like a tart and wiped my face with a dish towel.

It was the way Samantha looked sideways, batting her eyelashes at the
pimply teenage clerk, that let me know she meant trouble. Samantha once
had been just a dark shadow, taking up space but not attention in the halls of
the junior high, eternally depressed and weighty. Now she seemed determined to be seen.

When they got their milk shakes, Samantha and Nora walked past us
without so much as looking our way. They sat outside in the sunlight at an
umbrella table, sipping their shakes.

I was the first to speak. "Samantha's—different."

I wasn't sure how I should judge this change, and looked to Mona for
leadership.

Mona looked angry, dejected. She fixed a glare at Samantha through the
window and said, slowly, "She looks like a hooker, if you ask me. God, I wonder what happened to her over the summer."

Dawn agreed, wiping the chocolate off her face with a napkin. "I know.
I don't know what she's trying to prove. So she's got tits. Big deal. She
shouldn't dress like that."

I bit my lip and looked at my friends. I didn't say anything and went back
to sucking my milk shake.

THE BLACK KID, Stuart, was short and boxy, but good-looking enough,
with a strained, pleasing smile and a distinctive girlish laugh. His running-
back position on the football team deflected any trouble he might have gotten into as the only black boy in the school. In fact, the other boys seemed to
look up to him in a way. They called him "Bro" and talked in mock slang to
him, but he seemed used to the flak and would just laugh nervously and answer them in his tight New Hampshire accent.

At first the other kids shoved him toward Samantha, saying, "There's a girl for you, man. Look at her, man. She's a hot mama." But Stuart and Samantha seemed mutually disinterested, if not repelled by each other. In fact, they actively avoided each other, as if proximity might cause them to combust. Stuart wanted only Marcy, the chubby blond cheerleader, and Samantha was immediately transfixed by Matthew, the thin-lipped and freckled junior with an identical twin brother named Michael.

Over the course of the year, she became Matthew's girlfriend, in a way, though she always walked behind him when they were at school. He treated her with ambivalence, feeling her up in the hallways, talking down to her in public. I heard that one day at football practice he came into the locker room and had all the boys smell his finger, sayings, "Want a sniff of Samantha?"

The other boys, meanwhile, would snap her bra then run away hooting, whip her with their gym towels, make mooing noises and licking motions with their tongues when she passed them in the hall. And Samantha would frequently laugh along, a nervous laugh that bounced and echoed down the halls of the school.

The girls ignored Samantha with an active distaste. But none of them hated her with Mona's vengeance. Samantha not only received the attention which Mona craved from the boys, but also she was a majorette in the school band, a position Mona had wanted. Samantha was a wizard with her baton, and could do elaborate twirls and throw the silver wand what seemed to be miles in the air. Mona sought her revenge in nicknames for Samantha. Besides "Wilona," she called Samantha "Chunky Monkey," "Big Butt," and "Samanthapantha."

Mona liked to make up stories about Samantha and then recite them in public, where she would pretend they were the gospel truth. She said that Samantha had given the whole high-school football team blow jobs in the locker room after the big game. That Samantha had a night job as a nude dancer in a strip joint in Concord. That Matthew and Michael traded off having sex with her, pretending that they were both Matthew so that she wouldn't know the difference. Mona's favorite was that she had seen Samantha get picked up after school one day by her pimp, a "huge black guy with a gold tooth and a Jheri-kurl." When the other kids laughed and said they didn't believe her, Mona would pinken and look to me for confirmation. "Right, Jesse? It's true, huh?" And I would just laugh, a hollow laugh, and look away.

plastic
bubbles

Jim came into the living room and slumped down beside me on the couch. I stuck my nose in a book and ignored him. My mother was out at a student's house. Mona was in Saturday school detention. It was one of those rare moments when I couldn't avoid being alone with him.

Lately he had been stepping up his campaign to befriend me. I had resisted him for the past year and a half, and wasn't going to stop now. But it was getting difficult. He brought back comic books and fancy fudge from Boston for me each week. Whenever my mother refused to buy me new clothes, he was the one to sneak me off to the mall in the next town over. And I had to admit that he was the one who had gotten me up to speed on my math and science. He had taught me real science to supplement my mother's quackery about maggots. Jim stayed up many nights, bent over the kitchen table beside me, showing me the basics of algebra with a steady patience. It often struck me in those moments that my own father had never paid this kind of attention to me. But instead of making me warm to Jim, this fact somehow made me angry and more resistant to his efforts.

"So, kiddo," he said, spreading his legs out before him. "Whatcha reading?"

I mumbled, *"Ethan Frome."*

He was batting around a throw pillow, tossing it in the air and catching it. "Want to go out for a ride or something?"

I looked up at him. "In your car?"

"No, silly girl. On the horses. You know, show me some of those trails you're always disappearing to."

I shrugged. He'd been trying to get me to do something father-daughter for a while. I had to face the music sometime. Now was as good a time as any.

It was late November. The air smelled of burning wood, and the sky was a billowy white. I took Mr. Pleasure, Jim took Coffee. I led him to the trail that Nicholas had taken me on that strange afternoon. I hadn't seen Nicholas in more than a year; after his summer in Paris, he'd gone straight back to boarding school to begin his junior year. I had remained remarkably pure over the past year. I told myself I was waiting for Nicholas, but really, I wasn't sure if that was it. Mona had slept with several high-school boys over the summer, pretending with each of them that she was a virgin. She said she thought it would make it more special if they thought it was her first time. But they always grew tired of her once they were finished, which left me to comfort her in a sea of snot and tears.

Jim rode behind me, talking loudly about how important I was to him. "Jess, I know this has been hard for you. Your father's death. This move. And now me." I dug my heels into Mr. Pleasure to quicken my pace, but Jim was right behind me.

"But I just want you to know, I'm here for you guys. I'm not going to abandon you. You two are my family now. The first I've ever had."

I was embarrassed. I wished I had never agreed to go out alone with him. His words made me feel sad, defeated. The closer I got to him, the more foggy my memory of my father became.

"You're a tough cookie, Jess, and you've kept your mother going these past few years. You got her through the grieving. But everything's going to be okay now."

He came up beside me on his horse then. I hadn't even realized I was crying, but when he looked at me, I knew my face showed something I had been trying to keep secret. He looked terrified. "Jess, what is it? Did I say something?"

I wiped my cheek angrily. "But you don't understand. You can't be my dad. I already have a dad. And he was a whole hell of a lot cooler than you. Besides, we were doing just fine without you."

Jim stiffened and looked away. I could see he was hurt by my words. I

felt guilty and wanted to take them back. I knew how easy it would be to suc-
cumb to his gentle silly love, to let him be my father the way he wanted to
be. But I couldn't. Something in me resisted.

We were quiet on the ride back. My mother was waiting for us in the
kitchen. She had cooked a huge feast of rosemary roast potatoes, lemon
chicken, and asparagus. She wore a green apron with a Budweiser slogan
across the front and her hair in a loose bun. An open bottle of red wine sat
on the table beside two long blue candles. She was smiling, flushed, happier
than I had seen her in a long time.

She had planned the whole thing. She had wanted Jim to break through
to me so that we would be one unit. It took all my strength to tell her I
wasn't hungry. Her smile disappeared, and she looked behind me to Jim for
answers. I went up to my room and flung myself on my bed with my arm
over my eyes. I lay there for a while, listening to their muted voices, the
clinking of silverware, and reggae music coming from downstairs. I wanted
to go join them. I was hungry and lonely and tired of fighting. But I stayed
there, listening to my stomach growl and waiting for night to come.

At some point my mother brought me up a plate of food. I took it without saying thanks and set to eating greedily while she stood over me, watching me with a pained expression. She whispered, "You know, you could show
him a little compassion. He's trying his hardest."

I shrugged, keeping my eyes on the food.

"Anyway, I just came to tell you the good news. We were going to tell
you over dinner. We're going to New York City in a few weeks. The three of
us." When I didn't look up or even respond, she said, "God, you're becoming the worst kind of teenager. It's revolting, really. You used to be such a
great kid." Then she left, stomping heavily down the stairs.

After I finished devouring my dinner, I set the plate on the floor and lay
back down. I thought about New York City, feeling a tingle of excitement despite my desire to remain indifferent. It would be my first time out of New
Hampshire in a whole year and a half. I had visited New York once when I
was little and my parents were still together. It was a place I never forgot, although I was only six at the time. We had visited a cousin of my father's
named Josephine—a short, round woman who lived in a Harlem brownstone. That weekend a group of bashful, grateful men slept on her living-
room floor. Only later did I learn that she was running a safe house. The men

had seemed fun, and one of them, a tall, gentle man with acne scars and tired eyes, had taught Cole and me how to play gin rummy. I don't remember ever once touching the pavement that weekend. It seems that I saw New York only looking down from above, the small peppering of miniature bodies on the sidewalk, the bright-yellow cab roofs weaving in and out of one another like a herd of buffaloes.

The next morning at breakfast, they both acted normal. Jim cheerfully explained to me that it was a business trip—a computer technology conference to discuss the wave of the future.

"Boys with their toys," my mother said, rolling her eyes. She always acted slightly put off by his computer consulting business, but we both knew that we were living off the spoils, so she couldn't complain too much.

A part of me believed he was taking us to New York that weekend only so he could entrap us. I imagined he wanted to get us far from home so he could have us arrested away from the eyes of prying neighbors. I agreed to go only if I could bring Mona. It was partly just for the company. But also I wanted a witness if anything shady happened.

So two weekends later we drove in Jim's big Buick, and I watched the world transform outside my window. Mona had never been to New York— she had been on only two trips in her life, one to Niagara Falls and one to Somerville, Massachusetts, for her great-uncle's funeral. She transformed on the drive from the brassy teenager I knew to a wide-eyed and silent child. It seemed that the farther we got from New Hampshire, the younger she became, so that by the time we entered New York she was leaning forward in between my mother and Jim, pointing at the high-rises that greeted us, and shouting, "Holy shit, look at that building. Oh my God. This is craaaazy."

As we drove through the Village, I was quiet. I was feeling something else as I watched the blur of strangers go by. Coming into New York was like being brought back to civilization after years on a desert island. I scrutinized the city people with a kind of hunger, eating up their wild styles and furious features, faces that unearthed some part of me that had been buried for so long. My mother was quiet as well, and while Jim chattered on to Mona about what was what, I could see that my mother was pressing her hands against her purse to stop them from trembling.

We stayed at the apartment of an old friend of Jim's, a dancer with a picture of Billie Holiday over his bed. He was away on tour for a stage reproduction of *The Wizard of Oz* and had lent Jim his keys before he left. The apartment was on West Twelfth Street, in the Village. Mona and I got the pullout sofa; my mother and Jim the back bedroom. That first night, Mona and I stayed up late eating popcorn and watching a television rerun of *The Boy in the Plastic Bubble,* starring John Travolta as a boy who is allergic to everything and has to communicate with his parents and schoolmates from behind a plastic wall.

Later, on the pullout couch with Mona beside me, I listened to the honks and shrieks outside, feeling an anguished excitement. I wanted, suddenly, for the first time, really, to run away. I wondered about my father's cousin Josephine. If she still lived uptown. If she knew where my father was. If I tracked her down, would she remember me? Would she take me in? Hide me in her safe house until the coast was clear?

But instead I lay stiff while Mona whispered to me about the world out there.

"Dennis told me there are black guys on the streets of New York that are out for white girls, and that if they catch you, they'll sell you on the black market to a porn ring. That's what he said, anyway. Said he learned it on '60 Minutes.' I was thinking about it down at the subway stop today."

When I still didn't speak, she sat up and leaned over me. Her blond hair fell forward around her pale face, and the streetlights from outside gave her a haunted look.

"Why are you so quiet? I thought you were asleep already," she said, looking down at me.

I looked away. "I don't know. Just thinking."

"About what?"

I wanted to tell her. I even made up my mind to tell her right then. If my mother could have one confidant, so could I. But all I could manage was: "You shouldn't believe everything Dennis tells you. I mean, your mother calls him 'that fool' for a reason." I heard my weak reply and wondered if it was really my mother whom I was protecting with my silence. Perhaps I was protecting myself from something more obvious than my mother's invisible enemy—something Samantha faced every day.

Mona laughed. "Oh yeah, Ms. Tough Gal? We'll see about that."

My mother and Jim spent the next day wandering in museums, and Mona and I were forced to follow.

But after the third room of Impressionist paintings, I tugged at my mother's shirt. "Mona and I are going to wait for you guys outside, okay? On the steps."

"All right, but don't go anywhere else. Don't talk to strangers."

Outside, Mona and I bought a pretzel from the burly man on the corner. We settled on a park bench not far from the steps, and watched the people walk by us in bright-colored coats, their heads bent against the wind.

Before long, a group of black and Puerto Rican teenagers, just around our age, came and sat on the bench next to ours. They were smoking and goofing around and had a boom box. It played some kind of talking music, the first I had ever heard of its kind, and I strained to listen, as if it held some secret. Mona's chattering was beginning to annoy me—at first I had thought it was my imagination, but now I was sure. There was a note of fear, even hysteria, in her tone as she went on about some cousin of hers who had fed his guinea pig to his Doberman pinscher.

I blocked her out and stared at the teenagers. One of the boys, a lanky kid wearing a Kangol hat, stood up and started to dance. He jerked his body electronically and, with the encouraging shouts of the other teens, began to spin on one of his hands, his glove the only protection between his skin and the pavement. A chubby girl with straightened and dyed blond hair stood and clapped her hands, moving her hips. Her sweatshirt had her name, "Chevell," printed on it.

As well as I had adjusted to New Hampshire, I had never quite gotten used to the music, or the fact that people didn't dance. The parties the kids threw all focused on drinking, smoking, and making out. Sometimes I would try to move my body to some Pat Benatar song, or a Rolling Stones classic, and the kids would watch me and laugh nervously, saying, "She must think this is a disco." Disco was a four-letter word in New Hampshire. One of the boys in our class even had a T-shirt he sometimes wore that boldly read, "Disco Sucks."

But this music wasn't disco, though the underlying tune was somehow familiar, something I had known once, long ago. The kids were grooving now, and had drawn a small audience. They were competing in acrobatic leaps and dives.

I stood up, and Mona followed me to the circle of onlookers. I clapped my hands, laughing at their expertise, and began to move to the music. Mona stood stiffly by my side, her hands shoved in her pockets. I was surprised at Mona's transformation. She was so clearly uncomfortable, I almost felt sorry for her, but at the same time I wished she would get lost. She felt like a weight I didn't need.

Mona slipped her arm through mine. She whispered in my ear, "Didn't your mom and Jim want us to wait on the steps?" I was ashamed to be seen with her. I had imagined, vainly, that the whole of New York City was watching me, wondering who I was, and I wanted them all to think I was alone.

"Oh, who cares," I said, and pulled my arm away from hers.

It was dawning on me as I watched these kids dance how long I'd been away. Six years. I felt that I had missed some great party and was now hearing about it the day afterward. A lump of disappointment and envy rose in my throat.

I felt a hand on my shoulder. My mother's voice: "Jesse, don't run off like that. We didn't know where you were."

I turned around. Jim was grinning at me and stroking his beard, amused. "You were shaking it, Jesse. Can't leave you alone for a minute in this city, can we?"

My mother ruffled my hair, but she wore a severe look. It was a warning glance I had seen before, at Aurora, when I would start to talk to the women too much, when I would slip up and mention the earlier life. But she smiled for the sake of Jim, I suppose, and simply said, "Jess, there's a lot of dangerous people out here. Next time stay where I tell you to."

Jim watched the kids dancing, listened to the music for a minute, then shook his head. "Jesus, it's like some ancient African instinct that gets these kids dancing. Unbelievable. Doesn't sound like the reggae I used to listen to in Jamaica. But it's still got that bass. Always got that bass."

I looked at the ground, not wanting him to touch me.

He suggested, "Shall we get lunch? It's already one o'clock."

Mona and my mother groaned that, yes, they were hungry. Jim threw his arm over Mona's shoulder and said, "Now you're going to find out what a pastrami sandwich on rye is supposed to taste like!" As we made our way down the block, the talking music faded. I trailed a few steps behind my mother, Jim, and Mona, fantasizing for a brief moment that I didn't know them, that they were strangers to me, that I lived in this kaleidoscopic city, and that my name was Chevell.

WE GOT LOST the next night on our way back to New Hampshire. Seriously lost. Jim had refused to stop for directions at the gas station some ways back, and now we were beyond help. No gas stations or late-night stores in sight. We were somewhere in New Haven. That much we knew. Jim had wanted to show my mother a landmark near Yale, the school he had dropped out of once upon a time. But somehow he had taken a wrong turn.

He cursed and slapped the steering wheel. My mother was silent, her head resting against the glass. Mona sat next to me, pretending to read a *Teen Beat* article about Deney Terio. But I could see she was distressed. She thought we'd never get back to New Hampshire.

We had been around the same set of blocks four times. The houses were run down, graffiti-spattered, and there was a huddle of teenagers on the corner, drinking out of paper bags. They must have been sixteen or seventeen, three black kids, and I stared at them as we passed by. The third time around the block, I caught one of their eyes. He wore a wave cap on his head. He smiled at me, and I smiled back and waved.

He raised something in the air then, and I watched silently as he hurled it toward me. It was a rock, and I flinched only when it hit the back windshield. The window didn't break, but the rock left a small indentation, like a pellet wound, with little delicate cracks branching out from its center. I saw the boys laugh and turn away from us, quickly, as if nothing had happened.

Jim screeched to a halt and swore, "Holy fucking shit!"

My mother twisted around to see what had happened, and said, "Jess, you okay?"

I nodded. I was shocked, but not hurt in any way. I had felt detached watching the rock float toward us, as if it were a movie and I wanted to know what would happen next.

I glanced back. The boys were looking over at our parked car from the corner. Jim was struggling to free himself from his seat belt. He was breathing heavily.

My mother said, "What the hell are you doing? Just drive, idiot."

"No way," Jim said, wagging his finger close to her face. "I'm not taking that from a bunch of little fucking—" He didn't finish his sentence. He was out of the car then and storming toward the boys on the corner, with his hands on his hips. My mother got out of the car and stood at the side, watching. She ran a hand through her hair and cursed under her breath, "Oh, Jesus, he's stupid."

Mona had gone pale. She looked as if she were going to cry. "Mrs. Goldman," she called to my mother, "what's he gonna do? Those niggers are gonna kill him."

I punched Mona's shoulder hard and hissed, "Shut the fuck up. What do you know?" The reaction had been automatic, and I stared at my balled fist now, as if it were somebody else's. Mona gaped at me, open-mouthed, stunned. Then her face crumpled into a cry. I ignored her and stuck my head out the window. A few yards away, I saw Jim approaching the group.

I listened as Jim demanded to know which one had done it. The young men laughed sheepishly and looked at their feet. The one who had done it smiled over Jim's shoulder at me mischievously, daring me to tattletale.

"Who the fuck cracked my windshield?" Jim bellowed. "'Cuz you're going to pay for it. Now speak up!"

"Can you believe this clown?" I heard one of the kids say.

A stocky boy with braids walked up and stood close to Jim so that they were face-to-face. "Why don't you go home, man? You're not in your neighborhood now. Take your little wife and your little girls and get the fuck out."

I thought it was pretty sound advice. But Jim shoved the kid so that he stumbled into his friends, who caught him. Then I heard Jim say, "Listen, kid, don't tell me where I belong. I used to live in Jamaica."

There was laughter from the group, and it sounded almost jolly. But suddenly a punch was thrown. I don't know which of the kids did it, but I saw Jim hurtling backward and falling heavily onto the pavement. Mona was sobbing, "Oh my God, oh my fucking God. I shouldn't have come. Dennis told me not to come."

In a matter of seconds, my mother had slipped into the driver's seat, revved the motor, and swerved the car around to where Jim lay. The kids stood over him. "You want to mess with me, motherfucker? Pig-faced bitch. Come on!"

I slid low in the seat. I was scared, but also embarrassed. Jim looked like a fool lying there, holding his face and groaning. I didn't want the teenagers to think I belonged with these white people in the car. It struck me how little I felt toward Mona and Jim. It scared me a little, how easily they could become strangers to me. How easily they could become cowering white folks, nothing more, nothing less. But unlike them, my mother didn't seem frightened at all. She was back to her old self as she jumped out, stormed up to the teenagers, and dragged Jim to his feet. She said as she led Jim roughly to the car, "All right now. The fun's over. Enough of this silliness." The kids were still mumbling obscenities at Jim, but appeared satisfied with the one blow. They didn't seem to know what to make of my mother, this tall white lady who didn't behave in the least bit ruffled by their bravado. She didn't say two words to them.

She just shoved Jim into the passenger side, got in the driver's seat, and took off. We all were quiet as my mother zoomed toward a freeway entrance. It hadn't been that far away after all, making Jim's circular route seem all the more absurd. I heard Mona sniffling, but didn't look at her. Now that the threat was passed, I thought of something my father had once lectured to Cole over dinner at Bob the Chef's while I played with my spare ribs and mashed potatoes and listened in silence. "See, baby, white boys have a primitive fixation on black men," he had told Cole, who was busy reading a comic book under the table. "They envy black men and despise them and lust after them all at once. They want to be them, but first they have to destroy them." He had referred to black men as "them." He never brought himself into any of his theories. It was always about somebody else.

Jim cradled his face in his hands, and only when we were well on our way north did he look up. He glanced back at Mona and me. His top lip was cracked down the middle and was beginning to bleed.

"I swear, I try to be liberal," he said to no one in particular. "I try really, really hard. But when you meet fucking punks like that, you start to wonder. I mean, Jesus, what did we do to deserve that? We're on their side, and they don't even know it."

My mother turned to him. She wore an expression of extreme disgust. She stared at him for a minute. Then she shouted, "You didn't have to get out of the car, Jim. How idiotic was that? Trying to be a big man for a little crack in the window. They were children. Teenagers. Pranksters. I swear, sometimes your honky ass—"

She ate the words she was on the verge of saying and turned back to the road.

But Jim had heard enough. His face was the deepest crimson I had ever seen it. "What did you just say? My 'honky ass'? Who were you rooting for, anyway? Those ghetto thugs, or me? I mean, fuck, Sheila. Sometimes it's hard to tell with you."

She simply shook her head. "Jim, you're full of shit. We're all tired. The girls are terrified. Now let's just get home."

We didn't speak. Mona had stopped sobbing and was rubbing her shoulder angrily where I had hit her. I could see, out of the corner of my eye, that she was glaring at me, mouthing some vague threat that involved the words "kick your butt," but I didn't bother to look. I'd think of an excuse later. Damage control, as my mother called it. I'd explain that I had been scared and didn't know what I was doing. But for now I couldn't talk to any of them. Instead, I watched the darkness fly by outside, the yellow of cars coming toward us, the red of cars moving away.

I HAD SECRETLY hoped, listening to them fight, that Jim and my mother would break up. I had hoped that they would finally see each other for what they really were and fall promptly out of love. But it was as if the woman my mother had exposed to him that night—the brave, loud, foulmouthed one—had made her more attractive to him, not less.

By the following morning, they were giggling about the incident at the breakfast table. From my bedroom I could hear them talking. He was saying, "I guess I'm just a country boy trying to act city smart. But you were cool, babe, cool as a cucumber. Where'd you learn to act like that?" I heard my mother laugh, a Tinker Bell laugh that floated up to my bedroom, and I rolled over in bed, feeling a little sick.

When I came downstairs to go to school, my mother had already left for the professor's. Jim stood at the sink, washing dishes. He turned around, and I gasped. His top lip had swollen grotesquely overnight. He laughed at the expression on my face. "That kid sure knew how to throw a left hook. I still wish your mom woulda let me at him."

He threw a fake punch into the air and turned back to his pile of dishes, chuckling.

When I got to school, I expected to face Mona's wrath. But she only grinned when she saw me in the cafeteria at lunch, and waved me over to her table. She was in the midst of telling a group of girls the story of our New Haven adventure. As I neared the table, I heard her say, "Those fuckin' coons were out of control." When I sat down beside her, she put her arm around me and said she had forgiven me for my outburst. "Jess totally freaked out and socked me," she explained to the girls, pulling up her shirt sleeve to show us all the big purple bruise I had left her with. They oohed and aahed, impressed, and it seemed that all of them, including Mona, had newfound respect for me. Now I was not just Mona's sidekick, but her equal.

"Jesse's dad," Mona continued, "he was awesome. He got out of the car and told all these huge black dudes where they could shove it." She often referred to Jim as my dad. I'd grown tired of correcting her. The girls laughed and begged her to tell the story again.

Over the next few weeks, Mona obsessed over what had happened, and the more she talked about it, the more outrageously exaggerated the event became. One day I heard the story related back to me from a boy named Billy in my class. He said he heard that Mona and I had been attacked by a group of "crazy niggers in Harlem." Was it true?

I tried to explain to him that it hadn't happened that way at all. "They didn't attack us," I said. "Jim turned it into this big deal. And they were just kids, you know, playing around."

But Billy had wandered off already, bouncing a basketball down the hall, bored by my version of the events. When I asked Mona why she had been making things up, she just shrugged and laughed and said, "Well, it coulda happened that way."

By the time Christmas vacation came, I was barely speaking to my mother or Jim. They both tried, but I was sarcastic, cold, and sullen in their presence. One afternoon, my mother came up to my room. I was reading a novel and didn't look up.

"I want Christmas to be special this year, baby," I heard her say.

In response I mimicked something she once had said to me: "Christmas is a capitalist's wet dream. It's just one more chance to make poor people feel like shit."

I looked up to check her response. She stood at the door, holding a bitten apple. Her lips were wet, and she chewed slowly, frowning. When she didn't say anything, I shrugged and added, "Besides, I'm Jewish. I celebrate Hanukkah. Or don't you remember?"

She pursed her lips, looked around to see if Jim was anywhere near, then hissed across the room at me, "You're a cultural Jew. Not a religious one. And besides, your father's dead." She seemed tired as she added, "Let's make it good this year, baby. It's been forever since we had a real Christmas."

It had been five years. The first year after we fled Boston, we had had a pathetic little celebration in our motel room, complete with a fern dressed in tinsel and dime-store presents wrapped in newspaper. After we opened the gifts (a Magic Eight Ball for me, and a bottle of Bonnie Bell bath splash for her), we had gone out to a traditional meal of turkey and potatoes served at a nearby diner for only $4.99. The only other people taking advantage of the Holiday Special looked to me like either withered escapees from a nursing home, or serial killers. I had made us leave without dessert, because I swore a young man with a shaved head and sunglasses who sat at a nearby booth was laughing at us. After dinner we had avoided going back to our motel room. Instead, we had hidden in the escapist sanctuary of a movie theater, where we saw *Rocky*. My mother had cheered when the other boxer had beaten Sylvester Stallone to a pulp. The other people in the theater had hissed at us, and my mother had said loudly, "Look at them, Jess. They buy this crap."

After that, we had just stopped acknowledging the holiday. Not because I was Jewish, but because the holiday depressed both my mother and me. It had seemed designed simply to remind us of what was missing. So instead each year we'd find ourselves in a movie theater, taking refuge in the dark as some imitation of life blared down at us from the silver screen.

But Jim made Christmas different this year. He even bought a tall, crooked Christmas tree that filled the whole house with its scent. My mother and he spent hours listening to reggae and decorating it with old ornaments he had found in the basement of his cabin. He said he hadn't had a real Christmas in years either. They both went whole hog about it. There was a growing pile of presents for me under the tree, but I pretended to ignore it.

I was out of school for two weeks for Christmas vacation, and it was hard to avoid my mother and Jim. So I spent more and more time at Mona's trailer, lounging in the chintzy squalor of the trailer's boudoir while Mona tried on her mother's makeup, or playing video games in front of their big fake oak television. It was a strange solace I found at Mona's. Even as she and her mother and Dennis referred constantly to niggers and spics and dykes and gooks, things seemed clearer there. I didn't punch Mona anymore. Instead I would smile weakly and avert my eyes and try to tell myself what I had maintained from the start: I was a spy in enemy territory. This was all a game of make-believe.

When I woke on the big day, it did indeed feel like a real Christmas, the kind I saw only on television commercials. My mother had succeeded. Fat clumsy snowflakes floated slowly past my window, and the air was rich with the smell of coffee and my mother's famous huevos rancheros. I wanted to be immune to the holiday spirit, immune to their attempts at family, but despite myself, I felt happy, expectant, the way I used to feel as a little girl on Christmas. Back in Boston, when my parents were still married, Cole and I had always had to wait till after we had eaten breakfast to open our gifts, which made the meal unbearably long. When we did finally open them, I'd always finish first and would be forced to watch, with itching fingers, while Cole took her time, careful not to rip the paper. They often gave Cole and me identical gifts, but in different colors. Usually they got it wrong, mixed up our favorite colors, and I remembered Cole leaning forward over our new matching shirts and saying: "Hey, you got the purple one. Purple's my favorite. Here, let's trade. You can have the red."

I tiptoed downstairs, shivering in only a long T-shirt. In the living room, Jim was bent on his knees, placing presents wrapped in gold paper under the tree, and my mother lounged on the couch in a pink terry-cloth robe with the newspaper in her hands. Some Indian music floated through the air, whose haunting and religious words sounded like my mother's mantra.

Jim turned around then, and I knew something was different. Something had changed overnight.

The night before, sometime past midnight, I had heard my mother and Jim go out for a drive. They had disappeared for several hours. I had assumed they were at Jim's cabin having loud sex, or smoking by the lake.

But now I saw what their midnight drive had really been for. The news had been broken. Jim was grinning at me as if we were in on some secret together. And watching him watching me, I could see he wasn't a Fed, never had been a Fed. He wasn't and never had been dangerous in that way. From his expression, his slow-rising smile, I could imagine his reaction when she told him: dismay, fear, then a growing titillation as he realized that he was involed in something huge. The pieces—the parts that hadn't fit before—must have come into place for him, and he must have seen himself as a fool. But an important fool. He was beaming at me.

My mother lay supine on the couch, wool oatmeal socks on her feet and a concerned look on her face. She was trying to read my mood. I had a brief inexplicable urge to run out the door and through the snow to the Marshes'. But I knew they were away in Connecticut. Nicholas wouldn't be coming back for vacation until spring.

I stood still, watching them from the doorway, and we all were silent for a moment.

Jim broke the silence. "Hey, Jess—" He said the name awkwardly now, as if it lay heavy as a horse's bit against his tongue. "Merry Christmas, kiddo."

I stared at my mother. She was blushing. "Jess, babe. Come sit down with me." She patted the space on the couch beside her.

I hesitated, then went to the far corner of the couch, to the space at her feet.

Jim sat cross-legged on the floor, never taking his eyes off me. I shifted uncomfortably. He seemed to be searching my face for something, looking at me with a newfound curiosity, as if I were a jewel he had believed to be counterfeit and only now found out was real.

He said then, measuring his words: "Jess, I just want you to know that I'm going to stick by you and your mother. She's told me everything, and she was afraid I'd run. But I'm still here." He and my mother exchanged a meaningful smile. "And that's the way I'm gonna stay. By your side."

My mother sat up and reached for my hand. I didn't take it, but looked at it as if it were some strange foreign object being thrust my way. She started to say something: "Jess, he's with us. He knows who we are—" but stopped, just as the Indian music on the tape player stopped. The room was quiet, as if the stereo too wanted to hear my response.

I looked at Jim and gave a little cough of a laugh before I said, my voice rising into a pitch I hadn't used before, "This was supposed to be our secret. Now he's in on it? What the hell does he have to do with any of this? I thought we were waiting. I thought we were waiting for them."

Jim looked sad then and shook his head. "Jess, don't do this to your mother. To us. I know your mother's scared and brave and beautiful. And yes"—he sighed, as if he were speaking to a small child—"I know your father is black. I know everything, kiddo. And I think it's terrific the way you two have—"

I cut him off. My voice was loud and thick: "Oh, you *do* know everything? That my father's black? I feel so much better now. Did you know I was black too? And that I had a nappy-headed sister but my mother didn't know what to do with her so she sold her to the gypsies—"

"Birdie!" my mother shrieked. Her chin was trembling. I had finally hit a nerve.

I stood up, and they both looked frightened, like tourists staring up at a monkey in a tree, waiting for it to throw shit in their faces. Jim even stiffened as if to prepare for attack.

"Thanks, Mum," I said, "for sticking by the rules. Now I know who to trust," before dashing out of the room and up the stairs.

I BLASTED THE CARS and sifted through my shoe box of negrobilia, staring at the same old dusty objects, fingering the same old plastic pick, the same old Egyptian necklace that was tarnished and needed polishing. Outside, it had stopped snowing and the sky was a pale blue through the trees. The world seemed completely silent. I wondered if Cole missed white Christmases, if she missed my mother today.

I hadn't forgotten my father's words just before he had left. He had said to me at the door to the car, looking over my head: "Boston, America, is a fucking mess, and it's only going to get uglier. Black people need to start thinking internationally." He had also said that our separation was going to be "just for a while."

My box of negrobilia was getting so full it wouldn't close. Recently, for Mona's birthday, her mother had taken us out for Chinese food in the next town over. Dennis had come along and he had kept his hand on my knee under the table, licking his lips at me from time to time, when he didn't think his mother was looking. He had ordered a cocktail which had a little fat-bellied brown woman floating in it, the kind they used to serve at Aku-

Aku. After dinner, I had stolen the doll, slipped it in my pocket, and put it in the box when I got home. Looking at the dolls now it seemed a little crazy, an act of kleptomania. It reminded me of how my mother used to steal Snickers bars when we were little, embarrassing Cole, thrilling me. She didn't do that anymore.

Later in the afternoon, I sneaked downstairs. I could hear my mother and Jim whispering on the couch in the living room. My mother sounded like she was crying, and I heard my sister's name being whispered. It had started snowing again, and I bundled up in an old tweed coat of my mother's before going out into the whipping wind.

Inside the stable, Mr. Pleasure was cold to the touch, and I put a horse blanket on her. I pressed my face to her nose and inhaled. There was nothing better than the smell of a horse. It comforted me, and I rested my head there for a while, inhaling and thinking. In a way, I was disappointed that Jim wasn't a Fed. He was just a pothead with a goofy sense of humor. Maybe that was the more dangerous shade of white, I thought to myself as I kissed the velveteen nose of Mr. Pleasure. My father had said white liberals were a disease. At least you know what you're dealing with in an overt racist. But a liberal was more slippery. You could lose yourself. There was something to that argument. I had become friends with Mona and all the little racists. That way I would always know I was living a lie. Better them than someone who would smile in my face and make me believe I was at home. I was glad that I had resisted Jim's overtures to become my father. My real father, I decided, would be proud of me, if he ever got a chance to find out.

The day was almost all over. I considered going to Mona's trailer, seeing if she had gotten as drunk on egg nog as she had said she would. She had told me the night before that she was fed up with Samantha Taper and was going to "kick her black ass" one of these days. She admitted to me that she wanted Samantha's boyfriend, Matthew. "I mean, fuck, he's only the cutest boy in the school." I didn't want any of the boys in town. I wondered if there were something wrong with me. Permanent damage from those months at Aurora. I had told Mona that I had almost gone all the way with Nicholas, but really I had only touched him for that moment. Maybe I would never be able to go all the way with a white boy. Sex was the only time, outside of the womb, when a person became one with another, when two people really melted together, into one body. Allowing a white boy inside of me would make my transformation complete, something I wasn't ready for. I thought about Stuart Langley. Just the week before, he had winked at me during an assembly in the school auditorium. Perhaps I would lose my virginity to him. At least he was black. But the thought of it depressed me. His high-pitched laughter got on my nerves. Besides, he seemed to have a thing for blond girls. Maybe I would remain a virgin forever, never letting anything penetrate me.

Cole had a boyfriend the last time I saw her. A thin brown boy named Anthony. I remembered the first time he had kissed her. She had been twelve. She had slipped into bed with me, giggling. Her body beside me had felt different, softer, more alive, as she said, "Birdie, Ant kissed me today." I had closed my eyes, feeling sad but not wanting her to notice. I had felt her drifting away from me, into another world. I would always be three years behind her. That difference was forever.

I HEARD A NOISE and turned. There was a shadow at the door of the stable. My mother. She was shivering in Jim's big green parka and an old-mannish gray cap that shadowed her eyes. I didn't know how long she'd been there.

"Who are you talking to?" she asked.

I hadn't realized I was talking aloud. I just shrugged and looked back at Mr. Pleasure, stroking her silky brown nose.

"Listen, Jesse, I know you feel betrayed. But I had to let him in on it. I trust him. And you've been heroic, but I need more than just you in my life, baby. Really, it's healthier for both of us this way."

I turned to her, shoving my hands in my pockets. "What the hell is going on, Mum? Why are we here?" My voice surprised me. It sounded different—angry, adult, scolding.

She stiffened, her shoulders bunching slightly. I had asked it before, but there was more weight to the question this time. She laughed harshly. "So, you don't believe me. After all this time, you don't believe me."

I didn't say anything. I had never thought not to believe her. But now the possibility rose up between us, making me slightly dizzy in its implications.

She said, "It's strange. The only way you'd believe me is if I were in prison."

This was how she answered questions. Sideways.

It was so dark now that I couldn't see her expression as she came toward me and said, "It was illegal. Very. Nobody was hurt or killed. But I was a part of something big, and because of it, we had to split up. Your father and I. And we had to choose which one of you looked more like the other. We had to. In order for me to disappear. We had to choose." She sounded strange. Not drunk. More broken. Beyond crying as she said, "And the crazy thing is, your sister was the reason I did what I did. Having a black child made me see things differently. Made it all the more personal. It hurts to see your baby come into a world like this, so you want to change it." My mother did that sometimes, spoke of Cole as if she had been her only black child. It was as if my mother believed that Cole and I were so different. As if she believed I was white, believed I was Jesse.

She was in front of me, and her features looked beautiful, abstract, in the shadows of the barn. Mr. Pleasure was rattling her chains and snorting beside us.

I said something then, something I never knew I felt until the words came out: "She was your favorite. Wasn't she? You loved her the best. Both you and Papa did. She was the one you both wanted to keep."

Now that I had spoken it, it seemed so clear. Cole was the one my father and mother had fought for, not me. I was the one they both knew they could have without asking. And then I was crying. Sobbing. So that I couldn't breathe. And she was holding me to her, crying with me, saying softly, "That's nonsense, Birdalee. There, there, you're going to give yourself an asthma at-tack. Breathe, baby, breathe."

She had said that to me when I was little and was having a tantrum. The crying always made me wheeze, made my lungs close up.

"You miss her too," she said, stroking my hair. "Don't you? You miss her too."

It seemed a odd question. Odd that she would even have to say it. I just said, "Yeah, I miss her. And him."

I didn't think she'd heard me, but after a moment she said, "And him."

I smelled her hair. It smelled of green apples. Some new shampoo.

I pried myself out from her arms and looked down at our shoes, letting my hair fall forward over my eyes. I said in a small voice, "Did you even love him?"

She didn't pause. "I never loved a man more. Never will."

I was surprised. "Do you love Jim?"

She bit her lip and looked away. Then she shrugged. "I do love him, in a way. But not in the same way. Someday you'll love like I loved your father, and you'll spend the rest of your life recovering."

She draped her arm around me and led me outside into the cold white field. We began to walk back toward the house, which was lit up, smoke billowing from the chimney—the picture of a happy home. Merle Haggard played from the living room.

I wasn't sure I believed anything my mother had told me, but I put my head on her shoulder anyway and tried to imagine her as a young girl—fat and young and lost—on the verge of something beautiful in my father's arms.

the brown
and the pink

Mona leaned in and whispered into my ear, "Stuart Langley might be at the party tonight. Would you ever do it with him?"

I shrugged, not sure of the right answer. "I don't know. Would you?"

Mona licked her lips and said, "Me, I'd try anything once. But I know you. You're a baby. You'd be too scared of that big black cock."

I laughed and hugged myself against the wind of the open road.

The pickup truck belonged to Dennis, and the party was at his house. He was twenty-one, too old to be giving high-school parties, and because of his reputation, none of the other freshman girls was allowed to go that weekend. But my mother had simply smiled when I had asked her. She'd told me: "It's your choice, mush."

We'd be the youngest girls there, and Mona promised me that all of the upper-classmen boys would want us. I had only one boy on my mind. I had heard that Nicholas was coming back to stay. He had been expelled from his boarding school for good, though I still hadn't been able to find out why. His parents had mentioned it to my mother with grim expressions, saying, "If he wants to stay in this podunk town, throw away his opportunities, we're going to let him, goddamn it." My mother had reported this news to Jim and me over dinner. She had seemed impressed by Nicholas, his ability to get kicked out of an institution of wealth and privilege. She said, "He probably feels more at home around real people, not those snobs at boarding school. I can totally relate. I went through the same thing at his age. Good for him."

Nicholas had told me before he left: "Don't get too comfortable here." Back then, I still wore grass-stained Toughskins and my hair in twin braids. Nearly two years had gone by since then, and I wondered if he'd notice the changes in me.

Dennis lived on the outskirts of town, where he and his roommates could grow marijuana in the backyard, free from the eyes of nosy neighbors. The house was littered with junk—beer, garbage, underwear strewn over furniture.

Before the party began, I went into the bathroom to primp. I was just putting on some peacock-feather earrings that Mona had loaned me when Dennis opened the door without knocking. I was glad I hadn't been on the toilet. He stepped inside, leaving the door open a crack behind him.

He had a six-pack of beer in his hand. "Bud, Jesse?"

I shrugged. "Sure."

He winked at me. "You look good."

He was being nicer than usual, and he stood behind me, watching me in the mirror as I finished putting on the earring.

"You're growing up," he said, eyeing me in the mirror. "You're growing up real nice. You got a boyfriend, Jesse?"

I didn't like the way he was looking me up and down, and watched as he hawked and spit into his trusty brown-and-pink cup. "No. Not really," I answered.

"You will," he said licking his lips.

I blushed and tried to squeeze past him out of the bathroom to find Mona.

He stood in my path and slid his hand around my waist. "Aren't you going to thank me for the beer?"

I began to wheeze as if I were having an asthma attack, saying, "Thanks. I gotta go find my inhaler. I got asthma." Sweat tickled my armpits as I shoved past him.

I found Mona in Dennis's bedroom, where she stood before the mirror in a stuffed black bra and dingy gray Hello Kitty underwear. She was rubbing her cheeks furiously, trying to blend in the streaks of hot-pink blush. The room smelled of damp laundry.

"Hey, Jess, how does this blush look? I stole it from my mom."

I told her, "It looks fine. I mean, listen, your brother, Dennis—"

"Half brother, you mean."

"Half brother, yeah. He was acting kind of funny in the bathroom just now. I don't know—" I stopped in mid-sentence, hoping she would read my mind.

She sort of laughed. "Oh, was he trying to feel you up or something? Next time tell him to go jerk off."

Mona and I emerged from his room—full makeup, stuffed bras, skin-tight jeans, hardened hair—just as the party people started filing in, cracking beers, blasting the J. Geils Band, and slumping onto the furniture.

I stood in a corner for the first hour, by the keg, filling people's plastic cups and drinking out of my own. Although I had been taking occasional sips of my mother's beer and wine for as long as I could remember, I had never had this much, and before I knew it, I was dizzy. The people around me looked ghoulish, waving plastic cups in my face and belching. I told a buck-toothed girl in braces to watch the keg, and stumbled off toward the kitchen.

I peeked in the swinging door and breathed in quickly with shock, surprise, delight. Nicholas's hair was longer and hung around his face like a girl's. He looked intoxicated and was laughing hysterically with another boy, the black kid, Stuart Langley.

I stepped in, and the two boys turned to me.

Their eyes were red and doped. Nicholas didn't seem to recognize me at first, then a slow smile slid onto his lips.

"Well, if it isn't my little riding partner, Jesse."

He pulled me to him and knuckled my head. "Look at you, all made up like a little clown."

I blushed, embarrassed now at the mounds of powder-blue eye shadow, the streaks of hot-pink blush that Mona had encouraged me to put on.

He smelled like stale beer, and he playfully held me to him, saying to his friend, "Stu, this is Jesse. We go way back." He gulped from his cup, then turned back to Stuart. I noticed that he had acne now, on his neck—little red bumps. But he was still thin and delicate. "Did you hear I got kicked out? For mooning the headmistress. She was a fucking bitch. I'll tell you the whole story some other time."

Stuart was laughing. "Dude, you're a fuckin' riot. That's awesome. Well, it's good to have you here, anyway. Fuck all those rich kids."

Nicholas kind of grimaced and looked back at me. "So, Stu, my main man, what do you think of Jesse? She's gonna be mine when she's old enough."

Stuart looked at me and smiled. "She looks old enough tonight."

Nicholas pulled me into a tighter hug. "Maybe she is old enough. You think you're old enough, Pocahontas?"

I wanted Stuart to leave us alone, and as if he could read my mind, he said, "Nick, dude, I'm gonna get some more beer. Want anything?"

Nicholas said, "Nah."

When he was gone, Nicholas held me out in front of him, taking me in with his eyes, turning me around. "You look good—different."

I wasn't sure whether I saw disapproval in his eyes, so I said, "Yeah, Mona showed me how to do my makeup."

He nodded and punched me lightly across the chin. "I hope you didn't change too much." He paused, then asked, "Want to go outside? Where it's quieter? Onto the porch?"

"Okay."

We went onto the porch, where a couple of kids stood smoking weed. Dennis's house lay next to a forest, like the one near my house. Crickets screeched in unison over the rock music that wafted out from the party. I hugged myself and leaned against the railing, looking out at the vast darkness.

He pulled me close to him then, and I tipped my head up to his. The music that played now was "Centerfold" as I felt his tongue on my lips, his gentle mouth parting mine. Heard him say, "Relax, Jess," as he stroked my arms.

Mona had said that when a boy kissed her the right way, she "creamed" her panties. Although Nicholas's kissing techniques seemed fine, I still felt none of the cream that Mona had told me I would. Instead, I felt outside of myself, as if I hovered over the scene, staring down at these two bodies as their tongues darted toward, then away from, each other's. I watched myself—this stranger with the brown feathered hair, the thick meeting eyebrows, the one who no longer wore a Star of David—and thought how impressively she kissed. It was Alexis who had taught me this. Afterward,

Nicholas held me away from him and said, "I just want to look at you." In a flash of anxiety I wondered what he saw—if he knew that my perky breasts were made of shoulder pads.

Mona's voice broke into our moment.

"Jesse, I've been looking all over for you. I have to talk to you. Now."

She teetered before me, holding a bottle of Budweiser in one hand, tapping a cigarette with the other.

Nicholas winked at me and said, "See you around," then wandered off in the direction of the party.

I was annoyed by Mona's interruption, but she seemed upset. She pulled me into a corner of the porch.

"She's here," she whispered to me, smelling of clove cigarettes and perfume.

"Who?"

"That fucking bitch, Samantha. That's who. She's here and she's all over Matthew. You wouldn't believe it. Someone said she was giving him a blow job in the bathroom. I think I'm going to puke."

I wasn't sure if she was serious, but I moved away from her. She did actually throw up then. I watched it shoot, projectile yellow fluid, into the bushes in front of us. A little of it splattered on my shoes. When she was through, I held her arm and led her through the party to Dennis's bedroom.

On the way, I saw Samantha leaning against the wall in between Matthew and Dennis, while Michael rolled a joint near them on the couch. I could see why Mona was mad. Samantha looked good. She had let her hair loose for once, and it sat in black ringlets around her face. She wore a pink tank top that hugged her body, and a white denim miniskirt.

Dennis stood beside her, leering at her chest, his arm around her shoulder, running his finger up and down her arm. Samantha looked repulsed by him and seemed to be trying to pull away, toward Matthew, who was too busy chugging beers to notice.

In the bedroom, we shut the door, and Mona lay curled in a ball on the bed, sniffling into her hands. I sat on the bed, rubbing her shoulders. "It's okay, she's just easy. She's a slut. That's the only reason Matthew likes her."

Mona sobbed even harder, drunker than I'd ever seen her. "I want to be easy. I don't give a shit. I'd suck his cock. I think I love him."

She went on like that for a while until finally she seemed to pass out. I sat listening to the laughter and shouting from the party outside.

After covering Mona with a ratty blanket, I left her snoring on the bed. My mission was to find Nicholas, to finish what we had started. I looked around the house. Dennis, Matthew, and Stuart were standing over a girl who appeared to be asleep on the couch. They were trying to peek up her skirt. But I didn't see Nicholas. I didn't know anyone else in the room. They all were older than I, and they seemed to move in slow motion, heavy, lumbering movements, looking through me, not at me, as I walked over bodies, shoved past couples who made out against walls.

I had to pee and found the bathroom at the back of the hallway. Inside, two girls with eyes black and blue with makeup, faces dripping with beer, sat on the floor side by side, like Tweedledee and Tweedledum, laughing hysterically to themselves.

"Can I use the bathroom?" I asked, feeling dizzy all of a sudden.

They only looked at me and laughed harder. One of them pointed at me and said, "Fresh meat."

I stood outside the bathroom for a while, but they wouldn't budge. Finally, the pressure in my bladder got the best of me and I decided to go into the woods to pee. I was usually afraid of the woods at night, but tonight, with the light and clamor of the party behind me, I felt safe shoving through the brambles and stumbling over the sticks. The air was clear and cold and felt good filling my lungs. I hummed a song to myself. It was one of my mother's favorites. My voice sounded way off-key to me, drunk, and my body felt heavy, cumbersome, like someone else's.

I reached a clearing in the trees and stopped, balancing myself with one hand on the rough bark next to me.

I saw her before she saw me, and I must have been quite drunk because she appeared as someone else, someone melancholy and sullen and fluent in Elemeno. She appeared as my sister under the broken swatches of sky, and she stood at a distance, just buttoning up her skirt when I came upon her. My foot crunched on a twig, and she turned, not seeing me for a moment, her face frightened and smeared with aging makeup.

"It's just me," I said into the space between us.

Samantha's eyes adjusted to me, and she smiled slightly. "I thought you were a boy. You looked like a guy standing there in the shadows."

It only struck me right then as strange that we had never spoken. She was kneeling now, rifling around in her cheap leather purse. "Those girls," she said as she found a compact she had been looking for, "those girls aren't letting anyone near the bathroom. So I guess we all have to use the woods. As our toilet, you know." She laughed that same throaty, hollow laugh that she used with the boys. It was grating somehow, and I looked away. She was anxious around me. She knew I was one of them, that she had no friends outside of Nora and had better not try. She was putting on lipstick now, a light frosted pink that didn't suit her complexion.

I watched her, thinking of the kids dancing in New York. I wondered if she had ever been anywhere like that, seen any world outside of this, where people like her, like us, were not exceptions to some rule.

I spoke my thoughts out loud without meaning to. "Have you ever been to New York?"

She looked at me quizzically. "No. I'd be too scared. My dad says there are all kinds of weirdos there. Perverts, you know."

She put her purse over her shoulder and paused, waiting to see if I was going to talk more. "See you back there. Now I guess you can pee in peace." She started to walk away.

I shouted "No!" louder than I had meant to. I was drunk, and that must have had something to do with it, but I couldn't let her walk away so soon. I said in a softer voice, "I mean, could you wait while I pee? I'm kind of scared out here alone."

Relief spread over her features. She seemed surprised to have me speaking to her like this. Nobody but Nora spoke to her like this. "Okay, sure. I mean, I won't look."

And she turned her back to me, staring into the woods. I thought it was a funny modest gesture as I leaned to squat, letting the pee go trickling from my body into the dark soft earth. When I was done, I stood up and she turned around.

I said, zipping up my jeans and trying to steady myself, "Samantha, can I ask you a question?"

"Sure," she said, snapping on her gum in loud cracks.

I shivered. Suddenly, I wanted to go to her, to tell her who I was. I thought it might make her feel better to know she wasn't the only one.

But instead I said, "What color do you think I am?"

She was silent, staring at me in a new light, it seemed, taking in my features one by one. I tried to look different, more serious, and thought the word "black" to myself, hoping through telepathy to transmit the correct answer to her.

Finally she smiled kind of sideways, as if she were trying not to laugh. "Nora said you were Jewish. I saw you wearing that star thing they all have to wear. Yeah, Jewish." She repeated the words and they felt heavy, like drumbeats in my ears. Far off at the party I could hear them playing the Doors. *Hello. I love you. Won't you tell me your name?*

"Why do you ask?" she said.

I looked away. "I'm not really Jewish. It's a lie." I said it slowly, hoping to gather some kind of courage as I spoke.

She laughed. "What do you mean?"

I paused. My mother's words tickled my ears. *Trust nobody. You are Jesse Goldman. Everybody is suspect.*

"I mean," I said, feeling a sinking weight of resignation in my chest, "I'm not Jewish. My mom's not Jewish. She has to be Jewish for me to be Jewish, really, and she's not." As I said it, I wondered, for the first time, if the same was true with blackness. Did you have to have a black mother to be really black? There had been no black women involved in my conception. Cole's either. Maybe that made us frauds.

Samantha looked bored now, like she wanted to get back to the party.

She said, "Well, you want to start back?"

We walked, our feet crunching in unison as we made our way toward the loud burst of adolescent fever and debauchery. It had begun to drizzle softly, like a veil brushing my skin. I could hear the moisture touching the leaves of the forest; it made a mild hissing sound. Samantha held her hands over her hair so that it wouldn't get wet.

Just as we reached the lawn before the house, I pulled her to a stop and said, "One more question."

She looked impatient now. She didn't want to be popular this badly. "What?"

"What color are you?"

There was a prolonged silence, then she smiled sideways the way she had in the woods. She said so softly that I wasn't sure I'd heard her right: "I'm black. Like you."

A hoot of male laughter and a feminine squeal that sounded like Mona belted out at us from the house. "Fuckin' A, Dennis! Get off of me!"

Samantha glanced longingly back toward the house, the source of the shrieks, the windows which glowed yellow, revealing the hunched silhouettes of wanton bodies. It had begun to rain harder, and the hissing of the woods had turned to more of a slapping sound.

Her face glowed wetly, and her makeup seemed to run in little rivulets of paint down her skin. Her curls had tightened up from the moisture, making her hair appear shorter than it was. "So, are you coming inside with me, or what?"

I must have said no, because she shrugged, then walked away from me toward the party and the people, nearly slipping on the wet grass in her flat white shoes.

I WALKED THE TREK from Dennis's with my head bowed down to the asphalt, as if the only thing that mattered was that my feet kept moving, not where they led. It must have been about three miles, and by the time I reached my house, I was drenched.

Inside, a heavy silence filled the house. I crept up the creaking stairs to my mother's bedroom at the top, and stood outside her door. I felt a sob rising to my chest. I wanted to sleep with her in the big bed once again. I wanted her to be my mother right then, the mother she had been—heavy, angry, buck-wild, and dangerous. During our first year on the run, back when everything still seemed temporary, she used to tell me stories about the years I didn't remember—the years when Cole and I spoke Elemeno and my grandmother thought we were possessed. My mother used to describe those days to me in great detail, how Cole and I had walked in that goose step, me four steps behind Cole, our lips moving in incomprehensible babble. And she would recount the years when she and my father were so in love that their friends stopped coming over (it was boring, they told my parents, to be around two people so intensely focused on only each other).

She hadn't told me any of these tales in years, since we arrived at Aurora, really, when her silence began to set in. I wanted those stories. I wanted her to remind me of who I had been, who we had been. I opened her door.

Moonlight fell through the curtains, illuminating her bed. The duvet shone blue in the light. She lay with her blond locks spread around her face. She had stopped using henna, had let her hair go back to natural, a sure sign that the real danger had passed, even if she wouldn't admit it. Beside her was Jim, his big brawny arm thrown over her chest with the force of possession, his snore coming out clear and daunting. His back and shoulders were covered with gray hair.

I shifted, and the floorboard creaked. My mother grumbled something and flopped onto her other side. I waited to hear if she'd say anything else, but she was silent.

I watched them for a moment longer and felt that power one feels at being the only one awake in a room of sleeping bodies. I felt sorry for them. Then I left the room, closing the door softly behind me.

I packed the essentials—my box of negrobilia, a few pairs of underwear, a photograph of me and my mother during our first month in New Hampshire, when we still slept together, wrapped around each other like twin sisters. I took the Star of David as well, though I wasn't sure why. Downstairs in the kitchen, the refrigerator hummed as I shuffled around in our "emergency" drawer with trembling hands, looking for cash. I found it and stuffed it in my pocket.

Outside, I went to the stable. I woke Mr. Pleasure with a kiss to her velvety nose. I stood there for a while, inhaling her skin and fur, hugging her thickness and warmth to me. I don't remember if I cried. Just that I trembled all over. I left in the darkness, walking in long heavy strides. The invisible crickets and the mysterious electric hum of the forest made a kind of symphony in the night air. It struck me how clear the world was in the hour before dusk, how bright that last darkness was. I had left at this hour so many times before, trailing behind my mother, awed by how private that time was between us, intimate as a dream we had entered together as we moved forward on endless roads, side by side, silent and sleepy-eyed, in the cold drafty van. Now I felt a bit like her, taking to the road this way.

When I reached the center of town, all the shops were closed, the gratings pulled down, the streets bare, seeming slightly apocalyptic in their abandonment. Bing Bros. Guns 'n' Stuff, where I had shoplifted with Mona one morning, stolen a Swiss Army jackknife because it was the only thing not under glass. The billboard of the giant apple, the bite revealing an off-white pulp. The trails that wound around the edge of town, where Nicholas had taken me riding. Hans's Toy Shop and Doll Hospital, where I had seen dolls on a gurney. Those landmarks had looked so strange to me once, when we'd first arrived. Now each of them housed a memory.

There was a faint sound of laughter up ahead, and I thought I was imagining things for a moment, but around the bend, several cars were parked in front of the bar. The same bar where my mother had first spoken to Jim that night when Kenny Rogers played like a soundtrack to his pass. I missed the girl I had been then, so dirty and misfit and off-kilter. A girl raised by wolves.

As I got nearer to the bar, I passed a parked Suburban. Inside, I could just make out the shape of two bodies moving. One of the faces—the woman's—looked up long enough to notice me. I paused. Her face was familiar, and I blinked at it, trying to put together the features behind the glass. It was Mona's mother. Beside her, the bulbous red face of Gus, the bartender. Both of their expressions were completely blank, rubbed clean from the friction of flesh against flesh. I swayed before them, listening to the rock music that pounded out from the heavy red door.

Mona's mother turned back to Gus as if she hadn't seen me at all, and I moved forward, thinking of Nicholas and Mona, about Samantha and Nora. I suspected I would never see them again, and a shudder of grief passed through me. I wondered if my mother had felt that way leaving Bernadette and the rest of the women behind at Aurora. Or when she left Boston that morning in the dim dawn air, knowing she wouldn't see her mother, her child, her husband, for many years to come, if ever. I wondered, as I passed the clear abandoned lake—silver, still, silent—if I too would forever be fleeing in the dark, abandoning parts of myself that I no longer wanted, in search of some part that had escaped me. Killing one girl in order to let the other one free. It hurt, this killing, more than I thought it would, but I kept walking, repeating a pattern of words under my breath, words that I no longer understood but whispered just the same. *kublica marentha doba. lasa mel kin.*

compared
to what

chocolate city

It wasn't clear to me then why I had fled New Hampshire on that particular night and not another—whether my escape had been set into motion much earlier, in New York City, with the flying bodies on the pavement, or if it had begun just that night, with the half-nappy girl in the woods, and the rain that slapped the trees.

Later these questions would cross my mind, but for now, on that bus ride to Boston, I simply watched the world float by outside the bus window, beyond my own pale reflection, and thought that this was where I felt most safe—on a moving vehicle, rolling toward some destination but not quite there.

And when the daylight began to creep over the world and the twin dark forms of John Hancock and the Prudential grew visible in the distance, I considered staying on that bus, living on that bus, letting even this city, this vestige of my former life, roll on by. But I didn't have enough money to travel farther, and so I stood up with the rest of the red-eyed and rumpled travelers, fetched my backpack from the overhead rack, and stepped off the groaning vehicle and into the morning city, thinking how strange that this had been two and a half hours away all of that time.

I had nothing much to go on. Just the address I had found on the postcard in my mother's book. The address for Dorothy Lee. Aunt Dot. I fingered the postcard in my pocket. I had no idea when or how the postcard had reached my mother. And there was no guarantee Dot was still at the address she had given. The Dorothy Lee I had known had fled America in 1975, had gone to India with the words "permanent exile" as her only guide. It was improbable that Dot would still be living back here, in Boston, the very city that had sent her and so many others running.

A cracked and faded sign read, WELCOME TO BEAN TOWN! beside a Celtics leprechaun. Beneath that, a clock. Eight-thirty. My mother would be waking now, sitting at the butcher block table, the newspaper spread out in front of her and a cup of milky coffee growing cool in the handmade mug I had made her in arts and crafts. She would be curious to know how my big night had been. If I had a crush on anyone. She would be tempted to wake me for breakfast and find out the details, but she would wait for several more hours yet—several more hours to open the door to a sheet and a bed and an open drawer, clothes spilling out onto the floor.

The bus depot was filthy. Lumpen bodies slept under blankets made of newspapers. A tiny man who looked like Mickey Rooney was pulling open the grate that covered Dunkin' Donuts. I was slightly dizzy and thought it might be hunger. Or maybe it was just the alcohol. I had been drunk when I left New Hampshire.

It had been six years since I had been in this town. Six years since 1976, when my mother had taken me from bed and dragged us both into the dawn. Now it was March 1982, a whole new world of styles and sounds.

I had imagined Boston many times since then. In the Boston of my mind, streetlamps shone over cobblestone streets; swans in sneakers paddled around the Public Gardens; the Charles River glistened a silver white while crew boys glided swiftly across the water, their arms perfectly synchronized in motion; a raised black fist waved over a classroom of dashiki-clad children. Boston had remained to me as frozen as a body packed in ice.

But now, here it was before me—dull, muted colors, biting winter air, tacky signs advertising happiness. The faces around me seemed stony and mean, bitter and as closed as shutters.

The faithful pink-and-brown decor of the Dunkin' Donuts was all that was familiar. I went inside. A huddle of older men sat at the counter, drinking their coffee and joking with the waitress, a slim red-haired girl with braces. She looked underage. Her uniform was too large, with empty darts where her breasts should have been. I got a coffee with cream and sugar and a chocolate eclair, handing the girl a crumpled five-dollar bill. I had counted my money on the train. After the twelve-dollar bus fare, there were forty-five dollars left. It would get me to where I wanted to go, to that address which I had figured out was in the South End. Forty-six Montgomery Street. The place where Dorothy Lee was supposed to live.

I had the brief impulse to sit at the counter among the men, catch my breath, eavesdrop on their conversations about the Bruins spoken in thick local accents. My mother once had admitted a prejudice against just such accents. We had been lying side by side in a Motel 6 when she explained to me that she was prejudiced against three accents in the world: the German accent, the white Southern accent, and the Boston accent. All three accents made her suspect a person of great evil.

The Boston accent sounded a lot like the New Hampshire one. *Noo Hampsha.*

But in Dunkin' Donuts that morning, the Boston accent, even on these grizzly red-faced men, sounded comforting and welcoming to me. I wanted to stay for a while, just breathe in the fact that I was really here, in my old city where my mother once had said we would never safely set foot again.

M Y B O D Y R E M E M B E R E D the city. And outside, déjà vu hurt my eyes, made me squint as if to block out brightness, though the sky was gray. I scanned the stained bricks and cracked pavement with a vague longing. The eclair and coffee rolled around in my belly, seeming to clash and boil, causing a pin pressure just below my rib cage. Church bells rang somewhere not so far away. Nine strokes. My mother and Jim would be lying on the couch, doing their Sunday-morning ritual, half-reading the newspaper, half-massaging each other's feet.

I stopped. My body had led me to the T station. Copley Square.

Outside of the subway entrance was a map under glass, and I stared at it for a long time, at the lines of red and green and purple and blue and orange, a bright webbing of artificial colors, thick and primary. My father had told me once that those lines were racial codes. He said green led to Jews in Brookline and Newton. Red to Cambridge Wasps. The blue and the purple to the suburbs, where the Irish and Italian townies lived. And the orange line, he had told me, led to Chocolate City. To Dorchester and "the Berry." Roxbury. To your people, he had said.

People were passing me now. A gray-haired businessman with crumbs on his jacket banged against me as he made his way underground, and he looked back, annoyed. He seemed to do a double-take, and I felt a sharp tug of panic. I thought he looked at me suspiciously, as if I were something he had read about and was just now seeing for real. Had he seen my face on a post-office wall? I knew it was ridiculous, but I looked down just the same, letting my hair fall like a veil over my eyes. I turned to join the passing people in their march along Boylston Street, and when I glanced in a car window and saw my reflection, I understood the real reason the businessman had looked at me that way. I looked like a runaway. My clothes were the ones I had worn at the party the night before, the ones I had walked for miles in. They had partially dried on the bus and were musty and wrinkled. My makeup was smeared by rain and maybe tears, I couldn't remember—making my face appear blurred, like a photograph of someone caught in motion.

I FOUND MY WAY to the South End, where the brownstones sat stern and impenetrable, like troops before battle. Occasional laughter, footsteps on pavement, a brush of a passerby. Street cleaners pushed their brooms, and shop owners pulled up grates. My eyes rested on a house across the street, beyond the blinking red hand of the traffic light.

The brownstone that had housed a revolution.

As I got closer, I could see that the shutters had been painted a pale blue. A vase of paper lilies sat in the front window. My mother hadn't cared for such accoutrements. The dining room window was adorned with heavy red drapes, and upstairs I saw a soft light peeking out from my mother's old bedroom. I went up the steps slowly and read the name on the mailbox slot: "Thurman/Lewis."

I sat down on the top step and bent over, holding my head in my hands. I could feel the weight of its contents—my brain and the case it came in. My teeth had begun to chatter. I tried to envision a warm kitchen, with a cup of steaming hot chocolate and a wool blanket. It was a mind-control trick

Bernadette had taught me. Think warm, be warm. I rubbed my bare hands together and hunched forward even farther, letting my head fall upside down, so that all the blood rushed into it. I had a thick blue vein like a subway line etched in my forehead, which stuck out when I turned upside down. At Aurora, Alexis had told me once that it made me look like Frankenstein. I had liked that image of myself as a monster, an unfinished creation turned against its maker, and had terrorized a shrieking, giggling Alexis, walking toward her with my arms out in front of me, my legs stiff as wooden planks.

I had brought with me only a thin denim jacket. I wrapped my arms around my knees and rocked back and forth, my cheek pressed against my leg.

I had been lost in strange cities before, so many times, but always with my mother. She had turned danger and displacement into an adventure that we would solve together. I had believed then that my mother could take on anybody, do anything. And mostly I had been right. Few men messed with her. She wore an expression that said, "Don't fuck with me."

A voice cut into my thoughts.

"Hey, sister, you got any cigarettes?"

It was a singsong, taunting voice. A voice of royalty. I looked up. Some version of Diana Ross stood with her head in the air. She wore her long, black curls loose around a slightly ravaged mahogany face. A white faux-fur waist-length jacket wrapped around her slim form. Tight jeans and a pair of red, scuffed pump jemsons. There was a hoarseness beneath the voice, a thickness to her neck.

I found my voice. "No, sorry. Nothing." My eyes were fixed on the woman's feet. They were even bigger than mine.

The woman persisted, tapping her toe to the pavement in time as she said, "Well, how about some change? You got any? For coffee? I just need fifty cents. My head's a mess."

I saw something I liked in the woman's cracked mask. I dug into my pocket and handed her two quarters. I knew I should save my money, but the action had been automatic. Besides, I reasoned, fifty cents wouldn't make or break me.

The woman scooped the coins from me, and the tips of her nails tickled my palm. She winked at me and said, "Thanks, girl. I got no time for this headache."

She began to walk away, then paused and turned back around.

"You live here?"

I shook my head no. The woman examined me now, shrewdly, letting her eyes travel up and down my body. I automatically looked down, letting my hair swing forward across my eyes.

After a brief moment, she asked, "You all right?"

It was the hint of sympathy in her voice that broke me, and I cursed myself as I squeezed my eyes shut, feeling the warm wet tricklings against my cheek. I held my stomach and bit my lip as I rocked myself back and forth, trying to get ahold of myself. The woman came closer. I opened my eyes, and she said in a voice deeper than the one she had been using before, "You hustling?"

I shook my head, just now getting control of my breathing. My tears still streamed, and beyond them the street appeared to be floating.

The woman stepped closer and took my hand. "You're a runaway. This is your first night out here."

I nodded yes, then spoke in quick, halting sentences: "My aunt. She lives here. I mean, not here"—I gestured to the house behind me—"but in Boston, I think. I'm trying to find her. I used to live here—"

The woman cut me off. "Baby, you got an address for her, or something?"

I nodded and began to rifle through my backpack. The postcard came out, crumpled but still legible. The woman reached into her fur coat pocket and pulled out some glasses. They were drugstore reading glasses, decidedly granny-looking, and she put them on, reading the postcard with a turned-down concentration as she twirled a black curl thoughtfully.

After a moment, she looked up and smiled brightly, flashing a gold tooth with the letter C engraved in it. "Come on. I'll show you. It's not that far even. Buy me a coffee and I'll show you anything you want."

She called herself Corvette, and we walked through winding tree-lined streets together, arms linked, looking for the address while Corvette rambled on about her past to me. I was content just to listen.

"I ran away from home when I was your age. How old are you? 'Bout fifteen? Yep. You might not believe it but I come from a well-to-do family. In D.C. Uppity Negroes. You know?"

The streets around us were growing less posh. Corvette waved at an old man across the street and called out, "Hey, Louie! How's life treating you?" Then she continued: "My daddy was a doctor, mother was a bitch. Professionally, I mean. She was real pretty, though. Good hair. That's where I got my hair from. Anyway, though, my daddy didn't like me. 'Cause I was too fine, and I knew it. So I ran. First to New York. Then here. It's all right here."

She had found a cigarette in the bottom of her purse, and she lit it now and took a drag before continuing. "This neighborhood used to be all black and Rican. Now the white faggots are taking over. They're bringing in all the money. All the business. It's cool, 'cept when them teenage ruffians be fucking with us."

I didn't know who "us" was, but I saw a sign becoming clear in the distance. Montgomery Street. I pointed to it.

Corvette said, "Told you I'd find it."

Forty-six Montgomery Street was a narrow tenement with shingles the color of limes, a white trim, and a placard for a political campaign in the dilapidated front yard. Say Yes to some proposition. I turned to Corvette, handing her a couple of mangled dollars. "Well, thanks——"

Corvette smoothed out the bills, clearly pleased with the bonus prize. She dragged on the cigarette again. "Thanks. You want me to wait with you?"

I wanted her to, but at the same time felt an odd sense of pride. If Dot didn't live here, I didn't want Corvette to know. To see how lost I really was.

"Nah," I said, waving my hand and looking away. "I'll be fine. I mean, I know she's here."

Corvette took a suspicious drag of her cigarette, then said, "Okay, if you say so. But you come find me if you need anything. I hang out over in the park on Braddock Street. With my girlies. We'll set you up if you need it."

Then Corvette was gone, clipping down the street in her tipsy-topsy heels, fluffing the collar of her white fur coat as she moved out of sight. I felt an urge to chase her, cling to the hem of her jacket, anything. But I took a deep breath instead and made my way up the steps.

Inside, I took a moment to adjust to the dark. The front door to the building had been unlocked, and inside, the hallway smelled strongly of foreign cooking. Sunday smells. The address had said apartment number two, and I went up the stairs to the door at the top.

I was about to knock when I saw that the name on the door read "Ghalif." Not Lee. It was the wrong address, the wrong name, the wrong family.

I leaned my head against the door and closed my eyes. A wave of exhaustion and a growing pressure in my bladder, the intoxicants from the night before, Samantha's words, seemed to weigh on me with a sudden force. I could hear a television jingle inside. A child's voice singing along to a commercial for Cap'n Crunch cereal.

I had drunk that large coffee at the bus depot, and the pressure in my bladder was what made me knock finally. I knocked lightly at first. Then louder.

After a moment the door opened. There stood a child with reddish-brown skin and a head full of wild, blue-black curls. She had thick eyebrows and wore a red cape, leotard, and Danskins, with a tinfoil W safety-pinned to the front—a Wonder Woman costume.

"Who are you?" she asked.

I shifted. "I'm Jesse—I mean, Birdie. Birdie Lee. And who are you?"

"I'm Taj, and I'm gonna be four next month. You want to come to my party?"

"Sure, I'd love to," I said, imagining somehow that I really would come to her party, even if this wasn't Dot's house. I paused before asking, "Does Dot live here?"

The little girl shrugged. Then put out a small hand and said, "My mama lives here. C'mon. She's cooking me breakfast."

The apartment was warm and narrow. I glimpsed the living room when we passed through the hallway. Bright cloths hung over the furniture, sculptures from Africa and India were squeezed between huge tropical plants, and the floor was scattered with Legos and stuffed animals. Big Bird and Snuffelupagus were arguing on a small black-and-white television. The child named Taj led me, pulled me, toward the kitchen at the end of the hall, where heat and the smell of something good hit me in the face.

A woman stood with her back to us over the stove. She was singing something incomprehensible. Her hair hung down her back in thick ropes of dreadlocks.

She yelled with her back still to us, "Taj! Come get your food! It's gonna get cold." She turned then, with a plate in her hand.

Taj and I stood at the door together, still holding hands.

It was Dot.

She frowned at me for a moment, with a stranger's hostility. "What the hell—?" she started to say, then stopped in midsentence. Her hand came up and covered her mouth, and she dropped the plate to the floor, where it miraculously didn't break. The food splattered around her feet.

"Sweet Jesus. Is that who I think it is?"

I had imagined what I would say. I had a practiced speech to make Dot keep me. But now I was silent, afraid that if I spoke, everything would come out and I wouldn't be able to stop it.

Dot came toward me, and her eyes were wet as she held out her arms. She held me to her. She was bony, as always, and smelled of some kind of scalp oil. Something familiar.

She laughed as she held me and rubbed my back. "Baby Bird, where the hell have you been all my life?"

I PEED FIRST. Then I looked in the mirror. I looked tired and thin and rough. My denim jacket stank, and my jeans had dirt stains on the knees. My shoes had little splotches of Mona's vomit on them. I tried to run my fingers through my hair, but it was matted with tangles. There wasn't much I could do, so I just splashed my face.

When that was taken care of, Dot fed me. Eggs, cornbread, grits with hot sauce and butter, coffee with lots of sugar, lots of milk, just the way I liked it. She sat across from me, watching me wolf down the food, while Taj snuggled on her lap, sucking on a peach, never taking her wide, liquid black eyes off me. I wasn't sure if it was my imagination or not, but Dot seemed to be studying me with some degree of caution, suspicion. A voice entered my head, a voice of doubt, and I cursed it, knowing it was my mother. *Do you trust Dot with your secrets? Is she above the law, below the law, willing to go against the law and bring you into her home? Because you are against the law, Birdie Lee. Your body is a federal offense. Do you trust her with your secrets? . . .*

Dot was quiet, and I continued to shovel the food into my mouth—tasting its salty richness, but more intensely, tasting a metallic panic. I pretended to be too hungry to speak, and bowed my head, glancing up from time to time to smile greasily and say, "Yum." Dot would smile back slightly, twisting her own daughter's hair around a finger, and say, "Eat up, girl, just eat your food." I hoped if I took long enough to eat, she would forget to ask me where I had been, where I was going. That the question in her gaze would disappear, turn to something else. But it continued to sit there. I tried to remind myself that this was family. That this was the woman who had always loved me, who had loved me from the start, as I was.

When there was no more food on my plate to devour, I wiped my face and sat back in my seat. "That was so good, Dot. Thanks a million. I was ravenous." I heard the anxiety in my voice and felt a cool trickle running from under my arm down the length of my side.

Dot whispered in Taj's ear, "Tajikins, why don't you go watch television? Mami wants to talk to Birdie alone."

A song was stuck in my head, a song that reminded me of Jim's burly red and silver form, a song I couldn't shake. *You've got to know when to hold 'em, know when to fold 'em, know when to walk away, know when to run.*

Taj made a face and sucked her teeth, but slipped off her mother's lap without comment and went skipping down the hall. I could hear the little girl turn on the television. I wanted to go join her, to spread myself out on the sofa and watch cartoons all day long.

Dot folded her arms across her chest. She looked older, I could see now. There were crows' feet creeping out from the corners of her eyes, and small smile lines around her mouth. But she was still the same Dot, perpetually young in some way that would never be altered by time. I studied her, noticing for the first time our similarities, the invisible genetic twists that had skipped over my father and come to me through Dot. She had my wide shoulders and flat chest. My big, misshapen feet. And my exact fingers. Long, delicate fingers. Piano-player fingers, like wands, with big bony knuckles, only hers were the color of coffee, mine of café au lait.

I drummed the table with those fingers, a crazy beat, for a minute, looking around the kitchen for something to catch my eye, until Dot laid her hand on top of mine.

"Bird, where in the hell did you come from? You look like you haven't eaten or slept in forever. Look at you." She frowned. Then asked, "Does your mother know where you are?"

I tried to look casual, smiling as I patted the corners of my mouth with a napkin. My mother's training came back to me as it always seemed to in times of need. How to be crooked. How to tell a lie.

"Oh, yeah. She knows where I am. She's the one who bought the bus ticket." I waved my hand in the air, enjoying my own story. "You know how my mother is, so spur of the moment. She told me just the other morning that she thought I should find you. Of course, it was too dangerous for her to come with me, but she's hoping I can find Cole and Papa. That's why I'm here. To find them. My mom was sad and all that, but she said not to worry. When I found Cole and Papa, we'd be together again. She said to give you her love."

I looked at Dot and smiled, and I could feel how fake my smile was, how plastered on it must have looked to Dot.

I forced a giggle, saying: "Oh, Dot, let's not get into all of that right now. My life's a big bore. Now I want to hear about you. Where did this child—"

She cut me off again. "I don't think your life's boring at all." My game was up. She knew what she was dealing with, and the warmth she had greeted me with was gone, replaced with a kind of clinical concern. I regretted lying. She stood up then and said in a soft voice, the kind nurses use to subdue mental-health inpatients, "Listen. I have to take Taj to a recital she's in. Why don't you take a nap? Just sleep. Until I get back with Taj. Shouldn't be too long. And I think you need some rest, honey. Just till I get back."

Gently she led me by the arm into her bedroom. I didn't want to be left alone, and asked her if I could go to the recital with them. But Dot insisted that I stay and sleep. I had another flash of panic—wondering if she was going to get the cops—but then exhaustion took over and I didn't care. Just as long as I could sleep for an hour or two before they brought me to the police station. I changed into a white nightgown that she gave me, leaving my grubby clothes in a pile by the closet, then slipped under the sunflower-yellow comforter.

She leaned over me, and her dreadlocks tickled my shoulder. She kissed me on the forehead. "You better be here when I get back. I'm still not sure you're for real, kiddo."

Taj came in behind her, a small spot of red and silver at the door. She was scratching her knee. Her costume was falling apart, the tinfoil W curling down at the corners. "We're gonna be late for the recital. I'm gonna miss it."

They left me there with cheery, concerned good-byes, as if they thought I'd escape, as if I had somewhere else to go. The apartment was quiet when they were gone, so quiet I could hear the faucet dripping in the kitchen. I looked at the clock beside the bed.

Ten-thirty.

My bedroom door would be wide open by now, my mother would be standing there. Her first thought: *My child was raped and left for dead by that Dennis boy.* Second thought: *No, the Feds got her in the night. Came and took my baby right from that bed. They're going to use her for bait, going to use her as a negotiating tool.* Then the third thought, and the tears would have begun to fall now as she saw that the box of negrobilia was missing. That the Golliwog was missing. *She's run away. She's gone and left me. She doesn't want to play make-believe anymore.*

Or maybe she would find me there, in that bed—the other me, Jesse Goldman. Hung-over, giddy from the kiss last night, thinking only of how she wanted to call Mona and turn the party over and over in giggling whispers. Or perhaps Jesse was planning to run across the woods to the Marshes', where she would fall into Nicholas's arms and smother him in real-girl kisses. She would be as golden and casual and free as a prep-school girl. Maybe I was still there. It was too strange to think that Jesse Goldman was really gone, that I had erased her in just one night.

I felt salt dribbling into my mouth—my own tears—and used the back of my hand to wipe them away, then curled over and clenched my teeth to stop them. I could smell Dot in the pillows. Everyone had a scent. This one was like my mother's—some faint perfume that seemed to emanate from the bodies of all mothers. I wondered if Cole missed that smell. Strange not to have a father around, but even stranger not to have a mother. I felt a chill, suddenly, as if I could, for the first time, feel Cole's loneliness being channeled through my own body. She missed our mother. She cried herself to sleep every night for years before she hardened, grew to understand that her mother was never coming back. But the sore spot never left her, the wound in the center of her body as if something had been ripped clean away. If I closed my eyes I could see it: Cole lying on a cot in a hot Brazilian favela, the smells of food from some other family, some other mother, reaching her through the air, and sisters laughing together beyond her small window. I wasn't sure if the image had been a psychic explosion or if I was simply making things up again.

THE LIGHT HAD MOVED when I woke several hours later. It lay higher on the wall, and the clock beside the bed read noon. I couldn't remember what I had dreamed, only a vague sense that I had been falling through the air. My mother had told me that if you wake before you hit the ground, you'll be okay; if you hit the ground first, bad things are coming. I couldn't remember whether I had hit or not.

I was lucid, though, feeling none of the usual confusions of waking in a strange house. Corvette's face floated in my mind, a benevolent alternative to this world, just in case Dot turned out to be working with the Feds. Braddock Park. I'd have to remember that.

I sat up on my elbows and called out to Dot and Taj. A paper fluttered to the floor. It was a note from Dot. It said that they had returned but had decided not to wake me. They had gone shopping for groceries and would be back soon. I got up, steadying myself, before going to explore the apartment.

Dot's house was poor but classy. My mother once told me that some people were born with class, some people without it, and it didn't matter how much money you had or what your family name was. "Class comes from the soul, not the wallet," she had said. I had asked her for examples. She told me that Dot had class; my father had class; Redbone didn't; Jane, her old prep-school-turned-radical friend, didn't, despite her Boston Brahmin background. I wondered as I looked around Dot's room what this invisible thing called class was. I knew it when I saw it, but I couldn't describe it.

The living room was a cocoon of colors and soft light, in sharp contrast to the northern urban gloom that lay beyond the windowpane. Dot had transformed her home into a shrine to foreign lands, with bright cloths, buddhas, masks, tropical plants, and the persistent smell of sweet and smoky incense. There was a cluster of framed photographs on the mantelpiece. I stood in Dot's nightgown, studying the pictures one by one, the strangers that were now her life. Most were of Taj. Taj as an infant. Taj as a toddler. Taj as a terrible two on Halloween wearing a kitty-cat costume, a smudge of black on the tip of her nose. Dot nude and pregnant, a silhouette against a window, her balloon belly making me think of how my own mother must have looked. Dot as I remembered her, short-haired, skinny, at an airport ticket counter, a backpack on, smiling over her shoulder at the picture-taker. It must have been taken just as she left for India, and it was tucked crookedly in a cheap plastic frame. There were more pictures stuffed in behind it— photographs yet to get their own frames. Pictures not to be seen.

I pulled them out. The first one was of a handsome Indian guy holding Dot around the waist on a couch. Dot's hair is in a short afro and she wears next to nothing—a pair of underwear and a white tank top, the dark stain of her nipples showing thorough the thin mesh. She's laughing. The man is look- ing at her with a lusty grin. I felt embarrassed by the secrecy of their smiles, and turned to the next one. It was an old sepia photograph I had seen once before—of Dot and my father as children outside of a tenement. My father is about ten, Dot about seven, and they hold hands, looking a little haunted and destitute—like welfare kids. It struck me, looking at them now, how dif- ferent they were from each other. My father's mocha skin beside Dot's dark chocolate; his mixed features, hers clearly African; his hair curly and loose, hers nappy and stretched into tight braids. Neither of them ever spoke of their father. I wondered for a moment who he was, this man who could make multicolored babies out of one woman's dark body. I turned to the next pho- tograph.

For a brief moment I thought it might be some of Dot's friends from India. It looked hot, wherever it was—hot and Third World. But then I looked closer. It was my father and Cole—and Carmen standing next to them. In the picture, Cole looks angry, pouting, suspicious of the photogra- pher, the way she often does in pictures. Her clothes are ordinary, more American than I would have expected—shorts and a halter top and sandals. She's rolling her eyes at something my father's saying. He appears to be wav- ing his hands expressively, and has on a white button-down shirt with short sleeves and a wide collar, jeans, sandals. An outfit I would place in the late seventies. He looks sun-baked, darker than I'd ever seen him, dark and happy. Carmen is squinting at the camera and has her head wrapped high in a yellow cloth. She wears a long lime-green dress. She's put on weight.

My hands trembled as I held the picture.

I started at the sound of jingling keys in the front door.

I turned around, holding the picture behind my back. I half-expected to see two white men in suits. But it was just Dot, and Taj behind her, carrying a bouquet of daisies. She ran up to me. "My teacher said I stole the show. We got flowers and food to cook for dinner. Are you better now?"

I looked over at Dot, who rested a grocery bag on her hip. "What's up? Did you just get up?"

I nodded. "Just taking a look around."

She looked behind me at the row of pictures. Then said, "Did you find the one of Deck and Cole? In Brazil?

I gulped, surprised to hear their names spoken so openly. I held out the photo in my hand. "Yeah, I found it. Sorry. I was snooping."

She smiled. "What else would I expect from Sandy's little girl?"

She said no more. I followed them into the kitchen and placed the photograph face up on the kitchen table while I helped them unpack the groceries.

She was quiet for a while, then she turned to me, nodding as she said, "Yep. That's them, all right. My incredible disappearing brother. Taj, go change out of your costume. And wash that stage makeup off your face."

She turned on the small radio on the counter, a jazz station. Then handed me the perishables and told me to put them in the fridge.

I did as I was told. The photograph lay still on the table, begging the question.

Finally I barked it out, with my head submerged in the white glaring glow of the refrigerator: "Where are they, Dot?"

She held a can of soup in her hand as she shook her head. "I don't know, hon. Haven't heard from them in years—not since 1977, when I got a letter and this photo from Bahia, Brazil, saying they were doing just fine. I lost track of them. I moved to another part of India, and I did send them my new address, but I never heard from them again. I have no idea where they are. We lost touch. I don't know what else to tell you, Bird. I just don't know."

I had been traveling without a plan until this moment, not knowing what I was going toward, only what I was leaving behind. That was my mother's method. Her way of living. But now the disappointment I felt made it clear to me that I had been expecting an answer. I had been expecting six years' worth of letters for me here at Dot's, stamped from Brazil, letters that had never found me in New Hampshire, letters addressed not to Jesse Goldman, but to Birdie Lee.

And not finding these letters, I felt pitiful. I wanted Dot to tell me it was going to be okay, that Cole and Papa were on their way back. I wanted lies, sweet lies. Good lies. Lies made the world go around, my mother had taught me that.

I wondered what my mother was doing right now. I could see her supine on the sofa, her arm draped tragically across her eyes in old-movie-star fashion, while Jim paced before her, wringing his hands, trying to stay cool. He would want her to call the cops, to report me as missing—a logical solution to the problem on their hands. And she would laugh harshly, never exposing her eyes, and remind him, through gritted teeth, that she couldn't call the cops. "Don't you realize? The cops are the fucking bane of my existence. Did you miss that part of my story? They'd just love for me to call them so they can throw my ass in the slammer. So I can pay for my goddamn fucking sins against the system." And as she spoke, Jim would see that piece of her that leapt out at certain moments when alcohol or emergency were involved. The piece of her that had once stored ammunition and had talked about making pig meat of the Boston Police Department, pig meat for her dinner. He would see that she was bigger and braver and crazier than he had ever been himself. And he would see what he had gotten himself into, and feel a little dizzy.

Dot stood before me, arms akimbo. "Now," she said, "I want some answers."

WE SAT CROSS-LEGGED, facing each other on her futon, while I explained to her, in as vague terms as she let me get away with, that I had been living on the road for six years with my mother. I told her about our life on an unspecified women's commune, and about our life in an unspecified small Northeastern town. I told her that my mother was still on the lam, living under a different name. She listened quietly, and her expression was not as impressed or excited as Jim's had been that morning after he found out. She looked more concerned, more parental, more knowing.

I waited till the end to tell her that I'd been living as a white girl. Jesse. A white girl who wasn't even Jewish at the end of the day.

She was quiet. I hugged my knees and looked sideways at the man in the picture beside her bed. Taj's father. Dot's guru. The same man whose image seemed to be everywhere in this house—the man who seemed to watch us, crinkly eyed, seductive, enlightened. He had deep brown-red skin and straight black hair.

When I looked back at Dot, she took my hand and squeezed it. We let my words, my secrets, dance in the air around us. Let them settle on her, and it seemed that in telling her, I had grown a little lighter. Once spoken, the secrets seemed to lose some of their weight. The secrets that had owned me seemed to become my own all of a sudden—my history lesson to play with, to mold, to interpret and revise as I pleased. I wondered if my mother had felt this way when she told Jim.

Dot leaned back on her elbows and said, "Well, shit, Birdie. You went right into the belly of the beast, didn't you? Your mother took you for some ride."

She was twisting a dreadlock around her finger and thinking, her gaze turned toward the ceiling. She seemed to be calculating something, and finally she said, "So, why'd you run away? Why'd you leave?"

I looked at her. "I don't know. New Hampshire was—" I had let the state slip. Not the town, but the state was specific enough. I touched my hand to my mouth and shook my head. Damage control. "I mean—"

Dot was looking at me curiously, as if she were seeing me in a different light—a sorry light. "Bird," she said, "you don't have to worry about all that. Your mother's running from something, but it's not what you think it is. It's not what she thinks it is."

Her words reminded me of the night in the barn, after my mother had told Jim who we really were—the night not believing her had become a possibility. I asked, "What do you mean?"

"I mean," Dot said with a sad smile, "I don't think your mama's in—or has ever been in—the kind of trouble she likes to think she's in. All of us did things during that time that were a little wild—but the FBI is only interested in a few of us. And I truly doubt your mother was one of the wanted ones."

I felt strangely defensive, and twisted a loose thread around the tip of my finger, watching the red swollen bulb turn to blue. I blurted out: "That's not true. My mother did do something bad. Really bad. In the good sense.

And they do want her. She wouldn't have run for this long if it wasn't true. Besides, I saw her. In the night. With the guns."

Dot was frowning, her curiosity slightly piqued, but doubt in her eyes.

My finger had turned numb. "You weren't there, Dot, so how would you know?"

Dot only patted my hand. "Maybe, Bird, just maybe. Who knows? Right? But you can be sure of one thing. You don't have to be afraid of me. I love your mother and I love you."

She was trying to keep the peace, but I could see that she didn't really believe me. That she thought my mother was crazy. I untwisted the thread from around my finger and watched the blood rush down into the digit, turning my fingertip pink again.

I needed to switch the subject, turn the focus away from my mother. It was too much to think about. We both weren't ready. So we talked instead about her—where she had gone and why.

Dot told me, while the light faded around us into a pale winter blue, that she had left because America was poisonous that year. And she didn't want to let the poison enter her system. She had left in order to save herself. She wanted to go deeper than skin color, deeper than politics, to something more important. Something spiritual. Something she thought she could find only in India.

"I remember the day I finally left," she told me. "All my friends in their dashikis, with their raised fists, came to say good-bye. I remember thinking that they were so sweet and lost and stuck, and I thought I was so free, just leaving them all behind."

She stopped talking. She looked a little sad. Then she said, "I knew my people were screwed and I wanted to get as far away from them as I possibly could. Seems so evil. But that's the way I felt. Deck used to read Fanon to me when we were in college. He used to say, 'Wait'll you see the final stage of oppression. Niggers killing niggers.' And I thought I saw it happening all around me when I left. I had to go."

She told me she had lived with Raj and his followers in the mountains outside Calcutta. For four years she studied under him. And became his lover. She said she learned a lot from him, but even more from just being away from all that was familiar.

"I wasn't locked in a body anymore. I was a spirit, searching for something invisible. And I found it."

She told me of one night, when she was six months pregnant with Taj, when it was so hot outside that everyone—her "family"—slept on the floors of the ashram to stay cool. Dot had gone down to the river, just to cool off. She wore a nightgown as she waded in the water there, touching her belly, and it struck her how happy she was. She told me: "At some point I even started yelling out loud, 'I'm in India and I'm going to have a baby!' I couldn't believe it was me, Dorothy Lee, old ordinary skinny-legged, ashy-skinned Dorothy Lee from the Orchard Park projects, in the middle of the Holy Land acting like a fool. It was too much. I wanted to stay that way forever."

We both laughed, and I tried to envision her in the water, hollering into the blank Indian night. I looked at her, searching her features for my father's. There was something in the mouth, the high cheekbones, the forehead, but I wasn't sure if I was making it up, just seeing things. I had felt an aching in my chest as I listened to her describe the joy of being away from America. It was clear to me, hearing her, that my father and Cole had no possible reason to return. They were free. They were playing in the water, unburdened, no longer held back by that which they had left behind.

When I spoke, my voice was thick. "Did you miss here at all?"

Dot turned to me. She stroked my hair and smiled. "Did I miss America?"

She paused, then let out a low, long whistle, as if her answer were too complicated to put into words. "You know, I tried not to think of this place. I tried to let it go. To leave it behind. But it always came back to me, in my dreams. I'd dream about these details, these objects and people and places I'd left behind, and I'd wake up crying. I used to close my eyes before bed and see your papa's face, my mother's face, hear the Supremes playing distantly in my ears. Origins sure are powerful and shit. You can't shake them. I didn't want to miss America, but the truth of the matter is, in India, I was more American than I'd ever been at home."

"Why did you finally leave?"

Dot laughed and said it was the music that finally got her to leave India. She told me that she was sitting in Bombay one day, Raj at her side, Taj at her breast, when she heard Roberta Flack singing from some small radio. She hadn't heard black music in three years, and something opened up inside of her. Roberta, she said, was singing, *Try to make it real, but compared to what . . .* And Dot decided right then that she had to come home.

"I had been agonizing over the question for the past month, but when I heard that sound it seemed so simple, the answer. I didn't want to be so far from black American music, the greatest music in the world. I just suddenly felt this insatiable hunger for it. So I left."

"So, are you glad you came back?" I bit my nails and looked down, feeling as if something bigger rested on her answer.

Propping herself up on one elbow, she said, "It's funny. When you leave your home and wander really far, you always think, 'I want to go home.' But then you come home, and of course it's not the same. You can't live with it, you can't live away from it. And it seems like from then on there's always this yearning for some place that doesn't exist. I felt that. Still do. I'm never completely at home anywhere. But it's a good place to be, I think. It's like floating. From up above, you can see everything at once. It's the only way how."

casts
and die

I slept on the couch that night. I could see into the window across the street. A silhouette moved behind muslin curtains, a male figure hunched and attached to a telephone cord. Earlier that evening I had been given the chance to call my mother, and didn't. I knew I should have contacted her—from a pay phone, where I couldn't be traced, tapped, bugged—but I had chosen not to. This was the longest I had ever gone without hearing my mother's voice. This was the quietest my mother would ever be to me—but it was a not a peaceful silence. It was a silence heavy with her rage and anguish. Dot wanted me to call her, but I was afraid. Afraid she would make me come back to New Hampshire, and afraid I would go back, empty-handed, with nothing to show. When Dot persisted, saying that my mother couldn't make me do anything I didn't want to, I resorted to the old line reasoning: I told her that it wasn't safe, that a promise was a promise and that my mother had made me swear never to tell a soul where she was. Dot had rolled her eyes as if she knew, for sure, there was nothing to be afraid of.

The streetlights were keeping me from sleep. In New Hampshire there had been complete darkness. I had grown used to those pitch-black country nights. The sky here was a city sky, interrupted by concrete and wires. Dot had told me I could stay here as long as I needed. And it seemed the perfect solution. For me to move in with them, make them my new family. But something about it didn't feel right. It wasn't Boston I was looking for. It was my sister, whispering stories to me to help me fall asleep, holding my hand, telling me in Elemeno that everything was going to be all right. It was my father and my mother loving and hating each other somewhere nearby, their curses and their laughter ringing up through the vents of our house. I had come here on a mission, to find them.

And if I didn't find them—there weren't many options. Stay with Dot. Go back to my mother. Or find Corvette. She had told me she'd be hanging out at Braddock Park, and I saw myself suddenly, decked out in a silver dress with a fur stole and bright fuscia lipstick, a cigarette dangling from my lips, surrounded by a gaggle of similarly painted women. Waiting for some stranger to take me home. My feet were large. Perhaps they would fit Corvette's shoes, I thought to myself, before succumbing finally to sleep.

LATE THE NEXT MORNING I woke to the sound of my aunt's voice, one side of a telephone conversation coming from the kitchen. I lay languidly, fingering the tassels on the blanket, listening to the benign "un-hun"s and "oh, of course"s and watching the stream of rain that fell against the window. I felt a lightness, an excitement tinged with hysteria, that I was so far from New Hampshire and my mother.

Dot's voice came closer, and then I heard her say:

"Yes, Sandy—I know, sugar—She's—Well, of course you've been sick with worry—Are you serious? I'm so sorry that I waited even this long. I just didn't know the number. I found her school identification and tracked you down that way. Once I knew the town and the last name, it wasn't so hard. Not too many Goldmans up in those parts—Oh, well. I suppose so. The die has been cast."

I saw my aunt's slim figure coming toward me now, with a phone pressed to her ear, a small white bowl in one hand that emanated steam and the smell of coffee.

"Well, she's right here."

Then the phone was being extended down toward me. It was too early for this. I glared at my aunt, my best look of outrage. I felt my insides drop and my face heating up. I considered getting up and racing out the door, down the steps, into the Boston rain in only a T-shirt Dot had loaned me—a T-shirt similar to something Jim would wear—with the words "Reggae Sunsplash '81" across it. But Dot stood over me, forbidding, her dreadlocks piled up in a bun, the phone extended in her fist. She mouthed the word "Sorry," but her eyes were unrelenting.

I took the phone and sat up, shivering as I pulled the afghan around my body. I put the receiver to my ear.

"Hi, Mum."

I could hear her sniffle on the other end, pause, sigh. Then her voice came out, raspy: "Fuck you. Do you even realize what you've put me through, you little two-faced son-of-a-bitch—"

Someone—Jim, I suspected—took the phone away from her. A hand clamped over the mouthpiece, making a suction sound. I could hear some hissing argument taking place, and imagined that Jim was trying to calm her down.

Jim got on the line. "Jesse, it's me," he said. "Listen, kid, you know you screwed up. You know you should have told us what was going on. But we'll talk about that later. First we need to know when you're coming home."

"Never," I said. I glanced up at Taj, who stood draped in her mother's red-and-gold kimono at the door.

"Well, that's just not acceptable, Jess. We need to talk this over, when we're all a little less—"

He was cut off, and my mother's voice returned on the line. "Have you forgotten? I can't fuck around like this with your little adolescent rebellion. We're not like the goddamn Partridge Family. I've got bigger things to worry about. It's not just about you. You're putting us all at risk now. Jesus, Jess, I thought you understood that after all we've been through together."

Her voice had softened a bit. She sighed, then said, "Listen, we need to talk. When are you coming back here from your little vacation?"

I paused. "I'm not. Coming back. Dot said I could stay here as long as I need to. I'm looking for them. I'm not waiting anymore."

My mother was silent. Then finally she said, "Give me Dot. I can't talk to you right now. This is bullshit."

I handed the phone to Dot, glad to get away from it. Taj slid off her mother's lap, came over, and crawled under the covers with me. She said to me, "I like you. You're my sister now. Can I bring you to show and tell tomorrow?"

I was distracted, though, trying to eavesdrop on Dot's conversation with my mother. She had left the room with the phone. I heard her whispering, "Yep, I know, Sand. Of course. Well, okay. Let's talk then."

A pause. Then, "Baby, it's good to hear your voice too. It's been too long."

She came back into the living room, frowning. I started to say something, but she put up a hand. "Bird, let's give this some time. Stay here for a while, think about the situation you've put yourself in. Then we'll talk about it. I think you and Sandy just need a little time before you can think straight about this. Okay?"

She came toward me, pulling out a chopstick that had been stuck in her hair like a magic wand. Ropes of hair came flooding around her face. I hadn't noticed before, but her locks were gold at the tips.

DOT WORKED HARD. As much as she seemed to float above the world's problems, in her everyday activity she was totally grounded on earth. She taught English at a high school in Mattapan. She loved her job. She told me that in that cramped and dingy classroom she had found the meaning of all that soul searching. She left for work at the crack of dawn, taking Taj to kindergarten along the way. After a day of teaching, she usually went with Taj to some spiritual center in Cambridge, where she would meditate and socialize. She had friends all around Boston. Her friends were white and black and international, but they all were linked by a similar fixation on natural food and spiritual enlightenment.

A couple of them came by my second day—a lean, bearded black man in ethnic clothing, and a tiny pixyish white woman with pale, glowing skin. Dot introduced me to them as her niece, and they flashed me spacey smiles and asked me to join them for tea in the kitchen. I had grown shy, and slightly jealous that my aunt had friends outside of me, and retired to Dot's bedroom.

After they left, Dot came and lay with me on the bed. She told me that they were friends of hers from her religious center. As we lay there, Dot filled me in on her theories. She had plenty of them. They weren't like my father's theories, which had been based on bodies and where they fit in the world. Her theories were based on the soul, the spirit, and she said they were the thing—besides Taj—that had helped her survive over the years. Like my mother's mix-and-match school of religion, Dot's was a blend as well, of Buddhism, Hinduism, mystical Catholicism, and something of her own.

"You only meet five souls in your life, baby," she said that evening. "They come disguised in different flesh, different skin, different bones, and they float around you always in an invisible circle."

She said that people just look different. "Actually, they're a part of someone you've known before. Taj is a soul I've known before. I'd swear to it. I mean, she's only three years old. But I can tell. She's so damn familiar. Always has been. Like the taste of red wine. It's in her eyes."

I watched Dot as she spoke. When I was little, I had wanted to grow up to be just like her. Now we lay side by side, and it struck me that I was more like my father than I was like her. I wondered if I'd ever transcend the skin, the body. If I would ever believe in something I couldn't see. It seemed that in order to be as light as Dot, one couldn't afford to believe in evil. Not the way my mother and father did. They believed in evil they could see, and evil they couldn't. Dot believed only in good.

She was busy explaining to me her thoughts on color. "There's skin color, eye color, hair color, and then there's invisible color—that color rising above you. It's the color of your soul, and it rests just beyond the skin."

I asked for examples. Like my father, I too needed proof.

She was happy to oblige. She was silent for a moment, thinking. Finally, she said, "Okay. If my memory serves me correctly, your papa is green, your mama is blue, and your sister is most definitely purple."

I wanted to be skeptical. Her ideas reminded me too much of my mother's mantras. But something in her words rang true.

She told me Taj was orange, like a Creamsicle, and that she herself was yellow.

Then I asked Dot, "What color am I?" The last time I'd asked that question, I'd been in the woods of New Hampshire. Samantha had told me what color I was. She had said I was Jewish, but she had been joking, just playing along with what she knew to be a gag. Later she had told me I was black like her. At least that's what I had heard. Those words had made something clearer. Made it clear that I didn't want to be black like Samantha. A doomed, tragic shade of black. I wanted to be black like somebody else.

Dot hoisted herself up on her elbow and looked down at me across the darkness. She smelled of cocoa butter. I felt self-conscious, nervous about what she was going to say. But finally she smiled and said what I hadn't expected.

"I've got it. You, Ms. Birdie Lee, are a deep dark red."

WHILE DOT TAUGHT and Taj learned, I wandered the city. It was a cold March, and the wind froze in my nostrils, stiffened my fingers. The sky was the bleak shade of dirty snow, turning dark by four in the afternoon. I had been in Boston only three days, but I felt different. Each step I took forward made it more difficult for me to turn back. The city felt haunted—cold, merciless, unyielding. The same city my father had said was "suicide for a black man." Everything seemed smaller, dingier than my memory had allowed. There was Aku-Aku, the "tropical Polynesian getaway" where I had ordered the "pu-pu platter with toilet paper on the side." The swan boats in the Public Gardens. The roller disco in Kenmore Square, where Cole and I had zoomed around and around, hand in hand, while my father sat nearby, scribbling notes for his next book.

I pretended as I walked that I, like the stony-faced people who milled around me, had someplace to go, though really I was moving in circles. I kept my eyes averted from men in suits (my mother's lessons had stuck), but I stared hard into the faces of certain girls—light-skinned black girls, about eighteen years old: a frizzy-haired hippie girl wearing a long flouncy skirt and combat boots, who rode past me, giggling, on her blond boyfriend's back; a prim bespectacled girl wearing a Boston University sweatshirt, her hair straightened neatly, who glanced up at me when we passed each other; a pale girl with curlers in her hair, who sat in the backseat of a blue Chrysler LeBaron, nursing a baby while the driverless engine hummed and the radio played some classic soul melody. Looking at these girls, these possibilities, I caught my breath, thinking I had found Cole, only to see a stranger's face staring back.

NKRUMAH WAS DEAD. It was on my third night in Boston that Dot broke the news to me. It shouldn't have surprised me, but it did. I had hoped that my old school chums might know something about my disappearance, my sister's disappearance, my father's whereabouts. But, Dot told me, there was nothing left to go back to. She said the school had closed down in 1977. Lack of funding and lack of interest were the culprits. The old philosophies of Umoja and Ujamaa had lost their luster. In their wake lay a crumbling, rotting building with a "Do Not Enter" sign in front—a sign which homeless people soundly ignored, seeking shelter from the cold streets in the abandoned, dusty classrooms.

I had spent only one year at Nkrumah, but I was sad to hear it was gone. It was the one real link to my past, that part of me. But I also remembered my mother's wisdom: She always said we needed to be strategic, not nostalgic, if we were going to evade the Feds. I needed to do the same if I was to find what I was looking for.

The following day I had a new energy. I remembered Maria's old address in Mattapan, and was able to track down her number that way. But the sleepy woman who answered the phone informed me that Maria had moved to New York years before to live with her father and to attend a performing arts high school. When the woman asked who was calling, I told her nobody and hung up the phone.

It was Wednesday. I had been at Dot's only four days, but already I was feeling restless. Maria's life sounded exciting. I had seen the movie *Fame* a year before and at the time had wanted to escape to that fantasy, an urban hub where students spent lunch hour dancing on the roofs of taxi cabs and playing the tin-can drums in the streets. I imagined that Maria looked like

Irene Cara, and wondered if she knew any of the teenagers I had seen dancing that day in the city.

Ali was my only other hope. His father had been my father's best friend once upon a time. Ronnie Parkman, the documentary filmmaker. I recalled Ronnie's face, bending over me at Dot's party that night, assuring me in a gentle whisper that nobody was going to hurt my father.

It seemed like a long shot, but I called Information. The Parkmans had lived near us in the South End, on Dartmouth Street, and the operator found a listing for a Gloria Parkman. She was Ali's mother, a dainty dark-brown woman who wore fitted business suits, small gold hoops in her ears, and her hair in a neat natural. She worked as a public defender and always had seemed distracted when she came to pick up Ali from school. My father once had told my mother, "Now that's a strong black woman. You could use some of her backbone." He had often pointed to "strong black women" as evidence of my mother's inadequacy.

I called Ali's number and spent the rest of the afternoon in Dot's apartment with the television blaring in front of me and the phone to my ear. I let it ring over and over again for at least an hour. I must have fallen asleep that way, because I woke to somebody saying into my ear, "Hello? Hello!" There was drool on Dot's sofa and "Captain Kangaroo" on the television set. I jerked awake.

"Oh, hi," I said. I didn't know how long the person had been on the other end, listening to me snore.

"Who is this?" came the impatient voice on the other end. It was a boy. Somebody my age. Music played in the background.

"Is this Ali Parkman?"

"Yeah. Now are you going to tell me who this is?"

"Hi, uh, I used to know you." There was a heavy silence. I hesitated at saying my real name. "A long time ago."

Still no response. I half-hoped he would just guess who it was, but I knew that was crazy. So I said, "I'm Birdie. Birdie Lee."

It felt strange to say those two words. They had been forbidden for so long that I almost expected a bolt of lightning to crash through the living room. Instead, Ali spoke.

"Birdie Lee? For real?"

"Yeah, for real."

"Holy shit. I remember you. You were my first girlfriend. Over at Nkrumah."

"That's me."

"Where you been all this time? I remember you and your sis got taken out of school one day and I never seen you again."

A half-lie came forth as I fixed my gaze on the television screen, where Mr. Rogers was hanging up his jacket and putting on a cardigan. I said, "My grandmother sent me off to boarding school. And my sister went to Brazil with my dad. I lost track of them a long time ago."

Ali laughed a little. "Yeah, I knew it wasn't true. They was saying your mother went off the deep end, kidnapped you or something. People was freaking out about it for a while. Then the school closed down a year later and we all got sent back to public."

I felt vaguely defensive at the things they had said about my mother. The same way I had felt when Dot said she was running from nothing. But it was also a relief to hear that people had noticed I was gone, that they had been concerned.

I asked him if he wanted to come over and meet me. "I'm staying in the same neighborhood. We could go get a soda or something."

He sounded a little hesitant. "Um, like now?"

"Yeah, or later. I mean, whenever."

I felt stupid and wished I hadn't asked him.

But then he said, "Yeah, sure. That's cool."

After we hung up, I went and looked at myself in the mirror. I looked country. A girl Nicholas might like, but not Ali. Ali might be embarrassed to be seen with me. We were going to meet up at the pizza deli a few blocks away. I had only a few minutes to prepare. I brushed my hair and pulled it into a tight ponytail so that it masked the New Hampshire feathers. I changed into some of Dot's jeans and a long blue cardigan. I didn't want to put on my denim jacket and sneakers, but they were all I had.

I saw him from a distance, leaning against a concrete wall. As I neared him, I saw that his clothes were secondhand, his jeans stained with paint, and a backpack hung loosely off one shoulder. Even as I came closer, he stared past me, as if he were expecting somebody else, so that I had a chance to examine him before he recognized me. He had a young boy's face, though he was tall as a grown man. His skin was velvety dark, and he had his father's high cheekbones. His eyes were soft, deep set, his lips pink on the inner edge, in sharp contrast to the dark brown of the rest of his face. He was going to be handsome. For now, he was pretty, like Nicholas.

It wasn't until I was in front of him that he looked at me. "Ali, it's me."

He blinked at me, surprised. "Whoa. Birdie Lee. I forgot what you looked like." I wasn't sure what looked so different. I wondered if he had expected, somehow, to see a girl more like Cole.

We embraced without much affection and kept our eyes averted from each other's as we walked into the steam and smells of the pizza shop. We bought a couple of Pepsis and sat in a corner booth, across from each other, both fiddling with our straws. His hands were stained with splashes of colors—red and blue and yellow. He noticed me looking and explained, "I tag. Graffiti. You can see my work all over."

We chatted for a while about what had happened to other kids from Nkrumah. He said Maria had grown up to be "super fine" and that she had been told so many times that she could be a movie star, she had decided to try it out for real at the performing arts high school. Cherise was pregnant. Cathy went to his high school and had plans to join the Army in a few years. Mrs. Potter was running a program called METCO that bused black kids into the suburbs.

There was a lull in conversation, and then he said, "So, what was it like at boarding school?"

It took me a moment to remember my lie. "Oh, um, ever see 'The Facts of Life'? It was kind of like that."

He covered his mouth and laughed. "Seriously? With Tootie?"

"Yeah. With Tootie and Blair and the rest of them."

It didn't really feel like a lie, I had watched the show so many times. I saw myself with the cast, whizzing around the kitchen on roller skates, while the theme song played overhead. I wondered if it was still a lie if you could see it so clearly.

"So, why'd you leave?" Ali was asking. "What are you doing back here?"

I told him I was looking for my father and my sister. "They're still missing. I haven't seen them since, you know, we all left that day."

"Man, that's wild. Any leads?"

I took a deep breath. "Well, I was thinking. You might be able to help me. My dad," I said, trying to restrain the excitement in my voice. "Our dads. They were tight. Remember? They were good friends."

As I said it, Ali seemed to grow cold and distant, his lips thinning as he squinted at me. "So what?"

I hadn't expected this response. His body seemed to have moved farther away from me, though it was impossible. I persisted, remembering my mother's advice about being strategic. "Your dad might know where they are."

Ali only mumbled, "Yeah, well, maybe."

I looked around. The pizza joint was empty except for the young man in the pinstriped shirt behind the counter, who watched us while he leaned on the counter, talking sleepily into the phone. I leaned across the table and hissed to Ali, "I need to talk to your dad. And I thought you might be able to take me to him."

He laughed over my head. "Naw, Birdie. My dad's missing too. I think he might be dead. He left around the same time as yours. Weird, huh?"

I was quiet, taking in this news. Ronnie had never been as political as my mother. I didn't think he'd been up to any shady business of that magnitude. And I couldn't imagine him disappearing, leaving his son and perfect wife behind. Their family had seemed the antidote to mine. One color, one love, forever together. But I couldn't imagine why Ali would lie. All I could manage to say was "Oh, yeah? Sorry to hear that." I bit my lip, trying not to cry. I felt silly for being so disappointed, but I was. Ronnie had been my only hope. My father hadn't been close to very many people. There wasn't much else out there.

Just then there was a loud knock on the window next to us. We both started and looked. A bunch of teenage girls stood at the window, grinning in at Ali. He smiled and raised a hand. Two of the girls were black, one was white, and they all wore big bright bomber jackets, red lipstick, and tight jeans. The white girl's hair was in strawberry-blond cornrows, but her eyes were a pale blue. The girls squinted at me, their breath fogging up the glass as they tried to figure out who I was. They clearly didn't like what they saw, and went off, sneering. Ali smiled across the booth at me, bashfully.

"They go to my school," he muttered, by way of explanation. I got the feeling that he was tired of our conversation. He wanted to go. He was bored by me. By our reminiscing. He asked, "So, where are you staying?" It was a small effort, but false. I doubted we'd be seeing each other again.

"I'm staying at my aunt's. In the South End."

He nodded. "Well, maybe we'll bump into each other again. I hang out afternoons over at Downtown Crossing. Usually I'm there, tagging. Come visit some time."

I nodded, and said to Ali, "Yeah, sure," not really meaning it. We both got up to go.

We stood outside the pizza place for a moment. "Well, thanks," I told him. "For coming to meet me."

He looked at me. Smiled slightly. "You know, we wondered about you. For a long time, people was asking, 'What ever happened to Birdie and Cole Lee?' Maria was all sad, moping around the halls for a while. I'm glad you're all right."

I nodded. "Yeah, I'm okay."

The name Jesse had been a lie, but as I walked home that day, I wasn't quite sure the girl Jesse had been such a lie. I had felt out of place with Ali—less at home with him than I did in New Hampshire. Maybe I had actually become Jesse, and it was this girl, this Birdie Lee who haunted these streets, searching for ghosts, who was the lie. I missed Mona and Nicholas and my mother and Mr. Pleasure. I missed the soft country earth and the dingy little town I had come to think of as my own. The missing scared me. It made me feel a little contaminated. I wondered if whiteness were contagious. If it were, then surely I had caught it. I imagined this "condition" affected the way I walked, talked, dressed, danced, and at its most advanced stage, the way I looked at the world and at other people.

THAT NIGHT, I was too scared to sleep alone. Seeing Ali, hearing that his father was missing as well, had left me shaken. Nobody seemed to have stayed the same. No families intact. Dot, beside me on her wide futon, listened as I told her what Ali had said, and she shook her head. "Yeah, those were crazy times, babe. We lost a lot of good ones. Either died, went to prison, or left the country." She paused. "Or just disappeared, like your mom, into thin air."

Dot hadn't mentioned my mother since the second day, when she had forced me to talk to her. She hadn't mentioned whether I should stay or go. She had told my mother that I needed time, and that was what she was giving me. A part of me wanted to stay with Dot, pretend she was my mother, the mother I had never had before: slender, mahogany, sensible, a mother who didn't switch faces with the seasons, a mother who stuck to one spot. But I was certain she didn't need me, an extra weight, in her life. She had survived these years by keeping her baggage light, by floating, and I didn't want to ruin that precarious balance.

I spent the next day composing a letter to the Brazilian consulate, asking them to help me trace my father and sister. I even called a private detective I had found listed in the yellow pages and asked if he could help me. He said he might be able to, but he'd need five hundred cold cash up front, and I slammed down the phone. I stared at Dot's photograph of them, the last proof that they were alive, that they had ever existed after the night they drove off. I scrutinized my sister's face for signs of my own. The resemblance was there, but it wasn't easy to explain. It was something in the expression. Or maybe I was just imagining it. I played Dot's music. She had a mix of seventies soul and Indian religious music. I chose the soul and blasted Stevie Wonder, Roberta Flack, the Isley Brothers, and wondered what to do next.

Dot came home later that afternoon to find me watching television and listening to the record player all at once, with the contents of my box of negrobilia spread out before me. She stood watching me with a concerned look on her face. I wondered what she was seeing that disturbed her so much. I wondered how crazy I looked. Then she said that I needed to get out of the house, to get some fresh air. It was a Thursday and she sent me off to an organic food store in Cambridge with an elaborate list of vegetables, herbs, and teas.

When I was finished shopping, I took the bus home. I stared out the window at the raindrops eating one another on the windowpane and, beyond that, at a gloomy Harvard Square. It reminded me of my grandmother. I hadn't thought of her once since I had been back. I wondered if she were still alive. She had lived not far from where the bus was passing, in that big old house off Brattle Street.

Outside, a girl waited at a crosswalk. She wore her hair in Shirley Temple ringlets and carried a black umbrella with yellow sunflowers on it. It was something in her features, the mixture of hard and soft lines, that had made me pause. When she glanced up, it was nowhere near the face I was looking for, and my eyes stung.

Back at Dot's, I clambered up the stairs, leaving wet marks behind me. I heard voices from inside, but didn't stop to listen closely. I expected to see one of Dot's macrobiotic friends in a yoga twist on the floor.

Instead, my mother sat wide-eyed on the couch, with a cup of steaming tea in her hands. Beside Dot on the floor, Jim sat building a Lego truck with Taj.

There was a moment of silence, then Taj blurted out, "Birdie's in big trouble!"

As if choreographed, Jim and Dot rose at once and took Taj with them to the kitchen.

I listened to the door slam behind them. I steadied myself against the doorjamb and looked at my mother.

My first thought was that she had aged. Maybe her face had been as lined before and I simply hadn't noticed. But now she looked older, and a traumatic bewilderment had taken root in her blue eyes.

She was wearing her old stained Levi's and one of Jim's lumberjack shirts. Her knuckles were dirty and scabbed, I noticed, and I wondered why. She looked as if she had been crying.

Finally I said, "Isn't this dangerous? I mean, don't the Feds have a watch on Dot's house—"

She cut me off with a vicious "Shhhh. You should know better."

She was talking about bugs. She had lectured me on many occasions about the precautions a revolutionary must take, but this time her voice had a particular harshness to it. I wondered, perhaps for the first time, if she ever got tired of running, of living a lie, if she ever missed her mother the way I missed mine.

"Sorry." I sat across from her in Dot's denim beanbag chair, hugging my knees to my chest.

She sighed deeply and put a hand to her temple, rubbing it. She felt a migraine coming on, I could see it. She set the tea on the coffee table, then said after a pause, "What you did was unacceptable, Jesse. You nearly killed me. I was worried sick. Worried out of my fucking mind. Do you hear me?"

Her voice was rising, and I glanced around, an odd sense of decorum over-taking me. But it was too late for manners. She was shaking, and her left eye was twitching. "I've already lost one child to this war they call America. I refuse to lose another. Now I want to hear why the hell you would do this to me, without any warning. But first I want you to pack your bags and get downstairs, into the car. I don't want to stay here too long. There's too much of a risk."

I sat still with my knees drawn in, chewing on a strand of hair and drum-ming my fingers against my legs. I heard myself say, "I'm not coming, Mum." I saw myself look at her and say with a calm that surprised me: "I'm not going back to New Hampshire. You've got Jim. You'll be all right."

"Oh, Jess," my mother said, her voice cracking. "I know you've been miserable up there. But I can't lose you. Yeah, I've got Jim. But I don't know," she looked up at me, glanced toward the kitchen door. "He's scared. I'm not sure he wants to be in on this for much longer. I'm not sure I even trust him some days."

I kept my eyes on the floor. I thought if I looked at her, I'd be swayed. She was pulling out every trick in the book. She continued, in a breathless plea: "You're the only person in the whole world I trust, baby. You're every-thing to me. We can leave New Hampshire. We can go somewhere out west. To Berkeley. There's a lot of folks out there who would help us. You'd be hap-pier there. It's not so whitewashed. I know that's been hard for you. Don't think I haven't noticed. We can go anywhere you want. And if Jim wants to follow, fine. But it's you I care about. You've kept me alive. I would have died, sweetie. Don't you know that? I would have died without you. I had nothing else to live for."

I heard her words but fought hard against feeling them. I said, "I have to find them, Mum."

There was silence for a moment, then she stood up, smoothing her jeans with her hand. It was the freckles on her hands that made me hide my face. I knew her hands as well as my own, the pattern of the freckles and the dirt under her nails. I could see them clearly with my eyes closed.

"Come on, Jess. Get your things together, sweetie. We're leaving."

I sunk back a little into the beanbag and said in a small voice, "My name's not Jesse. It's Birdie Lee."

Then she came toward me. I had seen the expression on her face before. It meant she wasn't playing, that she had had enough. It meant that she was going to take you, force or no force. She reached for me, and in one motion I ducked under her arm and dashed across the room, out the front door of Dot's apartment, down the long staircase, outside into the cold, which hit my face like a much-needed slap. A barely perceptible drizzle moistened the air.

I heard her behind me, then felt her hands in my hair, her grip on my arm.

We tussled out there like two female mud wrestlers, not really hurting each other. She tried to get me onto the ground, while I tried to break out of her hold. We were on the sidewalk now, and a couple of people had stopped to watch the scene.

"Get in the car," she said to me between gritted teeth. "Get into the car, or I swear—"

I broke loose momentarily, and as she swung to grab me, she ended up belting me across the face. I saw yellow spots, darkness. Before I could get my balance, she had me in a headlock. I saw some lights go on in apartments around the street, silhouettes emerging at windows. Her arms were like steel clamps around my neck, and though my arms were free, I couldn't loosen her grip. She was stronger than she looked.

"Let go of me, Mum," I whimpered.

Just then Jim and Dot came rushing out the door together.

Dot tried to pull my mother off me. "Sandy, let go of her. We can talk this out."

Jim tried to reason: "Sheila, calm down. This isn't the right way to handle the situation."

She barked back, "Get lost, Jim. Just fuck off. This is between me and my daughter."

I struggled for a few minutes more, and just when I thought I was losing the battle, I felt her arm release my neck and looked up to see a police car cruise up beside us.

It rolled to a stop. I stood up straight and began to fluff my hair.

The driver was a chubby Puerto Rican with wavy black hair and pale skin, and beside him sat a redheaded younger officer with acne. They got out of the car slowly, adjusting their belts.

As they loped toward us, the Puerto Rican one said to my mother, "Ma'am, step away from the girl."

She forced a laugh, high-pitched, as she said, "This is a mistake, officer. She's my daughter. She was trying to run away from home and—"

The policeman put his hand on his holster. "I said, step away from her. We're getting complaints of assault and battery out here. That a blond lady was beating up a teenage girl. Now, who's gonna tell me what's going on?"

Jim spoke first, using his we're-all-good-guys tone. "Hi, officers. We were just having a little family game of tackle out here. Nothing serious. No problem."

The officer was looking past Jim, at me. I tried to control my breathing, which was coming out in rasps.

He said, pointing a chubby finger at me, "You, kid. What seems to be the problem?"

My mother started to talk for me: "She's just—" but the officer cut her off, wagging a finger as he said, "I'm not talking to you, lady. One more word out of you and I'll have to book you. Now, kid, what seems to be the problem?"

I stuttered, "No, sir. No problem. I mean, we were just playing around."

The younger redhead piped out from behind the other, "Playing around? You were causing a disturbance in the neighborhood. Do you know this woman?" he asked me, putting his hands on his hips. He was showing off to his superior.

"Yes, I know her," I told him, glancing at my mother now, who was standing in the crook of Jim's arm.

"What's your relationship?"

"She's—she's a friend of the family." I felt my face heat up. My mother was watching me with her mouth slightly parted, incredulous.

"Do you live here?"

"Yes, with my aunt," I said, motioning to Dot.

The cops looked back and forth between Dot and me, confused for a moment. The redhead said, "This lady's your aunt?"

I hadn't seen that double-take since I had last been with my father—that look of skepticism mixed with embarrassment. The look had once been followed by "Oh, she must be adopted."

I repeated, "Yes, she's my aunt."

The Puerto Rican cop seemed bored by the discussion and said, "All right, come on, Mike. Just keep the noise down out here. Or we'll be back." The two men left without taking our names.

After they drove off, my mother turned to me.

"I'm going to say this one more time, Jesse. Get in the car. Jim, get our coats from upstairs."

"Mum, I'm not going with you. I can't do this anymore."

Jim's voice: "Jesus, Jesse. Stop it now. This isn't cute anymore. Just get in the car. We can't stick around."

"No. I don't want to be with you anymore. It's over, Mum. Sorry."

Dot said in a hushed voice, "Birdie, you don't mean that."

When I didn't say anything, Dot let out a deep sigh.

There was a long silence while my mother and I just stared at each other, taking in each other's hair and skin and bones. It seemed at that moment that we had never really looked at each other like that, like strangers.

Finally Dot said quietly, "Sandy, I'll take good care of her. I promise."

Jim went upstairs to get their coats, while the three of us women stood out in the darkness, Dot holding my mother to her chest while she cried softly. I wouldn't look at her.

After a moment, Jim came out of the apartment with the coats piled over his arm. Taj peeked out of the doorway like a nymph, wearing just her pajamas.

Dot helped my mother put on her coat and whispered to her in comforting tones, "She'll come around. She just needs time."

When they were ready I stood with my hands in my pockets, staring at the pavement, not daring to look or move till they were out of sight.

I heard the slamming of doors, the sound of them kissing Dot good-bye, the sound of the engine, some muffled music—my mother's old Linda Ronstadt tape—coming from their radio. I allowed myself to look up only then, as their car pulled away from the curb.

She was looking back at me from the passenger window. Our eyes caught, and I saw her as she had been and would always be, a long-lost daughter of Mayflower histories, forever in motion, running from or toward an unutterable hideaway.

I stood outside for quite a long time, hugging my body, which was trembling now, transfixed by a spot of oil on the street below, where their car had been parked. I said aloud, "They have an oil leak." I stood, staring at that spot, which looked like a map of some distant nation, long after Dot and Taj had gone upstairs, until I was shaking with the cold and a soft rain came down around me.

A feather touch on my wrist made me turn. It was Taj, looking a bit frightened. I bet she had never seen a family like this one. She had come down to fetch me and was holding an orange in her hand.

"Are you crying, Birdie?"

I touched my face. It was wet.

"No, that's just the rain, Taj. I'm okay."

She patted my arm daintily, imitating her mother.

I laughed. My cheek still throbbed where my mother had hit me.

"Did the bad lady leave?" she asked.

I said, "She's not so bad. She's just scared."

"Scared of what?"

I looked at Taj, trying to think of the answer. "Scared of—I don't know. Something big and bad."

"Flying monkeys?" Taj suggested. She had been watching *The Wizard of Oz* the night before.

I laughed. "Yeah, flying monkeys."

Taj took my hand. "I want you to live with us forever and ever."

With her other hand, she was sinking her teeth into the skin of the orange, but not breaking through to the fruit. I squeezed her little hand. "Yeah, well, that would be nice." Taj had never really known her father. I wondered if years from now she too would be standing on some rainy street corner, searching the faces of strangers for the reflection of her own. Or maybe it would be easier for her. Maybe her father and her mother would share her between them and she would become the perfect blend of two rich cultures, moving effortlessly between the two worlds.

She said, "My mother said you should come upstairs or you'll catch pneumonia."

"I need to walk. I need to be alone. Tell your mom I'll be back later."

She nodded, but stood outside, watching me as I made my way down the street. I kept turning back and waving at her to go inside, but she would just wave back, opening and closing her fist.

I walked quickly, assuredly, though I had no idea where I was going nor how long I would be gone. Most of the children had been called in for dinner, and the streets were fairly quiet, though in the distance I could hear a joyful shout, and beyond that a siren. I was still shaken from the fight, and my mouth and cheek felt sore from the trauma of her punch. As I walked, I thought about my mother, her face in the car. She was the person in the world who was closest to me, the person who had been my other half all these years. But it hit me now how little I knew about her. In some deep way, she had remained a mystery even to me.

high soul burn

It was almost six o'clock when I found myself at Downtown Crossing, searching among the lean, slouched teenage boys for a pair of painted hands, for Ali's high cheekbones and soft eyes. I scanned the huddle of teenagers who loitered in front of the food court, scrutinizing their faces for something familiar. There were several imitations of Ali's general look, but none was the real thing. I tried to catch their eyes, but found no response. They didn't seem to see me. The girls wore scowls of indifference, helmets of straightened hair, and the boys stood posed in their candy-colored parkas, talking into the air, not to one another, with bashful smiles.

They all seemed to be waiting for something important, their faces tilted toward the sky. I followed their gaze to see what was coming, only to find the gleaming top of the John Hancock building. At this angle it appeared one-dimensional, a sheet of glass. A boom box on someone's shoulders played a song sung by a scratchy-voiced boy in the throes of puberty.

This was where he had said I could find him, so I wasn't surprised when someone touched my elbow and I turned to see Ali. He wore a green Army parka, a pair of paint-splattered combat boots, and a red scarf wrapped around his face so that only his eyes told me he was smiling. A small neat scar interrupted the dark smooth line of his eyebrow. I hadn't noticed it before. It saved him from being pretty. I glanced down at his hands to make sure it was really him. His fingers were tinged with gold, blue, and silver spray paint, though the colors had faded.

He frowned at what he saw on my face, his eyes moving over me with a slow dismay. "What happened to you?"

He reached out and gently touched my lip. I could feel that it was swollen. My scalp was still sore where my mother had pulled my hair.

"Who did this to you?" He looked protective all of a sudden.

I mumbled, "Just a crazy lady." I paused, calculating how much I could tell him without risking her safety. Then I felt silly for even hesitating. "I mean, my mother. She did it. But she's gone now."

A body emerged from behind Ali just then, a slim yellow girl with her hair neatly coifed into an elaborate twist, baby curls pressed into her forehead, lipstick bright and pink. "Ali," she said, snapping her gum and avoiding my eyes, "we're going to the movies. You coming?" She was sucking on a Slush Puppy, and when she opened her mouth I could see that her tongue was stained blue. She glanced at me. I had been caught staring. Her eyes were dark green, like sea glass—the color of Cole's eyes. She looked away quickly, and it struck me that I must have appeared a little out of control, with my fat lip and dirty blue jeans. She said, quieter now, to Ali, "We've got to go if we're gonna make it."

Ali glanced toward the girl, then back at me, as if trying to gauge how serious my situation was. I suspected that he had a crush on the girl, that he wanted to go to the movies, and I felt like a pest all of a sudden. He didn't know me anymore. I was just some strange girl who had gone to elementary school with him so long ago. And even then we hadn't really known each other. Now he was an ordinary teenager who had grown up in one place. The last thing he probably wanted to talk about were missing fathers and wayward mothers.

But he said to the girl, "Naw, Marcy. I'll catch y'all later. I gotta talk to Birdie."

She stood for a moment, indignance rumpling her features, then said something I couldn't decipher under her breath as she turned and clipped away. I watched her catch up with another girl, then the two girls whispered and looked back at us over their shoulders.

Ali watched them too—a little longingly, I thought—before turning to me. He shoved his hands into his parka pockets, the fur around his hood rippling in the cold wind as he said, "So, you want to go somewhere? To talk. You don't look too good."

"Okay. You lead the way."

He bought me a hot chocolate first, at the Friendly's across the street, as if he could tell that I needed something sweet just then. It warmed my hands as we made our way across the Common, our feet crunching in unison on the frozen grass. I wore only my thin denim jacket that still smelled of horses and New Hampshire and Mona's clove cigarettes. I wondered if the smell would wash out.

We reached the top of the hill. Across the street the gold-domed State House shimmered even in the fading winter light. My father once had told me that a little man polished it every morning to make it stay so shiny. Next to us sat the war memorial that my father had taken me and Cole to see as children. It was a sculpture of Robert Gould Shaw on horseback, colonel of the 54th Regiment of Massachusetts, surrounded by his "foot-bound Negro battalion" who, according to the inscription, died with him on Fort Wagner, South Carolina, July 18, 1863, in the name of "this great union." Shaw's name was the only one engraved on the stone, and a poem underneath him described his death.

But the High Soul Burns
On to Light Men's Feet
Where death for Noble Ends
Makes Dying Sweet.

My father had pointed to the foot-bound black soldiers behind Shaw and said, "These little nigger boys died in vain. And that white boy got all the credit."

The sun was setting around us now, and a diffused orange light hung over the city. It would be dark soon, but for now the sky was a dusty pink. My mother said dusk was the most beautiful time of day, filled with the possibilities of night. But I thought it was dreary, the bright colors that filled the sky somehow washed out and depressing. I liked the night better, when there was a clarity to the darkness.

If I squinted my eyes and ignored the modern cars and the Chee-tos wrapper by my feet, I could have been in any moment of history. Beacon Hill was well-preserved, a virtual museum of culture and class. It was the home of Boston's blue-blood elite—or at least those who could afford to pretend they were. My mother's brother, Randall, used to live on Beacon Hill, in the old family house on Louisburg Square. I wondered if he still lived there. And if he ever thought about his chubby younger sister with the appetite for trouble, the little sister who had once, in a fight, told him that he was "as effete as the rest of the Lodge boys." Or had he erased her from his history, and all the trouble that came with her?

Ali and I sat on the granite bench beneath the memorial. He turned to me and said, "So, I thought you said your mother disappeared. What's the story? You been telling lies?"

I hadn't been speaking because I was afraid I would cry, but the cocoa had comforted me. I looked at him. He was watching me, waiting, with a slightly suspicious smile. He was the same Ali who threw a spitball at me my first day at Nkrumah and hissed, *What you doin' in this school? You white?* His face had been rounder then, but his eyes were the same. I was feeling that itch—an itch I had felt many times before—to tell my story, the truth of where I had been. So far, Dot had been the only one to know, and even she didn't know the whole story. And now her words came back to me. *Sandy's not running from the law, baby. She's running from herself.* And if this were true, there had never been a danger at all. We had been hiding from only ourselves. And it was safe, then, to speak. This boy was waiting, and something in his face, the familiarity that brought me back to Nkrumah, to the chocolate milk drunk straight from a carton and the sound of sneakers against linoleum, made me speak.

I said it slowly, quietly, so that he had to lean in to hear me. I told him the facts, beginning with the last day he had seen me, Wednesday, in the cafeteria, May 17, 1976. He had pulled my braid in line for food, and I had been holding my tray, but then Cole had come up behind me and whispered in my ear, "C'mon Birdie, Mum and Papa are here. They want to take us to Aku-Aku."

And then I was gone.

And then I was gone.

"My mother, you see, she got this idea in her head that it wasn't safe to stick around Boston—and my dad had taken off by then, to Brazil, with my sister—so my mom and I had to go and I had to change my name." I glanced

at him. He was watching me, lips parted slightly, eyebrows raised. I hesitated. "Yeah, I had to change my name to—" I hesitated, then faltered. "To a
different name, and wear this Star of David around like I was Jewish."

I laughed, a hard embarrassed laugh, but he was quiet. So I went on.

I told him everything that I wasn't supposed to tell—about the
women's commune and even about my life in New Hampshire. As I spoke,
I saw my mother's image from before—in a Take Back the Night T-shirt,
laughing with Bernadette, a bottle of Rolling Rock in hand—and felt a pain
in my chest.

So I spoke as if in a trance, staring not at him but straight ahead, at the
dome of the State House as if it were a crystal ball that had hypnotized me,
had made me speak these forbidden words. I was conscious all the same that
I was breaking the rules, and my fingers trembled so badly I had to sit on my
hands.

But I kept talking, telling this truth, and it felt unnatural to do it. The
words seemed flat and unimaginative in their factual accuracy. I told him I
still didn't know if my mother was in trouble for something big or something
small, or if she had ever been in trouble at all—only that she was back in hiding and I didn't know when I would see her again.

When I was finished I looked into my cup, at the cocoa mix that had created a ring of darkness around the bottom of the paper, and said, "So, basically, I'm fucked. My mother's still on the lam. If I go back to her, I go back
to living this crazy lie. My dad and sister have dropped off the face of the
earth. And Dot has her own kid to raise."

Ali just kind of whistled a little when I was done. "Shit, that's some mad-
ness."

I nodded, biting my lip, looking around now for eavesdroppers. It
struck me how stupid this was, to tell him this story across from the State
House. I couldn't have picked a worse place to spill my guts. Ali put his arm
around me and knuckled my head with his other hand. My head was pressed
to his chest, and I could smell his sweat mingled with laundry detergent. It
was the same smell as Nicholas's—the smell of a boy whose mother still
washes his clothes.

I heard his voice say, "And you have no leads for your dad and sis?"

"Nope. Zilch. It's like they never existed."

Two silver-haired men walked past Ali and me at a fast clip. They wore dark suits and talked with their heads close, their brows furrowed over something important. They were officials of some sort, on the wrong side of history, as my mother would put it, that side that was well-documented and well-portrayed. I wondered if they had ever been angry enough about anything to bend the rules, had ever been tempted to forgo their birthrights and switch their fates the way my mother had. Her brother, Randall, had accepted the fate he was assigned with a smirk of indifference. He had become the man they all expected him to be, and his rebellions had been negligible, infractions within some boundary of forgiveness—some boundary my mother had crossed. It wasn't clear why she had been the one to cross over, cross out, and not Randall—if it was simply a roll of fat that had sent her to the other side, or something beyond that, something that she had understood about the world that the rest had been blind to.

Ali was quiet, and I watched his long dark fingers as they tore apart the paper cup he had been drinking from. They were delicate fingers, with big knobby knuckles, fingers I could watch all day. Gleaming silver cars swished by us on Beacon Street, and pale somber faces looked out at us from their heated chariots. They saw a dirty and bruised white girl and a black teenage hoodlum—the illusions that were our skins—sitting before a landmark, a historical monument, a Negro battalion.

Ali said, his voice breaking slightly, "They were friends, weren't they?"

"Who were friends?"

"My dad and your dad. They were friends."

Confused, I nodded. We had already had this conversation. I didn't feel like reminiscing about our fathers' friendship again, about two disappearances.

"They were real tight?" he asked, now turning his head away from me to squint into the distance, as if waiting for someone who was late.

I said, "Yeah, don't you remember? My mother used to call them Beauty and the Beast, 'cause your dad was so fine and my dad was so twisted."

He laughed a little, but it was a strained laugh, like his mind was on other things.

Finally, he looked at me and said, "All right, Birdie. I lied. My dad isn't missing and he isn't dead. He's alive and well and he lives not too far from here. So if you want to talk to him, you can. Maybe he'll know where your pops is." He looked down. "I'm sorry I lied and shit. I didn't know how serious this all was. I just don't talk to him no more. Can't stand the punk. But I know where he is. So you want to see him, or what?"

HIS FATHER'S HOUSE was within walking distance. I felt only a slight spark of hope as we made our way up Spruce Street in the toniest section of Beacon Hill. Ali's mouth was turned down in tension, and his eyes scanned the street as if he were trying to remember his way. I didn't know why he had lied to me, and for all I knew he was still lying. I knew only that I had nothing to lose by following him—no other leads. I tried not to think what I would do if Ronnie knew nothing—or simply didn't exist, was a figment of Ali's imagination. Then my father and sister would be truly lost to me, and I hadn't begun to imagine a future beyond that point.

Ali walked so fast I had to jog to catch up. Finally he halted before a small crooked townhouse with blue-gray shutters. Yellow lights filtered through curtained bay windows.

We stood for a moment before the house, our breaths visible in the cold air. It looked like Randall's old house. I wondered how Ali's father—a documentary filmmaker the last time I saw him—was able to afford to live here. I figured it was better not to ask.

Instead I whispered, "So, this is where he lives?" I wasn't sure why I was keeping my voice low, but it seemed appropriate.

Ali jerked his neck and seemed almost surprised to see me next to him. "Yeah. Pretty spiffy, huh? Well, come on."

I rang the doorbell, and we waited. After a few minutes, someone's crisp footsteps were heard, and there was a pause as someone peered at us through the peephole. I tried to look respectable. Ali looked at the ground. The door opened, and a silver-haired white man with sharp blue eyes, a white oxford shirt, and khakis stood staring at us. He held a tumbler in one hand and a cigarette in the other. Billie Holiday crooned behind him. He was not Ali's father. That was clear. Ali's father didn't exist, I thought, and saw my future in an instant: me, once again at Braddock Park, leaning into a Cadillac, my foot raised behind me to reveal the sole of a scuffed red pump jemson.

"Ali." The man had a British accent and he said the name slowly, as if he were making a statement of great weight and consequence. Ali just looked away, down the street, as if he couldn't bear to look at the man. I smiled anxiously to make up for Ali's clear disdain.

For a moment it seemed that Ali was going to change his mind, call the whole thing off, but then he spoke: "Is my pops here, Gideon? I need to see him about something."

A faint smile crossed Gideon's lips. "Of course. Come in."

I paused at the doorway, fighting a brief paranoid fantasy that Ali was leading me to the Feds. That would explain why he was acting so strange, why he avoided my eyes. He felt guilty to be handing me over to my captors. I imagined they had spoken earlier and decided this would be their ruse, their code message: to ask for Ali's pops.

But I entered the hallway behind him anyway, handing myself over to fate. The decor was familiar, a disheveled Wasp chamber like the Marshes' or my own fallen family's. But this was somehow brighter, as if it only referred to that shabby aesthetic, then strived beyond it. Gideon told us to wait while he went to get Ronnie. Then he disappeared, leaving us in a film of gray smoke from his cigarette.

Ali leaned against the doorway, staring at his boots as if they held great secrets. Since he wasn't talking, I wandered in and began to examine the pictures that lined the walls. They were familiar images: a boy dribbling on a basketball court; muscular young men on a street corner, turning hostile glances at the camera; a child picking at a scabbed knee; a group of girls playing double dutch. They were not original in their subjects, yet there was something macabre about the way they had been shot, something slightly haunting. The light fell on the bodies like a coat of ice, and the eyes were dazed, glassy. It looked as if Medusa were in fact the photographer and these unwitting subjects had been turned to stone, reduced to this moment, stopped in the act of whatever they were doing last.

From upstairs, someone turned down the volume of the jazz. After a moment, a man emerged from the shadows of the hallway to greet us.

Even as a child I had recognized Ronnie's beauty. Now I could see that it had deepened with age. There were only slight crows' feet at the edges of his eyes. He wore a white tank top, blue jeans that hugged his slender hips, and flip flops revealing perfect feet with neatly clipped, shaped, and buffed nails.

He leaned against the doorjamb as he took a long drag from his cigarette, then said to Ali as he let out a curling breath of smoke, "Surprise, surprise."

I felt myself fading into a backdrop. Ronnie said to his son, "To what do I owe this great honor?"

There was a thick silence as the two men surveyed each other, Ali with narrowed, contemptuous eyes, his father blinking, almost amused. Finally Ali said quietly, "I'm not here to see you. I'm here to introduce you to someone."

His father looked at me through a veil of nicotine as if he had just noticed my presence.

He came toward me, brushing past Ali, who flinched away from his father's body as if it held electric currents that would shock him. Ronnie extended a hand to me, and I took it.

He clearly didn't recognize me.

Ali was quiet, so I said, "I'm Birdie. Birdie Lee."

Ronnie blinked a little coldly for a moment, then a smile crept into his expression and he yelled, "My God, Deck's daughter! I remember you." And he opened his arm, engulfing me in an embrace. I felt the same sense of relief I had felt upon seeing Dot for the first time, upon her recognition of me.

Beaming now, I glanced back at Ali. He stood hunched and uncomfortable, hiding in the corner. He seemed to have lost his looks after entering the house. He had become small and tortured, a sneer of disgust marring his usually delicate face. He said to me, "Listen, Birdie, this is on you. I brought you here. Now I gotta go."

"Where are you going?"

"Back to my mom's. This shit is crazy."

I looked at his father, who just shrugged a little sadly. "Ali doesn't want to be seen near me. He finds me revolting." There was a hint of Gideon's British accent under Ronnie's voice, and I remembered then that he had been making a film on race tensions in Brixton the last time I'd seen him at the Nkrumah School. Back then he had been railing about the limits of black American politics, about how he, too, wanted to go international. He must have found Gideon on his travels.

I didn't want Ali to leave. Whatever I found out, I didn't want to be alone with it. I pleaded with him, "Just hang around for a while, Ali. Please? It's important."

He stared down at me a little coldly, looking just like his father in that flash of disdain. But I must have sounded desperate because he mumbled, "Okay, okay. But I can't stay long."

His father led us into the living room. A framed poster of Diana Ross, looking like an afroed and emaciated princess, hung over the mantelpiece, reminding me of Corvette. The decor had more funk than the hallway had let on. Candles stood in tall, gothic holders, and African cloths were strewn everywhere. An old hood from a yellow taxi cab was propped against one of the walls beside a lumpy green velvet sofa. Inside, the photographs continued, a series of portraits—all shades of black folks—with the word "Miscellaneous" scrawled in huge letters across their faces. Ali went immediately to a corner chair, slumped down, and stuck his nose into a book of primitive art.

Gideon appeared briefly to bring out a platter of wine and crackers with expensive, smelly cheese. He stood staring at Ali with a clear fascination. "The unprodigal son," he said before clucking his teeth and disappearing back into the kitchen.

After Gideon had gone, Ronnie settled back in his armchair across from us, cradling a wineglass in his hands, his legs stretched out before him.

I ignored the unfolding family drama and set into devouring the food and wine Gideon had placed in front of me. I hadn't eaten since breakfast, before my mother's near-arrest. I took large gulps of the wine, as if it were grape juice. I glanced up as I refilled my glass, and Ronnie was watching me. I felt self-conscious and slowed down on the food. I wasn't sure how to begin.

Ronnie said with a curious smile, "I always wondered how you and your sister would turn out. I remember your mother telling me how worried she was about you at the school, how the other kids were giving you trouble."

I hung on to his words, my own proof that I hadn't been making up this past. The wine I had put back so quickly made me slightly dizzy, a little queasy, but I strained to stay alert. Ronnie went on, not pausing to wonder why I was there.

"I used to see you in the crowd of other kids, when I'd come to pick up Ali." He gave Ali a meaningful look, then took a sip of his red wine. "You were like this pale speck in a dark circle. I remember thinking your parents

were such great mad scientists, embarking on this marvelous, ambitious experiment with you and your sister. I guess we all were back then. But I always
wondered how it would turn out."

He stopped laughing abruptly and said to Ali, "How's your mother? And
Lou?"

Ali glanced up from the book he appeared to be reading and said, coldly,
"Everything's fine. They're fine. But this isn't a family reunion. We're here on
business. I'm just trying to help Birdie."

A slight, barely perceptible hurt registered on Ronnie's face, then he
waved his hand at his son and said to me, trying to smile, "He'll regret all this
some day, when I'm on my death bed and he's got less testosterone flowing
through him. You'll see. He'll regret all of this childishness."

Ronnie leaned in close to me and whispered, "He saw me downtown the
other day. He was with a bunch of his little ruffian friends. I was with
Gideon. He ignored me. He looked right past me as if he didn't know me
from Adam. But some of his friends saw me and shouted names. Now that
was a sheer delight."

Ali rolled his eyes. "Yeah, well, you could act normal. You don't have to
act like such a fucking faggot. It makes me sick."

Ronnie sighed. "You're right, Ali. I don't have to act like this. I could do
what I did for all those years and play the straight man." He pulled out a cig-
arette and lit it. I noticed his hands were trembling. He glanced at me. "Shit,
I got so good at playing that part of the positive brother I could have won an
Emmy. But I'm not going back. This is the father you were born with, Ali.
I'm sorry."

I kept my eyes to the floor, twisting a napkin around my hand like a ban-
dage. Ronnie's was a familiar story to me. The women of Aurora often had
talked about what lies they had lived as Stepford wives—before they had become real, roaring, natural women. I thought about Bernadette and my
mother, their blatant kisses and hugs and nude romps to the lake. About
Alexis and me, our games of honeymoon. In the context of Aurora, it had
come to seem as natural as anything else. And it was my mother's affair with
Jim, not with Bernadette, that had disgusted me. I wondered if Ali would
turn against me if he knew my full story, if he knew all the worlds I had lived
in, worlds I still carried inside of me now.

Ronnie settled back in his chair, and we all were quiet for a few minutes.

"Well, whatever happened to Sandra Lee?" Ronnie finally said. "The blue blood turned black-and-blue blood." He chuckled at his own joke. "She was a real loose cannon. I always liked her for that."

His face turned serious, a little sad, as he said, "They all disappeared that year. We used to call them the Boston Four. Hassan. That Jane chick. Your mother. And of course, Linda, the Puerto Rican bull dyke. I heard rumors that Linda was turned in a few years ago—by her own lover, mind you. They were living in Berkeley together. Crazy. Heard she got fourteen years. She'll probably die in there. And for what? It's a shame, a crying shame."

I felt a sharp pain in my stomach and bent over. My mouth began to water. I was going to be sick.

Ronnie was still talking: "Such bullshit. I mean, really. Those Cointelpro motherfuckers killed the best people we had, or at least sent them into hiding, where they couldn't do shit to help—Hey, you all right?"

I stood and held the back of the chair to steady myself.

I glanced down at the half-eaten roll of cheese, green and blue lumps, a marshy smell wafting up from it. I put a hand over my mouth. "I'm sick—" I managed to say before rushing into the hall and into a small cubby bathroom under the stairs, instinct telling me where it was.

I threw up all of Gideon's fancy cheese, my hands resting on the rim of the toilet seat while my head grew heavy. After I was finished, I went to the sink to wash up. The bathroom wallpaper was made of red velvet; it gave my face a rosy tint in the antique mirror. I thought of Linda's fate—fourteen years behind bars. Was that the same fate my mother would have faced? Perhaps Dot had been wrong. Perhaps something real had made us run; it had not been just in my mother's head. I remembered her hissing to me one night in bed, while the New Hampshire air sat still and black and starry beyond the glass: *You think I'm making this up? You think this is some little game we're playing here? Trust me, these boys don't play. They want me. I know it for a fact. They want to make an example of me. There are political prisoners rotting away right now because they dared to stand up. People dying in prison. Women. They don't care if you've got children or a family. They're ruthless motherfuckers. Believe me.*

Deep down, I hoped my mother had done something. I hoped that she was bad and brave and guilty as charged. I wanted her to be involved in something that had changed history, not just me. And it struck me as I stared at my rouge reflection that I might have told Ali too much. For all I knew he was telling his father right now. I had no idea who any of these men really were—just who they once had been. My mother's words: *Trust nobody. Nobody is beyond suspicion. Nobody.*

I went back into the living room. Ronnie had vanished, and Ali sat with his head tilted back in the chair, his eyes closed. I didn't believe, really, that either Ali or Ronnie was to be feared, but at that moment I saw everything through the prism of my mother's rules.

I hissed, "Ali!"

He jumped awake with a start and looked at me. "Are you feeling okay?"

I nodded and glanced around me before whispering, "What I told you about my mother. Forget it. Everything I said. You hear me?"

He nodded, looking slightly frightened of me. My face was still dripping with water, and I was shivering.

I said, "Did you tell your dad already?"

"No," he said, seeming surprised at such a prospect.

"Well, don't—" I started to say.

Ronnie came back in just then with a tumbler of something more serious—Scotch, I could see, from the bottle he held in his other hand. He looked at me. "You drank too much wine. You were gulping that down like it was water."

I sat back down on the couch. "Sorry." I glanced back at Ali with my fiercest look of warning.

Ronnie said, "So, whatever happened to your mother? Or is that top secret—"

"I don't know. I mean, you tell me. She disappeared years ago." I paused. "Do you really think she was in serious trouble?"

Ronnie scoffed. "Of course she was. I don't have any proof. But there was talk that she was caught planning something big and had to split. Had to disappear. And you know, once you're on their list, you stay on their list. Forever. That's not the kind of thing they forget about."

Ronnie's words sounded like the truth. And his story fit in with what I remembered of Redbone and the men in the night. Dot had seemed convinced otherwise. But she always had been more spiritual than political. Most of her friends didn't even read the newspaper. It brought with it too much negative energy. Ronnie had been closer to the movement, I told myself. His story was the one I wanted to believe.

He asked where I had been all these years. And as always, my story flowed. "I've been away at boarding school. My grandmother put up the cash."

He seemed to know I was lying and winked at me as he said, "Well, I hope Ms. Sandy's safe, wherever she is. Give her my regards if you see her."

He glanced at his watch. "Now, what did you need help with? Gideon and I have plans for the evening."

I was running out of time. I said, "Have you heard from my father? I'm looking for my father and my sister. I know they're in Brazil, but I was wondering if you'd heard from them."

Ronnie stared at me blankly for a moment, as if I were speaking in tongues. Then he stood up and began to pace. Finally he turned to me and laughed a little abruptly, as if he saw something funny on my face: "Well, hon, as a matter of fact, I *saw* your dad."

I stopped breathing. "You were in Brazil?"

He looked down at me. I couldn't read his expression. "So, you mean you haven't seen them in all this time?"

I shook my head.

He turned away from me. "Baby, your papa didn't spend more than two years in Brazil. I bumped into him in San Francisco just a few years back. I was, you know, just walking down through the Mission when I saw this familiar figure coming out of a library, carrying a pile of books. I stared at him, then said, 'Shit, if it isn't Deck Lee!'"

I wanted to get up and leave then, just walk away from the story this man was telling me. For the first time, I wasn't sure I wanted to know the truth. Ignorance had been my bliss. Lies had become my only comfort. But something held me to the chair, and I watched Ronnie dumbly from my seat, not even blinking. Even Ali had perked up to listen in.

"Yeah, it was Deck, all right. I mean, he was always a little, well, how should I put it?" He flashed me a bright smile. "A little intense about his ideas. Well, girl, let me tell you, your pops was more obsessed than ever. With his own high-falutin' ideas about color and class and all that shit. He wouldn't talk of anything else. He didn't seem to notice how *I* had changed until about ten minutes into our conversation—or, I should say, his conversation—that I was wearing platforms and I was looking kind of fierce."

Ali made some racket behind me—a chair moving and a grunt in the back of his throat. He had his face in his hands now, and was rocking his head back and forth slowly, as if in great pain. I thought, a little guiltily, that I should have let him go home when he asked.

Ronnie shook his head, then continued: "Anyway, as I was saying, midway into this conversation, Deck looks at me—really looks at me—and starts to laugh, this weird inside kind of laugh. He said some shit that put me off—especially with us being old friends from the movement and all that. And then he was gone, down the street, blending in with the rest of the city. It was a strange encounter, but it was him, Birdie. He looked different—a little disheveled, unkempt—but it was definitely Mr. Deck Lee."

I spoke without feeling my lips move. "Did he say why he came back? Do you remember?" My fingers pressed into the cool glass in my hands.

Ronnie sat back down, squinting at the floor, searching his mind before he spoke. "Yeah, I do remember. He said he'd been back since, like, 1977, I think. Brazil was a bust. You know how he thought it was going to be this Xanadu, this grand Mulatto Nation? Well, he said he'd been wrong. It wasn't the racial paradise he thought it was going to be. There was some anthropological thing he had been looking for there called—what the hell was he calling it? Something crazy—your dad always was a genius. But he said the Brazilians were more racist than the Americans. He went on and on about it until he noticed my platforms. Then he wanted to get as far away from my faggot ass as he could."

Ronnie finished off what was in his tumbler and snorted, looking into the bottom of the empty glass as if to read tea leaves. "Your dad had changed. And I guess I had, too."

I blurted out, "Well, what about Cole? I mean, was he with my sister? Did he say anything about her?"

He shook his head. "I don't remember him saying anything about her. No mention of Carmen, either—"

I barely let him finish. "Did he give you his address? His phone number?"

Ronnie thought for a moment. "You know, as a matter of fact, I think he did give it to me. He said he was living in Oakland at the time. Who the hell knows if it's still the right one. This was about two years ago. Wait right here."

He left Ali and me in the living room together. Ali was watching me. His scowl had passed, and he seemed to have returned to himself. He came and sat beside me on the couch. "So, what's up with that, Birdie? What are you gonna do?"

I felt a little queasy still, and held my head in my hands. "I don't know. I guess go find them. In Oakland."

"Get there on what? That takes dollars."

He was right. I would need money to fly to Oakland. Dot had so little, I wouldn't want to ask her. And I was afraid to see my mother again, afraid that she would be able to stop me from leaving the next time, afraid I wouldn't want to leave. I looked down at the fancy cheese on the table, and the half-finished bottle of expensive Scotch. Their smells were mingling into one, a sharp odor of aging delicacies that knocked me back to my grandmother's house.

Ronnie returned with a napkin in his hand. He handed it to me. "Here it is. Deck Lee. Hope he hasn't moved."

I looked down at the napkin. It read, in Ronnie's childish script: "Deck, 24 Brighton Street, Apartment #1, Oakland." And a phone number.

"Thanks," I muttered, still staring in shock at the address. It seemed so simple and ordinary. Words and numbers on a napkin. No fireworks or smoke.

Ronnie shrugged. "Yeah, well, you tell your pops I said hi if you see him."

At the door, he kissed me lightly on the cheek and whispered into my ear, "Take care of yourself, little sister." Then he put out his hand to shake with his son. Ali hesitated, then accepted it, keeping his eyes fixed on their hands—his darker one, his father's lighter—as they pumped together. His face was tense, concentrated, as if he were fighting to stay true to some inner hardness, but something in his eyes was beginning to thaw slightly, against his own will.

Outside, Ali and I were quiet as we made our way past the Negro battalion, over the Common, and to the T station at Downtown Crossing. I was thinking. I had to call my father from a pay phone. Here and now. See if he really existed. Tell him I was coming to see him. Coming to be his daughter again.

When we reached the entrance to the station, Ali asked me where I was going.

I told him that I didn't know, feeling more comfortable in this lie than I had ever felt in the truth. I warned him one more time that my mother's whereabouts were a secret, and he nodded, solemn. I trusted him.

He scribbled his phone number on a Prudential matchbook and handed it to me. "If you need help or anything, just call."

"Thanks, Ali," I said, taking it from him. I crossed my arms and felt shy all of a sudden, as if I were saying good-bye on a first date. "I mean, thanks for bringing me to your father." I paused, looking for the right words. "It was everything."

He smiled kind of crookedly, seeming embarrassed. "No problem, B." He kicked the pavement with his combat boots. "It ain't that deep, you know? It ain't that deep."

I didn't know what he meant, but before I could ask, he was gone, striding away with his head bent against the cold, toward the Cheri 1-2-3 movie theater to meet his friends. He looked fragile from that distance, just a body buffeted by the wind, and I felt a burn of loss watching him go. I wished I had asked him to join me. But I hadn't, and I knew, deep down, that the job was mine to do alone.

After he was out of sight, I went in search of a pay phone. It was freezing outside now, and my throat felt raw. It was painful to swallow, and there was a pounding pressure in my ears. I didn't know if it was from the retching at Ronnie's house, or if I was getting some kind of flu. I found a phone at the entrance to an alley. At the far end, I could see a group of men huddled around a tin-can fire. Their laughter floated toward me, and it was somehow comforting in the night air. I held the phone in my hand for a while before dialing, whispering to myself, "Hello? This is your child. This is Birdie," over and over in different tones of voice. Finally, when my hand was stiff with the cold, I dialed the operator. It would have to be a collect call. He owed me that much. The woman took my name and the number, and then there was the sound of ringing. I was biting my nails, my cheeks burning despite the frigid air. I thought maybe I'd just hang up at the sound of his voice. All I needed to know was that he was there. That he existed.

Nobody picked up. After the sixth ring the operator told me I had to hang up. She said to try back later. I hung up and tried it again, twice, with two different operators. Both times the same thing happened. Nobody was home. Try back later.

I felt someone behind me and turned. It was a man in an Army coat, watching me from the corner. He had red hair and red skin and was grinning. Redbone. He had found me. It was over. My mother had been telling the truth.

But then, as my eyes focused, I saw it wasn't Redbone at all. It was a white man with a windburned face and scraggly blond hair coming out from his ski cap. He was walking toward me, still grinning, his hands in his coat pockets. I was transfixed, frozen by his image, and I smiled slightly back, relieved it was nobody I knew. He was only a few feet away when I looked down at the movement in his wrists. His coat was moving apart, and there was a flash of flesh, of bristly red hair. I turned and fled toward the light of the T station.

THE AIR AROUND Harvard Square, my mother used to say, has a particular smell. It's the smell, she said, of hypocrisy. A smell she didn't find in New Hampshire, among the working people who called a spade a spade, a spic a spic, a kike a kike. It was the smell of aging cheese and even older Scotch. A smell of dust embedded between yellowing history pages, of tobacco on stained fingertips. The smell of Cristalle perfume on a silk blouse, and lemon-scented cleaning solution on a pair of brown hands. That smell had been so strong to my mother that she was hardly able to breathe when she was around it, for fear of suffocation. She used to tell me and Cole to inhale when we drove for visits with my grandmother, over the Harvard Square Bridge that linked Boston to Cambridge; she would say, "Do you smell it, girls? Oh, God, it's strong today." And we would stick our faces out of the open window of the Pinto, the wind washing our faces, turning us numb as we tried to smell Cambridge. I did in fact catch something pungent hitting my nose then, and Cole did too. Bringing our heads back into the car, we would nod to our mother, wrinkling our noses, letting her know that she was not alone.

She said she could see it if she looked hard enough, a low rolling cloud rising up from the sycamores and weeping willows and making its way across the silver surface of the Charles River, through Harvard Yard, and into the dank corners of Lowell and Quincy streets, to Brattle Street, where it still lived.

The Square was bustling tonight with students and street musicians, a few homeless men waving freebie newspapers into the faces of the annoyed passersby. In front of Out of Town News, a crew of scruffy white teenagers in mohawks and ripped clothes smoked and performed dangerous tricks on skateboards. They reminded me of Nicholas—the person he might have been if he had escaped New Hampshire and his family. As I crossed Massachussetts Avenue, I scanned the faces for the Shirley Temple girl I had spotted just the day before from the bus window, but saw no one like her.

Soon I had wandered away from the bright lights, populace, and music of the Square and was heading down the darker residential streets that led to my grandmother's house. I felt nervous in the dark, alone, and imagined red-haired rapists dressed like Feds, waiting for me in the bushes. I found solace in trying to imagine my mother as she made her way home one dark night, after she had met my father, after he had asked her that question: *Do you drink coffee at night?* And I almost felt her beside me, young and fresh-faced and plump, carrying her copy of Camus's notebooks under her arm, asking, "But why?" to some unanswerable question.

MY GRANDMOTHER'S HOUSE hadn't changed much in the six years since I had seen it. The air around it was thick with the smoke of burning wood that floated out from chimneys. Her house was set far off the road and was hidden by the bars of sycamore branches, branches now bare and coated in a thin layer of ice. I shivered in front of the house, my teeth chattering, but the facts I had learned about my father distracted me from my body, from the flu I was now certain I had. Ronnie's words had at first seemed to sharpen my life, like a photograph coming into focus, but then had blurred it again, as if he had turned the lens just too far.

I made my way up the walkway. A dark-green Volvo sat in the driveway, my grandmother's ancient car which she had rarely driven when I was around. She would be in her eighties now, and I wondered if she drove at all anymore. The car was proof that she still lived here, that she still lived at all.

I crossed her lawn and reached the bottom of the steps leading up to her front door. On the first floor, the lights were on. My grandmother had been a grande dame of the social world of Cambridge—she might be having one of her famous dinner parties tonight. I imagined myself knocking, Edna answering, gray-haired now, and shepherding me into the dining room, where my grandmother would pause in mid-sentence at the sight of me, her long-lost grandchild. *The chicken has come home to roost.* The other guests would stare at me with bewildered expressions, wondering who this young ruffian standing before them was.

Instead of risking this scenario, I prowled around the side of the house, scraping myself against the line of bushes. In the springtime, those bushes bloomed lilac and pink and yellow roses. On one ill-fated visit, Cole and I, in a game of mad scientist, tried to make them into perfume. While my mother and grandmother argued on the veranda, we cut a bunch of her best roses, brought them inside, and put the petals in a sealed plastic baggie, which we placed between the pages of my grandmother's huge *Encyclopaedia Britannica*. We believed they would crush into a puddle of perfume. We brought the book to the top floor of the house and promptly dropped it out the window, where it sailed past my mother and grandmother on the veranda, and onto the lawn below. My grandmother scolded us harshly when she saw that the spine of the encyclopedia was broken; she told my mother we were being raised as savages and had no manners. But the roses did leave a kind of pasty perfume along the sides of the baggie, which my mother let us take home and put into a bottle with some water and alcohol. We soon forgot about it. Years later, we found the jar and opened it to the stench of mildew and fermented flowers.

I reached the back of the house, where a vast picture window looked onto the garden. Inside, the dining room was dark—no dinner party on the schedule for tonight. I pressed my face to the glass, which fogged up with my breath, and could make out the large silver teapot on the mantel. It had fascinated me as a child, the way I could see myself so clearly in it, only distorted, my head large and my body shrunken in its curved reflective surface. A few windows over from me, a light bounced out onto the bushes, and muffled music played from within. I sidled along the wall like a cat burglar. Inside those windows, I saw the television flickering and heard the familiar music of "Masterpiece Theatre." On the couch before the television, my grandmother sat, slack-jawed, sleeping in the glow of the room. She looked older and seemed to have grown smaller. I had remembered her as tall, towering, angular. Now she looked like the silver teapot in the next room, her head tilted back and her mouth open like a spout. Her hand rested on Delilah, her cat, who stared at me from her lap. The cat's eyes were gleaming yellow, reflecting the light from the television, and I was glad that she didn't know how to bark. The dog, Gory, had been old the last I'd seen him. I wondered if he'd died.

I knew I had to enter now, though I was terrified. I thought my mother would kill me if she could see me here. This was somewhere she had sworn we would never return to. I walked back, sweating with fever and fear, to the front of the house, the proper entrance. I rang the bell and waited for Edna to answer.

Instead, a new maid, a plump Irish woman, came to the door in a sweater that had crumbs littering its front. She smelled strongly of peanut butter and seemed to have a hard time talking through the food in her mouth. Her lips smacked as she said, "Yes, what can I do for you?"

She eyed me with a slight suspicion, I thought, as if she were trying to make out where she had seen me before.

"I'm here to see Penelope Lodge. She's expecting me," I told the woman.

She frowned, seeming anxious to get back to her snack. "Well, come in. You'll catch your death out there. Come in, dear."

There was something maternal in her saying this, and I smiled, trying to stop my teeth from chattering. She wiped her hands on her housedress and said in her lilting accent, "They say it's supposed to snow tonight. Thank God, you know. Snow brings the temperature up. Now, let me get Penny. She's probably fallen asleep by now. Who should I say is here?"

I hesitated. "Tell her it's her granddaughter."

The woman seemed to turn a little pale and looked at me with new-found interest. Finally she stuttered, "Oh, yes. I think I've heard of you. Hold on, please."

She shuffled off toward the living room, where I had seen my grandmother sleeping. I looked around. Nothing, indeed, had changed. There was still a clutter of ancestors lining the wall under the staircase. Cotton Mather's face peered out from a print—the same one that once had hung in our house, over our television, the one my father had said made Mather look like an octoroon dandy. The print had been framed properly, and the rips and stains that had marred it in our chaotic household seemed to have been mended. My grandmother must have taken all of our things after we evacuated.

There were no family photos in the hallway. The Lodge family considered it vulgar to have their family photographs exposed to the public, and liked to keep them hidden somewhere secret. They had been kept in the study just off the hall, the study that once had been my grandfather's. I stepped over to the study door and pushed it gently. It gave. I switched on the light. Books covered the walls, and there was a small manual typewriter on the table. Beside it sat a picture in a wood frame of Randall, older now, sitting in an Adirondack chair on a lawn, gazing off beyond the camera as if he is thinking of something important. Beside that, a picture of my mother, age fifteen or so, looking haunted, staring gloomily over a coffee mug. Through a trick of the camera she appears thinner than she really was at the time, not like herself—more like an approximation of what my grandmother might have wanted her to look like. She looked more like the woman my mother was now, only younger. On the bookshelf behind the desk I noticed a picture of Cole and me. Randall had taken it one gloomy afternoon when it had poured and we all were trapped inside to stare at one another. In the picture we look like gypsy children: Cole's hair is covered by a bandanna because it had gotten nappy in the rain and my mother hadn't been able to do anything with it. She is only about nine in the photo, but her eyes are like an adult's, cynical, unyielding. I am a child beside her, grinning, rambunctious, my overgrown bangs hiding my eyes. I am holding her hand tight.

A shriek came from the next room. Then the sound of a cat howling as it came bounding out from the living room and across the hall in a dart of gray fur. My grandmother's voice: "Good God, Doris! Don't joke with me!"

Footsteps. I quickly returned to the hall, closing the study door behind me and bracing myself.

She had a look of fear and hope on her face when she came around the corner. She paused there, her lips parting, then closing. "Birdie?"

I nodded. She was still tall, still imposing, even in her eighties. Her hair was frost white, no more streaks of black, and her face seemed slightly sunken. But awake, she was remarkably herself—still gaunt and well-dressed, in a pair of gray cashmere slacks and a dark-red cardigan, her hair pulled into a chignon. She was still vain at her age. She had a walking stick at her side, but didn't seem to need it now. She simply stared at me for a few moments, showing no emotion—her mouth set into a thin straight line.

Finally she said, "Well, goodness. You look awful—like Anne Frank. Come, sit with me in the other room. Doris, make me a drink. And something hot for the child."

I nodded and followed her into the living room, relieved now to be under a roof and out of the cold. She settled in her television chair, and I sat primly at the edge of the couch. She stared at me for a few more minutes, while I rubbed my hands together and tried not to meet her eyes. She had always acted stone cold toward her own family, flowering only in the company of near-strangers.

We were quiet while Doris brought my grandmother a glass of sherry with ice, and me a cup of lemon tea that I gulped too quickly, scalding my tongue.

When Doris was gone, my grandmother said, "Close the door."

I obeyed, and when I sat down, she spoke, looking dramatically out the window onto her own ghostly reflection. "So, go on. Tell me, please. I've been waiting for this. Now, go ahead. Where is that horrid daughter of mine?"

I hadn't prepared a speech. "She's safe and sound and she's got someone taking care of her. She's okay."

She sipped her sherry and fixed her eyes on me. "*Where* is she. Not *how* is she."

I looked down at my fingers. She was making me small again, turning me into the little girl I had been, who cowered before her as a child. I said in a small voice, "That's a secret."

My grandmother laughed harshly. "I have the right to know where my daughter is. If I've earned anything, it's that right. Now, speak it!"

I shook my head and remained quiet.

She was silent for a few moments, stunned, I think, by my audacity. Then she tried a new tactic: "You poor, poor child. We don't choose our parents. It's all terrible fate. I should have taken you away from her a long time ago. But she wouldn't have let me, you know. Sandy had a will of steel."

She had always said things like this to me, making me feel as if there were something pitiful about my existence. As a child, those words had made me feel ashamed. Now they made me angry.

"I'm just fine, Grandma. Really. Trust me. My mom's fine. I'm fine."

She shook her head, her eyes moistening as she said those words that were so familiar to me, words that had sent my mother into conniptions of rage when I was a child.

"It was doomed from the start. Tragedy in the making. Your mother should have stuck to her world."

I dropped my teacup and watched the dark liquid flow over the wood and into the cracks. She watched it too, as if it proved her theory right.

I remembered something my father once had told Cole when she complained about how my grandmother treated her. He had rubbed her little curly head and said, "Baby, don't pay that old lady any mind. She'll be gone soon. She's a dying breed. You're the future."

I snapped at my grandmother, and my words flowed with some rage I had been unaware of until now: "Oh, please. I'm not in the mood for this Victorian crap. You and all your ancestors are the tragedies. Not me. You walk around pretending to be so liberal and civilized in this big old house, but you're just as bad as the rest of them. This whole world—it's based on lies. No wonder my mother left. I mean, it stinks."

I was breathing hard and put my face in my hands. My head was throbbing, something banging around inside it, and I was shaking and sweating. But I felt better once the words were out of me. The words were aimed at my grandmother, but also at my mother, Jim, Mona, and the whole state of New Hampshire. They were the truest words I had spoken in a long time, and having said them I felt a little lighter.

I had meant every word of it. My grandmother had always loved me more than my sister. Or maybe it wasn't me she loved, but rather my face, my skin, my hair, and my bones, because they resembled her own. It wasn't a pure love, if such a thing existed. It was clear in her face every time she looked at us, every time she had reached out to stroke my hair. She believed that the face was a mirror of the soul. She believed, deep down, that the race my face reflected made me superior. Such a simple, comforting myth to live by. My father had explained that to Cole and me one morning while we wandered through the Isabella Stuart Gardner Museum. "Once they let go of that idea of their own innate superiority—and don't let them pretend they don't, deep down, believe in it—once they let go of that, it all begins to crumble. Things start to fall apart."

I heard my grandmother say after a moment, in a softer voice: "You're sick. I should have seen it. You're sick."

She was right. I was sick. But I didn't say anything. I didn't want any more of her pity. It made me nauseous.

I peeked at her through the bars of my fingers. She looked genuinely concerned. Her stern expression had faltered a bit, and her chin quivered slightly. "I didn't want it to turn out this way. She was so difficult. But I love your mother. I always loved her the best. She was always the smarter of the two. She was always the clever one. Randall was the great beauty, but never as intelligent as she was. She saw things no one else saw. And she was the only one to give me grandchildren. Randall might as well be a bugger."

I laughed abruptly, despite myself, at her description of him. A small smile crossed her lips. "It was too easy for Randall. I think that's a curse, really. To be given too much without even asking. Without having to work for it. It made him useless, weak. But Sandy, she cared about something." She leaned forward toward me, and I saw that her hands were shaking. "Where is she, Birdie? Where is she?"

I looked down at the cat, who was licking up the spilled tea. "I can't tell you where she is, Grandma. She's in trouble. You know that."

I said it but wasn't sure anymore if it was true. Dot had said one thing, Ronnie had said another.

My grandmother was trembling now, and I moved along the couch toward her, putting out my hand to her. She was old and she was scared and she had lost her child.

She took my hand and began to cry, quietly, seeming angry with herself for this cracking, but crying nonetheless. She stroked my hand, and the skin over her bones felt loose and soft. "Oh, God. I hope she's okay." After a moment she said through delicate sniffles, "Your sister. Do you know where your sister is?"

She had always referred to Cole as "your sister" and my father as "your father," as if she couldn't bear to say their names, couldn't bear to admit their relation to her. I restrained from comment this time, however, and said, "I'm not sure, but I think I might know where they are. That's why I'm here. You've got to help me. I've got an address where I think they live. My father and my sister. It's in Oakland, California, and I need money to get to them. I haven't seen them since we left. Could you help me get to them?"

She wiped away the wet streaks that lined her powdery face. She was back to herself, glacial, hardened. "No, no, no. Don't be silly. I wouldn't let you go there alone. That's not how to do it, Birdie. You'll live here, with me. I'm going to send you to Beaver Country Day School. Give you a proper education, if it's not too late. And then, when the time is right, you can write to them—a letter. It's far more sensible."

I sunk back into the couch, feeling deflated, trapped.

She yelled, "Doris!"

After a few minutes, Doris came in from somewhere, carrying a book, bifocals hanging from her neck. "What is it, Penny? For the love of Peter. I'm trying to get some rest."

My grandmother barked back, "Get a bed made up for Birdie. She's staying here. She's going to live with us."

Doris frowned, then gave me a questioning look. I shrugged. My flu had made me sleepy. I knew I should call Dot, tell her where I was, but all I could think about was my grandmother's guest room—the Irish linen sheets and goose-down duvet. A real bed in a real house, with my own bar of apricot soap from Crabtree and Evelyn.

So I followed Doris, who carried fresh towels and a washcloth, up to the guest room at the top of the stairs, thinking only as far as these bodily comforts.

THE WORLD OUTSIDE the window was as white as it had ever been. The clock over the desk said it was five-thirty. Doris had been right about the snow, and I opened the window beside the bed a crack, sticking my hand out into the fresh air, wiggling my fingers beyond the glass, where the snowflakes caught on them, then disappeared. The snow looked tinted with blue, the way totally white things sometimes do. It's the same with things that are deeply black—an Asian girl's hair, a drop of ink, a stallion's coat. They turn blue. I pulled my hand back in and gathered the comforter around me, watching the clumsy flakes float past the window in slow motion. I had been dreaming of Alexis, of us playing honeymoon after a day of climbing trees behind Aurora. Me on top of her, rubbing against her until that sharpness turned to melting. But we were not little girls in the dream. We were our current ages, and in the dream she was sad, her hazel eyes moist with worry. She lay beside me when we were done playing, and stroked my hair, saying, "You're right here, beside me, but I miss you."

The guest room once had been my mother's bedroom, when she was a high-school girl still obsessed with Camus. She had never chosen the pink-and-white decor that most girls her age had. Instead the room was a blend of melancholy colors—blues and grays and blacks.

I slipped out from under the covers and stood up, my feet bare against the cold wood floor. My head was still groggy, and I felt a little warm with fever. I went to the closet and opened the door. There were mostly men's clothes in it—my grandfather's suits that had been stored away since his death. But crushed behind those were skirts and dresses made for a sixteen-year-old fat girl named Sandy. I pulled out a checkered lime-green and white blouse and held it against my face. It smelled like stale clove smoke and mothballs. There were yellow sweat stains, like parchment, under the arms. I stepped inside the closet and pressed my face into my grandfather's clothes. They smelled like cigar smoke. My grandfather and mother had been the two smokers in the family, and after dinner each night they had been confined to the den together, where they would smoke with their heads conspiratorially bent toward each other's while they talked about the latest book they had read together—Sartre or Baldwin or Margaret Meade. It seemed somehow fitting that their clothes should be stored in this small space together. I wished I had known my grandfather. My mother said that if he had lived, things would have been different. I hadn't known what she was referring to exactly, but understood that in some way he had kept her on track, had kept her passions focused. I pulled out his heavy cashmere coat. In the dark of the room, I couldn't see if it was black or indigo, only that it was well-preserved, undamaged by moths. I draped it over the back of the desk chair and closed the closet door.

I dressed slowly, back into my blue jeans and thin sweater, as quietly as I could. I made the bed then with great care, redoing the hospital corners on the linen sheets and shaking out the gray duvet so it lay puffed like newly fallen snow. There was only the sound of the grandfather clock ticking down-stairs, but otherwise everything was utterly silent, as if the snow muffled our snores. I put on my grandfather's coat, over my clothes, and it draped heavily to my ankles. The sleeves covered my hands. I rolled them up, revealing a pale-blue satin lining, and reached in the pockets to find leather gloves, worn to the shape of someone else's larger hands.

I went to my grandmother's bedroom and knocked lightly. No answer. I pushed the door. Her face was sunken in, gaunt, so that she looked dead in the half light. She slept where she had always slept, in a big oak bed that had been passed down to her through the generations. My mother swore it was haunted; she had slept in it several times as a child and claimed that the bed had woken her up in the night, shaking, and she had turned over to find a chalk-white man beside her, grinning. Cole and I had been fascinated by the bed, conflicted between our fear of it and our thrill at the idea of sleeping in it, of maybe seeing a real live ghost. We never got the chance.

I whispered my grandmother's name: "Penelope."

She said something that sounded like an accusation. Dream talk. Her eyes stayed shut, but as I approached her, I could see the movement under the lids. I wondered what she was seeing.

I stood over her and spoke louder this time: "Grandma, wake up."

Her eyes blinked open, and she stared at me, terrified for a moment. I must have seemed to her the ghost of some child she once had known.

"Grandma, it's just me, Birdie."

She frowned and said, "What time is it?"

"Late."

She maneuvered herself onto her elbows and stared at me. Her hair was still in a bun, though loosening, and the stray hairs made her seem younger, softer. She wore a flannel nightgown, and a few buttons at the top had come open so I could see her collarbone, the delicate frame.

"What do you want? Why aren't you asleep?" She clicked on the light beside her, and we both blinked at its harshness. She saw what I was wearing— her dead husband's coat—and stiffened.

I hacked into my hand. "Grandma, please, could you give me the money? For a ticket."

She was fully awake now and was fiddling with her hair, trying to get it back into a bun.

"I've said no already, Birdie. This is outrageous. You waking me up like this. And why the hell have you got on Arthur's coat? Good God. You'd think this was a madhouse."

I blinked, about to cry, though I knew I wouldn't, couldn't. That wasn't part of my plan. I took a deep breath and said, "Listen, Grandma, I love you. But I don't belong here. I have to go now."

"But where will you go?"

"I need money to get to Oakland. Just enough to get there. One way. I know they're there. And I know you have the money." I paused and took a deep breath before saying it. "I'll tell you where she is."

She knew what I was talking about. Immediately. She said, "Your mother."

I nodded. I had my hands in my pockets now and was crossing my fingers where she couldn't see them. "Yes. If you'll give me the money. And I promise I'll be careful."

She sighed and looked out at the darkness beyond her lace curtains. Above her bed, she had a portrait, a sketch someone had done of Randall when he was in his twenties, when he was suavely handsome and had the world at his feet. He was sitting with a younger version of the family dog between his legs, a vague beach setting behind them.

She was quiet for a while. She was staring at me, considering my offer. Finally she said, with a slight note of approval, "You're a cold child."

We padded down to the study together. I remembered that she always kept cash handy in the safe, lots of it, ever since the Depression. I recalled how when I was little, my mother had told us to remember the combination, the birth year of Increase Mather, Cotton's father. But now, standing before the safe, the date escaped me.

My grandmother was quiet while she opened the safe, then pulled out the jewelry box. In it sat the family collection, a row of sparkling rings and necklaces and brooches. She had promised me something from that selection long ago. A ring, a pulsing red garnet. She had taken me, alone, into that little room on one of our afternoon visits, while my mother and sister played in the backyard. And she had whispered to me that it was our secret. That the ring was mine to keep someday. That it was worth a lot and was a Mather family heirloom. Something to be proud of. I remember feeling stung that she hadn't brought Cole in as well, that she hadn't had a ring for her.

She was pulling the jewelry drawer out now, to reach a false bottom. There was more money in there than I had expected. Twenties and fifties and hundreds. Rolls of them. She counted out six hundred and handed it to me. Enough, she said, to get me to California and back.

As she was packing up the jewels again, her eyes fixed on the garnet ring. She said, "That's yours, you know. I've saved it for you."

I nodded. She picked it up and turned it over in her fingers. "It's worth a lot. If I give it to you, you won't sell it, will you? That would be foolish."

I shook my head no. Really, I wasn't sure. It depended on what happened to me in Oakland.

She handed it to me and said, "Good. You're cold, but not foolish." It was too big for my ring fingers, so I put it on my thumb, where it fit but looked gaudy and fake.

She smiled weakly. "You can get it adjusted to fit. You're thin. That's good. Stay that way."

After she had locked everything away, she turned to me, and her expression had changed. She wanted her payback. Her tone was businesslike, formal. "Now, give me her address. And her phone number."

I bit my nails and looked around the room, fixing my eyes on the picture of Cole and me. Then she handed me a pad and a pen and folded her arms across her chest, daring me to refuse her.

I wrote an address. Not my mother's address, but one I made up. It was in Woodstock, and we had driven through there only once. I had to make up a street and a house number. The phone number I gave her was for nobody I knew. I felt a little guilty, but figured I'd contact my grandmother later, explain myself when I was out of her reach.

She held the slip of paper far from her face so she could read it, frowning at the words there. "Woodstock. Yes, I guess that's the sort of place she would end up."

She went to the kitchen to call the airlines, but returned a few minutes later to announce that there were no seats available till the next day. I blinked, surprised, somehow, though I should have known. I had thought that if only I could get the money, I would magically be transported to my father's doorstep. I had forgotten about the more practical matter of reservations.

My grandmother said she didn't mind keeping me another day; she said we'd call my mother together later, in the afternoon.

"Of course, you should be the one to speak to her first, so I don't scare her, calling her out of the blue."

I had to think fast. I had never flown before, but I knew enough about airports to be able to say I'd go standby. "I'll just wait at the airport until I can get on a flight. I'll wait all day if I have to," I said, sounding a little too eager. "I want to go today. I have to go today."

My grandmother shook her head, beginning to protest. But she must have seen some flash of desperation on my face, because after a moment she just shrugged. "Well, then, I suppose I'd better call a car service. Lord only knows how long you'll have to wait at that horrible place."

When everything was in order, she asked if she could fix me breakfast. "A crumpet and some tea? You look terribly weak, dear. You need something in your stomach."

I was hungry, but I told her I couldn't linger. It was already past six o'clock, and if I was going to catch a flight today, I needed to go now. I was jittery, worried that she'd figure out my lie before I left and take all the money back. I told her I'd call her from California, so she'd know I was safe.

When I came out of the study and into the hall, the cat, Delilah, sat on the steps, switching her tail, watching me with a playful stare, wondering why her mistress was up so early. She came to me and rubbed herself against my grandfather's cashmere, purring loudly. My grandmother watched, grimly. She said, "She recognizes Arthur's smell on the coat."

She seemed sad that I was leaving; her eyes were glistening. I didn't expect Randall came to visit her much. I told her, holding her hand in mine, that I would be back. "Cole and I, we'll come visit you this summer." I sounded more sure of it than I was.

She smiled a little. "You two were so close. You couldn't be with one without the other. You must miss her terribly to be doing this."

Then the Boston Coach beeped outside, my chariot to the airport. I glimpsed the car out the window. A gleaming black sedan with a man in uniform in the driver's seat. It looked a little like the Fed car my mother had described would come to get her someday.

I kissed my grandmother on the cheek, lightly. She held me close to her for a moment and said, "Please, be careful." There was a note of panic in her voice. I was surprised at how sad I was to be leaving her.

Then I left, moved forward, pulling the heavy oak-paneled door closed behind me as I trudged down the steps and into the blue-white morning.

wonders of the invisible world

Everything I had was in my shoe—a roll of my grandmother's cash pressed into the sole of my flat foot, creating an arch where there had been none. My last words to Dot had been that I'd return in a few hours. The evening had come and gone, and the night had passed, and the day was half over. I had finally made it on to a three-o'clock flight.

I'd spent most of the day loitering around the gate, eating junk food from the nearby vending machines, and watching strangers come and go. I'd also tried my father's number—six times, collect—and each time there was no answer. It was a strange relief. I didn't want to find out that he had moved, that this was the wrong address. If it was, I would have to go back, tail between my legs, to my grandmother. If she didn't know by now, she would probably know soon enough that Woodstock was a lie.

There were a few minutes left before boarding time. I had to call Dot. I had been avoiding it. I knew I should have contacted her earlier, that she would be worried sick that I had been missing since yesterday.

I expected no answer. It was two-thirty, and she was supposed to be at work, but she picked up the phone on the first ring and there was a thickness in her voice as she said, "Yes?"

I began to talk in a rush of words, an attempt to keep the conversation on an up note, as I explained to her all that I had learned since I'd last seen her. I relayed to her the news Ronnie had told me, and then, when she didn't respond, I attempted a laugh and told her I had tricked my grandmother.

"Do you do this to all the people you love?" It was a voice she had never used with me before. "Just like your father. Don't even bother to say good-bye."

"I'm sorry, Dot. I didn't mean to make you worry. I'm sorry I didn't call. But I've got his address now. I know where to find them."

She seemed only vaguely interested in my father's whereabouts, even less so in my encounter with my grandmother, and said only, "Birdie, why are you chasing ghosts?"

I was quiet and played with the metal phone cord. I watched the people milling about, businessmen on this flight west. They wore coats similar to mine, similar to my grandfather's, which I still hadn't taken off, despite the fact that I was beginning to sweat underneath.

When I didn't answer, she said in a whisper, so quietly that I barely heard it: "What possible excuse could Deck have for this?"

I had no answer. I hadn't dared to ask myself that, and could say only, "I don't know, I'm going to find out."

She said, authoritative now, "Listen. Come home. We'll work something out here. You can baby-sit for Taj, help me out around the house. We're your family, girl. Don't you know that?"

These were the words I had wanted her to speak over the past few weeks. But I was learning that people didn't invite you to stay until you were gone. And hearing her ask me now, from the other end of a pay phone while I waited for the announcement of USAir Flight 237, I knew it was too late. The comfort of Dot's home, Taj's fingers in my hair in the morning, the familiarity of that old city of Boston, were not enough. I closed my eyes, squeezed them shut so tightly I saw spots. I had started in motion, would stay in motion until I hit the truth or a wall, whichever came first.

"I know you're family, Dot. But I gotta go. Find them. Find out why. You know?"

She sighed then, resigned to my foolishness, not angry anymore, just dubious. "You call me when you get there, now. And your little ass better be careful." A sigh of something held back. "I don't want to lose you again."

Later, up in the sky, strapped down, a sweating plastic cup of Coke in front of me, I wondered, not for the first time since I left my grandmother's house, if I was, as Dot would say, "acting the fool." The fact that my father had been back in America since 1977 and had not seemed to want to find me was something that would be difficult to explain. Dot's question kept returning to me, even as I tried to block it out: *What possible excuse?*

But something told me to keep moving in this direction. It was partly the knowledge that there was no other direction in which to go. It was also a memory that kept coming back to me now. A memory of something that had never happened, something I could see all the same. My sister, wet-faced but dry sobs coming from deep within her chest as she grieved for her mother, for her sister. I could see her on a night in Brazil, foreign words—Portuguese, not Elemeno—filling the warm dark air around her, while she wondered where we were, why we had let the split happen. I saw her looking at Carmen one morning over breakfast and saying to herself, "You're not my mother. I want my mother." She wanted hard-boiled eggs out of chipped Lodge teacups and to sit in our mother's lap, which she imagined still to be wide and soft. She wanted to have my mother read her favorite book aloud, *Stuart Little*, while I pranced around in front of their twin serious solid forms, trying to get their attention. They had been mother and daughter once. I was not the only one who had been left behind.

The man next to me looked Indian. He was reading a book and occasionally sipping the water in front of him, clearing his throat. He wore a business suit with expensive cufflinks, and his hair was neat and shimmering black. He smelled strongly of cologne. For the first hour of the trip, he kept glancing at me out of the corner of his eye. When I'd feel him watching me, I'd frown at him and he would look away, nervously. He was in his thirties, and I doubted he was hitting on me, but I wasn't sure. I wished my mother were with me, that I could take her hand and lean in to her and say, "Mum, that guy next to me, he's creeping me out." And she wouldn't even need to do much. Her expression would be enough to scare him. She'd just lean forward and say, "Listen, man, you looking at my daughter?" She'd done it before. And the man would see something in her expression, something he knew he'd better not mess with. Something he didn't think fit with her blond hair and blue eyes and slender shape and aquiline features. And he would back off.

He was staring at my face, hard, as if he knew me. I turned to him and tried to assume my mother's hardest expression. He didn't turn away this time. Instead, he began to chatter to me in what sounded like Elemeno. It took a second for me to realize he was speaking his own language. And he was fully convinced that I would understand. He was asking me the same question, repeating it, with an expectant, friendly smile.

"Sorry, mister," I finally said. "I don't speak it. I speak English." Not only did I not speak his language—whatever it was—but I didn't speak Spanish or French either. My mother had left that out of our lessons.

The man raised his eyebrows, and said, "Oh, pardon me. I thought you were Pakistani. Indian?"

"Nope, neither," I said, shaking my head. "I mean, I'm American."

He laughed. "No, but where are you really from? Your ancestors. Where are they from?"

"Everywhere. I mean, before they got here, I guess they were from England and Africa. My mom's white. Dad's black."

His expression changed slightly. I had disappointed him, deeply. He had been homesick and had seen his home in my face. Now he turned away, no longer interested.

As I looked out the window and waited to land, it struck me that in all our wanderings, my mother had stayed fairly close to home. The farthest we had ever traveled was to Quebec for a few months when she claimed she could feel the FBI closing in on her and needed to make herself disappear. Mostly, we had kept to the eastern seaboard. We had never been to California, despite the fact that so many of her friends had gone there "after the drop." She said the West was where people went to make themselves over, to transform. But she hadn't taken us that far. She had New England in her blood and was like a child who runs away to the backyard of her very own home. I wondered if my father had come to the West to transform himself. Or simply to avoid me and my mother.

I slept fitfully for the rest of the plane trip. I dreamed that I was in India, wading in a river, pregnant, and that I knew I was supposed to be happy, being so far from the mess of America, but that I wasn't. Really, I missed someone, though I wasn't sure who, exactly, it was. My tears fell into the river, flowing away to the ocean. The dream deteriorated into a series of disconnected images. My flower-print underwear that I had worn the first day I got my period at Aurora, the faint brown stain in the crotch that I couldn't remove no matter how many times I washed it. Me walking across my father's back, trying to push the air out of his lungs. Bernadette smoking a cigar on the porch of the big commune house, while my mother, cross-legged a few feet away, tried to cornrow her own hair. The smell of someone's neck—I couldn't tell if it was Ali or Alexis or Nicholas—but it smelled good.

I woke up with the businessman beside me staring at me with a furrowed brow. He said, "You were talking in your sleep." I couldn't tell from his expression if he had understood what I had said. I hoped I hadn't given anything away.

I looked beyond his face, out the window. From behind the puff of clouds, something green and brown and expansive was emerging. We were dropping in latitude. The stewardess spoke in a pleasant drawl over the intercom, telling us to fasten our seat belts, straighten our chairs, put up our tray tables, to prepare for landing.

I NEVER ACTUALLY SAW the cabdriver's face head-on, only a sliver of it in the rearview mirror. There was a wall of plastic separating us. I stuck the address on the napkin into the change box and pushed it through to him. I half-expected him to tell me that the address didn't exist, but instead he winked at me in the rearview mirror and said, "Sure thing." And then we were off. I had decided not even to try my father's number again. There seemed to be no point.

The sky was the color of smoke without fire—charcoal, billowing, full. The rain was just a mist against the windshield, something that barely needed wiping. I recalled something my mother had once said as we had driven along an empty highway that took us away from Maine. It had been past midnight, and Carly Simon had been playing on the tape player. I had been half-asleep beside her but had heard her say, "America's a good place to get lost." She had said it wistfully.

The cabby's eyes, I could see through the mirror, were a grayish blue, and his hair was silver, slicked back into a ponytail. Barry Manilow played from his radio. He watched me, and I wondered what he saw on my face. I glanced away, down at the rip in the green vinyl seat, which revealed the dirty Styrofoam stuffing beneath.

"You visiting family out here?"

"Um, yeah, family. Kind of. My dad and my sister."

He laughed. "That qualifies as family."

While he rattled on about the weather, I glimpsed my face in his rearview mirror. I looked yellow, and my eyes seemed sunken, surrounded by dark-brown circles, the color of nicotine stains. I wished I looked better. I wished Mona had been there to make me up before this visit. I wished I had taken a shower at my grandmother's, as she had offered. I looked dirty and sick.

"Are they expecting you?"

I felt my face flush. He knew, somehow, that I was lost. I looked away. "Of course, they're expecting me."

He nodded, his eyes still on me in the rearview mirror. I changed my mind and said in a small, tense voice, "No. Actually, that's not true. They aren't expecting me at all. They haven't seen me in six years. I don't even know if they'll remember me."

The driver was quiet. I suspected that he didn't care. Truth or fiction, it made no difference to him. He had just been making small talk. But it had seemed important for me to say.

He shrugged and said only, "Well, kid, I wish you luck."

The music on the radio turned to Neil Diamond. Something verging on Muzak. My palms hurt. It sounded so crazy—me coming here, unexpected. It was so clearly a bad idea. I could die here, on Western soil, so far from anyone who had ever loved me. I could become one of those girls who turns up in a Dumpster and whose identity stays a mystery for twenty years, or forever. They'd have an open file on me that some fat detective would obsess over. Staring mournfully down at my file, he'd say, "It could have been my daughter." White girl, fourteen, flat feet. In her backpack, a box containing queer useless objects—Black Power junk from the seventies, and a Star of David, the only object that seems to make any sense. That's all they'd know of me once I was gone: the lies of my body and the artifacts of my life.

I had him drop me off at the corner of the street where the address had been listed. He told me to take care of myself. I gave him a big tip, and then stood on the curb, waving foolishly at him, until the car was out of sight. I turned and made my way up Brighton Street, squinting at the numbers on the houses. I found what I was looking for about halfway down, and it was the oldest and most dilapidated apartment building on the block. Its blue paint was flaking to reveal an undercoat of pink. Objects littered the overgrown lawn—a beer can, dirty diapers, the head of a black Cabbage Patch Kid, its pugnacious face dimpled with laughter even in decapitation. The block itself was bustling with children coming home from school, screeching and tugging up kneesocks, while jiggling-armed women pulled their laundry out from the rain.

I stood surveying the house from across the street for a while, maybe fifteen minutes, looking into the faces of every man who made his way down the street, to see if he were the one.

Finally, a white Cadillac pulled up in front of the house. Because of the reflection against the windshield, I couldn't see who was inside, and I held my breath when the door opened. An obese white man stepped out, hiking up his sagging jeans, running a hand over his glistening bald head, and I laughed for a moment at my mistake. It seemed that every man who walked down the street—Asian, white, black, tall, short, thin, or obese—was some imposture of my father, some crude imitation that caused me to wonder if I really even remembered what he looked like. It seemed that now, in particular, his image had faded, dusted over, and I knew only the vital statistics, those facts so impersonal as to be written in a police report: black, six feet, thin, medium complexion.

People walking by cast curious glances at me, and I hugged the coat tighter, looking away in some absurd fear of recognition. At one point, a skinny blond woman, strung out, wearing flip flops, flew past me, looking back only to shout, "Get lost, you fucking bozo!" and I watched her as she strode down the street, laughing to herself, wondering who she was, how she had come to this.

The mist in the air remained, but the sky had brightened into a pale film, as if the sun were struggling to come out into the rain. It struck me only now that I had come this far from home. The air even smelled different. I had a twinge of excitement and fear. I wondered what had drawn my father to this particular neighborhood, the same part of the world, I recalled Ronnie telling me, where Linda had lived before she was turned in by her lover. My mother had once said that Oakland and Berkeley were haunted, always living in the shadow of some unfinished revolution. In California, she had said, even the ground moves. And indeed, as I crossed the street, looking down past the bottom of the hill to the bay, there did seem to be a sense of something lurking, not willing to die.

I knew I had to cross the street, ring the bell, sooner or later. But I wasn't ready; my entrance felt too sudden. I wished I had done something sensible like written a letter first, as Dot and my grandmother had recommended. I couldn't even be sure if Ronnie had actually seen my father, and if he had, that my father still lived in the same place two years later.

The address Ronnie had written on the napkin said apartment number one. The first floor. I stared at the nameless mailbox and buzzer for a moment before ringing. Then I waited. It seemed like forever, but when I looked at my watch it had been only two minutes. I rang again and waited a few more minutes, kicking my sneaker into the mat on the ground. There were menus hanging on the doorknob, from Chinese restaurants and pizza joints. Someone didn't care enough to throw them out. When nobody came to the door, I turned to see the street, almost empty now, the light seeming to have dimmed considerably. If he didn't live here, if he didn't exist, I would be alone for the night. I couldn't imagine going back to Boston, to my grandmother, without an answer. It would confirm everything she believed about children like me.

I tried to imagine what my mother would do in this moment, and that's when I decided to go around the back.

My shoes sank into the mud as I slithered between the fence and the side of the building, trying not to rustle the branches that hung in my path. When I finally reached the small fenced-in backyard, I stood on my tiptoes and peered into a room, which was hidden only by crooked and broken venetian blinds. It was a living room, with a television running, and a dog snoozing on the couch.

There was another window about ten feet away, and I moved slowly over to it. It was open a crack.

A shortwave radio on the windowsill marred my vision, and it crackled a BBC news brief in a female British accent. Beyond the radio, I could see that the room was someone's study. I stood to full height and took a better look. A typewriter and stacks of papers and books covered the desk at the far end. There were a few framed posters on the walls, but nothing I recognized. The one closest to me was a reprint of an Impressionist painting of women with parasols at a picnic.

Despite the chattering of the radio, nobody seemed to be at home. I had no clue whether my father lived here. It could have been anyone's house, from where I stood. I needed to get inside. I knew if I hesitated, I would never do it. So in one swift motion I pushed open the window and clambered through.

The apartment smelled of strong European cigarettes, the kind my mother's brother, Randall, used to smoke on Beacon Hill. The smell was overlaid with a kind of sweet, thick, musty odor.

On the far wall, a large bulletin board announced the words "While you were out . . ." in bubble letters across the top. Instead of messages, though, there were newspaper clippings tacked to the cork below, some yellow and dated from the mid-seventies, others more recent. They were on a wide variety of topics, from science articles debating gene-tissue research to Central American death squads to Soviet missiles. But the majority of the clippings were articles about famous black people—scholars, athletes, entertainers, scientists—with select phrases highlighted in green marker and with black lines drawn from one person to the other, creating a kind of web pattern among the clippings. There were a couple about one man in particular, a notorious black scholar whose name, Chip Dewey, was vaguely familiar. One was a rave review of his latest book on race in the popular culture. Another was an interview which included a photograph of him seated in an armchair, books and degrees surrounding him. Scribbled beneath the picture in somebody's tiny handwriting were the words "Chip the Janitor." I wasn't sure if it was my father's handwriting. It was too small to tell.

I sat down in the swivel chair at the desk. The seat was comfortably worn to the shape of someone else's behind. The typewriter on the desk was an old-fashioned Olympus with several of the keys missing. Reams of manuscript pages littered the tabletop. A mug on the desk held the cold remains of coffee. I took a sip, and it was sweet and pale—too much milk, too much sugar. A page sat in the typewriter, blank and ready. I typed in the name "Birdie" and sat staring at the word for a moment. The house was oddly barren and impersonal, despite its messiness. Yet everything seemed to point to him. I thought I even smelled him in the air. Mothers have a particular scent, but so do fathers. My father's was sharp and smoky and serious.

I heard a clicking noise and looked over. The dog from the living room stood at the door, wagging his tail, watching me with a goofy smile. It was a puppy, maybe one year old. A black-and-tan mutt with long legs and over-sized paws and ears. I put out my hand to him. He came to me, licking me as if we were old friends. "Is this where Papa lives?" I asked aloud. The dog just groaned excitedly before pattering out of the room. I stood up to follow him.

The dog led me to the bedroom. It was as bare as the study had been. There were no photographs, no sign of anyone's personal taste—just a lumpy full-sized bed with a flowery polyester comforter across it. On the night table sat a dying brown fern by the window, a half-empty glass of water, and a book about the history of Liberia. I picked up the book and turned it around in my shaking hands, flipping through it for clues. It was unmarked. I spoke softly to the dog, asking him what the book meant. He just tap-danced around me, laughing, it seemed, at my situation.

Next I headed for the bathroom. The dog was following me now, whin-ing anxiously as if he wanted to play. The bathroom was basically empty, ex-cept for a ratty white Budweiser towel and a roll of paper towels beside the toilet. At the edge of the tub sat an industrial bottle of cheap green shampoo and some soap-on-a-rope. I opened the medicine cabinet. There sat a large bottle of Pepto Bismol and an asthma inhaler, the kind both my father and I used. I took out the inhaler and turned it over in my hands, then looked at myself in the mirror as I inhaled from it, sucking in three times until my chest expanded and my head lightened and that familiar jittery excitement set in from the steroids. The mutt was looking up at me expectantly. I reached out to scratch his forehead, and said, "I think we've got our man."

The kitchen was small, with dirty curtains looking out onto the street, which had grown dark. The refrigerator held only a carton of milk and a can of dog food, but the freezer was stacked with frozen dinners. The orange light of the coffee maker was on, and a ring of scalded sludge sat at the bot-tom. I turned it off and leaned against the counter, trying to imagine my fa-ther in this house. He had never been particularly interested in the domestic world. But he had usually had a woman to clean up after him. When he was single, it was Cole and I who scrubbed his toilet. Looking around at the apartment now, I knew one thing. It was a house without a woman. Neither Carmen nor Cole would have let him live like this.

It was then that I heard the door open. The dog took off clicking down the hall, and I stood utterly still, coffee maker still in my hand. I thought briefly of running, jumping out the kitchen window. The apartment could belong to any old psychopath. The possibilities flashed through my mind from all the horror movies I'd ever seen. I listened without breathing to the sound of someone locking the door behind them, putting bags down, and then a man's voice that was too familiar to be anyone else: "Hey there, Spanky. Pissing on my floor again, you dirty mongrel?"

Then footsteps, heavy and hard-soled, coming toward me, in the kitchen, where I stood by the counter, holding the coffee maker.

He stopped at the doorway, his lips parted, and the words just escaping: "What the—?"

Then he was silent and we watched each other. There was no mistaking him. He was the same, only thinner, more bedraggled, with the salt just starting to creep up at the temples of his pepper hair. Dot was right. We did have the same eyes.

Finally I managed to say, "It's me."

His expression changed only slightly, a barely perceptible twitch at the corner of his mouth as he looked down at me with widened eyes. I touched my hair, self-conscious under his stare.

He didn't say anything for a minute. He just looked at me. When he spoke, it was quietly, almost a whisper. "I told her you'd show up sooner or later. I told her." Then, after a pause, he cracked a slight and sad smile and said without much enthusiasm, "So, welcome home."

He came to me with outstretched arms, awkward and seeming vaguely embarrassed by this moment. We hugged, the coffee maker still in my hand behind him, and I closed my eyes, stifling a sob. His body smelled like cigarettes and newspaper ink, the way it had always smelled, and yet he was a stranger to me. When we split apart I saw that he had a strained expression on his face, and he looked away rather harshly, saying in a tight voice, "Well, have a seat. You look tired."

IT SEEMED AS THOUGH he had been expecting me, that in fact we had decided on this exact date to meet up again, as he said, "I'll put on some coffee and then we can think about dinner. Hungry?"

While the frozen macaroni-and-cheese dinners thawed in the oven, he fixed us some instant coffee. He said he was out of fresh. We sat across from each other at the small table, our hands clasping our coffee mugs. The dog, Spanky, had come into the kitchen and sat with his head on my father's lap, staring up at him, forlorn.

Dot's words again: *What possible excuse?*

I wanted to ask, but there was only one question I really could give voice to at that moment.

"Where's Cole?"

"Cole. She's doing her own thing now." I thought I heard disapproval. Then he said, "She's in Berkeley. Just down the road."

Berkeley. It was so close, the next town over. We were breathing the same air. "I need to see her," I told him. "When can I see her?"

He seemed nonchalant. "Oh, anytime, I suppose."

I was sitting on my hands, rocking back and forth slightly in the chair, trying to keep myself calm. He wasn't what I had expected. He wasn't the man in Dot's picture, the happy, brown, healthy, glowing man. He wasn't the man who had escaped America, who had found freedom. His was a face that got little sunlight. He was still young—forty-three, I calculated—but he seemed older. A person who had been so distracted by thought, he had neglected his body.

I said, "How long have you been here?"

I still didn't really believe what Ronnie had told me, and waited for my father to say something that would explain his absence.

He sipped his coffee and pondered the question for a moment. "I moved into this place about three years ago. The other pad was too small. I needed my own office—"

"No," I said, cutting into his sentence. "I mean, when did you move back to America? From Brazil?"

His eyes flickered surprise. "Oh, that. Back in 'seventy-seven. Years ago."

It was late March 1982. That meant he had been back five years. Ronnie had been telling the truth.

I picked at a loose piece of linoleum. Underneath, it was grimy from the food and grease that had slipped under the crack. I finally managed to say, "What do you mean, 'years ago'? Why didn't you come get me? Why didn't we get back together? Like you promised?"

He was watching me from what seemed a wide distance, the way a scientist looks at an amoeba through a telescope. He said, "Hey, are you okay? You look like you need to lie down, maybe—"

I cut him off: "You said you'd come back to get me. You said it was just for a little while."

He sighed and pulled a handkerchief out of his back pocket. He ran it along his brow, though there didn't appear to be sweat. "Well, Birdie, it's complicated. You know, your mother was underground, really hard to trace. I thought by the time I got back, your mother would have come up. But word on the street was that she had stayed down. I'm sure that the danger she was in had long passed, but I guess she liked it better down there. Sandy was always such a nut. Anyway"—he glanced up at me, then away toward the window—"I asked around, even tried calling some friends from Boston. But it was going to be difficult—a real project."

So, according to him, my mother was out of danger, running from only her own demons. Ronnie said she was in definite danger. Dot said she never had been. My father said she might once have been, but no longer was. I added his to the different versions of her. She was at once a hero, a madwoman, and a fool. It was too confusing. I wasn't sure it mattered. The fact was clear: He hadn't tried to find me.

I just stared at him. "What do you mean, 'a real project'?"

He stood up with a screech of his chair and went to the window. It was dark beyond the pane, and I could see cars streak by on the street. He spoke with his back to me. "I mean, a big time commitment. True, I had some leads your mom left me with, but really now. I figured if she wanted to find me, she could." He turned around. "Your mother wanted to disappear, Birdie. That's not to say she wasn't doing some shady shit in the basement, but she needed to believe something was after her. Because there was nothing for her to come back to. She started to fall apart after we split up. You must know that. She just couldn't handle the fact that things had changed. She wanted them to stay the way they had always been. And when they didn't, she broke."

He went on, oblivious to the expression on my face: "Anyway, it wasn't like I had a lot of time on my hands to go searching for someone who didn't want to be found. I've been working on this book. The book is all I've been able to do for the past few years. And I had all this information I'd gotten in Brazil, data I needed to put into writing. The book just devoured me. Ate me alive." He paused, laughed shortly. "Seven hundred pages, baby. It's done.

Pretty much, that is. Except for the footnotes on the last chapter. I think it's ready." He smiled at me. "You can see it if you want."

He was speaking, but somehow I wasn't registering his words. "See what?"

"See the book, baby. Don't you want to know what I've been doing all this time?"

He reached into his back pocket and pulled out a crumpled pack of foreign brown cigarettes. "I don't show it to too many people anymore. I mean, not after that derivative son-of-a-bitch, Chip Dewey, tried to tout my ideas as his own. I try to keep it pretty quiet. You learn your lessons the hard way. But I'd like for you to see it." He lit up his cigarette, squinting into the haze. "Come on."

Then he was striding toward the study, Spanky and me at his heels.

The study was dark now, with only a bar of light from the street making the silhouettes of objects visible. The window where I had climbed in was still open, and from the shortwave radio came the voice of a British reporter—a man, this time—talking in quick excited tones about the massacres in Central America. My father turned on a lamp in the corner and went to a battered black file cabinet, which he unlocked and began to rifle through.

He finally pulled out his manuscript—the whole thing. He handed all seven hundred pages to me, smiling, as if it were a gift, as if I would be ecstatic to receive it. I took it with both hands and looked down at the cover page.

The Petrified Monkey:
Race, Blood, and the Origins of Hypocrisy
by Deck Lee

And beneath all of that a big copyright sign beside the year 1982.

He said, "There's been some interest, but people are scared of this book. They know I'm on to something. All those Negroes in the academy publish the same old drivel every year, talking the same tired talk year after year, and nobody wants to hear something new. Man, those fools are a broken record, singin' the same old song, dancin' the same old dance we've been doing since 1863."

He seemed to remember I was there and said, "Anyway, this is what I've been doing all this time. It really did take over everything. Ask Cole. She'll tell you."

I looked at him. He was smiling rather sweetly, as if he truly believed that this had made up for his absence.

I cleared my throat, just now finding my tongue.

"Papa, do you even know where I've been? Do you even care? I've been living as a white girl, a Jewish girl. I've waited and waited, and I kept the box of crap you gave me. But you never came." I paused. I was hugging myself, my fingernails digging into the thickness of the coat, but still I wasn't crying. "I passed as white, Papa."

He was frowning at me, and I thought he was going to go into a tirade about the evils of passing. But he only shrugged and said, "Of course I care where you've been, Birdie. I want to hear all about it. I love you. Of course. But baby, there's no such thing as passing. We're all just pretending. Race is a complete illusion, make-believe. It's a costume. We all wear one. You just switched yours at some point. That's just the absurdity of the whole race game." He was turning professorial on me again.

He began to talk about the fact that race was not only a construct but a scientific error along the magnitude of the error that the world was flat. "That's how big a fucking blunder they've made, baby," he said. "And when they discover their mistake, I mean, truly discover it, it'll be as big as when they learned the world was, in fact, round. It'll open up a whole new world. And nothing will ever be the same again."

Listening to him talk, it struck me that the most terrifying thing about my father was not that he was wrong, but that he was right, no matter how rarely he actually looked me in the eye.

Now he looked me in the eye, disarmingly. I was taken aback. He said, "And the worst thing is when you realize your whole life's work is going to have to be about correcting somebody else's four-hundred-year-old mistake. Now if that don't cause some existential angst, I don't know what will." His voice sounded thick and weary as he added, "I'm telling you, it's the myth of fucking Sysiphus."

He looked old to me, older than his years, and I had a brief pang of worry that he was sick. His skin didn't look as brown as it once had. More gray. And his eyes had a yellowish cast to them. While he once had seemed tall to me, he now looked stooped and slight.

He smiled a little and said, "Let me show you something."

He took my arm and led me toward the living room, the one room I hadn't had a chance to investigate. It was shabby, but neat, with a plaid sofa and a small fake-wood coffee table. There was tinfoil on the television antenna, and the news was playing with the sound turned off. On the wall near the bookshelf hung an elaborate chart my father had made, a chart with the words "Canaries in the Coal Mine" written in black magic marker at the top. It depicted a row of pictures of mulattos throughout history—some of whom I remembered from the walls of the Nkrumah School, others from my father's old study at Boston University. I recognized Alexander Pushkin, Phillipa Schuyler, Nella Larsen, Jean Toomer—Xeroxed photographs of their sallow faces above the dates of their lives, and beneath that their "fates," brief descriptions of their desolate or violent deaths: Pushkin, shot in a duel; Nella Larsen, obscure and poverty stricken, with no records of her birth and no obituary to mark her death; Phillipa Schuyler, the child genius of the Harlem Renaissance, passing as white, in a firefight in Vietnam. The last column of the chart was a snapshot of Cole and me when we were eight and eleven, holding hands and grinning in front of my father's house in Roxbury, a grainy and slightly blurred photograph revealing the street around us as dilapidated and urban. On the chart, my father had handwritten our names, Birdie and Cole Lee, beside our birth dates. For Cole, 1964; for me, 1967. Under the last column, where the others had their fates written, there was a blank space.

He explained to me his theory—that the mulatto in America functions as a canary in the coal mine. The canaries, he said, were used by coal miners to gauge how poisonous the air underground was. They would bring a canary in with them, and if it grew sick and died, they knew the air was bad and that eventually everyone else would be poisoned by the fumes. My father said that likewise, mulattos had historically been the gauge of how poisonous American race relations were. The fate of the mulatto in history and in literature, he said, will manifest the symptoms that will eventually infect the rest of the nation.

He pointed to the chart. "See, my guess is that you're the first generation of canaries to survive, a little injured, perhaps, but alive. And," he said, smiling, "it's a good thing you showed up—"

Something in my face made him stop.

"What is it?" he said, reaching out to touch my hair.

He was as mad and brilliant as Ronnie had described. He was the same father who had started me, who had begun but had never finished me. The same father who cared more for books and theories than he did for flesh and blood. There was a smell of burning in the air, burning Stouffer's macaroni and cheese, but neither of us moved to get it.

I heard myself say, "Fuck the canaries in the fucking coal mines. You left me. You left me with Mum, knowing she was going to disappear. Why did you only take Cole? Why didn't you take me? If race is so make-believe, why did I go with Mum? You gave me to Mum 'cause I looked white. You don't think that's real? Those are the facts."

I knew I sounded out of control, but I couldn't stop myself. I scoffed, looking at the chart, my face and Cole's face on the bottom of this row of history's victims. Something that had been pushing from the inside cut through just then. The words came out of my mouth, fast and harsh, like my mother's. "You think this makes up for anything? This silly chart? Your big book of numbers? I waited for you all this time. I believed you were coming back. But you never even planned to. You knew it was for good, but you didn't care. Mum's right. You are an overintellectualized creep."

He frowned at me for a moment. Then he glanced at the chart beside himself as if to find answers in the faces of those ragged specimens. Not finding them, he said, "The food's burning," and turned to go to the kitchen.

I followed him and stood against the doorjamb, staring at a spot on the linoleum, while he tried to resuscitate dinner.

He pulled the macaroni out of the oven and began to scrape the burned edges off as he spoke, haltingly, his face turned down.

"It wasn't just me. You're mother was in on it, too. It was a decision we made the week before we split. You'd go with her, I'd take Cole. We didn't know whether we'd be able to meet up again. Things were dangerous then, bad as they'd ever been in Boston. Worse than it was after the Civil War. It was the only way. Cole couldn't have gone with your mother. Not just for safety issues, imagining there were any. But also because it just wasn't working out. Cole needed a black mother. It was important to her."

He turned to me, his hand in a flowered cooking mitt, the now-mangled TV dinner thrust toward me like some strange peace offering. He looked me in the eye, and I thought I sensed some sadness as he said, "Man, in America, that's the kind of decision you gotta make."

He let out a sound that wasn't quite a laugh, then said to himself, "And wouldn't you know it? Cole turned out to be as different from me as any child could be."

We just watched each other silently, and I saw that the food in his hand had begun to tremble. His face was a browner, older version of my own.

He put the food on the counter, seeming exhausted. "So, you want to see Cole."

I nodded. "Yeah. I want to see her."

"Well, let's eat first."

He fixed me a plate and poured me a glass of Coke. We sat at the small table under the bright glare of the kitchen light, eating our macaroni and cheese in a polite, strained silence. The Coke was flat, but the food was good in an artificial kind of way. I was hungry, but there was a lump in my throat that made it hard to swallow. He ate the way he always had, with one eyebrow raised and his head cocked to one side, as if weighed down with thoughts. He glanced at me from time to time, scanning my face, then looked back at his food. When we were finished he said, "You know, you look a little like my mother. I never noticed that before. Same skinny body, broad shoulders. Same eyes."

HE INSISTED THAT he drive me there. He said he wouldn't want me out on the Oakland streets alone, and besides, I was sick. Even he could see that. It was raining softly now, a pattering of moisture on concrete. He put on a gray Members Only jacket, a fashion that had gone out of style many years before. I noticed that all of his clothes were like this—an assortment of styles that were three years too late, and that fact somehow touched me, warmed me to him, against my will.

He brought out an old-fashioned big black umbrella, and the two of us huddled together under it as we made our way to his brown Chevy Citation. Inside, it smelled like cigarettes and stale air freshener. I wondered what had happened to the orange Volvo after he had left for Brazil. This car was so different, so American, like something Jim would drive.

I rested my head on the glass of the window as he started up the engine.

I asked him, "So, what happened to Carmen?"

He snorted through his nose as he pulled away from the curb. "Carmen. She's long gone. After we got back from Brazil, we had had just about enough of each other. We didn't have much in common, you know. She didn't care about ideas. She just wanted the comforts of life. I guess she's still living in Atlanta, down near her folks. Last I heard she got married to some clown, a radio celebrity."

The thought of her—the way she had made me want to disappear—still angered me. I wondered if my father knew. Someday I'd tell him.

He drove me around for the next forty-five minutes, weaving through the streets of Oakland at a snail's pace. I fidgeted beside him, afraid I'd miss Cole if we didn't get there soon. Afraid she'd disappear into thin air. He said he was taking me on the long route so I could get a chance to know the neighborhood, but really he didn't seem to notice the neighborhood. He was too busy talking, lecturing to me about the world, politics, race. The same thing he had always done. This time, though, it seemed he was actually speaking to me, rather than to the air or to my sister or to Carmen.

He talked in circles, pointing at people on the streets as if they proved his theories right—women dragging their children roughly behind them, men lined up around a block for a soup kitchen, beggars pushing grocery carts full of junk. He told me that the only ones who had benefited from the civil rights movement were the black middle class and white women. He said that the movement had failed the poor. He said racism mattered, but that it was being exploited by the elite. "Birdie, do you understand what I'm telling you? These overeducated pompous Negro fools in the academy have everything, and still want to feel like victims. They're addicted to racism, because once you got money and the approval of the white academy, you *need* something to remind you that you're not a total sellout." He said it was the same with rich white women who had black maids at home, caring for their children. "They need to talk about sexism because without it they'd have to admit what side they're really on. You get what I'm saying?"

I got what he was saying, but I also knew what I had seen and heard in New Hampshire. Who I had become. That was as real as anything else. I looked at the projects we now passed. Mothers with baby carriages and grocery bags tried to get in from the rain. Looking at them, I remembered how when I was little, I used to think that socialism meant that everyone got free umbrellas when it was raining outside. I thought that in a socialist country, whenever it rained, a big truck would drive through the center of town throwing black umbrellas and yellow raincoats to the people in the streets. I don't know where I'd gotten that picture. I don't know why I'd fixated on umbrellas.

"Have you ever read Fanon?" my father was saying. I nodded. My mother had drummed Fanon's teachings into me when we were on the road. I opened my mouth, about to quote *Black Skin, White Masks*—to show off just how well I knew Fanon—but my father cut me off. He said that Fanon hated black women and only wanted power over them. He said that Fanon was proof of what Simone Weil wrote: When the weak get together, they mimic the actions of the formerly powerful. "Now Simone Weil," my father said, "she was a real radical. You should read her if you want to hear what a truly great mind has to say."

I smiled slightly to myself, thinking how alike my parents still were. My mother had read aloud to me from Simone Weil one night in the parking lot of a Ground Round. I had been too tired to listen, but remembered her name just the same. We had been planning on sleeping in the van that night, behind the Ground Round, but sometime past midnight we were awakened by a security guard banging on our window. He told us he was going to call the cops if we didn't move. My mother had sped away, shouting curses and waving her middle finger at him.

My father went on, making me a little dizzy as he discredited one revolutionary after another. After a while I didn't really register what he was saying, just the sound of his voice bouncing off the glass, and the rhythmic squeal of the windshield wipers. Eventually he seemed to tire of talking, seemed to be broken by the weight of his own thoughts. He grew quiet, pensive. He drove like an old man, signaling long before the lights.

I stared out the window at the crooked streets and miserable pedestrians who huddled under bus stop awnings. The lights and colors seemed somehow seedy and beautiful in this black night. My father turned on the radio to a news station and listened to the woman speak about Reagan's latest welfare cuts, with his head tilted to the side, his brow furrowed in grim concentration.

He broke the silence for only one brief moment, when we sat at a stop-light on University Avenue. "Your mother. How is Sandy these days?"

I had seen her face just the day before, but it seemed long ago, some other girl's life story. I had glimpsed her face behind the car glass, moving away in Jim's Buick, and she hadn't seemed well at all. But I said to my father, "She's okay. She's got a new man. She's doing just fine."

"Where is she? Did she settle down somewhere?"

I looked out the window at a bag man on the sidewalk. He stood like a sculpture, hair matted into dripping dreadlocks, feet great stumps of brown cloth, a trash bag wrapped tightly around him. I wondered where his mother was. Who had let him come to this. I knew where my mother was, but wasn't allowed say. I didn't trust my own father with that information. So I said, "I don't know."

He was quiet, tapping his fingers to some beat against the steering wheel. We started to move at the green light, and he said, "I miss her."

COLE LIVED IN A wood house that was set back from the narrow ram-shackle street. As my father pulled in front of Cole's house, I tried to imag-ine this sister I would meet. No image came to mind. It was as if all those fantasies that had kept me moving had dissolved upon seeing this flesh father, this crumpled cerebral outcast.

I turned to him. The motor was still running.

"Are you coming inside?"

Even as I said it, I hoped he wouldn't. I still remembered that whenever they came together, I disappeared.

He looked at me across the darkness of the car. "No, Birdie. You go alone. She'll want to see you alone."

"Okay, then."

He paused. "You can always come back to my place tonight, if you need to. If you don't want to stay here. You got enough money for a cab?"

I nodded.

I couldn't make out his expression, but his voice cracked slightly as he asked, "Will I see you again?"

Something told me to say no, to tell him I didn't want to see him ever again, that he had been a bad, neglectful man, that he had let me go once and hadn't earned the right to see me again.

But then my mouth said the words that seemed far more true: "Yes, Papa."

We didn't hug good-bye, just looked at each other as if agreeing on some unspoken rule, before I stepped out of the car.

And then he was gone, down the street at his old-man's pace, cautious now as he had ever been.

I stood in front of the big house, looking up at the darkened windows, then went up the stairs. I hadn't really slept in days and was moving on automatic. I felt a little lightheaded as I knocked on the door.

A woman who was not my sister answered. She was chubby and dark, with a big-toothed smile. She wore a long braid down her back and a man's oxford shirt over jeans.

She waited for me to speak, and when I didn't, she said, "Can I help you with something?"

"I'm looking for Cole Lee. Does she live here?"

The woman looked me up and down now, curious. "Sure does. But she's not here right now."

I choked the words "Please, I need to see her. It's important. Where is she?"

I had expected somehow that the woman wouldn't trust me, but she just smiled warmly. "Oh, not far. She's studying for tests tomorrow. She's at that café up on Shattuck. The one next to the bank." She gave me directions. I could hear now that she had a slight Spanish accent. Then, perhaps realizing after the fact that she should have asked who I was, she said, "You a friend from school?"

I shrugged and looked out onto the street, where the parked cars sat wet and gleaming under the streetlights. "Yeah. We used to go to school together a long time ago."

She looked ready to ask something when I abruptly thanked her and turned, stamping down the steps and into the rain.

I walked briskly in the direction she had pointed, over the shimmering asphalt, my hands shoved deep in my pockets. When I glanced down, I saw that worms carpeted the sidewalk, small lumps of unformed life waiting to be crushed. The sight of them, helpless, soft, identical, revolted me, and so I walked down the middle of the street to avoid killing them. I walked in long strides, nearly running, and at one point a car came around a corner and toward me, its lights on bright, blinding me for a moment. I stopped to let it pass, leaning against a parked car, but it splashed me just the same. The driver honked as it drove by, and I looked after it, the red taillights fading into the distance.

The rain against my face felt warm and dirty. It had soaked through the cashmere, so that my grandfather's coat had grown heavier and cumbersome to walk in. This wasn't how I had wanted her to see me. I looked at my reflection in a nearby car window. My hair had come out of its loose ponytail and hung in wet clumps around my face. I didn't think she'd recognize me. The last time she'd seen me, I'd been neat and pressed, my hair in a tight braid, gold hoops in my ears. Now I looked a tattered wreck, gaunt and perilous and lost.

But I was there already, at the corner of Shattuck, and I saw the soft light of the café that the woman had described, saw that it was filled with people seeking shelter from the rain.

I hesitated, not sure whether to go inside. I considered just waiting outside, catching her on her way out. Just then, I wasn't sure I wanted to find what I was looking for. But the cold was creeping in under the cashmere to my skin, and I had a pounding headache, like great waves crashing in my skull. So I walked into the café, letting the warm, rich smell of coffee surround me.

The door swung closed behind me, jingling a string of bells, and a few strangers looked up. They didn't seem to see anything remarkable or horrifying in my face, and went back to their conversations without much pause. I stood there, stock still at the door, and scanned the room of hunched figures curved over newspapers and books and one another, steam rising up from their mugs, smoke from the cigarettes perched between their fingers.

She sat toward the back of the café, in a connected area with a glass roof, like a greenhouse. I recognized her immediately. She had my mother's high forehead, my grandmother's deep-set eyes—only on a light-brown girl with a tumble of thick black curls to her shoulders. She was sitting at the table with another girl, and she was laughing, a quiet laugh, at something the other girl, whose face I couldn't see, had just said. She was sitting curled in on herself and holding a coffee mug between two hands like a prayer. She was the same at eighteen as she had been at twelve—the same anxious serious eyes, the same face that knew it was being watched—only her body, I could see even from that distance, was softer, a fuller and more womanly body than my own.

I remained at the door, blocking the entrance, my hands still in my pockets, just watching her across the steamy clutter of bodies. And I felt oddly content, as if I could stand there all night just watching, never being seen.

But she looked up then, abruptly, searching into the faces of the strangers who surrounded her, as if she had heard someone call her name. And as her eyes moved over my face, I felt a slight heat, like a match held close to the flesh, but not touching. Her eyes kept moving, past my face, not recognizing me, turning back to her friend with a lonely smile. She had seen me and not known me from the foreign bodies that surrounded her. And I thought I would leave then, just turn and walk into the unknown city, disappear like my mother. Perhaps it was enough to know where she was, to know she was safe, to know she was laughing with a friend. But then she glanced up from her table again, almost shyly. She glanced toward the girl at the door, the thin pale girl in the big man's coat, at me, where I stood shaking and dripping and holding my breath. Her smile faded and she watched me, squinting, her eyes scrutinizing my features, searching them for something. Then seeing it, and lips parting and something breaking, a hand moving to touch the girl beside her, the girl whose face I couldn't see, as if to warn the girl of some great danger. And we just watched each other then, watched for that minute when the whole restaurant seemed to grow quiet, grow still, the bodies around us melting into one another, into a blanket that surrounded us, and then I began to float toward the back of the café, like an apparition, a memory of myself, toward my sister, who rose to meet me.

WE PRESSED OUR bodies together for a long while, not talking or crying or trying to make sense out of anything. I could smell the oil from her hair, could feel the shine and crunch of her curls tickling my cheek. I saw nothing then but those yellow spots against the darkness of my eyelids, but I heard everything around me with a crystal clarity, the public noises that were somehow reassuring—spoons lightly clinking the sides of cups, an old man coughing up phlegm, the tinny rock music from the radio behind the counter. Those ordinary sounds solidified my sister in my arms.

When we parted, her face was wet and she looked crushed. She held me away from her and stared at my features hard, then at my hands, examined my long ones with her own delicate and trembling ones. Today she wore a bulky Irish sweater, and her eyes had turned a similar gray, with flecks of green still showing through. We hadn't spoken yet, and it didn't seem necessary. She held my hands (hers were warm, mine cold and stiff) and turned me toward the girl at the table, whom I hadn't seen yet. The girl was the color of well-steeped tea and wore thick horn-rimmed glasses and her hair short like a boy's. She smiled at me as if we too had known each other once before, and said to Cole, "She's the one in the photograph, isn't she?"

And Cole nodded, still clutching my hand, shadowing her eyes with her hand now, as if blocking out a bright light. "This is her," she said in a quiet, throaty voice. "I'm going home with her now. We've got some catching up to do."

The girl laughed, and squeezed my sister's hand. "Of course you do." She looked at me. "Cole's been waiting for you. For a long time now."

COLE DROVE A BUTTER-YELLOW Karmann Ghia with a punched-in nose and jungle-print seat covers. As she unlocked my door, she glanced at me, shy suddenly, and said, "You're really big. I somehow thought you'd still be a kid." Inside, the car smelled of dust and must, along with a slight lingering of something pungent and chemical, like development fluid in a darkroom. The rain made a hollow tin pattering on the roof.

As we sat waiting for it to warm up, I explained, "Papa brought me to your house. Your roommate told me you were here."

She nodded. "He always said you'd come back, looking for us. But I didn't believe him. I thought we should have been looking harder, you know. Not just waiting." She looked at me. "I'm sorry, Bird. I didn't know how. They made it so hard."

I looked out at the café, at the bodies inside, sheltered, happy under that bright light, then repeated her words: "They made it so hard."

We drove the short distance to her house without any more words, and she kept looking over at me, away from the road, as if afraid I would evaporate.

She was renting a room in the house on Grant Street, and inside it was comfortable, shabby, politicized. Two women—one black, one the heavy-set Latin-American woman who had answered the door—sat around the kitchen table, smoking and talking when we came in, a half-finished bottle of Chianti on the table beside a plate of chips and salsa. The older black woman had a toddler on her lap, a little boy with a wild dusty afro. His face was puffy with sleep.

Cole stood with me at the door, her arm around my shoulder. They looked at us and said expectant hellos, and the little boy screamed, perking up, "Cole! I'm Superman!" I thought of Taj in her Wonder Woman costume, and I missed her. I could see her and Dot here with me. I remembered I had promised to call them when I got here. Right now, though, I could talk only to Cole. I would call them tomorrow, to tell them I was safe. I knew I would have to contact my grandmother as well, but was dreading it. I would have to face up to my lie.

The woman who had answered the door earlier said to me, "Oh, good, you tracked Cole down."

I nodded. Cole held me by her side as she said, beaming, "Alma, Simone, Jay, this is my sister. Birdie."

They all paused, wide-eyed, and I could see they had heard of me. Cole had been able to talk about me to strangers. She hadn't had to erase me completely. The women seemed excited to see me in the flesh, and gushed about how they had been hearing about me for so long. They offered me a cup of tea and some dinner, but I didn't think I'd be able to hold anything down. I was still sick. I needed sleep. Cole took my hand and said to them, "We're going upstairs now. Birdie's tired. And we need to catch up."

Her bedroom was at the top of the stairs. It was different from the rest of the house—austere, bare, and colorless, with a pale-blue duvet on the bed like the ones in my grandmother's house. On her dresser were two photographs framed in silver. One of an older, thin, and ravaged man whom I now recognized as my father. Another of us at ages five and eight, in Halloween costumes. She's Bugs Bunny, I'm Daffy Duck. My mother is crouched behind us with a tall, pointed witch hat on her head and a silly grin on her face. She had dressed up as one of the Salem witches that year.

I picked up the picture of my mother, Cole, and me, and looked at it, feeling a twinge of resentment that Cole had been able to keep everything exposed. It seemed strange to see us all together, out there in the open. My mother looked happy in the photograph, happy and fat and married to a man she loved, with two children she loved. I wondered what she was doing now. If she had come back to fetch me from Dot, or if she had been scared away by the run-in with the cops.

When I turned around, Cole was sitting cross-legged on the bed. She smiled softly. "There's so much to say, huh?"

I nodded. "I know. I don't know where to start."

I went to her. We lay on the bed, facing each other. She began to speak to me then in broken Elemeno. At first I didn't understand it, but then it began to come back to me.

simapho. nooli stadi. beltin caruse mestiz jambal. kez wannaba. fello maotao burundi. simapho. ki wo fela.

We talked about where each of us had been. I kept my story short. There was too much to say, so I settled for not saying much. There would be time for details later. I told her that my mother and I had traveled for years without going anywhere far, and that I had passed as white, if such a thing were possible.

She told me some of her story—how she, my father, and Carmen had gone to Brazil with such high expectations. But over those first few months in Rio, it had slowly dawned on them that the poor people living in the favellas resembled Africans, the rich people in power resembled Europeans, and everyone in the middle was obsessed with where they and their children would fall on the spectrum of color. Our father's disappointment over this realization had tainted everything; he was no longer able to see what was beautiful about Brazil. And over time, Carmen had grown bored with his obsessions; she spent her days complaining about stomach pains, the lack of plumbing, and the flying cockroaches. Cole had been forced to spend most of her time alone, yearning for America, for Black America, whose pathology she at least could call her own. When they did finally return, Carmen had taken off to be with her family in the South. Cole had come to Oakland with our father, and had been living in the Bay Area ever since—just an ordinary American girl.

"But why didn't you come to get me?" My throat went dry as I asked the question.

She had a lot of reasons, and she rattled them off while I listened, not convinced that any one of them was good enough. For a time, she believed our mother had killed herself when they left. Then she believed our mother was alive, but wouldn't want her anymore. After all, why would she have let her go in the first place? And then there was always our father's reasoning, which she had accepted as her own: It would put us in jeopardy if they searched for us.

I didn't say anything. It wasn't that I didn't believe Cole. I did. I understood that it was a mixture of fear and lethargy that had kept her away. But the bottom line was that she hadn't tried to find me. She had gone on with her life. I hadn't been able to.

I had believed all along that Cole was all I needed to feel complete. Now I wondered if completion wasn't overrated.

Cole looked at me. "Mum is okay, isn't she?"

I nodded. "Yeah, Cole. She's okay."

She hugged a throw pillow to her chest. "I hated Mum for a long time. For leaving me. For letting me go. Then I hated myself. I blamed myself because I was so stupid and teenage and so mean to her. I picked Carmen—this woman I didn't even know—over Mum 'cause she could do my hair and she looked like a woman who could be my mother, and she wore lipstick and didn't make scenes in public."

As she spoke, I studied her face. She had something of me in her, though it wasn't as visible as a bend in the nose, a curve of a lip, a slant of the eyes. It was something hidden, untouchable—an expression of someone who will always be waiting.

She said, looking away now, biting an already gnawed fingernail, "Did Mum want to find me?"

"Of course. She was never the same after you left," I told her. "She did mantras every morning. She always believed you'd be back. But she was too scared to go looking."

Cole stared up at the ceiling and sighed heavily. "There are others like her. Ones who did get caught. The sacrificial lambs of the movement. They're the ones who made everything else possible. And the FBI is ruthless. They haven't given up. They'll let you die in there if you're not careful. It happened to Timothy Dove, it happened to Maria Cabrera. I believe Mum. I do." Cole wiped a tear away. "But mantras, Birdie? That wasn't enough. She should have done more to find me. To contact me." She was crying freely now, her face in her hands, as she said, "They should have stuck together. They should have tried harder."

I felt for her. I, too, hoped our mother had been for real. I wanted her to be one of the radicals whose names she had toyed with using that morning in the Maine diner: Grushenka, Tanya, Angela, Sojo. Instead she had become Sheila Goldman. And while her friends, at least some of them, had paid for living out their beliefs, my mother had gotten away with it. All I'd been left with was the charade itself; she'd been that good at it. It was strange, but her conviction could be her only vindication—the only way Cole and I would ever know for sure what her role in history had been. But at the same time, if she was for real, neither Cole nor I would ever want to see her caught.

I could see the night outside Cole's window. It was thicker now, a more solid starless black. It had stopped raining. There were sycamore trees outside her window, and they brushed against it, the branches making tapping noises like fingers against glass.

I said, "I know they should have. And you know something? Now Papa says I'm not black or white anymore. He's changed his tune completely. He's stuck on this canary thing. It's too much to keep up with."

She laughed through the crying. "I know. Canaries in the coal mine. Choking on all the fumes."

I giggled, thinking of the picture of Cole and me at the bottom of his chart. "He says there's no such thing as race."

She shrugged. "He's right, you know. About it all being constructed. But"—she turned to me, looking at me intently—"that doesn't mean it doesn't exist."

"I know it does," I said, nodding. Something seemed to clarify as I looked into her face. I thought of Samantha, in that thick forest, with her cheap white shoes and blue eye shadow. I thought of Stuart at the party, laughing along to all those jokes spoken to him in fake slang. That was how they had learned to survive it. Everybody had their own way of surviving. My mother had her way, my father had his, Cole had hers. And then I thought of me, the silent me that was Jesse Goldman, the one who hadn't uttered a word, the one who had removed even her Star of David. It had come so easily to me. I had become somebody I didn't like. Somebody who had no voice or color or conviction. I wasn't sure that was survival at all. I spoke my thoughts aloud. "They say you don't have to choose. But the thing is, you do. Because there are consequences if you don't."

Cole shrugged. "Yeah, and there are consequences if you do."

We were silent on her bed for some time. I could hear her housemates laughing downstairs, the little boy squealing madly in a hyperactive burst, and bass-heavy music. It sounded like a party, and I turned to ask Cole about her roommates, but she was somewhere else, twisting a curl and staring out into the night.

Finally she said, staring down at her fingers, which fiddled with a loose thread on her sweater, "Where is she?"

I thought of my mother's words: *Nobody can know where I am. Nobody.*

And I smiled, thinking that this was the one exception in the world to that rule. The one exception she hadn't needed to tell me, because we both had known it all along. So I said, "She's in New Hampshire. Hiding out still. You should call her. I have her number."

Cole didn't think it was safe to call from her house, so we went for a walk into town. As she put on a flaking leather jacket and a bright turquoise scarf, she explained, "Mum wasn't fooling around, you know. The FBI—the government, whatever—wanted her bad, wanted to set an example. I mean, I'm sure she did something really wicked. I'm certain of it. Who knows if they're still after her, but you can never be too careful."

I nodded, but really I was thinking that Cole couldn't begin to know what it was to be too careful. She hadn't lived the way I had lived all these years. She hadn't known what it was like waking up at three in the morning in order to flee, learning to see danger in the face of every stranger, cultivating paranoia. She hadn't known what it was to live as a fugitive, all the while looking longingly for the person I missed every day—her.

Of course, I couldn't ever really know what she had been through either in Brazil or in Oakland, living all these years as my father's daughter. We were sisters, but we were as separate in our experiences as two sisters could be. I had to face this, if I could. I didn't know if I could.

"No, you can never be too careful. You're right about that," I said to her. "About anyone or anything."

I pulled on my musty and leaden coat, explaining to her as we went out that it was our grandfather's. I giggled and told her what I had done at our grandmother's, but she seemed distracted, tense, her mind already on the phone call. I was still sick with the flu. My head felt hot, and yet I shivered. My mother, if she were here, would make me drink ginger tea and eat graham crackers. She would put a wet washcloth on my forehead and hand me a book to read. My mother believed books were as good a medicine as any.

We found a pay phone at the North Berkeley BART, and Cole seemed hesitant, unsure, as we approached it. She bit her lip and turned to me. "Is she still fat?"

I shook my head. "No, she lost all that weight after you and Papa left. It was like she didn't care enough to eat anymore. The running wore her down."

She nodded and looked away, up toward the sky. "I dreamt about her a lot. That she was thin and that she was different. She lived in this little white house in a nice suburban neighborhood, and when I came to her door, she didn't recognize me. She thought I was a Jehovah's Witness trying to convert her, and wouldn't let me in. I had to explain to her who I was."

She put out her hand, which was trembling, and I wrote the number on the back of it with the pen we had brought. She looked at me then, and I knew she wanted to do it alone. So I said, "I'll be waiting at the corner."

I watched from a distance as she dialed. Occasional cars swished by, but the night was otherwise empty, a blank slate waiting to be written upon. She stood hunched over, still twirling her hair, her eyes hidden. She was calling collect, and I heard her say, "Cole," loudly.

After few moments, I heard her say, "Mum? It's me." And then her crying softly, muffled words that I couldn't understand.

I saw my mother seated on the couch, reading glasses on, opera playing faintly from the television. The phone rings twice, and she is nervous, doesn't like phone calls this late into the night. She picks up on the third ring and says, "Hello?" Operator says, "Hello. Collect call from Cole." And for a moment she wonders if it's me playing tricks, and she says, "I accept." And then a voice that is not mine comes through, crackling, a street noise behind it. A voice that is her firstborn. A voice that is her. And she feels something long buried come rising up to meet that voice, she feels someone waking deep inside her. And she is holding the phone so tight that later her hands will ache, when she is beside Jim in that wide country bed, staring into the silent night. Then she will close her eyes and see the New Hampshire license plate with the words "Live Free or Die" imprinted across the bottom, and will know it was never as simple as that. But she will know that her daughters are safe, sleeping together under one roof, and that will allow her to rest tonight.

MY MOTHER AND COLE agreed that the three of us would meet in the summer, after classes ended. Cole and I would meet her in New York, at Penn Station, where we wouldn't stand out.

Cole held my arm as we walked to her house, and seemed lighter. Some of the sadness had disappeared, at least for the time being. She told me she wanted to go to Guatemala after we met our mother; she was part of a group of women that planned to bring food and supplies to friends working there. Hearing this, I panicked, reminded of the last time people I loved had left the country. I told her I wanted to go too. She said she'd think about it. She worried it would be dangerous.

She asked me questions about where I'd been, and when I told her about our time at Aurora, she shrieked a laugh and said, "Papa would keel over! He's pretty uptight about anything outside of race."

As we walked arm in arm back to her house, Cole asked me to stay with her, to live with her. I said yes and tried to picture myself living in this house, with Cole and these strangers, my father skulking around the edges with a notebook in hand and a hypothesis on his tongue. It was still hard to imagine myself settling down anywhere.

She told me, "You should to go to Berkeley High. That's where I went." She chuckled and said, "If you ever thought you were the only one, get ready. We're a dime a dozen out here."

I saw myself as a teenager in a high school with a medley of mulatto children, canaries who had in fact survived the coal mine, singed and asthmatic, but still alive. Then I thought of Samantha and felt a wave of sadness. I wondered what would happen to her.

When we got back to the house, the woman named Alma was up watching television, with the little boy asleep on her lap. The others appeared to have gone out. There was a big half-finished banner on the kitchen table that said, "No Nukes." Cole pointed to it. "There's some rally tomorrow. I'm supposed to go."

I remembered that Jim had been hysterical about nuclear bombs and like to fantasize over dinner about what he'd do in the event of one. He had always struck me as the type who would build a hole in the ground and hide there with cans of soup, just to save himself. But it had been the one issue he seemed really to care about, the one subject I could bear to hear him go on about.

I took a long-awaited shower while Cole got ready for bed. I scrubbed myself hard, washing away the grit and grime of my travels, before slipping into the plaid flannel shirt that Cole had given me to wear as a nightgown. When I went upstairs, Cole was lying in bed, flipping through some textbook. She wore reading glasses that made her look older. She glanced up at me over the tops of them and said, "I keep expecting you to vanish."

I WOKE CONFUSED. There were green glow-in-the-dark stars on the ceiling, and for a moment I thought I was back in New Hampshire, on Nicholas's bed. It was only when I turned and looked beside me that I realized where I really was.

Cole had stolen all the covers and had spread her limbs out across the bed the way she had always done. I shivered at the edge of the mattress, on the verge of falling off. My stomach was cramped with hunger. The morning light was just beginning to seep through her lace curtains. I slipped out of bed quietly, without waking Cole. My clothes were musty, so I put on some of hers—a pair of jeans, which were too baggy, and her Irish sweater from the night before, which still smelled of her perfume. The money from my sneakers was crumpled into a moist, smelly ball on her dresser. I took it and went off to buy breakfast food.

Outside, it wasn't clear yet what kind of day it would be. The air was crisp, and the sky above was a bruise of colors from the just-rising sun. As I made my way up Virginia Street, the hills in the distance were only partially visible, hidden behind the morning fog. I passed a bike shop at the corner of Martin Luther King Boulevard and glanced in at the bright bicycles that hung upside down, their wheels stagnant in midair. The houses I passed along the way were crooked and tumbling, with political placards and winter blossoms shooting up from overgrown gardens, half-destroyed cars parked out front.

As I turned onto Shattuck, a big, old-fashioned school bus sat idling at the curb, boarding a herd of noisy kids, and I looked at them, surprised, somehow, that children still went to school, that children went on with their lives. The bus was closing its doors, and I peered up at the faces just settling behind the windows. They were black and Mexican and Asian and white, on the verge of puberty, but not quite in it. They were utterly ordinary, throwing obscenities and spitballs at one another the way kids do. One face toward the back of the bus caught my eye, and I halted in my tracks, catching my breath. It was a cinnamon-skinned girl with her hair in braids. She was black like me, a mixed girl, and she was watching me from behind the dirty glass. For a second I thought I was somewhere familiar and she was a girl I already knew. I began to lift my hand, but stopped, remembering where I was and what I had already found. Then the bus lurched forward, and the face was gone with it, just a blur of yellow and black in motion.

A c k n o w l e d g m e n t s

There were so many who inspired and supported me during the writing of this book. I would especially like to thank the following: my wonderful editor, Cindy Spiegel, whose critical vision was essential in bringing this book to fruition; my agent, Binky Urban, for believing in, and finding the right home for, this book; Farai Chideya, and my cousins Rebecca Quaytman and Jeff Preiss, who all opened their homes to me when I needed the space to live *and* write; Omar Wasow, minister of information for the Mulatto Nation, who showed me the mestizo imperative; Joeritta and Adjoa Jones de Almeida, for opening up worlds for me; Nelson Aldrich, for sending me in the right direction; Maya Perez, for her support and warm enthusiasm; my colleagues and professors in the writing program at UC-Irvine, particularly Geoffrey Wolff and Judith Grossman, for their generosity and wisdom; and a special thanks to Phil Hay, a great reader, writer, and friend, who was so much a part of this process.

All my thanks and love to my sister and brother, Lucien and Maceo, my East and my West, who give me strength, joy, and especially laughter. And to my father, who showed me that in matters of color, there is always more than meets the eye.

And finally, deepest gratitude to my mother, an incredible woman and writer, who taught me what really matters.